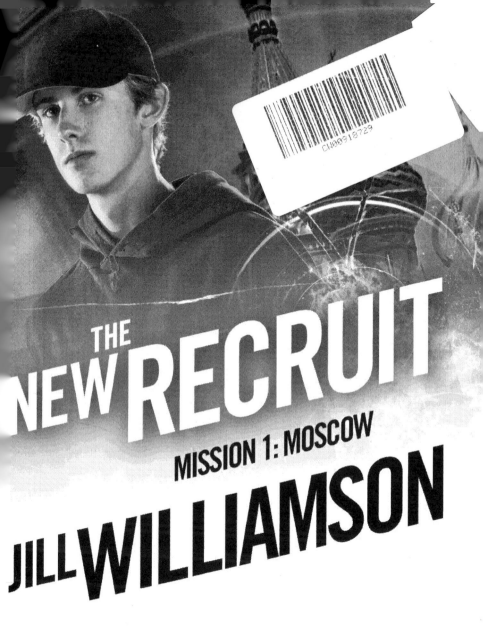

THE NEW RECRUIT

MISSION 1: MOSCOW

JILL WILLIAMSON

N
teen

The author is represented by MacGregor Literary Inc. of Hillsboro, OR.

Cover Designer: Kirk DouPonce
Editor: Jeff Gerke
Moscow Map Illustrator: Nichole White
Mission League Logo and miscellaneous images: Jill Williamson

Library of Congress Cataloging-in-Publication Data
An application to register this book for cataloging has been filed with the Library of Congress.

International Standard Book Number: 978-0-9962945-6-0

Printed in the United States of America

RESTRICTED ACCESS

YOU HAVE ACCESSED THE
INTERNATIONAL SERVER FOR
THE MISSION LEAGUE.

THESE FILES CONTAIN CLASSIFIED INFORMATION
ON THE ORGANIZATION, AGENTS, CRIMINALS, PROCEDURES,
TRAININGS AND MISSIONS.

GOD HAS CALLED. YOU HAVE ANSWERED.

Other books by Jill Williamson

The Mission League series
The New Recruit
Chokepoint
Project Gemini
Ambushed
Broken Trust
The Profile Match

The Blood of Kings trilogy
By Darkness Hid
To Darkness Fled
From Darkness Won

The Kinsman Chronicles
King's Folly
King's Blood
King's War

The Safe Lands series
Captives
Outcasts
Rebels

RoboTales
Tinker
Mardok and the Seven Exiles
The Tiny Cyborg

Stand-Alone Titles
Replication: The Jason Experiment

Nonfiction
Go Teen Writers: How to Turn Your First Draft into a Published Book
Storyworld First: Creating a Unique Fantasy World for Your Novel

To Ricky Fruchey, for being my very first reader.
Thank you.

REPORT NUMBER: 1

REPORT TITLE: I Get Recruited To Be a Spy
SUBMITTED BY: Agent-in-Training Spencer Garmond
LOCATION: Pilot Point, California, USA
DATE AND TIME: Friday, April 25, 4:27 p.m.

WHAT CAN I SAY? I'M A MORON.

I knew better than to play ball in King Coat's territory. Maybe I was looking for a fight, wanting to blow off steam after my "talk" with Principal McKaffey.

But there we were, me and three guys from the public school, playing two on two on the court in Alameda Park. It was around 2:20. The elementary schools hadn't let out yet. Then C-Rok and his wannabe gangsters showed up and asked to join in. Someone called "no blood, no foul" defense. C-Rok held my shirt, stepped on my feet, pushed, and shoved.

So I did too.

And I *might* have talked my share of trash. My mouth has the tendency to get me in trouble. Especially on the court.

Before I knew it, I was flat on my back on the hot asphalt, C-Rok straddling me, his gang buddies holding me down. The three public school guys took off, leaving me alone with the gang and the California sun.

"Get off!" I yelled.

C-Rok leaned in so close I could count the hairs on his attempt at a soul patch. "You talk to the popo, *Rojo?* Huh?" He slapped my face. "You tell them King Coats push for Vanderson? Huh?"

Richie Vanderson, a millionaire post production studio executive, was my buddy Sammy's dad. He was also a bit of a drug dealer in Pilot Point.

But who was I to judge?

"I don't squeal." Anymore. I'd made that mistake back in middle school.

And C-Rok knew it. "You lie!" He slapped me again. "The popo picked up Príncipe. You tell them where we live?"

I knew C-Rok's little brother—whose real name was Paco—from our days at Thirty-Second Street Elementary. We used to be good friends. "I didn't talk to anyone about your brother." I blame the searing asphalt for my next comment. "You gonna get offa me now? *Carlos?*"

I admit, mocking C-Rok's accent had been a bad move. Plus, he really hated being called *Carlos*.

That's when he pulled the knife.

"Laugh it up, Rojo. I'm-a give you a warning you better not forgit. X marks the spot, y'hear? I find out you talked to the popo, I'm-a go target shootin'."

And then C-Rok carved an X into my forehead.

Okay, maybe *scraped* would've been a better word than *carved*. I had the tendency to exaggerate. But it sure felt like a carving.

● ● ●

Thankfully, Grandma wasn't home when I got there. I ran straight for the bathroom to survey the damage.

Grandma's two-bedroom house had been built in the 70s. The place was covered in cheap wood paneling and orange shag carpet. Grandma had accessorized with crocheted yarn pillows and blankets, except for her wall of fame in the living room that was filled with framed pictures of old rock stars.

The bathroom had a tiny tub with frosted sliding shower doors, a really low toilet, and one of those scalloped pedestal sinks—all in goldenrod porcelain. I always felt like I was standing in a dollhouse.

I hunched a bit and squinted at my reflection in the bathroom mirror, hands still shaking as I held the hair off my forehead. I looked pretty gruesome. The cuts weren't deep, but bright red blood trailed through my eyebrows and down both sides of my nose. It pooled momentarily above my top lip before running around the corners of my mouth and down my chin like something out of a horror movie.

I turned on the water and washed my face, then dabbed at the wounds with wadded up toilet paper. The paper disintegrated, leaving doughy clumps stuck to the cuts. I wiped them off and patched myself up with gauze and Band-Aids.

My hair wouldn't cover the bandage, so I dug my Lakers cap out of my backpack, moved the snaps on the back to a

wider setting, and carefully slid it onto my head. Perfect. I
started rinsing the blood out of the sink, but the ringing of
Grandma's ancient phone jolted me away from housekeeping.
When that thing rings, it's like artillery.

I ducked out the bathroom door and ran to the living
room. I reached for the receiver and froze.

What if it was McKaffey calling about detention? My vice
principal probably had Grandma's number on speed dial. Or it
could be Kip, wanting me to get online for a *Planet of Peril*
raid. Kip's pilot character, Badios, could never do anything
without my bounty hunter, Kardash.

The phone rang again, the jarring metal bell almost
deafening me.

Or maybe it was Sammy calling to fill me in about his dad.
Something big had to have gone down if the cops had arrested
Príncipe.

Another ring. I snatched up the receiver. "Yeah?"

"Spencer? This is Lillian Daggett."

The low, rasping voice of Grandma's closest friend made
me relax. Not McKaffey. Good. "Grandma's not home."

"I'm looking for you, actually. I have your lawn mowing
money," Mrs. Daggett said. "Could you stop by sometime this
evening? If I keep it any longer I'm afraid I might spend it on
more fabric." She chuckled, but it sounded more like someone
gasping for breath.

I perked up at the mention of money. I'd been saving up
for a decent USB headset so I could talk to Kip while playing
Planet of Peril. "Yeah, sure. I'll be right over." I hung up,
excited about the cash. Mrs. Daggett hadn't paid me in so long
she owed me, like, fifty bucks. If all went well, I'd be talking
live on *PoP* tonight.

Before leaving, I called Sammy to see what was up, but he didn't answer his cell. I left a message, then hunched down to look in the round mirror between Bob Dylan and John Denver on the wall of fame, double checking that the cap covered my bandage. If Mrs. Daggett saw it, Grandma would hear about it. Those two shared a brain.

And if Grandma found out I'd gotten in another fight, I'd be the next cadet at the Carlsbad Military Academy. As if Pilot Point Christian School wasn't bad enough. At least they had a good basketball program. I shuddered to think what kind of competitive basketball they played in military school.

Probably none.

Which reminded me, if I was going on a walk, I needed my ball. It had rolled under Grandma's fancy tassel lamp after I'd dropped it on my way in last night. I got down on my hands and knees to retrieve it. Prepping for college ball was a 24-hour job, and the more I held my ball, the more my dribbling, shooting, and ball handling improved. I tucked the faded Wilson under my arm, opened the front door . . .

And stopped.

A police cruiser idled in the driveway behind Grandma's green Lincoln. This couldn't be good.

Grandma and two men headed toward the house, Grandma leading like a crossing guard in her fluorescent green tank top. Behind her, Officer Dave Kimbal, my school resource officer, walked beside a stick of a man who was dressed in a navy suit like some kind of lawyer.

Again, not good.

My brain tossed up a volley of curse words and settled on the worst-case scenario. They'd come to ask me about Mr. Vanderson. Like C-Rok, they thought I knew something. And if

Grandma thought I was mixed up in some drug bust, I'd have a shaved head and a pair of combat boots quicker than you could say, "Drop and give me twenty."

Grandma opened the screen door. The tension rod wheezed like a *PoP* warrior charging his blaster. The sound made me want to defend myself. But what could I say? I stepped back, my heart banging inside my chest like it wanted out.

"Here's Spencer." Grandma smiled as if this was going to be a good time. The hot pink sequin flamingoes on her green shirt distracted me from my fear for a millisecond. That, the metal bracelets, and her spiky, short white hair cinched it.

Eighties rock star wannabe.

Odd that Grandma's fashion had progressed as far as the 80s, but the house hadn't.

The men climbed the porch steps. Six foot five, pale, and freckled with bright orange hair, Officer Kimbal could pass for my relative—only I didn't have any relatives, except for Grandma. Not that my near-orphan status stopped the kids at school from calling me Kimbal, Jr.

I'd never found that very funny.

Kimbal's eyes pinned me like two blue searchlights. He'd been on my case a lot lately. Kimbal didn't like my idea of fun.

The guy in the suit squinted in the sunlight. His hair was oiled back, and a thick moustache hid his mouth. Was this guy the dean of the military school? The city prosecutor? Hitler in need of a trim?

If they asked me about Sammy's dad, I wouldn't know what to say. Crazy as the man was, if he went to jail, Sammy would be stuck in a foster home. He and I needed to touch base before I talked to anyone, figure out what to say.

"Come inside, gentlemen," Grandma said. "I'll get you something to drink, then you can talk with my grandson."

I flattened against the wall of fame as Grandma and the men filed inside.

Kimbal slapped my gut. "You missed detention this afternoon, Garmond. Had someplace better to be?"

"Uh . . . I forgot."

"That don't sound like you."

Grandma's voice drifted out from the kitchen. "That's Spencer's excuse for everything, Officer Kimbal, I'm sure you know. It's a wonder he remembers to get dressed before he leaves the house each day."

Officer Kimbal and I looked at each other. I hated the way he could read me, how he knew me better than anyone, how he was the one adult I literally had to look up to, since I was only six foot three. It made it hard to slip something past him.

I wanted to ask why he was here, but I was too afraid of what else he might say in front of Grandma. I had to get lost. Hide somewhere. Now. Before things got ugly. My mind whirred. None of my friends lived nearby . . . The school gym was closed . . . C-Rok's boys might be watching the park . . .

But Mrs. Daggett was expecting me. And I could use the cash to hang somewhere until Kimbal and his shadow left. Then I could convince Grandma that I had nothing to do with Mr. Vanderson's little side business.

Which was true. I didn't do drugs. Anymore.

I set my basketball on the orange shag and slipped outside, holding the screen door so it clicked shut instead of banged. The afternoon sun high in the sky, instantly warming my skin and causing the bitter smell of hot asphalt to overpower the scent of the flowers in Grandma's garden. I jumped off the porch and edged down the driveway, past Grandma's Lincoln, past the squad car—

The driver's side door of the squad car popped open, scaring me back into the flowerbed edging the driveway. I tripped over a plastic pinwheel and fell into soft dirt and daffodils.

A pink-faced bald man with a tiny double chin climbed out of the car. He had a gut that hung over his belt and was wearing tan military gear. He peered at me through thick, coke-bottle glasses. I'd seen him somewhere before. But where?

"Spencer," the man said in a deep voice. "You okay?"

The screen door whooshed open, and Kimbal stepped out onto the porch. "Where you going, Garmond?"

I scrabbled to my feet. "I don't know anything. I swear." I sprinted across the lawn, ignoring Kimbal's protests drifting after me.

I hurdled the white picket fence that boxed in Grandma's yard and tore down the street without looking back. Right on Maple. Left on Elm. The Daggetts lived in a one-story peach stucco home halfway down the block. I'd spent hours of my elementary life at their place, getting babysat while Grandma was at work, watching John Wayne movies with Mr. Daggett. The guy was obsessed.

After I got the cash, I'd take the bus to Kip's house, call Sammy for the scoop, and play *PoP* or *Guitar Star* until this all blew over. Man, I wished I had a cell phone.

I took the three front steps in one leap, but before I could knock, the front door swung in.

Mrs. Daggett was huge, a wrinkled lineman in an Eagles-green housecoat. She flashed her pasty dentures in a smile that looked like a grimace. "Hot out today, isn't it? Come in and have some lemonade, Spencer."

I ducked inside the dark and musty living room and was greeted by a merciful blast of air conditioning. I breathed deeply and sighed. The place was bigger and newer than Grandma's but always had the same old-house smell mixed with the smell of Mr. Daggett's pipe tobacco.

I took in the familiar hardwood floors, white walls, and the ugly brown and green velour furniture. Dust-caked knickknacks, old-fashioned toys, crafts, and books were crammed onto every available surface and clustered on the floor around the furniture. Heavy brown drapes hid a wall of windows as if the sun was a nosy neighbor. A hallway stretched across the house from the front door to the laundry room with doors shooting off both sides like a hotel.

Mrs. Daggett led me to the kitchen the long way around, through the cluttered living room. I stepped carefully, knowing better than to knock over any priceless junk. I stopped beside the circular table in the kitchen-slash-dining room as Mrs. Daggett pulled a pitcher of lemonade out from the fridge. A sheet of flowery fabric covered all but one edge of the dining table. Mrs. Daggett's sewing machine sat in the clear spot, fabric bunched up behind it in waves.

Mrs. Daggett snagged a glass from a dish rack. She cracked two ice cubes into it, poured the lemonade, and handed it to me. "Sit, sit. I'll get your money."

I perched on a dark wooden chair at the table and sat on something awkward. I popped back to my feet and found a stack of quilting magazines on the chair. Standing, I guzzled half the glass of lemonade. Good stuff. A clock ticked somewhere, but I couldn't find it in the mess. I checked my watch: 4:38. I wanted to get moving.

"I've got some fabric for Alice," Mrs. Daggett said from somewhere down the hall. "It's just the thing for her log cabin project."

Fabric? No. I didn't want any fabric. Just the money, thanks, and I'd be on my way.

The phone rang, electronic, almost musical. If only Mrs. Daggett could teach Grandma that antiques weren't meant to be used.

Mrs. Daggett picked up on the second ring. "Lillian Daggett speaking . . . Oh, hello . . . Yes, he's here. I'm sending him back with some darling yellow calico that will be perfect for . . . Is that right?"

I swore under my breath. My hand shook, the ice cubes clinking against the side of my glass. I shoved the fabric back and slid my drink onto the table. I crept toward the hall. Mrs. Daggett's voice had lowered to a whisper. She and Grandma were plotting. Time for plan B. Somewhere close I could hide for free. The mall?

The doorbell burst into a chimed version of "Amazing Grace." The sound sent me jogging down the hall toward the laundry room and back door, but Mrs. Daggett stepped out from her sewing room and grabbed my shoulder, her grip like Kimbal's. She'd make an intimidating SRO.

She grin-grimaced up at me. "Someone's at the door, Spencer. Would you mind?"

I shook my head. No way was I going to military school.

"Oh, don't be such a ninny-pinny. They aren't going to hurt you." Mrs. Daggett pushed past me. I slipped into the bathroom but peeked out to watch.

Mrs. Daggett opened the front door. "Dave! Lovely to see you."

Officer Kimbal ducked inside. "Where is he?"

"Glen didn't tell me this was a recruitment day." Mrs. Daggett closed the door behind Kimbal. "Is this secretive nonsense really necessary?"

"*Lil.*" Kimbal stretched her name out in a warning tone.

"Oh, relax." Mrs. Daggett lumbered through the living room toward the kitchen. "You must be excited. Will you finally tell him? After all these years, how do you think he'll react?"

I frowned, confused by Mrs. Daggett's strange comments. Kimbal's head turned, scanning the living room. "Where, Lil?"

I could no longer see Mrs. Daggett but heard her voice as she moved through the house. "He's just having some lemonade. Would you like some? It's fresh squeezed."

I wanted to run, but my thoughts kept me frozen. Mrs. Daggett knew Kimbal from church, but what secret could she be talking about?

It didn't matter. Curiosity wasn't worth the risk. I had to leave. Now.

Kimbal drifted through the living room toward the kitchen, so I seized the moment and snuck toward the back door.

"Spencer?"

Heat flooded my veins. I whirled around just as Mrs. Daggett stepped out of the kitchen doorway.

"You didn't finish your lemonade," she said.

I backed into the laundry room. Just a few more steps, and I'd be golden.

Kimbal darted into the hall behind Mrs. Daggett. I whipped around and knocked a pile of towels of the dryer, then jumped a laundry basket and crashed into the back door. I fumbled with two deadbolts and flung the door open to a wall of heat.

Kimbal yelled, "Wait!" but I slammed the white wood on his fingers. Kimbal growled through clenched teeth and the metal screen. "I just . . . want . . . to talk."

Forget that. I fled through the back yard and banged out the side gate. I sprinted across the street, right in front of the patrol car. It whizzed past and screeched in a reckless U-turn. I heaved myself over a metal fence and ran through someone's back yard, vaulted the fence on the other side, and continued on.

The cruiser turned at the end of the street. I ducked between two houses and stopped for a moment, panting. Barbecue smoke drifted from the yard to my left. A four-foot brick wall fenced the yard on my right. I climbed up and walked it like a tightrope, then dropped down on the other side. I ran around a bean-shaped swimming pool and crept up the side of the house toward the front yard.

Kimbal jumped out at me. He grabbed the front of my shirt and thrust me against the side of the house. I might be tall for fifteen, but Kimbal's muscular upper body was twice my width. It was over.

"You shut my fingers in that door, Garmond," Kimbal said, his voice calm but firm. "I could take you in for assaulting a police officer."

I let my head fall back against the side of the house. "Oh, come on!"

"Talk. For five minutes. Don't make me cuff you."

The cruiser pulled up at the curb. Kimbal grabbed my elbow and led me to the car. He opened the back door. "Get in."

I gritted my teeth and complied. Dread churned as I ducked inside and met a blast of frigid air conditioning. The Hitler wannabe sat in the back seat behind the driver. I slid in beside him on the molded plastic seat, every muscle tense. Kimbal slammed the door then climbed in the passenger's seat.

I glanced at the driver through the open window in the Plexiglas that separated the front from the back seat. It was the bald guy with the coke-bottle glasses. He hit the gas.

"Cozy back there, Prière?" Kimbal looked over his shoulder and tapped his knuckles against the barrier. "You should recruit in a squad car more often."

"*Mais oui*, it is quite *différent*," the Hitler wannabe said. His thick accent sounded European. Maybe French.

A dozen knots formed in my stomach. I'd been in a squad car only twice before. And even though I'd been arrested those other times, I'd never been as freaked out as I was now. Because I hadn't done anything this time.

I slouched back on the seat as far as I could and adjusted my legs, trying to fit in the small space. I felt like a pipe cleaner inside a Hot Wheels car.

The driver shot me a crooked smile over the front seat. Sunlight flashed off his glasses. "I think you scared him."

Ya think? I glared out the window. It looked like we were heading back to Grandma's place.

"I am named, Prière," the Hitler wannabe said. "*Monsieur* Kimbal, him you already know. Pat Stopplecamp is there, driving the vehicle. He is called by his students, Mr. S. My apologies for frightening you, Monsieur Garmond. We came to your house to speak privately. Our wish was not to be making you uncomfortable."

Too late, pal. I wiped my sweaty palms across my jean shorts. "Pree-air?" I looked in the man's squinted eyes. "You a lawyer?"

"*Non*, Spence—may I call you Spence?"

Spence? I blinked and adjusted my Laker's cap carefully over my cuts.

"I have come here to recruit you."

I narrowed my eyes. "Look, I'm *not* going to military school. I don't get into trouble. Anymore."

Kimbal snorted a laugh. "That's not what Mr. McKaffey told me."

I leaned up to the window. "Officer Kimbal, detention is no big deal. Everybody gets one sometimes."

"Sure. For being late to class. For chewing gum. Not for talking back to their teachers. Not for foul language. Not for threatening to beat up a seventh grader who—"

"That was a joke! We were just messing with him."

Mr. S chuckled from the driver's seat, his voice airy and soft. "Gee, I've never heard that one before."

I glared at Mr. S—more like *Mr. Chess* with those thick glasses and that pink face. I suddenly remembered seeing the guy at a school assembly last fall doing some talk about Africa. "Hey, aren't you the mission club guy?"

"'It takes a wise man to recognize a wise man,'" Mr. Chess said.

"Psalms?" Kimbal asked.

"Xenophanes of Colophon," Mr. Chess said. "Often seen as one of the first monotheists in the Western philosophy of religion."

Say what?

"Spence, have you ever thought that you would enjoy being a spy?" Prière asked.

I stared at him for a long moment, putting the pieces together. "Oh, no. I'm not going to be your rat. I don't know nothing. And I'm not going to spy on my friends, or wear a wire, or anything like that. I know my rights. Legally, you can't even ask me this stuff without Grandma here."

"Garmond, you're not in trouble, okay?" Kimbal said. "This is the real deal. We think you got the stuff to be a secret agent. Now, I want you to listen to what Prière's got to say. Can you do that for me?"

Kimbal might be a cop who was always busting my chops, but I trusted him. "Sure." I leaned back on the molded plastic seat, glad to know I wasn't about to be interrogated. Or arrested. "But I'm not spying on my friends."

"But of course," Prière said. "Monsieur Garmond, I represent *une organization* that trains adolescents to be spies. They meet daily, une *heure* before school and after. They do also travel to a foreign country every summer lasting for eight weeks. Is that appealing to you?"

"Wait, this isn't about drugs at school? You're talking spies? Real spies? Like Jason Bourne?"

"Not exactly Jason Bourne," Kimbal said, "but yes."

"For real?" I pictured myself dressed all in black with a transmitter in my ear, creeping into McKaffey's office and changing Kip's and my Ds in Bible History to Bs. That would be sweet. There had to be a catch.

"Why would the CIA want a guy like me?" I glanced at Kimbal. "A guy with a juvenile record? I'm not exactly good at upholding the law." Even in my daydreams I was breaking into McKaffey's office and changing grades.

"We aren't with the CIA," Kimbal said. "I promise you've never heard of this organization. But it's been around since W WII. And we don't care about your record. That's not how we pick—"

"You're one of them?" I asked Kimbal. "Aren't you a cop?"

"I'm both," Kimbal said.

I looked back to Prière. "Why pick me, though?"

"It was not *I* who choose you, Spence. Mais non! The Lord spoke to me your name in my times of *intercession*."

I looked from face to face. It felt real, but . . . "Come on." I rubbed my eyes, feeling like a complete tool. "You guys had me going there for a minute."

"He's not joking, Garmond," Kimbal said. "The Mission League is an international intelligence organization that does the Lord's work. And you've been chosen for the Juvenile Agent Development Program."

I blew an airy raspberry. "Chosen by *you*, you mean." And probably Grandma. It all made sense now. *Mission* League? This was a churcher thing. Kimbal went to our church. He and Grandma must have set all this up. "Thanks, but I've got better things to do than hang out with a bunch of Jesus Boy Scouts."

Kimbal shifted sideways to face me through the Plexiglas. "God has plans for you, Garmond. You're smart, athletic, and your family has a history in the organization."

I scoffed. "My grades are barely Cs, you know that. And I live with my— Wait, my family? What? Grandma's no Bible agent or whatever you call them."

Prière smoothed out his moustache. "Not always are things as they seem to be, Spence. Think it over. And remember, six o'clock Monday morning, the Barn, Harris Hall—if you choose to join our little band, oui?"

"Wii, yeah, whatever." Wish I had a Wii. Or X-Box or PlayStation . . . But I had no intention of seeing Prière again. Ever.

Mr. Chess steered into Grandma's driveway. Kimbal let me out. I took the front steps two at a time and burst inside the muggy house.

REPORT NUMBER: 2

REPORT TITLE: I Am Given the Ultimate Ultimatum
SUBMITTED BY: Agent-in-Training Spencer Garmond
LOCATION: Grandma Alice's House, Pilot Point, California, USA
DATE AND TIME: Saturday, April 26, 12:18 p.m.

I WOKE AT NOON ON SATURDAY, eyes stinging. A nightmare of a wolf chasing me through a forest had kept me awake half the night. I yawned so hard my jaw ached. The chatter of Grandma's quilt club drifted through the wall separating my room from the living room. I pulled the blankets over my head, but it didn't drown out their voices.

The bizarre events of Friday afternoon replayed in my mind.

"I have come here to recruit you."

For a crazy Bible club? I glanced at my poster of Lebron James. Why couldn't basketball scouts recruit me? If I could take my team to state next year, maybe I could follow in

Lebron's footsteps: Skip college ball and go straight into the NBA. Someday some kid might be staring at a poster of me on his wall.

Clearly Grandma knew all about this Mission League club. She probably knew Prière too, but she was refusing to answer my questions until I agreed to join the Mission League, which I was *so* not about to do. At least she hadn't mentioned military school, my skipped detention, or the drug bust on Sammy's dad.

The weird thing was . . . Prière, Kimbal, Mr. Chess, Grandma . . . I could tell they were serious. They actually thought their Mission League thing was some kind of God Squad.

I dragged myself three steps to my MacBook on my desk and logged on to *Planet of Peril*. I scanned the screen names for Badios but didn't see him. Kip was probably still sleeping.

Man, I wanted that headset. How much longer would I have to wait until Mrs. Daggett paid me now? I sighed, thankful for a computer and Internet access at all. Still, *Planet of Peril* would be so much cooler if I could talk. And it would block the noise a little, so maybe Grandma couldn't hear what I was doing. She didn't like me playing "those violent cartoon games."

Grandma's house was like stepping into a time warp. Antique furniture. No TV, microwave, or answering machine. And forget cell phones. My MacBook had been mysteriously delivered two Christmases ago. It was my only connection to the technological world Grandma hated. I played *PoP* until hunger drove me to the kitchen.

Grandma caught me rummaging for food. "About time you woke up. The girls want to see you."

"I'm hungry." I dug inside a box of cereal and dumped a fistful of corn flakes in my mouth.

"This will only take a minute." Grandma snatched the box away and set it on the counter, the metal bracelets on her wrist clanging.

Today Grandma wore a dark purple sweater with yellow sequin swirls, black pants, and purple and silver beaded sandals.

She wet her hands at the sink and reached her glossy, red-tipped nails up to smooth out my hair. She was two heads shorter than me. "Bend down so I can make you presentable."

I stuffed another handful of corn flakes into my mouth and inclined my head, too tired to argue. Her cold, probing fingers pushed back my hair and leaked icy water onto my scalp.

"What happened to your face?"

Heat flashed over me. I looked up, cursing and squirming inside.

She leaned close, eyes narrowed, and ripped the bandage off my forehead.

"Ow!" I stepped back and mumbled over my mouth full of cereal, "Wha you do tha fo?"

She sucked in a sharp breath like I'd just insulted her mother. "Did you do that to yourself? Is this some kind of macho boy thing? Like a tattoo?"

I swallowed my bite of cereal and huffed a laugh. "You caught me. I wanted to look like Harry Potter."

Grandma's entire face went slack except for her left eye, which squinted just slightly. Her signature death glare. It always sent a chill up my spine. "Don't be smart with me."

"It's nothing, Grandma."

"*Spencer.*" Her tone held a warning.

I am so not a morning person. I mean, where *was* my head? And why'd she have to wet my hair anyway? Making it neat wouldn't make the horrendous orange color any more "presentable."

Her stare stabbed into mine. It was icy blue and gave me a chill. "You didn't get into another fight? Did you?"

I stared at the smiling boy on the cereal box, wishing I were him. Unable to think up a decent lie off the top of my head, I mumbled, "Just a dumb argument."

Silence.

I didn't dare make eye contact. I didn't want to see that look.

"Where's your basketball?"

My posture slumped, my jaw tightened. She always took my ball. Every time.

"Fine!" I stomped to my room and grabbed the basketball out from under my desk, where it had faithfully served as a footrest all morning. Then I stomped back to the kitchen and chucked it at Grandma a little too hard.

She caught it with a loud smack. The yellow sequins on her sweater scratched against the leather. "Watch yourself, young man, or you may never see it again. We'll talk about this when the girls leave." She set the ball on the counter, paraded me into the living room, and settled into her brown armchair.

I stood in the center of the room. A drop of water slid down my temple from my sopping hair. I wiped it away with my thumb.

I towered over the circle of women like some sort of skyscraper. Only three of Grandma's quilt club friends were present today. Mrs. Daggett more than filled Grandma's rocker. Mrs. Martin and Mrs. Bogarth were sitting on the sofa. Both were a few decades older than Grandma and drove motor scooters around town together. The only way I could tell them apart was that Mrs. Martin wore glasses. The ladies hushed at the sight of me, their hands frozen above the quilts in their laps.

Mrs. Martin tilted her head down, peering over her bifocals. "Alice tells us you're going on a vacation this summer."

"Not a vacation, Edna," Mrs. Bogarth said, "a missionary adventure."

"That's what I said."

"No, you said, 'vacation.' That's different." Mrs. Bogarth looked up at me. "Where are you going?"

"He doesn't know yet," Mrs. Daggett said.

I was a bit peeved that Grandma was telling her friends I was going on the mission trip. But at least now I knew what Mrs. Daggett and Kimbal had been talking about.

Mrs. Bogarth raised her finger toward my waist. "Be sure to take sun lotion. With your fair complexion, you'll burn."

"Sunscreen, Fran, not lotion," Mrs. Martin said.

"Oh, they're the same thing," Mrs. Bogarth said.

"You need an SPF of 45 or higher, Spencer," Mrs. Martin told me.

Right. I suffered in polite silence, desperate to escape. The ladies asked question after question before their babble shifted to quilting topics. My stomach growled. I'd left the cereal box in the kitchen.

"Spencer, be a dear and hand me those scissors." Mrs. Martin pointed to a wicker basket in the center of the floor.

I passed her the swan-handled scissors.

"I need a finger!" Mrs. Bogarth sang like she was offering a special treat. I remembered a time when I eagerly sat with these women hoping to help. I could probably make a quilt on my own if I wanted to—which I didn't. The mere thought made me feel girlish.

I trudged over to Mrs. Bogarth and put my finger in the center of her string. After three tries, she managed to tie the knot.

The doorbell rescued me.

It was the FedEx guy. I signed for a package from Notion Commotion, threw it on the sofa, and dashed out to the driveway—past the twin motor scooters—to shoot around in my portable hoop.

Then I remembered that my ball was being held hostage. I practiced anyway, dribbling and shooting with nothing but air. It was good for my form and conditioning. When I got tired, I snuck into the kitchen through the back door. I grabbed a loaf of bread, a jar of peanut butter, and a knife and hid in my room.

I ate sandwiches and played *PoP* until an ominous knock shook my bedroom door in its frame. I'd forgotten to lock it, and Grandma didn't wait for permission to enter. She barged in and sniffed the air. Her shrewd gaze landed on a pile of clothes at the foot of my bed.

"Are those clean or dirty?"

I shrugged.

"Up." She nudged me out of the chair, almost onto the floor, and closed my MacBook. "I want this room cleaned." She fell into my seat. "What am I going to do with you, Spencer? You think raising a boy your age—at *my* age—is easy?"

I shoved a wad of clothes into my laundry basket, no clue

if they were clean or dirty. I just wanted Grandma to leave, and compliance was the first step.

She gestured toward the jar of peanut butter with the messy knife sticking out. "How many times have I said no food in here?"

I kicked a shoe under my bed. Silence was always the best answer with Grandma. She liked the sound of her own voice.

"You broke our deal, Spencer. One more fight, I said, and military school. I don't *want* to send you there. Your father went when he was your age, you know. You really are turning out just like him."

I twitched. I hated being compared to my father—the man who abandoned me and my mom just before she died. Not that I could remember any of this. And Grandma never shared anything else about my parents despite how often I'd asked for details over the years.

I'd stopped asking a long time ago.

I channeled my anger into action and heaved the overflowing laundry basket to the door.

Grandma's nails dug into my arm. "Wait."

I set down the basket, keeping my eyes glued to the orange shag carpet.

"Is military school what you want?"

I shook my head. "I want to play ball."

"Of course you do." She pursed her lips, eyes dancing. "Make me a deal. You can stay at Pilot Point Christian School and play basketball . . . if you join the Mission League. If not, Carlsbad Military Academy."

My jaw dropped. Not fair. I blinked, searching for some wise comeback to change her mind. But I had nothing.

"It's settled, then." Grandma jumped up. She grabbed the

bread and peanut butter and made for the door.

"What about conditioning and summer league?" If I got dragged on some eight-week trek into the wilds of West Africa, I'd miss them.

"That's a sacrifice you'll have to make if you want to stay."

A scowl burned into my face, the wrinkles in my forehead pinching the X C-Rok had carved there.

"Take this to the kitchen and sort it." Grandma kicked the laundry basket with her beaded sandal and glided out the door.

I stared at the tangle of clothing, thinking how much it resembled my life: a jumble of dirty laundry trapped in a cage and desperate to be free. No matter how much I tried, I couldn't get rid of the slimy feeling that no one—especially Grandma—cared what *I* wanted.

The size of the congregation at Calvary Baptist Church made it easy to get lost in the crowd. I counted on that. Suffering through the Sunday school class, the choir's singing, and the pastor's sermon without falling asleep was hard enough without worrying about dodging do-gooders.

Every week the youth pastor shook my hand and told me about upcoming teen events, like I might actually come sometime.

Yeah, sure. Whatever, buddy.

I used to like church. When I was a kid, I looked forward to Sunday school, bringing my quarters for starving children in Africa, making cross crafts out of popsicle sticks, memorizing Bible verses, singing songs with hand motions, and showing

Grandma the cartoon story in the take-home paper.

Somewhere along the way I just lost interest. But I'm glad, you know? Because when I look at the people who are my age—those churcher teens—I don't want to be one of those people. Those happy, peppy, "Yay, God!" types. I've got my friends. I don't need all that . . . joy.

Yet Grandma makes me go, so I go. And now she's going to make me go on a mission trip. So I'll go. But I'm not going to become one of those people.

No way.

Before going to bed Sunday night, I searched online for information about this Mission League. I found lots of pictures but no official website, no stories, blogs, or articles. Googling "Agent Development Program" led only to a website for real estate training.

Seemed odd. Everybody had a website these days. It took five minutes to build one. But a lot of churches were stuck in the past—like Grandma. So it didn't surprise me that the Mission League might be anti-technology too.

One thing was certain. This mission club was bigger than just a group at Pilot Point Christian School—I found images of people all over the world. But nothing explaining what they did or even how to join. They all looked like Boy Scouts, though . . . or Girl Scouts. Churchers.

But girls were a big plus. The Mission League appeared to be co-ed. Maybe I'd get lucky and there'd be girls on this trip. Churcher girls, but still . . .

I popped over to check my Facebook and saw I had a new e-mail. I clicked it open.

Spence,

I am sensing that you have not yet discovered what you are searching for online. *Bonne chance* tomorrow.

Prière

A creepy feeling ran up my arms, as if I'd heard a noise in the dark after watching *Jolt 3*. I snapped off the light and dove into bed. I slid my index finger over the cuts on my forehead. Just scratches. It had better not scar, or C-Rok would get his. I mulled over the fight in the park, the chase, Prière . . .

Grandma still wouldn't say how she knew him.

Churcher spies. What a joke. But if I did this, at least I'd get out of town, away from Grandma and the quilt club. And I'd avoid military school. The question was, where would I get out of town *to*? Eight weeks in the Kenyan jungle being eaten by bugs—or eating bugs—wasn't exactly my idea of a vacation.

Unless they had a basketball court.

Lord, have mercy.

REPORT NUMBER: 3

REPORT TITLE: I Take a Spy Class with Bible Geeks
SUBMITTED BY: Agent-in-Training Spencer Garmond
LOCATION: Grandma Alice's House, Pilot Point, California, USA
DATE AND TIME: Monday, April 28, 5:30 a.m.

I DRIBBLE HARD TO THE HOOP. I stop, jerk my body up, but keep my feet planted. Bodies burst into the air around me like fireworks. As they fall back to the floor, I jump and slam the ball through the hoop. I hang from the metal rim with one hand until the floor beneath me clears.

The roaring of the crowd is deafening.

I look to the bench, past the row of jumping cheerleaders, over the heads of my yelling teammates, and wink at the scouts from duke, Michigan State, and Syracuse. All NCAA schools. All far from Pilot Point, California.

The stadium shrinks, morphing into a restaurant. Still clad in my uniform and sneakers, I stand in the aisle amid lively customers. My sweaty body shivers in the air-conditioning. The meaty smell of sausage is mouth-watering.

A beautiful blond woman wearing a red blouse sits at a table with a guy my age. She speaks to him in a language I can't understand. My hopes of playing NCAA basketball crash when the hauntingly familiar surroundings take shape.

An alarm sounds, but the hungry guests take no notice. The woman keeps talking. I look for the fire. The alarm blares louder. I cover my ears.

My eyes opened to darkness. I clicked off my alarm clock and groaned.

Mission League day.

In less than five minutes, I got dressed, slammed together three peanut butter sandwiches, and was trudging through the dark morning. The cool breeze rustled my hair and helped to wake me.

Why did the Mission League have to meet so early? And where were they meeting, again? Prière had said Harris Hall in The Barn and The Barn was a utilities building at the far end of the football field. I found it locked, so I circled the building checking the other doors. Only a janitor closet opened. Where was Harris Hall, anyway? I checked my watch: 5:48. I was early.

I scanned the field and saw movement. A black guy—upperclassman—in a school uniform strode toward me with a spring in his step, his thin cornrows were tied into a low ponytail. He wore a navy blue bowtie instead of the required blue and red-striped necktie. One arm clutched the strap of a leather bag that hung over his shoulder. I had at least four inches on him. Student government, if I remembered right. James. Jace. Something with a J.

"Looking for Harris Hall, Kimbal, Jr.?" J's lips twisted in a smirk.

I retaliated with my own half insult. "What's with the bowtie?"

"It's a sign of intelligence."

I honked out a louder-than-intended laugh. "It's a sign of nerd-dom."

"Winston Churchill wore bowties." J bounced past me and stopped in front of the broom closet. "This is the place right here." He pulled the door open and stepped inside.

I stayed put. "Dude, it's a broom closet."

"It is that, but it's also much more." J grabbed my arm and yanked me into the mess of brooms, mops, and cleaning supplies. He shut the door, leaving us in blackness, which was a bit freaky.

I held my breath. The room reeked of disinfectants and Jake's toxic cologne. Metal tinkled against glass, and a light clicked on. A swinging chain hung from a bulb overhead.

J pointed over my shoulder. "The button's behind the bleach."

I turned to a shelf covered with cleaners and spied a dirty white button on the wall. "Seriously? How could anyone ever find that?"

J's grin widened, his teeth glowing in the dim light. "That's the point." He rummaged through the cleaning supplies. "I'm Jake Lindley, by the way."

Jake, that was it. "What are you doing now, Jake?"

"Well, there's this rule about your first day—it's kind of unfair, but if you don't play along, trust me, you'll never live it down."

An initiation? "What's the rule?" I wanted this morning to

go as smoothly as possible.

Jake pursed his lips. "The thing is—ah, this'll do fine." He held up a broom. "The thing is, League agents have been meeting in this bomb shelter since the fifties. There's a certain respect for the facility, and everyone likes to know that new recruits are sensitive to that. Pay their dues, know what I'm saying?"

I didn't have a clue. This closet was a bomb shelter?

Jake thrust the broom into my hands. "Just sweep the room and everyone'll know you respect our place."

I wasn't sweeping no bomb shelter. I did enough housework for Grandma. "What if I don't care what people think?"

Jake's perma-grin faltered. "I'm sorry, did you just say you don't want to be here? Because I would *not* go downstairs sporting that attitude. I'm just trying to help, man. It's up to you. "Now, close that door." Jake pointed behind me. "The inside door won't open if the outside one isn't shut."

I climbed back up and pulled the outside door shut.

Jake reached past me, behind the bleach, and pressed the white button. A soft buzz came from below. Jake pushed the wall of mops and brooms inward and stepped through a secret door. He turned back. "You coming or not?"

I gaped at the flight of cement stairs that led down to who knew where and expressed my surprise with a few swear words. "Are you kidding me?"

"I suggest you watch that mouth in front of Mr. S." Jake jogged down the stairs like he'd done it every day of his life. "He docks points for swearing."

Of course he does. I carried the broom down the steps. At the bottom, faded black letters on a tan metal door read:

Harris Hall. An old keypad with big silver buttons was hooked to the doorknob.

"We meet in the school in the afternoons for our mission trip cover." Jake looked up at me. "Room 401. Anyone who sees us coming or going from here assumes we're on a clean-up detention or something."

"Right." Clearly these people were mentally unbalanced. Why would missionaries need to hide in an old bomb shelter? Who were they hiding from?

Jake punched a code into the keypad. "Seven, three, one. Remember that. And start sweeping right away. When you're done, sit anywhere."

Jake cranked the doorknob and strode in. I followed. Three faces turned toward the door, a guy and two girls. I avoided looking directly at anyone and took in the tiny, chilled room. It was no bigger than a two-car garage with white cinderblock walls and a plain concrete floor. A teacher's desk sat vacant in the front corner. A dozen student desks crammed in the center with two round tables squeezed in behind. Black metal cabinets filled the entire back wall.

Jake fell into a seat. "Sweep."

I fixed my eyes on the cement floor and started sweeping. The room was quiet except for the sound of straw on cement. *Whoosh. Whoosh. Whoosh.*

A girl giggled. Someone else snorted.

"Oh, Jake," a sweet voice scolded. "Why you so cruel?"

Heat flashed down the back of my neck. Jake had tricked me. I propped the broom in the corner and strode to a seat in the back before looking up. I locked gazes with Jake, who sat kitty-corner to my left.

Jake's smile split his face. "Hey." He rubbed his fancy

black Oxford over the floor by his desk. "You missed a spot."

"Nice," I said, annoyed I'd fallen for his dumb prank.

A muscular blond guy, who was so tan he looked like an ad for PacSun, rose from the seat in front of Jake and headed my way. He wore baggy plaid shorts, flip-flops, and a yellow T-shirt that was so faded I couldn't read what it said. I'd never seen him before.

"Name's Isaac." He held out his fist. "Whenever I meet someone taller than me, I make friends, 'cause I don't want them as my enemy."

"Good one," I said, knocking my first against his. "At least you didn't call me a giraffe." There were about five tall jokes I'd heard nearly every day of my life since third grade. "You don't go to PPCS, do you?"

"Homeschooled." Isaac's hair hung just past his eyes, and he shook it aside. "Well, I'm glad you're on my team for more than your size. Last thing we need's another *wahine*." Isaac cast a mischievous grin toward the girl in the seat to my right. She was slouched down in her chair, reading a book titled, *Creation Evangelism*. He lowered his voice to a whisper. "Actually, we could use more girls, but what can you do? 'Called by God' and everything."

The girl lowered the book and revealed choppy, chin-length hair that spilt right down the middle, half candy-apple red, half black. She looked like Melitah, an alien smuggler from *PoP*. She was kind of cute. I didn't recognize her either. Maybe she was homeschooled too.

She sat up, her posture ramrod straight. "I got to PPH," she said. "I'm Jensina Hicks."

"*Quita!* I want to meet him too," another girl said.

Isaac stepped aside to reveal a curvy Latino girl. Thick,

flowing curls framed her face. She gazed at me, big brown eyes edged in lots of black makeup. I swear my temperature rose ten degrees. I'd seen this goddess before. Isabel Rodriguez. Sophomore. Came from some foreign country. *Way* out of my league.

"I'm Isabel. What's your name?"

I swallowed. She'd said her name all exotic-like—*Ee-sabell*—with a faint accent, the same sweet voice that had found Jake *so cruel*. I gawked, my mind blank, my brain melting in those chocolate eyes. "Uh . . ." I rubbed the back of my neck. "Ahh . . ."

Isaac slapped my back. "You'll have to excuse his drool, Isabel. I haven't got him trained yet."

Isaac's voice broke the spell. "I'm Spencer."

"I'm glad you're here, *Es-pensor*." The way she said my name tangled my thoughts. She flashed me a wide smile and returned to the center front-row seat.

I straightened in my chair, wanting to follow her, then snapped back to my senses. Why did that always happen? Whenever a pretty girl talked to me, my brain went to screensaver.

Isaac returned to his seat, snickering. Jensina raised one of her eyebrows before disappearing behind her book.

"What?" I said.

The door creaked again. A stick of a girl dragged a mop and bucket on wheels into the room, her unibrow furrowed in concentration. Well, well. At least I wasn't the only new recruit. I recognized Arianna Sloan from my homeroom class. She was a missionary kid that everyone called *Mission-Ari*. Instead of the regulation pleated navy uniform skirt, Arianna somehow got away with wearing floor length ones. Today, hers puffed out like a feather duster.

A cute girl with a ponytail loped in behind Arianna, her sneakers scuffing over the concrete floor. She was wearing black sweatpants and a pink T-shirt that read, "Don't let pink fool you." She leaned close to Arianna's ear. "Start in the corner by Mr. S's desk."

Arianna pushed the mop bucket across the room, wheels clicking over the floor. The girl with the ponytail turned her back to Arianna and mimed laughter. I put my fist to my mouth to hide my grin.

It was a riot when it wasn't happening to me.

Ponytail girl took the seat in front of Isaac's, closest to the teacher's desk. Isaac tugged on her ponytail, and she turned around and slugged his bicep. I flinched at the smack of skin against skin. Yikes. Tough chick.

Isaac just laughed, but once the girl turned back around he winced and rubbed his arm.

The door opened again. Mr. S entered the room, pink-faced, and wearing starched, high-waisted jeans and a baby blue polo shirt that clung to his pudgy gut. A woman and a teenaged boy, who had to be her son, followed. Both had curly black hair and glasses, though the guy's glasses were black: Buddy Holly frames. Buddy had been one of my great Grandpa's favorites, so his picture held an honorary place on Grandma's wall of fame.

The Buddy Holly guy slid into the desk behind Isabel.

"Hey, Gabe," several voices chimed.

Gabe's smile revealed gleaming silver braces that deflated his cool just a bit.

Mr. S regarded Arianna, who was mopping with fury, then faced the room, hands on his hips. "Who is responsible for this?"

Everyone pointed at me.

I froze in my seat, mouth gaping. "Excuse me?" Was this another prank?

"I see. Agent Sloan, I thank you for your hard work this morning." Mr. S took the mop from Arianna and set it beside my broom. Arianna beamed and took the front-row seat by the door. Mr. S folded his arms and surveyed the class until his coke bottles locked onto me. "Agent Garmond, come to the front, please."

Agent Garmond? A chill flashed over me. "What'd I do?"

Mr. S just stared through those thick lenses. "We're waiting, Agent Garmond."

I shuffled to the front of the room, my face hotter with each step.

Mr. S pulled the chair from behind his desk to the center front, facing the class. The wheels clacking over the cement floor seemed deafening in the silence. He motioned for me to sit. "Interrogation, Agent Garmond."

I sat, rigid, and focused on the metal cupboards along the back wall. Isabel's face blurred in my peripheral vision. I swallowed, trying to forget she was watching me.

Mr. S stepped in front of me, and I could no longer see Isabel. "Agent Garmond, did you ask Agent Sloan to mop the floor?"

"No."

He leaned over me, his eyes glimmering behind his glasses. "'The truth is always exciting. Speak it, then. Life is dull without it.'"

"I am!"

"It's true, Mr. Stopplecamp, sir." Arianna looked almost

boyish beside Isabel, despite the feather duster skirt.

Wait. Mr. Stopple-who? No wonder they called him Mr. S.

Mr. S walked to Arianna's desk and patted it. "Bear with me, please." He spun to face me. "Agent Garmond, I want to know who tricked Agent Sloan and"—he pointed to the broom in the corner— "who tricked you."

Oh-kay. It was a game, right? I glanced at Isaac, who winked. The rest of the class sat in freeze frame. I shrugged, determined to play along. "I just felt like cleaning."

"*Really?*" Mr. S raised a dark eyebrow. "Agent Schwarz. Please assist your teammate by stating the four types of interrogation an enemy could use on a captive."

Isaac leaned around Ponytail Girl's bicep to meet my gaze. "Drugs, torture, threats, and deals—oh, and saying 'please.'" Isaac swept the hair out of his eyes. "But bad guys often forget their manners."

Jake snickered and held a fist over Isaac's shoulder. They knocked knuckles. I glared at them. How nice that they were enjoying themselves.

Mr. S crouched in front of me, his eyes brown and magnified behind his glasses. "Excluding drugs, torture, and threats— which would get me in a whole lot of trouble—if you tell the truth, Agent Garmond, I *will* offer you a deal."

I glanced at Jake, who barely shook his head in warning.

"Confess who put you and Agent Sloan up to playing *janitor,*" Mr. S said, "and I'll tell you who gave you a MacBook a year and a half ago."

The blood drained out of my face so fast it left my cheeks tingling. "Uh . . . well, Jake said I had to show respect for the facility." I pointed at Ponytail Girl. "She came in with Arianna."

Jake threw his head back. "I knew it!"

Ponytail Girl pounded her desk.

"Deals." Mr. S straightened and ran a hand over his bare head. "Everyone has a price. Make sure no one knows yours."

"Wait, you said you'd tell me who gave me my computer."

"Sucker," Ponytail Girl said.

"How do you keep people from knowing your price, sir?" Arianna asked.

"That's one of the things I'll be teaching you. Take your seat, Agent Garmond. Diakonos team loses twenty points for Jake and twenty for Beth."

Isaac cackled.

"And since Spencer broke under interrogation, Alpha team also loses twenty points."

Isaac sobered and looked up at the ceiling. "Aw, man!"

I stood and faced Mr. S. "So who gave me the MacBook?"

Mr. S's cheeks crinkled in a smile. "Lesson two, Agent Garmond. Criminals rarely make good on their deals. Once they get what they want, they kill you. How about I let you live, and we'll call it even?"

"That's not fair!"

"Nor are criminals generally fair. Take your seat, please."

I stumbled to my desk, dazed, and tripped on Isaac's backpack in the aisle.

"*Careful,*" Isaac said in a worried tone. "My porcelain unicorn collection is in there."

The class laughed, but my mind was distracted as I sat down. How could Mr. S know who gave me my computer? Was he bluffing? Had he been talking to Grandma?

"Let's open with prayer." Mr. S bowed his head, the halogen lights illuminating his scalp.

I stifled a groan. Here were go. Church time.

"Heavenly Father, thank You for our new members. We're grateful they've answered your call. We pray for our journey to Moscow this summer. Prepare us to serve you there. In Jesus' name, amen."

Moscow? Well, that was better than Africa. In Moscow they at least had running water and cars. They had basketball too, Olympic team and all. Might not be so bad.

Mr. S gestured toward the curly haired woman, who now stood behind the teacher's desk. "This is my wife: Kerri. We are your instructors. Spencer, you'll join Alpha team with Isaac. Arianna, you'll join Diakonos with Jake. Let's break up and acquaint our new recruits with what we do."

I stayed put until Isaac coaxed me to a round table in the back. I sat between him and Gabe. Jensina sat across the table from me, still reading.

"Hey, Jensina. You play *Planet of Peril*?" I asked.

She looked up, cocking that same eyebrow. "Is that a card game?"

"Never mind," I said. Isaac had gone over to Mr. S's desk, so I shifted my gaze to Jake's table where he sat with the other girls. Exotic Ee-sa-bell wasn't in my group? The outrage! If I were in the Diakonos group, at least I'd have Isabel and Buff Beth for aesthetics. Not that Jensina, the ice fairy, was all that bad.

Isaac returned with a stack of papers and sat down. He drummed his hands on the table. "What to say . . . ? Well, we'll be learning Russian. That's no beach break, take it from me. It's a hard language. Mornings, we study trainings. Afternoons, we study language and culture. Looks like we're gonna hang at a homeless shelter in Moscow and—oh! We get to visit the field office. So we'll see all kinds of cubicles, file cabinets, and copy machines."

I looked at Isaac until the cool air forced me to blink. He may as well have been speaking Russian. "What's a field office?"

"It's just like a regular office, but in a field," Isaac said. "They sit in a shack on some hay bales." Then he cracked a smile. "Naw, I'm just messing with you, newb. Think CIA branch office but for the Mission League."

CIA? That cinched it. These guys were nuts. "If we're all CIA-worthy, why would we be working at a homeless shelter? Shouldn't we work at the field office? Aren't we supposed to be secret agents or something?"

"Agents-*in-training*," Isaac said, as if that made a huge difference. "But don't forget, homeless assassins need to eat too."

I blew out a noisy breath and took in the room again. There were no posters of Zimbabwe or African orphans, but I didn't see any Bibles either. Perhaps someone *had* stolen them. "Okay, I'll bite. How do you become real agents if all you do is feed the homeless?"

"A little social justice never hurt anyone," Jensina said.

"Didn't we just cover the homeless assassins?" Isaac said. "Look, newbies just get thrown in to see how you swim. We'll review some trainings before the trip, though. So you probably won't die."

"What's a training?"

Isaac exaggerated a deep breath and spoke fast. "Lie detection, tailing, *reports*, bugs, spiritual warfare, *reports*, hacking, stakeout, *reports*, languages, hostage, escape, defensive driving, *reports*."

Gabe peered at me over the top of his glasses. "My dad

likes reports."

Mr. Chess was this guy's dad? Pity. Gabe seemed cooler than that. Buddy Holly frames vs. those coke bottles Mr. S wore. And a whole lot of hair.

Only a matter of time, perhaps.

Isaac tipped his chair back on two legs. "Trainings reveal your skills. And your senior year, you get called to a path and post. I'm going Special Forces."

"Because you're insane," Jensina mumbled.

"Because I'm *awesome*." Isaac leaned toward me and whispered. "Jensina likes an office."

She peeked over the top of *Creation evangelism* and rolled her eyes. "What I *like* is a mental challenge."

I sighed. It was all very cute, but they had to be delusional. "We've already got the CIA and FBI and the military. Who needs missionary agents? You don't get guns, right? What's the point?"

Gabe's eyebrows shot above his Buddy Holly's. "It's not the point of the CIA or the FBI to carry guns."

"But it *is* a sweet bonus." Isaac's chair thudded back on all fours and he leaned forward, shaggy blond hair falling in his eyes. "We're an international organization funded by INTERPOL. Ever heard of them?"

"Sounds like a comic book," I said.

"We're *exactly* like a comic book, but with less Spandex," Isaac said. "We fight spiritual battles. We pray. A non-Christian CIA agent can't do squat against a demon. We go undercover to investigate *cults*. We find out how they recruit. What promises they offer. Is there demonic activity going on? How can we help? Not that we want to promote demonic activity, but you know what I mean. The Mission League takes on the forces of darkness to expose the truth."

I shifted in my seat. Forces of darkness? What was this, Jedi training? I bet they had an arsenal of plastic light sabers in those black cabinets. Maybe a few storm trooper masks for the *demons* and a chess board or two, just in case they got bored investigating cults. Maybe they should look in a mirror.

Isaac went on to explain about team points and homework. Certain trainings could only be done by upperclassmen and only with enough personal points. Isaac was the only senior. Jensina, Jake, and Buff Beth were juniors, and Gabe, Isabel, and Nick—whoever he was—were sophomores.

As if reading my mind, Mr. S spoke from his desk. "Does anyone know where Mr. Muren is this morning?"

Wait, Nick Muren? Please, no.

When no one answered, Mr. S said, "'Absence sharpens love; presence strengthens it.' Unexcused absences are a ten point deduction—unless anyone can tell me who said that."

"Thomas Haynes Bayly?" Jake said, wincing a hopeful grin.

"A fine guess, Mr. Lindley. But it was Thomas Fuller."

Jake groaned and ran his hand over his cornrows. Beth banged a fist on the Diakonos table, making her ink pen bounce off the fake wood surface.

I couldn't believe that Nick Muren was a part of this thing. Why would the Lex Luthor of PKs hang with these Trekkies? You'd think they had some sort of screening process. But then again, they picked me, so they clearly didn't.

Mr. S walked to the front of the class. "Our motto is, 'Expect great things from God, attempt great things for God.' I hope you'll embrace that theme in your lives. God has called, and you have answered."

I raised my hand.

"Yes, Agent Garmond?"

"I didn't hear any mystical *call*." What I really wanted to say was that I sat in this chair under threat of being sent to military school and no basketball, but I didn't want Isabel hearing that.

"God speaks to each of us in His own, perfect timing. Prière received your call and extended it to you. You in turn—"

"Wait, God talked to someone else about me? Why didn't God extend it to me? I mean, I'm just saying."

"Well . . . that's not how it works. The intercessors receive the names, and they extend the offer to the juvenile."

Juvenile sounded like an SRO word to me.

Mr. S seemed to sense that I wasn't buying any of this. Chalk that up to his being a spy. "I'd understand if you had some questions, Agent Garmond. I'd be happy to talk those over with you after class."

"Naw. That's okay." I didn't want to stay in this room a minute longer than was necessary.

"It's good to question things. We only ask you to keep the covert side of the organization to yourself so that—"

"You want me to lie, then?" I asked, without really thinking it through. "Give a song and dance about feeding the homeless and scrubbing Russian toilets?"

Mr. S blinked, his eyes magnified behind his maximum prescription lenses. "Proverbs 21:23 says, 'The one who guards his mouth and tongue keeps himself out of trouble.' We'll never ask you to lie outright, but we mustn't publicly proclaim the true nature of our involvement in this organization. It belongs to God, and we respect his authority by maintaining its secrecy. If asked, simply play up the angle of our missionary cover, because on our trips you *will* feed homeless and you *may* need to scrub a toilet or two."

No way was I scrubbing a toilet, but I kind of liked that I still had him talking when he'd tried to shut me up. "So the whole school sees us meet in Room 401 in the afternoons, and they think we're all going on a mission trip."

"That's right."

"But we also meet here in the mornings, and if anyone sees us, they think we're delinquents on detention?"

"Umm . . ."

"And what if someone else wants to go on this mission trip? Someone not *called*. You tell them they can't? That doesn't sound very P.C."

"We explain that there are a limited number of spots available on—"

"And they buy that? No one sues?"

"Anyone can apply for our mission trips, Agent Garmond. I received sixty-two applications this year."

"Well, I didn't apply."

"Your grandmother filled out your application."

That shut me up. "Seriously?"

"We must appear to be doing everything by the book." Mr. S walked back to his desk and stood beside his wife, who had taken his seat. "Arianna, Spencer, come and see Kerri before you go. The rest of you are dismissed. See you all this afternoon in Room 401."

I dragged myself to where Mrs. S sat by two stacks of books. My eyes bulged. It made sense, though. Geek agents needed books. Got to look the part.

"Don't worry," Kerri said in a gushy, reserved-for-kindergartners voice. "I know it looks like a lot, but the non-Russian books stay here. Most of your homework is studying language and memorizing Scriptures." She set two sheets of paper on both stacks of books. "Here's an assignment chart and a memory verse list. Do you have any questions?"

I blew a soft raspberry. "Yeah. When will I do my regular homework?"

Kerri giggled. "Funny guy, Spencer. I'll see you later, okay?"

I scratched the back of my neck. "Can't wait."

Arianna stepped up beside me, her feather duster skirt brushing my leg. She scooped up the top two books and cradled them. "Better go or we'll be late."

Homework for no credit or grade? What was the point?

Avoiding military school.

Right. I sighed through my nose, reached out, hesitated, and finally shoved the paperwork and the two Russian tomes into my backpack. I slung it over my shoulder and followed Arianna up the steps and through the broom closet.

Outside, dawn had lit the campus in pale light but not enough to raise the temperature. I poured on the speed, hoping to ditch Arianna.

Unfortunately, she jogged to keep up. "How long did you use the broom before you realized it was a prank?" she asked.

"Not long."

"Isn't this neat? I hoped I'd get called. I speak three languages already, but that doesn't guarantee—"

"How come you wear those weird skirts?" I asked, hoping rudeness might shut her up.

"You like them?" Arianna said, glancing down at her skirt. "I think our uniforms skirts are immodest, so I—"

"They go to the knee," I said. As did our cheerleaders' skirts, unfortunately.

"Exactly," Arianna said. "So I petitioned to get rid of them. Mr. McKaffey turned me down but said I could wear a longer skirt if I wanted to, as long as it was navy blue. So I sewed up a dozen different styles. This one is my favorite."

"Wow." And I meant it.

"Every year I ask God to give me a word, and this year he gave me the word *service*. And now this opportunity has come! It's such a God thing."

Arianna dove into an oration on being a servant of God, as if that would somehow make me want to be one too. Weird strategy. I ignored her babbling while zigzagging through the mob. I turned down the freshman hallway, which was filled with rowdy students and clanging lockers.

Arianna stopped off at her locker. "See you in homeroom."

That settled that. I'd skip homeroom for the rest of the year if only to avoid any more heart-to-hearts with Mission-Ari Sloan.

A bigger group than usual had crowded in front of my locker. I cleared my throat. "Look out, people. Coming through."

The crowd parted to reveal Nick Muren leaning against my locker like some kind of Mr. McKaffey wannabe. "Well if it isn't Spencer 'The Snitch' Garmond."

Just what I needed, a blast from my past.

REPORT NUMBER: 4

REPORT TITLE: I Take a Pop Quiz and Pass!
SUBMITTED BY: Agent-in-Training Spencer Garmond
LOCATION: Freshman Hall, Pilot Point Christian School, Pilot
Point, California, USA
DATE AND TIME: Monday, April 28, 7:18 a.m.

"WHAT'S UP?" I SAID TO NICK in a pathetic attempt to pretend this wasn't going to get ugly.

Nick just smirked. As always, his face, clothes, pose, and perfectly gelled hair looked like something from the cover of *GQ* magazine. He was tall and thin, but I had four inches on him.

Nick's friends—an even mix of henchmen and hotties—clustered around, expressions awestruck, as if their very breath hinged on what might come out of Nick's pretty-boy mouth next.

I didn't really care. Nick was in my way, and I was taller. He and I had been friends once too, but things went bad. "You mind stepping aside, Muren? You're blocking my locker."

"Guess what, jockstrap?" Nick stepped forward—partially on my foot. "You're *not* one of us."

I lowered my eyes to Nick's suede designer sneakers and ripped my foot free. "Dude, tell me about it. This is the third year I applied for the Nick Muren Fan Club and still, nothing. Think you can put in a good word for me?"

As if he could get any closer, Nick took another menacing inch forward. Though it was hard to be menacing when he had to look up at me. I stepped back and bumped into Jeb— another shadow from my past. Jeb was a meaty wrestler with a face like a gargoyle. He rammed my back, bumping me closer to Nick.

Nick's voice, barely audible, made goosebumps pop up on my arms. "Not this group, you moron. The *mission trip*. It must be a mistake. *You* must be a mistake."

Spending the morning with churchers who thought they were spies was one thing. But having Nick Muren get all in my face about it, like I stole his *American Idol* audition, topped the weirdness scale. I was done with all of this.

I stretched my spine, making myself as tall as I could, and looked down on Nick. "I didn't ask for this, okay? I know you don't like me. Newsflash: I don't like you either. Now beat it, will you? I want to get to class." I thought of Mission-Ari waiting to inform me of how a servant's heart should be humble. "Skip class, actually."

"That's quite a mouth, little freshman," Jeb said, as if his being a sophomore gave him the right to patronize me.

Plus, I always liked hearing I was little from a guy shorter than me. I gave Jeb a curt nod and my best John Wayne. "Well, thanks, little pardner."

Nick's eyes cut into me like *PoP* laser vision. "I don't trust you, Garmond, and I'm telling Mr. S that much."

I lifted my hands out to the side. "If you think that'll make us even, you go right ahead and tell Mr. S whatever you want. I've got nothing to hide."

Nick leaned so close I could smell his minty breath. "You don't belong in this group, Garmond. We're like a family, and if I'm not mistaken, you don't have one. Quit now before you make a fool of yourself."

The mention of my lack of parents boiled my spit. Nick just had to go and make it personal. I clenched my fists and considered the best way to make Nick eat his words. But a nasal voice cut through my visual of laying Nick out like concrete.

"Fighting is a poor way to serve the Lord, Nick."

I turned my head. Arianna wedged her thin self through the wall of bodies.

"Stay out of this, Mission-Ari," Nick said.

Her eyes went wide. "Ooh, good one, Nick! Like I haven't heard that in the last two minutes." She grabbed my arm and pulled. "Come on, Spencer. Time for class."

Speechless, I allowed the Pixy Stix to pull me away from what would have been a suspension.

"Saved by his girlfriend. How sweet!" Nick's jeer floated after us, followed by a round of laughter from the henchmen and hotties.

I flushed and jerked free from Arianna. The last thing I needed was rumors of me and Arianna circulating the halls, especially when I hadn't managed to say two words to Isabel yet.

Outside the doorway to our homeroom class, Arianna

turned and propped one hand on her hip. "My advice? Keep out of Nick's way. He can get—"

"I don't plan to get *in* his way, but if he's blocking my locker, and I'm thinking about going to Moscow with him, were bound to run into each other."

"Thinking about? Spencer, God chose you for this."

I couldn't help but notice that Arianna had some serious peach fuzz on her upper lip, which drew my gaze to her unibrow. The girl could use some tweezers.

"Spencer," she reached out and grabbed my arm as if to anchor me to some sort of reality, "you can't run from God."

"Wanna bet? I can run pretty fast."

She rolled her eyes, then pushed past me into the homeroom class.

With Mr. Miller standing just inside, I couldn't ditch. Still, I waited a good ten seconds before going in so no one would think I'd been walking with Arianna.

I slouched into my usual seat in the back corner just as the bell rang. Arianna chattered to a girl in the front row and tucked a strand of short, brown hair behind her ear. She wasn't very pretty. And that peach fuzz . . . I shuddered. I wished Isabel was in my group, but then I would've said something dumb. The prettier the girl, the less I functioned like a normal human.

Given the chance, would Isabel lecture me too? Try to reform me? I grinned and let the thought occupy my mind until the bell rang.

After homeroom, I returned to my locker to switch books. It appeared that Nick and Company had found more important things to do than harass me. I crouched and dug through the pile of papers at the bottom of my locker, looking for my Bible.

Yes, I owned one. It was required for students at PPCS.

I sat back on my heels and reached for my notebook. Before I could touch it, my locker slammed shut, scraping my knuckles. I swore and scanned the crowded hallway, just catching a glimpse of Jeb darting into the bathroom. As soon as I managed to open my locker again, Pete knocked it shut. I had to open it three times before Bible history class, and I barely beat the bell.

I didn't care what I'd said to the cops three years ago: Nick Muren and his lackeys were messing with the wrong guy.

I made my way to class and found my seat next to Kip. We knocked fists.

"Missed you on *PoP* last night," I said. "Where were you?"

"Megan Barnes's place." He waggled his eyebrows.

"You lucky dog. You hear from Sammy?"

"His dad's keeping him home. I guess some reporter chick stole Sammy's phone and took him for a ride. Now Sammy's on lockdown."

Sammy lived up in the hills and went to Pilot Point High. If he wasn't coming in for school, I might not see him for a while. "His dad okay?"

Kip shook his head. "Out on bail. There's going to be a trial and everything, but not for a few months, Sammy says."

"What's he want us to say if we get questioned?"

"We don't know anything about any drugs at Mr. Vanderson's house. He's a great dad." Kip punched my arm. "Dude, what's this talk of you going on some mission trip?"

I grunted, annoyed that Kip had heard this in rumor form already. That meant people were talking about it. About me. And it didn't involve basketball. "Grandma's making me go."

"What about conditioning?"

Mr. Hearn closed the door, his signal for absolute silence. I mouthed the word "Later" to Kip and slouched down in my seat.

"Esau, Isaac's firstborn twin, a hairy redhead, a hunter," Mr. Hearn said, his voice like the grating hum of a tractor. "Favorite of his father, he is none too bright and has sold his birthright to his brother, Jacob, for a bowl of stew."

I doodled in my notebook as Mr. Hearn went on. I was glad that Sammy was still with his dad and relieved to know what I was supposed to say to help him out. I didn't know what would happen to Sammy if his dad went to jail.

"Then there is Jacob, Isaac's second born twin, a homebody, a *mama's boy*, the brains."

I tuned out Mr. Hearn, a strategy I'd developed for sermons and lectures. I stopped listening, my vision blurred, and I traveled to the basketball court in my mind to work on my mental game.

At lunch, I grabbed my tray and started for the table in the far corner, where the basketball guys usually sat. Out of nowhere, Jeb plowed into me, knocking my plate of spaghetti onto my white shirt.

Jeb's chiseled face morphed into an evil grin. "Sorry, man."

I was just about to throw down my tray and tackle him when Arianna appeared again, like some wispy, ever-present bodyguard.

She grabbed my arm and dragged me away. "Sit with us."

I don't know why I went with her. I always sat with Kip and the basketball team, in spite of Grandma's objection to Kip's, uh . . . influence. I glanced at my table where Kip was sitting. Megan Barnes, a cute basketball player, was laughing at something he said.

I hope it wasn't about me going on a mission trip.

Nick sat down at the next table, right behind Megan, and shot me an I'm-the-king-of-the-school look. I so didn't want to deal with Nick. Maybe it wouldn't hurt to sit with these churchers, just for today. Maybe Isabel would sit here, and I could say something to make her laugh. And then . . .

Arianna forced me onto the bench beside Gabe. "Be right back." Arianna nudged Gabe. "Make him stay."

"Spencer, Arianna says stay." Gabe flashed his metal smile and looked at my shirt. "Ooh. What happened?"

"Jeb Beary happened." I flicked spaghetti off my striped necktie. "I hate school uniforms."

No sign of Isabel yet. My tray looked like roadkill. I shoveled spaghetti into my mouth anyway, keeping one eye on the entrance for exotic Ee-sa-bell.

"You normally sit with the basketball team?" Gabe asked.

"Yeah," I said, opening my carton of milk.

And suddenly the goddess stood before me, giggling with Arianna. They'd come from behind me. Arianna snorted a laugh, her eyes filled with tears. But like a slow-motion scene out of a music video, Isabel tossed her hair and smiled. Her face glowed like bronze, her eyes sparked.

"What's so funny?" Gabe asked.

Arianna's expression sobered. "Do you have room for Bill and Bob?"

Isabel linked her arm with Arianna's and murmured,

"*Mande?* Which one is me again?"

"You're Bob Rod, remember? I'm Bill Slo," Arianna said.

"Ah, *si.*" Isabel leaned toward Gabe and stuck out her hand adorned with glossy, claw-like fingernails edged in white. Her brown curls tumbled over her shoulder—again with the slo mo. "*Me llamo* Bob."

Gabe shook her hand, one eyebrow raised. "Nice to meet you, Bob."

I stared at her flawless cheeks as I stuck out my hand. "Spencer Garmond."

She turned her eyes on me, and it felt like the heat of the bat signal. She shook my hand. "Me llamo Bob."

She let go all too soon, and, like a cloud crossing over the sun, the heat vanished. The girls sat across from me and Gabe. At least now, if Kip saw me, he'd understand why I ditched him. He and I had talked about the goddess before.

Arianna leaned across the table and whispered. "We worked out undercover aliases in case we need them this summer."

"So you came up with Bill and Bob?" I asked.

The girls burst into hysterics again. I didn't get it, but watching Isabel laugh was not unpleasant.

Gabe ripped off the end of his straw and blew the wrapper at Isabel. "You don't need aliases yet, Isabel, don't worry."

"*Yo sé.* It's only for playing." She wadded his straw wrapper and flicked it back.

I wished I had a straw wrapper to flick. I must have lost mine when Jeb attacked.

By the time lunch ended, Arianna had bestowed goofy aliases on all of us. The big secret consisted of a short 'B' name followed by the first three letters in the person's last name. I became Biff Gar. Gabe became Bo Sto.

Ingenious . . . and completely lame. But the time had not been wasted. I'd also learned, mostly from Gabe, that Isabel had come here from Cuba two years ago, that she had a younger brother named Lukas, and that her mother owned a salon called *Peluqueria Rodriguez.*

I know, right? Score one for reconnaissance.

After school, I went to Room 401. The classroom held a teacher's desk, two round tables, and a stack of chairs. The place was wallpapered in international posters. Swaziland, Germany, Puerto Rico, Greece, Turkey, Saskatchewan . . . Where on earth was Saskatchewan? Oh, and sure enough, a World Vision poster of an African waif hung behind the teacher's desk. I smirked. Now this was more like it.

Most everyone had arrived. Mr. S and his wife, Kerri, were talking beside the teacher's desk. I carefully chose my seat at the Alpha table to give me the best, non-obvious location for staring at Isabel. Gabe sat beside me, humming to himself. Jensina was reading her Russian textbook. I pulled mine out of my backpack, propped one elbow on it, and gazed at the back of Isabel's head.

How did girls get their hair so silky? Must be the magic of the hair salon.

It was probably for the best that I wasn't in Diakonos with Isabel. I'd undoubtedly make a fool of myself within seconds. Then where would I be? At least in Alpha group I could observe and plot from a safe distance.

"Why do you people need an alias?" I asked Gabe. I mean, *James bond* was one thing. But *biff Gar*? Another thing entirely.

"*You* don't," Gabe said. "Not until your second summer—before your first red card." He huffed a laugh. "Bo Sto isn't going to cut it."

At least Gabe could see that much. "What's a red card?"

"An intercessor-assigned mission. That's probably why Isabel is considering aliases. Who knows why Arianna's doing it. She's—"

"You pick an alias, yet?"

Gabe faked a cheesy smile that showed off his braces. "Maybe."

"I hope it's better than Bo Sto."

"It is. But if I told you, I'd have to kill you, and I kinda like having you around."

This coming from a guy with a little boy face and braces who spoke so softly I could hardly hear him.

Kerri handed me a packet of paperwork. "It's tradition for new recruits to take a spiritual gifts survey. You may know some of your strengths already, and some may not develop until later in life. But we like to get you thinking about how God has gifted you and how you might apply those gifts in your life. I'll score the test tonight, and you can discuss them with your groups tomorrow."

A test? Who ever heard of a pop quiz on the first day?

The class got quiet. Everyone was studying their Russian books except me, and probably Arianna. I drew around the staple in the top corner of my test until I ripped through a layer, then I wrote my name on the top and traced over the letters until they were nice and thick. Gabe flipped a few pages in his Russian textbook. I sighed and read the first question.

1. My enthusiasm and excitement about the things of the Lord is evident:
a. always; b. often; c. sometimes; d. not at all

Well, that was an easy one. I circled *d*.

Day two in the basement of the Barn. I fought to keep my eyes open. School started too early as it was. Having this 6:00 a.m. business every day would be torture, especially when vivid dreams woke me at least twice a week. Last night's dream had again been about the blond woman at the foreign restaurant. I yawned and shook her face from my mind.

I sat at the round table in the back, staring at the survey Kerri had handed me. *Prophecy-13, discernment-13* was marked in red at the top. There was no letter grade. For some reason, Arianna sat beside me at the Alpha table, poring over her own survey. Today she was wearing a navy blue floor length skirt that clung to her legs and was pleated like the guts of an accordion.

"Ooh!" Her eyes glowed. "Healing is interesting. Teaching and knowledge—knew I'd get those. But healing. Hmm." She leaned close, smelling like herbal tea. "What'd you get?"

I passed her my survey.

"Wow!" She raised her eyebrows. "Prophecy *and* discernment? Impressive."

Didn't feel impressive. "What's it supposed to mean?"

"Discernment is sensing good from evil, truth from lies. Prophecy is speaking God's truths. Sometimes you could even have God speak through you to predict—"

"What truths?" There was no way I was predicting anything about God.

"You joke about everything, Spencer?" She gave me an appraising smirk, then looked back to my test. "Those are wonderful gifts."

I didn't like the little flutter of pride in my gut at Arianna's praise. I didn't believe in any of this, so why should I care what the test said?

I scribbled around the staple where I'd left off yesterday, making a bigger ink blob and separating the top sheet from the rest. Could I spend the summer with these people without looking like a complete moron? Could I fake discernment? I'd have to Google it.

I'd Googled INTERPOL last night. It turned out to be the world's largest international police organization. They employ about 650 staff members. From my math, the Mission League would have way more agents than that. And, of course, there was no mention of the Mission League on the INTERPOL site.

I didn't know what to think of these people.

Maybe military school would be better. I wouldn't have to live with Grandma or hang out with any über Christians. But PPCS's varsity point guard was a senior, leaving me in prime position to make the starting five next season. I had to make this work.

Arianna moved to the Diakonos table as the rest of Alpha group arrived. Still no sign of Isabel.

"Hey, newbie." Isaac snatched my survey and studied it. "Hmm, good for Special Forces, good for Special Forces. But those gifts are good for other paths too, if you're not into Special Forces." Isaac showed Gabe my paper.

I clicked the top of my pen up, down, up, down, up. "What's Special—"

"Nice," Gabe said. "I've never seen anyone get top scores in discernment and prophecy. Have you ever felt called in these areas?"

I didn't answer. If I felt *called* to do anything it was to leave the room.

REPORT NUMBER: 5

REPORT TITLE: The Day Pasha Met Anya
SUBMITTED BY: Agent Ryan Matheson
INTERVIEWEE: Pasha Ivanovich
LOCATION: Café Moo Moo, Arbat Street #45/24, Moscow, Russia
DATE AND TIME: Wednesday, April 30, 5:04 p.m.

THE SMELLS OF HOT FOOD teased Pasha's empty stomach. He missed his mother's cooking, especially her borscht. Maybe he should make peace with Father and go home.

Café *Moo Moo* served home-cooked Russian food, and they did it buffet style. The place was decorated like a farm inside: black and white décor with red accents and cartoon cows.

Pasha carried his order to one of the red plastic tables and sucked some strawberry compote through the straw. It had taken him all day to panhandle enough money for a meal. He sat down and stuffed one of the sausages into his mouth, then a salted cucumber wedge. He sat back and chewed, sighing through his nose, thankful for the tasty blessing.

A slender blonde passed his table, gliding along with the posture of a ballerina. Pasha straightened and breathed in her spicy perfume. He took another bite of sausage, but the food no longer satisfied.

The blonde turned and blinked long, dark lashes at him. "Privyet." *Hi.*

Pasha stopped chewing and gave an awkward wave. She couldn't be interested in him, could she? At sixteen, he stood nearly six feet tall, but he was all bones topped with an oily black mop and a nose too big for his face.

He washed down the sausage with a gulp of compote. A woman like her and a goofy looking kid like him? He snorted a laugh, sucking cold liquid up his nose. Now everything stung: nose, eyes, throat. He gasped, and his vision blurred through watering eyes.

The woman sauntered toward him and stopped at his table. She ran her long, red fingernail along the back of the white plastic chair adjacent to his. Her eyes searched his, green and intense, and her platinum hair draped around her shoulders like a movie star's. "Is anyone sitting here?" she asked in English.

Pasha shook his head, blinking away tears and embarrassment. Was she American? A tourist?

She slid into the chair across from him. "Menya zovoot Anya." *My name is Anya.* Her accent was flawless in both languages.

He gave her a half-smile, absorbed by her presence. "I am Pasha."

"I know." She took a sip of his compote, leaving a red lipstick smudge on his straw.

How she knew his name didn't matter. She reached out to shake his hand, and when their skin touched, an unnatural chill coursed over his body.

A meal and a beautiful new lady friend in the same day? Maybe Pasha's luck was changing.

REPORT NUMBER: 6

REPORT TITLE: I'm Attacked By Masked . . . Men?
SUBMITTED BY: Agent-in-Training Spencer Garmond
LOCATION: Driveway, Grandma Alice's House, Pilot Point,
California, USA
DATE AND TIME: Saturday, May 10, 2:47 p.m.

I DRIBBLED TO THE EDGE of the driveway and brought the ball up for a ten-foot jumper. Before I shot, a shadow streaked across the concrete. I whipped around.

Two figures wearing black clothes and ski masks rushed me. The taller one grabbed my wrist, turned, and flung me, twisting my body in the air.

I landed on my back on the driveway—stunned—and moaned into the cloudless sky. Before I could move, my attacker's fist came down, punching me hard in the gut. My body seized, and I wheezed for air.

The smaller figure grunted at the other, then reached for me.

I scrambled to my feet, ignoring my throbbing gut, and darted out of the smaller figure's grasp. They both came at me again. I landed a punch in the tall person's face. The smaller one kicked the back of my knees. I went down. He wrenched an arm around my neck—securing me in a headlock—and squeezed slightly.

The pressure of the headlock cut off my air. I dug my fingernails into my captor's eye. He screamed—high pitched, like a girl—then pushed me to my chest, keeping hold of my neck until my face pressed against the hot concrete.

Something dug into a major pressure point on my back. I growled but couldn't move an inch. My attacker emitted a rhythmic string of grunts.

Some sort of signal?

The concrete seared my cheek, and all I could do was watch as my basketball rolled slowly into the flower bed. The taller person squatted in front of me and ripped off a chunk of duct tape.

I panicked, flooded with hot fear. "Grandma! Gran—"

Duct tape went over my mouth, bound my ankles, and secured my wrists behind my back. A red pillowcase was pulled over my head, dousing everything in the color of fire. I thrashed in rage, heart pounding as they dragged me away.

A hinge creaked, and I pitched forward. My limbs crashed against cold, corrugated metal, shooting pain through every nerve. A door slammed, and everything went black.

I struggled against the tape, but the smallest twist pulled the hairs on my wrists and ankles like tiny needles pressing into my skin. A motor vibrated to life. Was I in a van? Some kind of truck? My body surged to the right as the vehicle peeled away. I took deep breaths through my nose to compose myself, and I smelled fabric softener on the pillowcase clinging to my face.

I had to calm down. Think.

I rolled onto my side and bent my knees, bringing my feet up to my hands behind me—quite uncomfortable. I worked at the tape doubled around my ankles until my arms and legs ached. Finally the tape started to give, then ripped in half.

"Hey!" The voice was female.

I struggled to sit, pushing back with my feet until I hit something solid. Voices hissed in the darkness, but no one touched me. I tried working my hands under my rear to get them in front of me, but before I could manage, the vehicle jerked to a stop.

Metal creaked. Everything lit up red. Someone grabbed my arm, so I started kicking. I made contact several times before he or she or they dragged me out.

A dog barked. An ice cream truck chimed in the distance. A residential area? If I could get them to drop me, maybe I could run. Someone might see me—or a car might hit me. I wriggled like a fish out of water, but my ankles were wedged against something soft. A door squeaked, and the chill of air conditioning made my skin tingle. I fell suddenly onto soft carpet. The room smelled like fresh cookies. Why was someone baking?

"What happened?" a bass voice asked.

"He's a wild tiger," a low feminine voice said.

They were disguising their voices. It sounded ridiculous. I made to stand, but someone pulled me into to a sitting position and propped me against another body—a whimpering girl by the sound of things. The kidnappers employed the duct tape again, binding me to the other person.

"Free their mouths," the bass voice commanded.

Fingers reached inside the pillowcase and ripped the tape from my mouth. Air prickled my skin where the tape had been. I stretched my lips to stop the burn.

The girl bound to me started begging. "Listen to me, please! My dad will pay you. Call him! 555-3248. I promise you, he—"

"Arianna?" I took a deep breath and caught the light scent of herbal tea. Plus I'd recognize that nasal voice anywhere.

"Spencer? That you?"

"No talking!" the bass voice said.

Arianna whimpered.

"You." It was the bass voice again. He batted at my face. "Give me the names of the members of Alpha team, your instructor, and the intercessor."

A different person asked Arianna the same question about Diakonos.

Arianna screamed. "Please don't hurt me!"

"Tell me what I want to know, and I'll stop," her interrogator said.

"Leave her alone!" I yelled, then called him a few choice names.

"Spencer!" Arianna said, sounding shocked.

Well, she may be a freak show, but that didn't mean I was going to let some psycho beat her up if I could help it.

Someone whacked my arm, and the bass voice repeated his request. I sat still for a minute, listening to the sounds around me. Bass Voice smacked me a few more times, but he wasn't even trying to hurt me. Something was off here. I mean, come on. Who would kidnap someone to find out who was in the Mission League? Everyone knew—about the cover story mission trip to Russia anyway. It wouldn't take a genius to put two and two together.

My breath caught. *It's a test!*

Arianna was sobbing now. "Jake Lindley, Isabel Rodriguez, Beth—"

"Arianna, shut up!" I elbowed her. "It's Mr. S. They're messing with us!"

Cheers and groans rose around me. A few snips and pulls released the tape from my arms and wrists. Someone yanked me to my feet and lifted the pillowcase from my head. The light made me wince.

I squinted and blinked until my vision focused on Isaac. He was wearing a black T-shirt and black jeans.

"And that's how it's done! Yeah!" Isaac wadded the red pillowcase and pelted it at Jake, who sat on a long, brown leather sofa between Isabel and Beth.

I looked around me. I stood in a spotless living room with forest green carpet. A baby grand piano sat beside the sofa. A portrait showing five people—four with black curly heads and one bald man—hung over the sofa and revealed that this was the Stopplecamp's place.

Jake and the girls were dressed in black too. Isabel's hair was tousled. And Buff Beth held a tissue to her nose. Tendrils of brown hair clung to her forehead. Deep red scratches swelled under one eye.

I frowned. Had Beth put me in that headlock?

Okay, that was weird . . . and scary . . . and disturbing that a girl had thrashed me like that.

And also kind of . . . hot.

Gabe—also wearing black—and Mr. S sat in matching leather recliners in front of a wall with a huge picture window that looked out onto a trim lawn. Opposite the couch, Nick and Jensina were sitting at a dining table, dressed like a couple of burglars.

The final wall was split by a kitchen counter. Kerri—Mrs. S—stood behind it, wearing baking mitts and scraping cookies onto a cooling rack.

"You guys hungry?" she asked.

I leaned against the wall and crossed my arms, unsure if the cookies were another test. I peered down at Arianna. She still sat on the floor, scowling.

"An Alpha victory all around," Mr. S said. "But 'it is the fight alone that pleases us, not the victory.' Blaise Pascal."

"And I would like to add," Isaac said, "that 'a date without a goodnight kiss is like a doughnut without frosting.' And that quote is *all* me."

Laughter, including my own, bubbled around the room. "Spencer, Arianna," Mr. S asked, "you okay?"

I nodded, wondering if there was room for four on that couch.

Arianna sniffed. "What a lousy trick. Wait 'til my dad hears."

Jake cackled, his arms draped along the back of the sofa behind Isabel and Beth, who'd tied the red pillowcase over her head like a bandana.

"Your padre knows, wahine." Isaac picked up scraps of duct tape from the beige carpet and rolled them into a ball.

"We have to inform a League Agent when we're going to train on their property," Jake said.

"Or kidnap his daughter," Isaac said.

"It's the standard initiation test," Jake said.

Arianna huffed and got to her feet. "It's a little scary, don't you think?"

"You need to be aware of what you're getting into with this organization," Mr. S said. "It's not all classroom studies."

She folded her arms. "I still think my dad wouldn't have let you do this. He wasn't even mad?"

Isaac shot the duct tape ball into the kitchen trash and grabbed a handful of cookies off the counter. "He gave me a house key and told me the best time to nab you. So, no. Not mad at all."

Jake bolted upright and glared at Isaac. "You're a cheater!"

"I . . . used my resources," Isaac mumbled through stuffed cheeks.

Jake pointed at me. "I've been following Spencer for the past three weekends. Mr. Sloan shouldn't have helped you. That's unfair."

I slid behind Jake and stole his seat between the girls. "I never saw you around my neighborhood," I said, smiling at Isabel, then Beth.

"Because I'm good. Now, get out of my seat, newbie!" Jake said.

"No way!" I said, pressing back when Jake tried to pull me up.

"Isaac grabbed me?" Arianna asked.

Isaac tossed Arianna a cookie, which she failed to catch, and sat on the arm of Gabe's recliner. "You cool with that?"

Arianna held her scowl for a moment before saying, "You didn't really hurt me. Scared me half to death, though."

Jake let go of me and went to get cookies. I eyed Beth. "Who got me? 'Cause that hurt!"

Isaac spun to face Beth. "Hey, Beth: rule 18b!"

"What? He's alive." Beth smiled at me, still holding a tissue under her eye. "Nick's the one who broke protocol. And Tiger fought back big time." She elbowed me.

I looked to Nick at the dining table. A big red welt blazed on his cheek.

Serves him right.

Nick stared my way. "He kicked me."

Beth raised her voice. "After you punched him. I had him subdued without harm. All you had to do was tape him."

Nick stood. "He got the tape off his ankles. It was self-defense."

Beth rolled her eyes. "Sprained my finger. Tiger should train in LCT for District. After I'm gone you're going to need someone good." She elbowed me again.

LCT? I looked at Beth, and she winked at me, a dimple forming under her eye. My heart pumped faster to compensate for the blood rushing to my head.

"Looks like the newbie can take care of himself." Isaac inspected Nick's cheek with mock concern. "Should I call 911?"

The group laughed.

"Diakonos and Nick lose twenty points for breaking protocol," Mr. S said. "They're not supposed to inflict harm. But real captors may. Not that there's a reason for anyone to abduct you simply for being a part of the Mission League. We do this test early so you know what you're getting into. Sorry for the scare."

I still couldn't believe a girl had taken me down—put me in that headlock. I'd gouged her eye, and she'd complimented me? I sat between Isabel and Beth, happy, yet torn.

Things in the Mission League had just gotten interesting.

REPORT NUMBER: 7

REPORT TITLE: Pasha Joins Bratva
SUBMITTED BY: Agent Ryan Matheson
INTERVIEWEE: Pasha Ivanovich
LOCATION: Bratva Headquarters, Moscow, Russia
DATE AND TIME: Sunday, May 11, 10:54 p.m.

PASHA GULPED. HE SAT IN A reclining chair, shirtless, in a dark room on the seventh floor of Bratva Headquarters. Anya sat on a stool. She switched directions, and her sleek blond ponytail flew through the steamy air like a whip.

"You won't regret this, Pasha," she said in English. She unclamped a lid on what looked like a pressure cooker and took out a needle. "This mark proves your loyalty. You can never completely remove a tattoo. The ink is permanent."

She was lying, wasn't she? There were ways to get rid of a tattoo. She just liked scaring him. At first she had captivated him with her beauty, then impressed him with her toughness. A girl like her had worked hard to make a place for herself in an organization like Bratva. She had a dark side, though, and he didn't fully trust her. The way she towered above him now, needle in hand, sent a shiver down his arms.

Anya snapped on a pair of rubber gloves and wiped alcohol on his bicep. "Ready, Pasha?" she all but sang.

No. Get up. Leave, you fool.

She reached toward him, and he pushed her hand away. "I don't know."

"Pasha." She took a deep breath and kissed his cheek. "Your father despises you. You are not a part of his world, and therefore you are useless to him. Bratva needs you. I need you. Please don't deny me."

She kissed him then, and for those few moments, he forgot why he'd wanted to leave. But then she broke away and flipped on the machine. A soft motor whirred, and Pasha's stomach tightened.

His English was not as good as hers. "You are not needing to draw design?"

Anya cackled. "No. I've done this hundreds of times. Each one is a little different, like art. I like to mark people, Pasha, it's my hobby. Are you sure this is where you want it?"

He wasn't sure he wanted it at all, but he nodded.

She put the needle to his arm, and he flinched. "Hold still. It'll be a while." She didn't try to be gentle. Typical Anya. She enjoyed inflicting pain.

So why did he let her? Her eyes were wild as she punctured him over and over with that needle, and for a moment she terrified him. But soon the sharp twinges of the needle dulled, and he got used to them. The guilt however, only increased.

Lord Eesoos, what have I done?

REPORT NUMBER: 8

REPORT TITLE: I Get a Letter from My Dead Mother
SUBMITTED BY: Agent-in-Training Spencer Garmond
LOCATION: Grandma Alice's House, Pilot Point, California, USA
DATE AND TIME: Wednesday, May 14, 2:15 p.m.

WHEN I GOT HOME FROM SCHOOL, I found Kimbal's patrol car in the driveway. A shiver flashed over me. I didn't want to know what he had to tell me about today. The initiation abduction had changed things. Girls who could take down a six-foot-three guy didn't hide out in basements to play chess.

Girls like that meant business. The guys too.

Curious, I went inside and found Grandma, Kimbal, and Prière sitting in the living room. "Now what?"

"Your *cérémonie d'initiation* is complete," Prière said, "so I have come to you to confirm your desire to continue training with the Mission League *organisation*."

I glanced from face to face. They were all staring at me, waiting for an answer. Grandma's face was stoic. "Do I have a choice?" I asked her.

She leaned forward in her armchair, the top of her spiky head like an angry, white porcupine. "There's no wishy-washy 'my grandma made me' in the Mission League, Spencer. If you want to stay in, you take this seriously."

I narrowed my eyes. "Want to stay in? So, now I get to decide?"

Grandma pursed her lips and nodded. "Yes. It's up to you."

"And no military school, even if I say no?"

Her jaw tensed. She glanced at Kimbal out of the corner of her eye. "No."

I dropped my backpack on the floor and leaned against the wall, flanked by the pictures of Babs and Duke. "How do you know so much about all this anyway, Grandma?"

She'd ignored this question dozens of times, but today she leaned back in her velour armchair and answered. "I'm a retired agent," she said, as if it were no big deal. "I used to be an Internal Profiler for the Los Angeles Field Office."

I blinked. Grandma, preschool teacher and the head of the quilting club, was a what? "I don't get it."

"What's to get? I am what I am."

I gritted my teeth. "Unbelievable!"

Prière cleared his throat. "Come now, Spence. Alice only has been trying to follow protocol of the Mission League."

"I couldn't compromise my secret until I was sure about you," she said.

My anger boiled over. "You don't trust me? I'm not the one keeping secrets!"

Grandma sighed. "Those are the rules. First there's the initial recruitment. If you show interest and attend classes, as you have, they move to the next phase: initiation. The initiation is done to give you a taste of the seriousness of things. Then, if you're still interested—"

"You made me join! You blackmailed me into it." I ran my hand through my hair and paced to the door. "And how am I supposed to join something I don't even . . . You people act like I should be excited or something. I don't even know . . . One day I'm memorizing a Bible verse, the next day people are duct-taping me in the driveway!"

"The thing is, Garmond," Kimbal scooted forward in his chair, "it doesn't usually happen this way. The call tends to run in the family, not always directly, but the students who are called usually know something about the organization already, so that when they receive their call, they . . . well, they know."

My mind processed this information. "What were you, again, Grandma?"

"Internal Profiler. I investigated for leaks, spies, and traitors."

Missionary traitors? "Like Internal Affairs?"

She nodded. "Exactly."

"Did Grandpa Earl know?" I asked.

"That's how we met. He was director of the LA Field Office."

"He was great man," Prière said.

Director of the LA Field Office? What would Gabe think of that? Probably already knew. Isaac and Jake too. Everyone probably knew. I'd hardly known the man. He'd died when I'd been five. A question crossed my mind, but I didn't want to ask it in front of everyone.

Had my mom and dad known?

Grandma peered at Kimbal and forced a cough.

Kimbal jumped to his feet and started for the door. "Let's go for a walk, Garmond."

I pinched my eyebrows together. "Why?"

"Just go with him!" Grandma snapped.

I stormed out of the house. I stopped in the driveway and whipped around. Kimbal was right behind me. "So? What else?"

Kimbal shoved his hands into his pockets and strolled to the mailbox. "There's a lot you don't know, and I'm sorry for that. I never meant for things to be like this, but there's more at stake here than my feelings or yours. Sometimes, Spencer, you have to do hard things because they serve a greater good."

I stared at a trail of ants crossing the sidewalk.

"The thing is . . ." Kimbal stopped and looked at me, his eyes watery. "I'm your dad's little brother. Your uncle."

"Come on," I said, but a shiver washed over me as I thought back to the things Mrs. Daggett had said. The secret Kimbal would finally get to reveal.

"It's true." Kimbal blew out a big sigh, as if telling me had been difficult for him.

Dozens of questions assaulted my mind. I didn't bother holding them back. "Why didn't you say so? Wait, do you know where my dad is right now? Why he left? Do you know how my mom died? Why do I have to live with Grandma? Where do you live? Can I—"

"Hold on. I'll answer what I can, one at a time, but I can't talk too much about your parents. Most of it's classified."

"Are you kidding me?" I thought of what Kimbal—Uncle Dave—had said a few moments before. "So, me not knowing I had an uncle serves the greater good of . . . what?"

Kimbal leaned against the wooden fence that edged Grandma's lawn. An Oldsmobile drove past, and Kimbal's head turned with it. "Keeping you alive."

"From who?"

"I can't say."

"Why not?"

"Protocol."

I kicked the fence. "That's stupid."

"What I can tell you is both your parents were League agents. A certain group wanted to turn your mom—to convert her to serving the enemy. She was too tough, so they went after your dad. My brother was never the strongest guy when it came to outright temptation, so he was an easy target. They used him to get to your mom and . . ." Kimbal's lips pressed into a thin line, and he looked down the street. "They killed her."

The air pricked my eyes, but I couldn't blink, I couldn't swallow, I couldn't breathe. Grandma had said my dad had left when I was a baby, but she'd never said how her daughter had died. I'd always assumed a car wreck or cancer or something like that.

I sucked in a long breath. It was sweet from the flowers in Grandma's garden. "Where's my dad now? Prison?"

Kimbal winced and looked me in the eye. "We don't know."

"Why didn't Grandma tell me? Do you know what it's like living with her?"

Kimbal propped his hands on the fence. "Cut her some slack. You're all she has in the world, and you look just like your dad—not all that different from me. Hadn't you noticed?"

"Kimbal Jr. wasn't too far off, I guess."

He chuckled. "Anyway, having us around all these years, reminding her of the man responsible for her daughter's death—it couldn't have been easy."

"But I'd never seen you before I came to Pilot Point Christian School."

"Yeah, well. I've been around. When you started getting in trouble, I went undercover with the Pilot Point PD. But I've been assigned to protect you ever since you came to live with Alice, just in case your dad came looking."

"He left. Why would he come looking?"

Kimbal shrugged and watched another car drive by, this one a silver Lexus. "You're his only son."

Bogus. Kimbal wasn't spilling the whole story. "Do you follow me around?"

"Yup."

"You tell Grandma everything I do?"

"Sometimes."

"Nice." No wonder Grandma always knew things she couldn't possibly know. I looked to the house and saw her and Prière standing at the window. "Why tell me now?"

"You deserve to know, especially if you're thinking about not joining the League. Your parents lived for this organization. If you'd grown up with them, you'd have been excited when you got your call. I just want you to have the facts before you say no. At least give it the summer, go on the first trip."

I didn't even want to think about the trip right now. "Where do you live?"

"A couple blocks over. Screenland Drive."

Screenland Drive was only six blocks from here. I

pondered the idea of a home where the decor wasn't made from yarn . . . Maybe Kimbal had a TV and central air. Two guys hanging out could be cool. "Why can't I live with you?"

Kimbal laughed. "Because I'm assigned to watch you. If I'm your caregiver, there's a lot I can't see. I'd be distracted. It's safer this way. Plus, I don't know nothing about raising a kid."

"I'm not a kid. I'm fifteen. And I can take care of myself."

"Yeah, I've seen that. How's your cheek and forehead?"

"Whatever." Another thing didn't add up. "Why do I have Grandma's last name, instead of my dad's? Grandma would never say."

Kimbal looked uncomfortable. "When she took you in . . . Because of what happened . . . well . . . You're both in a witness protection program of sorts."

"Are you kidding me?" I looked at my hands. I didn't even know who I was?

"Look, take a few days, take as much time as you need, but—" Kimbal pulled out a worn purple envelope from his back pocket. "This is confidential, along with everything I just told you. Keep it to yourself. No one would believe you, anyway. I mean"—he huffed—"Christian spies. Who'd believe that?"

I smirked as I stared at the creased envelope in Kimbal's outstretched hand. The top had been slit open. "You read it?"

"It's my job. HQ reads everything first anyway."

I looked into my newfound uncle's eyes—blue, like my own. Something inside burst. I wanted to run fast and far, but my body wouldn't cooperate.

Kimbal grabbed my wrist, pulled it forward, and forced the envelope into my hand. "I'll be inside if you need me." He slapped my shoulder.

I sank against the inside of the fence. I ripped open the envelope and jerked out a single sheet of white paper. The ink was purple.

Jonas,

If you're reading this, it means I'm dead. It's so strange to write such a thing when I'm alive and you're so little, but that's the job, I guess. I'm so sorry.

Try to understand that wherever you are, whoever you're with, it's for the best. Since I can't predict what's happened to me, I can't give you more assurance than that.

It was always our prayer that you would be called to serve in the Mission League someday like your father and me. If that's the case, I encourage you to become the best agent you can. Trust God always. He's in control, and His plans are perfect. Stay close to Him in prayer, for that relationship will be your best protection in any circumstance and your only hope of seeing me again.

I love you with all my heart.

Mom

Jonas?

I gazed at the loopy purple writing, my mind reeling with overload, my new name—old name. Nothing made sense. Some people had tried to turn my mom? To what? And why had my dad betrayed her? What temptation couldn't he resist? Why would he want to hurt me? The questions begged for answers.

Grandma had said this was my choice, but how could I quit now? All I ever wanted to do was to play college ball. I'd never given much thought to a career beyond that. Sure, NBA would be nice, but I wasn't delusional. Even if I did play college ball, I'd still need to pick a major. Maybe this League thing would pan out, and I could transfer to the CIA or something.

My name was Jonas?

I suddenly ached for my ball. It always felt good to channel my frustration toward the hoop. But I didn't want to go in and get it, so I got up and played with an imaginary ball instead.

The sky was grey when I climbed the steps and went inside. The house smelled like gravy, and my stomach growled. Grandma was in the kitchen. Kimbal and Prière were sitting in the living room, Prière on the sofa, Kimbal in Grandma's armchair.

Kimbal saw me first. "How you doing?"

I ran my hand through my hair. "I'm in."

"Dinner first, then you can sign the contract." Grandma pulled on baking mitts. "Go get washed up."

I didn't move. "Contract?" These people were intense. "I want to sign it now."

"Oh, all right." Grandma removed the mitts from her hands and switched off the oven. "We'll eat after."

Kimbal got up and offered me Grandma's chair. "Sit."

I did. Prière opened a brown file folder. Inside was a stack of paper I figured must be the contract. This contract was ten pages, the last six filled with rows and rows of blanks for me to initial.

Prière sat silently on the couch while I read the thing over. I was committing to juvenile service only, apparently. A new contract would be offered if I chose to make a career of it.

"Much more *difficile* are the choices then," Prière said. "There is much to be sacrificed as an adult agent."

I didn't want to think about that now. I only intended to stick around long enough to learn what I could about my parents, maybe study LCT with Beth. Maybe make a move on Isabel.

But the contract seemed to require me to be squeaky clean perfect. No alcohol, drugs, witchcraft, sex, pornography, unnecessary violence, or crime of any kind. Not that I set out to get in trouble. Anymore. Still, if Mr. S did any kind of monitoring at all, I'd be kicked out by the end of next week.

On pages eight and nine, the contract got real technical. Maintain C average.

Needed to do that for basketball already.

Must attend a church service on a weekly basis.

Grandma saw to that.

No swearing.

Yikes! I was in big trouble there.

No inappropriate dress.

Not sure what they meant on that one.

No tattoos. No piercings.

"What's with all these rules? Aren't spies supposed to go undercover and stuff ? How are we supposed to blend in if we all look like choir boys and Girl Scouts?"

"The rules are différent for adults," Prière said. "Now you are training. There is much more, ah, how do you say . . . red tape in the *juvénile programme*."

I snorted. "Of course there is."

The list went on and on. I initialed every blank, signed each page at the bottom, and gave the whole pile to Kimbal, who signed on the last page as a witness. Prière also signed. Two witnesses. Protocol. Bizarre.

So there it was. God had supposedly made the call, and I had supposedly accepted, strange as that still sounded. Maybe I was nuts, but knowing a little piece of my past made it all seem right somehow. I wasn't going to become a churcher, though.

"*Félicitations*, Spence. "I wish to offer you one caution. Try to hold tightly to your temper when you are playing the sport of basketball *à la gym*. This I know is strange to hear, but sometimes these things come to me. In my dreams." He tapped his temple. "Think about my warning, oui?"

The dude was dreaming about me? Creepy.

Prière tucked the contract under his arm and shook my hand. "I look forward to working with you over the next few years."

"Yeah." As long as I didn't get kicked out before then.

But I had to stay in. My mother had died for this loony organization. I'd do whatever it took to live up to her sacrifice, at least until I found out who "they" were.

And made them pay.

REPORT NUMBER: 9

REPORT TITLE: I Lose My Temper, Big Time
SUBMITTED BY: Agent-in-Training Spencer Garmond
LOCATION: Cafeteria, Pilot Point Christian School, Pilot Point,
California, USA
DATE AND TIME: Friday, May 16, 11:42 a.m.

TWO DAYS LATER, I SAT at the basketball lunch table with Kip, eating pizza and dreaming about kicking Nick in the face—by accident of course, now that I'd pledged myself to non-violent behavior and butterfly collecting. But Nick seemed to have no scruples about skirting the Mission League rules, so why should I? His cronies had harassed me all morning. I'd been pushed and tripped, and I'd been the recipient of so much trash talk, I felt like a landfill. It was a miracle I hadn't fought back.

"So you going to ask her out or what?" Kip asked.

"No way." I'd been telling Kip about Isabel, not that there was anything to tell, but his jealousy amused me. I hadn't mentioned Beth. Turns out she was homeschooled, and since I couldn't talk about LCT, I didn't know how to tell him about her. Isabel was challenge enough. I glanced at the door. Still no sign of her.

"What's the matter with you, fool? Ask her!"

"I like talking to her," I said. "If I ask her out, I figure one of two things will happen. She'll say no, and then I'll feel stupid around her. Or she'll say yes, and it will be Sherry all over again."

"She's not Sherry, man," Kip said.

"It's not worth the risk." I took a big bite of pizza, caught sight of Sherry a few tables down, and shuddered.

Gabe set his tray beside mine and sat down. "How's it going?"

I almost choked on my pizza. What was Gabe doing? This was the basketball team's table. He couldn't just sit here.

Kip stared at Gabe too, then glanced at me. I shrugged.

"I saw some senior push you in the hall this morning," Gabe said. "That happening a lot?"

"You could say that." I held up my left hand. My first and middle fingers were bruised purple-grey. Jeb had slammed my locker shut on my hand.

Gabe winced. "You should tell McKaffey."

"Nah." Nick was Golden Boy around PPCS. Plus he'd been careful about not doing his own dirty work, so far. I hadn't told the churchers that Nick was behind the assaults. They'd go straight to Mr. S and tattle, squeaky clean do-gooders that they were. I wanted to deal with Nick my own way. If only I could snag a pair of handcuffs off Kimbal. Get Beth to help me.

"Someone messing with you?" Kip asked.

"Later," I said, jerking my head toward Gabe. I'd given Kip

the cover story mission trip version of the Mission League. But I had no problem telling him the truth about Nick. Kip would understand. He'd been with me the day Nick and I had ceased to be buds.

Arianna pranced up to the table. Today her skirt was navy blue and all sparkly, like a prom dress. She sat down on the other side of the table, right next to Kip.

Kip's face paled, and he shot me another look. All I could do was shrug. I mean, I agreed with him. We'd worked hard to earn our place at this table. Then these churchers show up with no regard for social hierarchy. It was disgraceful. Like breaking a high school commandment or something.

Arianna unpacked a brown paper lunch sack, placed a sandwich, an apple, a milk, and a bag of chips in a square formation in front of her, and began shifting them meticulously, like a photographer setting up a still life scene. "I can't believe we're going to Moscow in two-and-a-half weeks! Got your passport yet? I've had mine for ages."

I half-listened as Gabe bowed his head. A lot of the kids at Pilot Point prayed before their meals, so it didn't surprise me. But it made me tense. Like it meant I wasn't as good of person as they were, or something. Arianna's question caught up with me. "Yeah, mine came last week."

I loved my passport. Just holding it made me feel like James Bond. I mean, it didn't even have my real name—Jonas—on it anywhere. Maybe I really was going to be a spy. The day after I'd signed the contract, Grandma had taken me to get my passport picture taken. I'd scowled for the camera, trying to look tough, which had driven her nuts. She'd made the photographer take four pictures before giving up, and she still hassled me over *that horrible scowl*.

Now Arianna was praying.

"Dude? What are we—flypaper for freaks?" Kip shot me a look that said I should do something about this. But I didn't know what to do. This was bad. Worlds were colliding.

So I took a huge bite of pizza. I swallowed it too fast, though, and the lump inched down my throat. I coughed so hard that I grabbed my milk carton to help wash it down, but I'd finished it already.

Gabe smiled at Kip, unfazed by the insult, and passed me his unopened carton of milk. "How are you today, Kip?"

"How do you *think* I am?" Kip motioned to Arianna, who was *still* praying. Not even Grandma prayed that long.

I gulped Gabe's milk, urging the pizza down.

"Dude, this is nuts. I'm out of here." Kip stood up. "I'll be outside."

Gabe opened a bag of chips and offered Kip one. "You should probably stay in the building. It's pretty hot out today."

Kip stared at Gabe as if the guy had two heads.

"*Que pasa?* Got room for me, *Gabriel?*" Isabel stood behind me, holding a pink fabric lunch sack. Her thick black lashes seemed to blink in slow motion.

Gabe pushed his stuff over and squished closer to me, making a spot for Isabel, but she sat on my other side. Ha! Garmond-1. Stopplecamp-0.

And I just have to point out: When Isabel said Gabriel's name, it sounded like Gabrielle, which is a girl's name. I'm just saying . . .

"Yeah . . ." Kip said, his eyes roaming over Isabel like a searchlight. "It *does* look kind of hot outside." He sat back on the bench. "Kind of hot in here too."

I snorted a laugh. Kip took great pride in the cheesy

pickup lines he dealt to girls. The sad thing was, they worked half the time. I secretly hoped Isabel was smarter than the girls Kip usually hit on.

"Es-pensor, what church do you go to?" Isabel asked.

"Calvary Baptist," I said, thankful for the first time that Grandma made me go so I could provide the goddess with a pleasing answer.

"Me, Gabe, Arianna, and *Neek*, we all go to Cornerstone Christian Center. You should come to our youth group sometime. It's on Wednesday nights."

Yeah, right. Like I'd ever set foot in *that* place again. Nick didn't like me, and neither did his dad, Pastor Muren. Yet this was Isabel inviting me somewhere.

"I'm sorry, were you talking to me?" Kip asked Isabel.

She looked across the table. "Uh, no. I was asking—"

"Would you like to?" Kip asked.

She frowned. Apparently not quick enough to catch his meaning.

Kip flashed her a cheesy grin. "I'm just asking because my friend Spencer here wants to know if you think I'm cute."

I rolled my eyes.

Isabel pursed her lips and tipped her head to the side. "Well, what is your name, Es-pensor's friend?"

"You can call me Kip if I can call you tonight."

This time Isabel chuckled. "Oh, you're a funny one."

Kip tapped his fingers on the table in front of my tray. "Dude, did the sun come up or did she just smile at me?"

I laughed too. I couldn't help it. When Kip got going, only a slap to the face could stop him. And I had to give him credit for using his clean lines on Isabel. I guess he could tell she was too nice to be raunchy around.

Or maybe he just didn't want her to slap him.

• • •

There were only three days left of the school year. Somehow I'd made it through the last few weeks without swearing in public or getting into a fight, but the stress of finals, learning to speak Russian, and Nick's subtle torments had me ready to snap.

P.E. class was my only reprieve from the chaos, because Mr. Lawler, the gym teacher, never gave finals. When he divided the class for a basketball scrimmage, I pulled on a red jersey and soaked up the potential bliss. Nick and Jeb were wearing blue.

I was going to spread them over the floor like peanut butter.

Only five minutes had passed when the whistle blew for the seventh time.

TWEEEEET!

"Foul, Mr. Muren!" Mr. Lawler shook his head. "Take it easy. That's a bonus already."

I went to the free throw line smiling. My side hurt from where Nick had elbowed me, but I didn't care. He could foul me all day, as far as I cared. I never missed free throws.

Nick glared from the side of the key. "You suck, Garmond."

I dribbled the ball without looking at him. "Hey, I'm busy now, Muren. Can I ignore you some other time?" I sank the first free throw, and Mr. Lawler tossed me the ball again. I crouched to aim and—

Nick punches me in the gut. I fall to my knees at the free throw line.

89

Warmth spread through my body. What was that? It was as if I'd seen it happening from outside myself.

Right where I was standing now.

I waggled my head to clear my thoughts. Nick was crouched, watching the hoop, poised for a rebound. Was he going to hit me?

Jeb cleared his throat. "Today, Garmond!"

My shot bounced off the rim. I ran for the other end of the court in a daze. I missed? I never missed free throws!

Nick brought the ball down and tried to be fancy but didn't have the skill. I swiped the ball away and glided to my end for an easy lay-up.

That was more like it.

Nick raced down the court, out of control, and air-balled a three point attempt. I chuckled. I couldn't have picked a better way to beat Nick. If only Isabel had been in the crowd to cheer me on.

I brought the ball down and passed it left. I started through the key to the hoop, but Jeb slammed against me like a punching bag. I pivoted in the crowd of bodies, and suddenly Nick was right against me. With Jeb's body shielding Nick from the Mr. Lawler's view, Nick drove his fist into my stomach.

Pain shattered my concentration. I staggered and fell to my knees at the top of the key, wheezing.

The whistle blew somewhere in the distance, muted by the pounding in my head. I slumped onto my side and rolled to my back, staring at the caged lamps hanging from the ceiling. Nick towered over me, sneering.

Was this a dream? Nick looked real. My aching gut felt real.

"I admire you, Garmond, know why?" Nick crouched over me and lowered his voice. "Because *I've* never had the courage to be a liar, a cheat, and a backstabber." Then he spat into my eye.

Like a flash I scrambled up and stalked toward him. Nick jogged backwards, grinning, his sneakers squeaking on the glossy floor, his arms out to the side, beckoning me to bring it.

So I swung at him. But he leaned back out of my reach. He punched my shoulder, then swung for my face and missed.

"Hey, boys!" Mr. Lawler yelled. "None of that, now."

I lunged forward. I grabbed Nick's jersey and pulled him close. Punched him in the eye. He spun away, but I held onto the blue fabric, even when it ripped down the front.

Mr. Lawler pushed between us. "That's enough!"

Nick tripped over Mr. Lawler's leg and landed on his side. I darted around Mr. Lawler and pulled Nick toward me. He slid over the court, right up to my feet.

I drove my fist into any part of him I could hit, breathing through my nose, slowly and loudly, like I was trying not to puke.

Nick screamed for me to get off, punched at my legs, my arms, but I ignored him. I was too far gone. I lost count of the blows I landed before Mr. Lawler and Jeb and who knew else pried us apart.

REPORT NUMBER: 10

REPORT TITLE: I Play with Night Vision Contacts and Bionic Ear
SUBMITTED BY: Agent-in-Training Spencer Garmond
LOCATION: My Bedroom, Grandma Alice's House, Pilot Point,
California, USA
DATE AND TIME: Wednesday, May 28, 6:09 p.m.

I WAS DUNKED LIKE A BASKETBALL in Lebron James'
hands.

I lay on my bed that night, my gut still tender, hating
myself, yet loving the memory of Nick's black eye. I couldn't
help it. We'd been due to have it out. Ever since that day I'd
told the cops that Nick had let us into his dad's church.

For one horrible moment in McKaffey's office, I knew he'd
expel me. But Mr. S had showed up, and it turned out that
people had donated funds for me to go on the Moscow
"mission trip," and the school didn't want to penalize the
donors. So McKaffey suspended me and Nick for the first three
days of next year.

On the way out of McKaffey's office I'd asked Mr. S about my breaking the rules in the contract.

He said, "'Sin does not stop God's grace from flowing.'"

I thought they were nuts, sending me and Nick anywhere together. But, for the sake of my transcripts, I was glad they hadn't expelled me. I needed good grades on my finals, or I could kiss a college scholarship goodbye. To play for the schools I wanted, all four years of my transcripts had to look at least half as good as my game.

None of that would matter if Grandma grounded me for life. And she wouldn't be happy about the fight. She was off at some quilting thing with Mrs. Daggett. Hopefully I wouldn't see her until the morning.

I tried not to think about what had happened in my head before Nick punched me, but it wasn't normal to see stuff like that—the future. I'd had weird dreams all my life. Images filled my mind just thinking about it: the blond woman at the foreign restaurant, a snarling wolf, a baby born in a dirty cabin, an exploding office building, a pretty Asian girl swimming in the ocean. Random scenes that came again and again, knocking me dizzy and keeping me from sleep.

But they'd meant nothing. Until now.

Because if the little Nick daydream had come true, did that mean the others could too?

And what about what Prière had said that day I'd signed the contract?

"Try to hold tightly to your temper when you are playing the sport of basketball à la gym *. . . These things come to me. In my dreams."*

I didn't like the idea that Prière and I had things in common. Not at all.

• • •

At lunch the next day, everyone had already heard what had happened with Nick. The Mission League kids had infiltrated the basketball table . . . again. I really wasn't in the mood to deal with them, Isabel excepted.

Grandma had lectured my skin off this morning. I still felt raw. She wasn't a bad lady. She just didn't listen. Didn't care. Wanted me to be perfect. Which was *never* going to happen.

"I say we tell C-Rok that Nick ratted on Príncipe," Kip said. "Let the King Coats take him out."

That got a snort out of me.

"You'd have been smarter to walk away," Arianna said as if scolding a puppy. "But this is still an answer to prayer."

Kip gaped at Arianna. "You prayed Spencer would get into a fight? Now that's my kind of praying."

"No. I prayed, as I do each day, that whenever Spencer gets into trouble, he'll get caught quickly."

I turned slowly to face the Pixy Stix.

"Yes," she said, smiling at me as if she'd given me a gift. "That way, you can suffer the consequences and move on. When you don't get caught, you carry around the secret, and that builds into guilt and remorse. That, and you get the idea that you can get away with things. Both of which make a person liable to get into trouble again."

Unbelievable. Arianna's cryptic lectures weren't helping my mood.

Kip snorted. "And people wonder why women have been historically oppressed . . ."

"That's not nice, *Keep*," Isabel said, her lips pursed into a cute pout. Then she turned her supermodel gaze my way. "Ees *no problema*, Es-pensor. By the time you come back from Moscow, I bet your grandma forget all about it."

Isabel's voice calmed my soul, as did the fact that she didn't judge me for getting into a fight. If only I could play her voice like an MP3. What could I say to keep her talking? I'd already asked about her family.

"Yeah," was all I could manage. Smooth.

Yet Arianna seemed to have no trouble finding something to babble on about. "I heard that you and Nick used to be friends," she said to me. "Want to talk about that?"

"No. I don't. And don't ever mention it again."

"Okay." Arianna rolled her eyes. "But you really should work on your temper. Self-control is a fruit of the Spirit."

I glared at Arianna. "You really should work on keeping your mouth shut."

Gabe's jaw dropped. "Whoa!"

"Sor-ry." Arianna's eyes brimmed with tears. "I knew *Kip* was a bully, but I thought you were different." She seized her things and left.

Isabel scowled at me and followed.

Perfect.

"Some people bring happiness wherever they go," Kip said, sighing dramatically. "She brings happiness *whenever* she goes."

"Come on, man," Gabe said. "She wasn't trying to be mean."

I stabbed a chunk of broccoli with my plastic knife. "She's always nagging and bossing me. Who does she think she is, my grandma?"

"Whatever." Gabe stood. "I've got to get to band. See you."

I stabbed another broccoli. No one seemed to care that I'd never asked for any of this. How had my life gotten so complicated all of a sudden? I squished the macaroni on my plate through the tongs of my fork. Mutilating my lunch was more fun than eating it. I didn't want to listen to Arianna's lectures, and I didn't want any judgmental friends. I really just wanted to be left alone.

But Kip was still with me. "Maybe the babies will all go get a waahm-burger and some French cries."

The joke—lame though it was—diffused my anger instantly. See, that was why I hung with Kip. I just wasn't one of those churcher types. I'd never be one of them, either. I had my own friends. They were all I needed.

Clothes, books, and cheap souvenirs from America covered my bedroom floor. I was sitting in the middle of it trying to repack the suitcase Grandma had loaned me. It was an ancient beast made from olive green pleather over something hard, making it look like a turtle shell. Someone knocked on the door.

"Yeah?"

The door swung in and hit the suitcase. Kimbal squeezed through the crack and shut the door behind him. He held a shopping bag full of something in his hand. "Packing?"

"There's no way I can take all these blankets."

Grandma had crocheted five bulky afghans for me to give away to homeless people in Moscow. She'd waited until the last minute to mention them.

"Let me try." Kimbal set down the shopping bag, pulled

the suitcase toward him, and crouched in front of it. He started rolling clothes and stacking them snugly inside.

I leaned against the bed and spun my basketball on one finger. I lost control of my spin, and the ball flew off my hand and bounced over the suitcase. Kimbal picked it up and sent it back to me by rolling it down one arm, behind his neck, and off the other.

I caught it. "You play ball?"

"Used to."

"Want to shoot sometime?"

Kimbal rolled a pair of jeans. "Sometime."

I eyed the shopping bag. "What's in the bag?"

"I don't think you have room for it."

I snatched up the bag and pulled out new purple Lakers cap. "This for me?"

"Only if you have room."

I pulled off my old one and tried on the new one. "I'll wear it. Thanks."

"You've got some pretty sharp clothes here."

I couldn't take credit. "Grandma asks the clerks for help."

Kimbal huffed. "Clerks. Right."

An idea came to me. "Wait, you're the clerk?"

"Don't tell Alice you know. She likes you thinking she has good taste in clothes."

"You gave me the MacBook, didn't you?" It made perfect sense.

"There was nothing Alice could do when she saw the look on your face. You beamed for days."

I suddenly felt immense friendship with this man. My uncle. "What about my other grandparents. Are they alive?"

"They died when your dad and I were little." He tucked

some socks into a crack in my suitcase. "We were placed in foster care with a League family. Our parents had both been agents, so I guess they figured the odds were high we'd be called someday. Plus I think they wanted to keep an eye on us."

"Why can't I live with you?"

"Right now is a good reason. I'm breaking protocol just by being in here. If a bad guy was out there, ready to make a move, I wouldn't know because I'm in here packing your suitcase instead of out there doing my job."

"What bad guy would want to make a move on me?"

"You'd be surprised." He pointed at my towel. "Hand me that."

I passed him the towel. "Wait, are you coming on the trip? Don't you have to be there to follow me around Moscow?"

"Nope. There will be plenty of people to keep an eye on you in Moscow. I'm going on my first vacation in thirteen years."

"Dude, that is the worst thing I've ever heard. It must be so boring guarding me. What, do you sleep in a car outside my house? Don't you have a family?"

Kimbal shook his head. "Just you, and you were rarely boring." He shut the suitcase and flipped the latches shut. "*Voila.*"

"Thanks," I said. "Still, wouldn't it be better to go after bad guys and save the world or something? Watching me seems like a lame assignment."

Kimbal looked up and smiled. "I don't mind."

The eye contact made me feel uncomfortable, so I changed the subject. "You ever have to hot-wire a car or escape death like spies on TV?"

"Where do you watch TV?"

"Online. Does the Mission League have cool gadgets like watches that explode or pens that are really knives?"

Kimbal looked at me again. His freckles, eyes, and hair were so like mine that it was like looking into some sort of future-mirror.

"Okay," he said. "I'll play the cool uncle for ten more minutes, then I've got to go." He stood, reached into his pants pocket, and tossed a few things on the carpet: a penny, a stick of gum, an allergy pill, a contact lens case, a paperclip.

Kimbal hit the lights, and the room went black except for a tiny beam: Kimbal holding an ink pen flashlight. "It's no knife, but I like it." He shined the light at the items on the floor. "Here you have the standard field ops kit. Nothing too obvious. That's always the challenge. A smart adversary will take everything off you, but if you're lucky, these things go unnoticed." Kimbal picked up the contact lenses. "Night vision contacts. Amazing technology." He tossed it to me. "Try one."

I removed one contact from the container, and after four tries, managed to get it into my eye. I blinked and closed my other eye. My room was illuminated in electronic green. I expressed my delight by uttering a few colorful metaphors.

"Better watch that mouth around Stopplecamp. He's not kidding about that contract. A couple write-ups for swearing, and he'll send you home."

"I can't help it!" And I couldn't. The poetry just flowed. I took out the contact.

"You might try a made-up phrase instead. Train yourself to say something clean. I'm particularly fond of "mother pus bucket."

I laughed and laughed and laughed at that one. "I guess I could try that."

"Anyway, the gum is actually C4. So, you know, don't blow any bubbles." Kimbal picked up the aluminum-covered stick. "The wrapper is the charge. Turn it inside out and cover the C4 in the foil, and you've got about ten seconds before it blows. Nothing big, but it'll break open most standard locks. Don't try it on a handcuff, though. You'll lose a hand."

"Whoa! What does the penny do?"

Kimbal elbowed me to hold the light. I took it from him, and he grabbed the coin. I leaned in close. "Set Lincoln's head on one finger and press your thumbnail between the center pillars on the Lincoln Memorial." A tiny click, and Kimbal lifted the bottom off the penny. "Bionic ear."

I got up and flipped on the lights to get a clearer look. Inside the penny a coil of black wire lay on top of a tiny rubber suction cup.

"Stick this baby to a door or wall, and you can hear through it. Suction only lasts about ten minutes and won't pick up anything over ten yards away." Kimbal clicked the penny back together. "The allergy pill is concentrated ipecac. Take it right away if you've been poisoned."

"People might poison you?"

Kimbal shrugged. "I've never used it, but you never know."

The idea that my life could be in so much danger that I'd need this stuff was both thrilling and enough to make me sick.

"What about the paperclip?"

"Yeah, that's just a paperclip. They're always handy."

"You ever use any of this stuff?"

"Years ago." He swept up the gadgets and stuffed them back into his pocket. "The job's been pretty quiet for the past thirteen years."

REPORT NUMBER: 11

REPORT TITLE: Pasha's Visit to the Moscow Field Office
SUBMITTED BY: Agent Ryan Matheson
INTERVIEWEE: Pasha Ivanovich
LOCATION: Mission League Field Office, Moscow, Russia
DATE AND TIME: Tuesday, June 3, 12:08 p.m.

PASHA SHIFTED HIS BACKPACK from one shoulder to the other as the elevator passed the third floor. He wiggled his fingers at his sides and checked his watch.

Three weeks ago, Anya had taken him to dinner at Johannes, one of the best restaurants in Russia. She'd been sweet to him— right up until he'd refused to do this job. His hands trembled at the memory of her anger.

Fourth floor.

He regretted being here already. He was a fool to do Anya's bidding, especially in a place like this. Getting caught would be a nightmare.

The elevator stopped on the fifth floor and slid open. He

walked out into the lobby of *Leega Missionerov.*

"Privyet, Pasha!" the receptionist said, buzzing him through the first door.

"Katerina." Pasha nodded and plodded down a long, narrow hallway, passing the computer room on his left. If all went well, he'd stop there on his way out. That way, if anything went wrong, at least he'd have the copies. He'd cased the place for weeks and snooped in every file in Father's office. He knew precisely where to find everything Anya wanted.

Pasha peeked through the window at the Administration Office door. The receptionist had gone to lunch right on schedule. Excellent. He pulled his father's spare clearance card from his pocket and swiped it through the card reader. The door clicked, and he entered.

He rounded the corner and stopped in front of the door to the director's office. Father's secretary, Ivanna, still sat at her desk. She should have gone to lunch already. Pasha tapped on the door and waved. The door buzzed and he entered.

"Privyet," Ivanna said.

"Is Father in?" Pasha asked in Russian.

"You just missed him."

Yes, but he couldn't make copies with Ivanna watching. "Can I wait?"

"He'll be at least an hour."

"That's okay. I brought a book." He turned so she could see his backpack.

"Wait if you like, I'm going to lunch." Ivanna grabbed her purse and started toward the door. "See you later."

Relieved, Pasha entered his father's office and settled into the big leather chair. He turned in a circle and put his feet up on the mahogany desk. Two minutes passed on the clock before he turned toward the window. He tapped his fingers on the armrests and stared out at the parking lot. Finally, Ivanna appeared down below. Pasha smiled and removed a pair of black leather gloves from his backpack, which he pulled on, just in case.

He quickly found the files Anya needed. He pulled the folders out halfway to mark their spots then took the contents to the copy machine. He smiled as the copies slid out one after another. Slow elevator. Fast copy machine.

In less than ten minutes, everything was back in place and the copies were hidden in his backpack. He stuck a prewritten note on his father's computer screen and hurried out the door.

Just missed you.
Pasha

He held the wireless USB adapter in his hand as he approached the door to the computer room. All he had to do was push it into an USB slot on one of the servers, and Anya would do the rest from her remote location. He peered through the window in the door. Empty. Relief flooded him. He needed only ten seconds.

Pasha swiped his father's card again. He slipped inside, reached around to the back of the nearest computer server, and pushed the adapter into place. He checked the window again and hurried out, slowly closing the door behind him to muffle any noise. He strode down the hall, this time headed out. Air spread through his lungs. It seemed like he hadn't breathed since his arrival.

Someone walked toward him. Igor. Worked in computers. Probably headed back there now. Close call.

"Privyet."

Pasha didn't stop. "Igor."

"You cold or something?" He pointed at Pasha's gloves.

Rats!

Pasha turned, continuing to walk backwards. He held up a gloved fist. "Nyet. My girlfriend gave them to me. You like?"

Igor raised his eyebrows. "Not really."

Pasha didn't breathe again until he was on the elevator and the door was shut. As the elevator crept down, Pasha tucked the gloves into his backpack, relieved it was over. Would this be enough, now? Would Anya be satisfied? Pasha doubted it. Anya always wanted more, and Pasha would do it.

He'd do anything for her.

REPORT NUMBER: 12

REPORT TITLE: I Fly Halfway Around the World
SUBMITTED BY: Agent-in-Training Spencer Garmond
LOCATION: Grandma Alice's House, Pilot Point, California, USA
DATE AND TIME: Wednesday, June 4, 11:45 a.m.

GRANDMA MADE WAFFLES FOR BREAKFAST, my favorite. Slathered with peanut butter. She perched on the edge of the table, sniffling, and watched me eat. I glanced at her between bites, hoping she wouldn't bawl.

"Don't mind me. I'll be fine." She pulled a white gift bag out from under the table and set it beside my plate. "A little something for your trip."

Grandma never gave the best gifts, except for clothes—the ones Kimbal picked out. I cleaned my plate then reached into the bag and pulled out a little black velvet box.

Uh-oh. Jewelry was for girls. I winced and cracked it opened. A silver chain glittered inside. "It's a necklace."

"It's a cross necklace. The clerk helped me pick it out."

Clerk? I bit the inside of my cheek. I'd have to have a word with *Clerk Kimbal.* It was silver—a little shield with a cross on a bead chain. The back of the shield was engraved with Joshua 1:9 "I will be strong and courageous. I will not be terrified or discouraged, for the Lord my God is with me wherever I go." Guys wore similar chains at school. But a cross? For me?

I don't think so.

"I thought you'd like to have a symbol of your faith to wear on your trip."

A symbol of *her* faith, maybe. "Thanks, Grandma."

She whisked the box out of my hands and fastened the chain around my neck. I bit back sarcastic remarks and wiped a glob of peanut butter off my plate with my finger.

She came around front and took my face in her hands. Tears pooled in her eyes.

Oh, come on.

"I'm so proud of you, Spencer. I know I've been strict, not letting you see your friends, making you do so many chores." She straightened my collar. "But look how it's paid off ! Your mother would be proud too. I know she would."

I guess so. But the chain hung cold and heavy around my neck like a leash. It was probably Grandma's way of controlling me from the other side of the world, of guilting me into staying out of trouble.

I'd take it off the first chance I got.

"Expect great things from God, attempt great things for God."

I muttered the Mission League motto along with everyone else, though the others were chanting it with excitement. Our small group stood in a circle, holding hands in front of the departure gate at the Los Angeles airport. I barely held Gabe's shirtsleeve on my left and firmly gripped Isabel's soft warm hand on my right.

There were eleven of us—Mr. and Mrs. S and the nine students—thirteen, if I counted the Stopplecamps' twin girls. I wasn't sure why kids got to come on a spy trip. But I guess eight weeks was a long time to find a babysitter.

Mr. S monopolized the next hour with mini speeches about staying together and behaving on the plane. He split us up into buddies. I was with Gabe. When Mr. S finished, I sat in one of the seats in front of the large windows overlooking the runway and stared at the Boeing 737. I'd never flown on a plane before. It looked like a toy I'd had years ago.

My stomach churned with dread and excitement, like the night before a playoff game. I imagined chasing after Nick on the streets of Moscow and using field ops gadgets to apprehend him. I smiled at the thought.

Speaking of which . . . Nick passed by a moment later, soda in hand. I'd given him quite the shiner in our fight. "Stay away from me this summer, Garmond. I don't want to have to hurt you."

"Like you could, Black & Decker."

"*Boys*," Mr. S warned from the seat behind me.

Yeah, yeah. We'd behave. As long as Nick stayed out of my way.

Gabe set his backpack and guitar in the seat beside me. I mean, really? Mr. Goody-Two-Shoes Churcher with the Buddy Holly glasses was a musician too? Go figure.

Mr. S had requested we wear nice but comfortable attire. I'd worn a pair of Dockers and a short-sleeved white-and-black plaid shirt. And sneakers, of course. Gabe didn't look comfortable in black slacks and a dress shirt and tie. He looked ready for an interview more than a flight across the ocean.

A few rows away, one of Gabe's twin sisters sat down beside the other. Their curls, as tight as Gabe's, hung past their shoulders. They were identical, except that the one who had just sat down was eating a doughnut.

"Your sisters are really coming with?" I asked him.

"Yeah, they always come. Don't freak out, but I should warn you: Mary thinks you're cute."

"Who wouldn't?" But I suddenly felt awkward about being admired by a little kid. I glanced at them again. "How old are they anyway? Eight?"

Gabe laughed. "They're twelve. Twins are sometimes smaller. Thankfully, if they get called into the League, I'll be long gone. You'll be a senior, though."

I caught the one with the doughnut staring. She grinned—her mouth full of teal braces—and wiggled her fingers in a flirtatious wave.

"One of them is waving at me."

Gabe looked up. "Yup. That's Mary. Told you. Don't worry. Mom will keep them away from us. And no offense, but Mary likes every guy she meets. I'm hoping she grows out of it before she ends up like you."

I sat up straight. "*Excuse* me? What about me is not to like?"

Gabe looked at his loafers and rubbed his throat. "I just think you should be careful. I mean, Beth, Jensina, Arianna, Isabel . . . they're nice girls. Not your type. Plus, going after all of them at once makes you look like a jerk."

I drew back. "Okay, first of all, I'm *not* going after Arianna." I shuddered. "And second, I'm a jerk? What'd I do?"

Gabe rolled his eyes. "You're not as bad as Nick or anything. I'm just saying that girls don't like being treated like a slab of meat."

"Meat?" I couldn't help it, I laughed so hard I started to choke. When I managed to breathe again, I made myself clear. "I've never treated a girl like meat."

"What about Sherry?"

Flames kindled in my gut. Must. Not. Murder. Teacher's. Son. Must not. Not. I gritted my teeth. "What do you know about my life?"

Gabe looked at me then, and it wasn't a look of anger or hatred or disgust, but of simple facts. "Sherry's in our youth group."

I was speechless and steamed that this loafer-wearing, braces-sucking, four-eyed mama's boy had the nerve to get all up in my business. At the same time, questions were screaming in my head. What had Sherry told these people? Had she made stuff up? What had I done that was so bad?

But before I could excuse myself to the bathroom and beat up a stall door, a woman's voice announced it was time to board.

It was going to be a looooong eight weeks.

The airplane had three rows on both sides of the aisle. I was in seat 28A, which was against the window just behind the left wing. Gabe sat next to me, and Arianna was on the aisle next to

Gabe. Trapped alongside the Prude Patrol and Miss Bossy wasn't the best way to start the summer, but it was better than having to sit with Nick . . . Or Mr. S.

I shoved my backpack under the seat and looked for the other girls. Isabel, Beth, and Jensina were in the row behind us on the opposite side of the plane. This seating arrangement ruined any opportunity for chitchat.

Gabe would be so pleased.

I'd been so excited last night after Kimbal had showed me the gadgets. I'd daydreamed a hundred ways I'd save the day and get the girl. But my own personal secret mission of kissing at least one of them had just been cracked open by Gabe and his perfect mind-reading intentions.

And Grandma's stupid necklace was making my neck itch. I took it off and slipped it into my backpack.

"This is so exciting!" Arianna said. "I've never gone anywhere without my parents. Can you believe how embarrassing that is?" She was holding her Russian textbook on her lap.

"You're not going to study on the plane, are you?" I asked.

She turned her head but looked at Gabe instead of me. "Have you ever gone anywhere without your parents, Gabe?"

"Nope."

"Someday you will. I'm so excited to serve God this summer. Gabe, did I tell you He gave me the word *service* for this year?"

Gabe played with the nozzle above his seat. "Yeah, you told us in Sunday school."

"Have you ever prayed for a word, Gabe?"

Gabe shook his head. "My mom does it."

"What's her word for this year?"

A shrug. "You'd have to ask her."

Arianna Sloan was the poster child for a missionary agent, and I told her so.

She sighed, keeping her gaze on her Russian textbook. "Your words sound nice, Spencer, but I'm sure you're just making jokes."

"You're still mad at me." How long did girls hold grudges? Not that I really cared if Arianna never talked to me again. But this seemed an opportune moment to prove that I was a nice guy. "I'm sorry I was a jerk, Arianna. I was really angry about the fight and took it out on you. That was lame." I raised my eyebrows at Gabe. Stick that in your pipe, Prude Patrol.

Mr. Show No Emotion Man just stared.

But Arianna smiled so big I could see her gums. "I forgive you, Spencer! I sometimes get mad too, but it's good to apologize when you hurt someone. I'm so glad we're friends again. You can practice with us." She cracked open her textbook. "Okay, *Amerikanets, Amerikanka, Amerikantsy.* What's the difference?"

"Uh . . . Amerikantsy is plural, for a group of Americans," Gabe said.

I glared out the window. Leave it to Mission-Ari to make a long flight longer.

The plane started down the runway, and I liked the way my body slammed back against the seat. Takeoff was surprisingly smooth. I studied the landscape out the window as we rose into the sky. Eventually we passed through clouds until it looked like we were flying on a field of cotton balls.

By the time the drink service came and went, Arianna and Gabe were deep into conjugating verbs. Isabel passed by, headed toward the bathroom, and I kept watch, hoping to make eye contact when she came back through. Unfortunately, Nick was sitting kitty cornered ahead of Gabe and got to her first. As she passed by his seat, he grabbed her hand.

She looked down and smiled, her curls tumbling over her shoulder. "*Hola*, Neek."

"You want some gum?" Nick asked, smacking on a piece of his own.

"No thanks."

Nick pulled Isabel onto his lap. "Switch with Isaac." He leaned close to her ear. "*Tee khrupkaya.*"

Arianna snorted. I didn't know what was so funny, but seeing Nick with his hands on Isabel made me want to give him a matching shiner on his other eye.

"No, thanks, Neek." She squirmed off his lap and paused at our row. She glanced at Arianna's book. "You guys studying?"

"*Da*," Arianna said.

Isabel's gaze passed from me to Gabe then back to me, her eyes sparkling. She tilted her head to the side and frowned. "What happen to your chain, *Beef?*"

Beef? I stared at her in mesmerized silence, the soft tone of her voice hypnotic. Arianna elbowed me, and I realized Isabel had asked me something. Oh right. I'd forgotten my secret code name was Biff Gar.

"Huh?" I said to the goddess.

She scratched her fingernails against her collarbone. "You wore a cross before, no? I liked it."

The goddess had noticed me! She had to have been looking at me to see my necklace. A necklace she liked. "Oh. Yeah. Uh . . . took it off. Didn't want to lose it." I fought to keep a straight face over *that* lie.

"Is the clasp broken?" Arianna leaned around Gabe to look at me. "I can maybe fix it. I make my own jewelry."

"Ees true," Isabel said. "Arianna makes beautiful jewelry." She flashed her perfect smile and continued to her seat.

"Let me see it, Spencer," Arianna said.

To please Isabel I handed the chain to Arianna. "Pretty cross!" She examined it a moment before handing it back. "I don't see anything wrong with it. Make sure it hooks all the way the next time you put it on. Want me to help?"

I took the chain back. "Naw, I can do it."

Nick twisted in his seat to peek at me. "Are you serious? Garmond wearing a cross?" He burst into laughter.

"Don't do that stuff, Nick," Gabe said. "It's not nice."

"What? Laughing at Garmond?"

"Touching Isabel like that. Plus, if you're trying to tell her she's beautiful, you're saying it wrong. You told her she's fragile, like she's a lamp or something. If you want to say, 'You're beautiful,' say '*Tee krasivaya*.'"

"What do you know?" Nick asked.

"I know embarrassing her is mean."

And the Prude Patrol strikes again.

Nick smacked the gum in his mouth. "Huh. Well, I was going to tell Garmond all about his dad and the LA Field office, but I guess I won't. I wouldn't want to *embarrass* him."

My head tingled as blood rushed toward my heart. "You *what*?"

Gabe turned to me. "Your dad was in?"

Nick popped a bubble. "Same time as my dad."

I couldn't have heard right. "*Your* dad was in?"

Nick smirked as if this placed him ahead of me in some secret competition. "The League knows the truth about your parents too. They know everything."

I leaned over Gabe to get a better look at Nick. "What do you know about my parents?"

But Nick only cackled and turned to face the flight attendant, who was offering another round of beverages.

I thunked my head above the little window. Nick had to be messing with me. No way our dads could have known each other.

Isabel's soothing voice drifted from a few rows back, but I couldn't make out her words. And when I tuned back in to Arianna and Gabe, they were talking about serious God stuff.

"My dad said Asians don't understand who God is because their culture has many gods," Arianna said. "To serve as missionaries, you have to understand the country's history and culture before you can teach the gospel."

"I went to Germany once," Gabe said. "Most people believe in God there, but they don't live for him. Kind of like Americans."

The more they talked, the more I wished I was anywhere else, at least sitting with Isabel and Beth. I plugged my headphones in and watched some of the movie they were showing on the little TVs in the back of the seats, but it was a chick flick, so I plugged into my lame little MP3 player instead and visited the basketball court in my mind. It worked until Arianna and Gabe appeared on the sidelines, telling me how much I needed Jesus in my life. I screamed in my head and wished Grandma had let me bring my MacBook.

I dug out the latest Dean Koontz novel and started reading it. Grandma didn't like me reading books that she hadn't read first, so I'd checked this one out from the library. It would be way past overdue by the time I turned it in, but whatever.

Every so often I looked back at Isabel and Beth and Jensina. Their giggles haunted me throughout the flight. Was Gabe right? Was I a dog? And Sherry . . . I tried to remember back to the beginning of the school year. We'd lasted only six days. And we hadn't done anything but make out. I wondered what she was telling people.

Gabe's little warning wasn't going to stop me from talking to the girls. I put my necklace back on in hopes it might spark another conversation with the goddess.

We had a short layover at the JFK airport in New York, then boarded a bigger plane. This plane had three rows of seats, five seats in the middle row and two on each side. Our group was clustered on the left toward the front. I was still sitting by Gabe, but this time he was by the window, and I got the aisle. Jake was across the aisle from me.

Isabel had the seat in front of Jake, kitty cornered from me. No window this time, and yet I had the best view!

Now I just had to think of something to say to her that wouldn't backfire. Grandma had once said that the way to a girl's heart wasn't with chocolates or jewelry but with listening. So if I could come up with the right question, all I had to do was shut up.

The moment she pulled out the book, I knew. I gave her a moment to get immersed then reached across the aisle and tapped her elbow. "Hey, Isabel, what you reading?"

She turned and held up a book with a girl on the cover, then blessed me with a gorgeous smile. "*Angel Eyes*."

For a moment we just stared at each other. Then I asked a follow up question. "What's it about?"

"Ees about a girl who suffered a horrible tragedy, and she's grieving, but then she meets a boy who ees so cute and nice and warm, and she likes heem. But he ees being raised by an angel, and they get caught up in a spiritual battle. Ees so good, Es-pensor. You should read it when I finish."

"Sure," I said, without thinking. Wait, had I just agreed to read a chick book?

"You believe in angels and demons?"

"I guess."

"Ees real, Es-pensor." She turned back and opened her book again.

I wanted to say, "Don't go!" but all I could do was settle back in my seat and try to think of another question to ask.

Claustrophobia. I'd never understood the full meaning of that word until now. Coach seats were not meant for guys over six feet tall. At least I had the aisle to stretch my right leg, and I'd gotten up and walked to the restroom so many times, I'd likely paved a groove in the floor. There were quite a few Russians on the plane, and Gabe and I had fun eavesdropping and trying to translate what they were saying. I was pretty stoked that I could half understand them.

I finished my book and desperately tried to sleep, hoping for a good basketball dream, but sleep wouldn't come. After the twelfth time I asked Gabe how much longer, I was convinced we were hovering over the ocean. Or doing circles.

I managed one more conversation with Isabel about who painted her fingernails. Turns out her mother did them at the *Peluqueria Rodriguez.*

I was pathetic.

It had to be a billion hours later when the pilot finally announced our descent into a sunny Moscow where the weather was thirty-three degrees Celsius, whatever that meant. I actually laughed out loud at the news.

The plane landed with a quick bump at the Moscow Sheremetyevo International Airport at 12:15 p.m., a day after we'd left Los Angeles. Explain that one to me. Well, it sure felt like we'd been in that plane a whole day or more.

Once we were all off the plane, Mr. S gathered us in a group. "Everyone with your buddy?" He scanned our faces. "Good. First, we're going to stop at the currency exchange. I want you to be careful with your money. Don't spend it all. But realize that few places take credit cards in the city, and almost no one will take American dollars. So if you want to have money, you need to get some here."

"Can we get something to eat?" Isaac said.

"Ivan Petrovich and his daughter are going to meet us down in baggage claim. They're going to feed us dinner when we get to the apartment, but that will be a few hours, so if you're hungry now, you can grab some food before we leave the airport. But no one wanders off without telling me, and no one goes anywhere without their buddy. Got it?"

"Got it," several chimed back.

And so I heaved my backpack over my shoulder and made my way across the airport with the Pilot Point Mission League.

I was ecstatic to be off the plane and walking. I absorbed my surroundings as I trudged down a long, beige corridor in the terminal. Waffled metal covered the ceiling, brown tile covered the floor, and pale sunlight flooded through a wall of windows on my left.

We exchanged currency, and I loved looking at the Russian money. The bills were colorful and fat, and the coins were thick, different sizes, and made of different metals: some solid brass, some solid nickel, some nickel in the center with a brass ring around the outside. I shoved my fortune into my backpack and put it over one shoulder.

We passed under festive red, blue, and white banners begging us, in English and Russian, to visit the Duty Free shop on the other side of the airport. Posters of perfume, cars, and alcohol covered the walls.

Mr. S stopped at a food stall called *Kroshka Kartoshka* that had a cartoon logo of a chef holding a massive potato. I ordered a baked potato filled with feta cheese, bacon, and sour cream and a bottle of Coke. Once we'd finished eating, we made our way toward a descending escalator. A blue and gold banner above the stairs welcomed us to Moscow.

The customs line moved quickly. My guy was hunched but looked no older than thirty. I said, "Privyet," proud of my first attempt at communicating in a foreign language, but the dude never spoke. He just took my passport, looked at it, looked at my face, typed something into his computer, stamped inside my passport, and handed it back.

And that was that. I was in!

The airport seemed to go on forever, but we finally found the baggage claim. The bags weren't there yet, so we stood around and waited, looking like tourists, no doubt. A grey-haired man in a charcoal suit approached us. He was holding a card that read *Stopplecamp*. He had a face that was starting to get Sharpei wrinkles but still instilled a respectful, don't-mess-with-me fear.

A young woman stood beside him. She had wispy brown hair and the gaunt cheekbones of a fashion model. I guessed she was in her mid-twenties.

"Ivan!" Mr. S said, and I wondered if they'd met before.

The two shook hands. Mrs. S gave the girl a hug.

"Dobro pazhalovat' v Maskvoo," the guy said. "I am Ivan Petrovich, director of Moscow Field Office. This my daughter Tatyana Ivanovna, who will be working with you. I am hoping your flight was well."

I smirked at the guy's broken English. Maybe no one would notice my lame Russian.

We finally got our bags, and Ivan led us toward the exit. Everyone had suitcases with wheels—including me. But mine was not the same. While their suitcases had handles that pulled up out of the bag so that they could drag them along on fat plastic wheels as they walked, my suitcase had four Hot Wheels-sized wheels on the spine, and I had to pull the thing with a dinky pleather strap. I also had to hunch down to pull it, because if I lifted the front wheels off the ground even a millimeter, the turtle shell would keel over onto its side.

Grandma and her antiques. Anyway, I eventually gave up and carried the pleather beast.

When I finally stepped outside, I was surprised at how warm it was. We were way far north of the Equator, yet this felt and looked like home. I could barely see the sun, a white ball blanketed in thick grey smog. Grey sky and concrete met my gaze as far as I could see. Taxis had crammed into the loading zone, their drivers pleading for customers.

Our mob had slowed, so I put down my suitcase and tugged it along inch by inch, giving my shoulder a rest. We passed by the eager taxi drivers to four black sedans with tinted windows. The cars stood like royalty beside the late model foreign cars and taxis crawling through the loading zone.

Tatyana pushed her hair out of her eyes as a warm breeze blew past. "The field office is helping with transportation."

"Do we have to wash them when we're done?" Isaac asked. I chuckled.

Mr. S divided our group among the sedans, and I followed Tatyana. Someone bumped me from behind. My suitcase flipped onto its side, jerking my arm and causing me to drop my backpack.

"Oh, pardon *me*." Nick pushed past, his fancy rolling suitcase gliding along behind him.

Figs and jam!

In an effort to take Kimbal's advice, *figs and jam* was my new non-swear phrase. I clenched my teeth and set my suitcase back on all four Hot Wheels wheels. I twisted around looking for my backpack and found one of the twins holding it out to me.

"You dropped this." Her voice was soft, like Gabe's. She blinked thick, dark, make-up free eyelashes. Pretty brown eyes.

I recoiled at that thought and snatched my backpack from whichever very, very young girl this was. "Thanks." I heaved the turtle off the ground and walked toward the last car in line.

Jensina shrieked. I jumped at the volume of her voice, almost losing my bags again. She threw her arms around the waist of a giant man with wavy brown hair. He was built like one of the forwards for Duke's Blue Devils. Looked about six-foot-five. He had long, ape-like arms and an overbite that kept his mouth open constantly, like he had a cold and couldn't breathe.

"Wild hair!" The guy inspected Jensina's red and black, bisected hairdo.

Gabe's eyes were wide. "That's Ryan!" he said as if he were seeing the real Santa Claus. "He used to go to my church."

"Really." The dude looked Russian to me. I heaved the turtle into the trunk and climbed into the back seat with Gabe and Arianna. Gabe got stuck in the middle this time. Soon, our little black caravan pulled away and left the airport.

"Dad says Ryan works at the Moscow Field Office," Gabe said. "He and Jensina's parents have been friends for years."

"Did he play ball at Pilot Point? He's tall enough to play college ball."

"Yeah, but he quit in high school. Said it conflicted too much with the Mission League."

I didn't like the sound of *that*. Because if it came down to this or basketball, no way this was going to win.

Tatyana turned in the front seat. "Kak bwil polet?" *How was your flight?*

"Long," Gabe and Arianna said in unison.

I absorbed the scenery through the window as we swerved around corners en route to our home for the next eight weeks. If I wasn't half asleep, I might have been a little freaked at the crazy driving. Like LA, the city of Moscow kept going and going. Roads were jammed with cars, sidewalks with people, and an endless display of billboards loomed above. Moscow seemed to be in the midst of an extensive renovation. Scaffolding hedged the buildings on nearly every street.

The city held one contrast after another. Orthodox cathedrals towered beside crumbling buildings. Fancy boutiques and trendy cafés were wedged between empty shops. Down side streets, grey residential areas sprawled out with an occasional shiny teardrop dome reaching above. Hip-looking young people on cell phones pranced around the elderly, who sauntered along wearing bland clothing that matched their bland expressions.

"Pepsi!" Arianna pointed at a billboard displaying a bottle of the American soft drink and two athletes holding a soccer ball.

Our car passed familiar golden arches. "McDonald's!" Gabe shouted.

The billboards on my side of the car were for Russian products, until I saw the words *Jolt 2* and a familiar face.

Brittany Holmes, a young American actress, stared at me from the side of a building. She wore a silky black robe over a black bikini—or maybe it was underwear. It was hard to tell the difference. A black utility belt hung low on her hips, loaded with the tools of a beast hunter: a wooden stake, a vial of salt, a crucifix, a pentagram, a canteen of holy water, a devil's trap, and a rope of garlic bulbs. She clutched a bloody dagger in her hand, likely having just offed a werewolf. The billboard read: "Some *thing* disturbed her beauty sleep."

I wolf-whistled. "Yes it did, but she put that beastie in its place!"

Gabe leaned over to look out my window. "Who is that? She looks scary."

I chuckled. "She *is* scary. Don't worry, though. The Light Goddess only kills evil beasties. That's Brittany Holmes from the *Jolt* horror movies."

"Your grandma lets you watch those?" Arianna asked.

"Uh . . . no. I watch them with Kip."

"That's dishonest, Spencer," Arianna said. "I don't think your grandmother would appreciate that very much."

"I guarantee she wouldn't." I craned my neck to watch Brittany as the car moved away. That poster is better than the ones in the US. Wonder if I can get one here?"

It was early afternoon when the cars stopped on a narrow street that dead-ended about fifty feet before a T-shaped intersection. We were in an old neighborhood with brick buildings all around us, about three to six stories high. The area was paved in brick too, including the cross street, which looked like some sort of Universal City Walk tourist attraction. We all piled out, and the driver helped us unload our luggage. Techno music blared in the distance, and I could smell fried grease on the air.

"Arbat ulitsa is pedestrian street," Tatyana said as she led us over the brick-paved ground. "No vehicles permitted."

I carried my suitcase. No point trying to pull the turtle over *that*.

"There's a Starbucks!" Nick said, and Jensina squealed.

"'Let the first impulse pass,'" Mr. S said. "You can come back after we get settled in the apartment."

Tatyana led us across Arbat ulitsa, away from the Starbucks. We trailed around a kiosk filled with paintings of landscapes and a few still lifes. Vendors shouted over the pedestrian chatter, trying to sell their bizarre souvenirs. Plywood stalls along the street held small brooms decorated with dried flowers and homemade dolls with beards. A few panhandlers begged for change. Arianna gave them each something.

Tatyana was leading us toward the door of what looked like an old apartment building made of grey brick. It was five stories high, and had wrought-iron balconies.

Tatyana held open the oak door for our group. I stepped inside a small foyer and adjusted my eyes. Low watt bulbs cast a yellow glow on the off-white walls. A narrow staircase covered in brown tile led up the back. Ivan and Tatyana led us to the stairs, and up we went. By the time I lugged my suitcase up four flights, my arm had turned to Jell-O.

Ivan led us out of the stairwell and down a narrow hallway. He turned his back to a door where the hallway right-angled around a corner. "These three apartment are for you stay." He motioned to the door behind him, then the ones on either side. "Boys will be taking first room, girls will be taking last. Between is kitchen, TV, and room for Stopplecamp family. When you are settled, come to kitchen. My wife is preparing dinner."

"If there's a bed, I call it!" Isaac opened the door to the boys' room and went inside. "Nope, I call the couch."

I followed Gabe into a stuffy room that was only slightly bigger than my bedroom at home. The place was bare except for two bunk beds on the entry wall and a funny looking couch that sat under a narrow window on the far wall. Our sneakers scuffed and squeaked over a white tile floor. The room smelled like fresh paint, and the same low lighting yellowed the bare walls. An open door on the left wall led to the center apartment. A door in the back led to a bathroom.

I half expected a nurse to walk in and take my blood pressure.

Isaac tossed his suitcase on the couch. Jake climbed on top of the bunk bed in the corner. Gabe claimed the bed underneath Jake. Before I could think about where to put my stuff, a flip-flop flew past my ear and landed near the door.

"Forgot to take off my shoes," Isaac said. "You know what they say, when in Russia . . . Heads!"

I backed up as Isaac threw his second flip-flop. I kicked off my own sneakers beside the door.

Nick heaved his things on the remaining top bunk and went into the bathroom.

I groaned when I realized the only remaining bed put me under Nick.

"This is great!" Gabe beamed at me. "Last year we slept on the floor the whole summer. It was a hard floor too. We were lucky to have that in Swaziland. Most people had dirt floors in the village we stayed at."

I shoved my suitcase below the bottom bunk, lay down on the hard bed, I stared at the mattress bulging between the bars above. At least I could keep an eye on Nick from here.

My head throbbed. My body ached. It felt like it should be bedtime, though it was only 3:46. I closed my eyes and listened to Gabe describe a slimy green creature from Swaziland, his mellow voice lulling me to sleep.

OUR APARTMENT IN MOSCOW

REPORT NUMBER: 13

REPORT TITLE: I Get Two Thumbs Down for My
Observation Skills
SUBMITTED BY: Agent-in-Training Spencer Garmond
LOCATION: Arbat Ulitsa, 43, Moscow, Russia
DATE AND TIME: Thursday, June 5, 6:34 p.m.

GABE WOKE ME FOR DINNER before I could sleep long enough to make a dent in my fatigue. The smell of something meaty got me moving. I followed Gabe through the door that led into the center apartment. It surprised me how the colorful room contrasted with the sterile whiteness of the boys' sanatorium cell.

This room was a long rectangle with a green and yellow kitchen on one end by the front door, a brown living room on the other end where the windows and wrought-iron balcony looked out over Arbat ulitsa, and a dining area in between. The kitchen had one of those extra wide counters with three bar stools on the outside. Behind the stools, two long tables finished off the dining area. They had green and red plaid tablecloths that made me think of Christmas. The tables were crammed with platters and bowls of food and surrounded by people in conversation.

Since all the seats were taken, Gabe and I made for the stools at the kitchen counter. I claimed the one by the wall. Isabel was sitting between Beth and Jake.

Glossy yellow cabinets with forest green accents lined the kitchen. A short, round woman with an orange and red floral scarf tied over her head bustled around, stirring bubbling pots and peeking into the oven.

Ivan took the woman's arm and steered her toward the tables. "I would like to introduce to you all my wife, Yelena."

"Please, we are all friends," she said. "Call me simply Lena."

"The food smells great," Isaac said.

Yelena bowed her head and smiled. "Priyatnova appeteeta. For you to eat. Enjoy."

Ivan prayed for the meal, then I had to wait until Isaac passed each dish to Gabe and me. I heaped my plate with scalloped potatoes, roast beef, something called *kielbasa*, cheese, bread, tomatoes, and sliced cucumbers. Lena offered tea, juice, or bottled water to drink. No milk or soda, so I took water.

I ate until I was full, then I ate more when Lena came by and refilled my plate. The conversation bounced around. Ivan and Tatyana asked about America, and the Americans asked Ivan and Tatyana about Russia. Lena buzzed around the tables like a waitress. I just stuffed my face.

"I noticed there were a lot of homeless right outside," Arianna said.

"Yes. The homeless problem is very growing," Tatyana said. "Job training is needed because many young people are not affording college and are having no qualification for work. They are ending up on street, lost into alcohol, gangs, or Mafia."

Jake's eyes bulged. "There's a Mafia in Moscow?"

"*Al Caponeovich?*" Isaac said.

"Konechna," Ivan said. *Of course.*

While Ivan explained the Russian Mafia to Jake and Isaac, I glanced at Nick, who was sitting beside Isabel. Maybe Nick could join the Mafia for the summer. He'd be a shoo-in for an internship. I laughed to myself and finished off my potatoes.

Tatyana opened her mouth three times during Ivan's Mafia explanation and finally won back the floor. "Over one hundred thousand are homeless in Moscow. In winter, hundreds are freezing to death without proper clothing, food, and medical care. We are hoping our training will provide them future." Tatyana's eyes sparkled as she spoke, as if hanging out with a bunch of homeless people was a good time.

After dinner, I jumped over the back of a beige sofa that ran parallel to the bar stools. Three identical beige sofas sat in a U shape around a 70's looking TV built into a wooden console. If Grandma ever got a TV set, she'd probably pick something like that.

Mr. S was kneeling before the TV, flipping through the channels. Arianna sat on the center sofa, trying to translate whatever Russian she heard.

I tried to get comfortable as I watched the shows flick past. The sofa felt wrong. It was too deep. If I sat all the way back, my knees couldn't bend, like I was a little kid. I jumped up and darted in front of the TV set to sit in a wing chair in the far

JILL WILLIAMSON

corner and found it a better fit.

I couldn't see the TV from here, though. So I glanced out the sliding glass doors to the balcony where Nick and Isabel stood looking down on the street. I growled inside. Isabel's be-nice-to-everyone personality put her in Nick's company more often than I liked to see. I needed to start thinking offensively.

What did Nick know about my parents, anyway? And more importantly, how could I get him to spill it?

Once the Russians left for the night, Mr. S called everyone into the living room. Isaac and Jake claimed the couch adjacent to my chair. On the other side of the living room, Jensina and Beth sat down on the couch I'd abandoned. Gabe settled on the floor in front of their legs. The girls started playing with his hair. I suddenly wished I had crazy hair that *sproinged* and *boinged* and made girls want to touch it.

Isabel and Nick came inside. Isabel sat beside Gabe on the floor. Nick elbowed Beth aside make room. She elbowed him back. The pained expression on his face made me grin.

"Ivan and Tatyana's English is better than Jake's," Isaac said.

"Oh, that's real nice," Jake said.

"Most Russians know some English," Mr. S said. "Still, try to speak Russian to them as much as possible for your own practice."

Isabel leaned her head on Gabe's shoulder. "I don't like those meat noodle thingies. They were gross."

"You didn't like those?" Isaac let out a raunchy burp. "Ooh! I did."

"The dumplings are called pelmini. They're served at special occasions." Kerri closed a door to a room I hadn't explored and settled down on the sofa between Arianna and her husband. It hit me that Gabe's sisters were around here somewhere—maybe in that room Kerri had come out of.

Mr. S's gaze swept the room, the light flashing off his glasses every so often. "You all did well tonight. Lena was happy to see such hearty appetites."

Gabe raised his hand. "The juice was good. What was it?"

"Yuck!" Beth tapped Gabe's head with her palm. "That chunky stuff made me gag."

"It's called compote," Kerri said. "It's cooked fruit."

For the next hour, we discussed the food, the country, and our hosts. I'd never spent much time with any of these churchers outside of school. They talked and laughed freely. No secret who was the outsider here.

I listened until the talk got too preachy. Topics like redemption, repentance of sins, and holiness turned me off. The basketball court in my imagination was calling.

After what felt like three hours, Mr. S asked Isaac to close in prayer, and he sent everyone to bed.

There was a line at the bathroom. Forget that. I could brush my teeth in the morning. I climbed under the covers on my bunk, but the bed was so small that I had to curl on my side to fit.

I dozed off until Isaac's voice jerked me awake. "I'm hitting the lights. Everyone in?"

A few guys grunted, and the lights flicked off. All was not dark, however. On the bunk across from me, Gabe lay reading his Bible, his glasses off, a book light clipped onto the binding. I rolled my eyes.

Above Gabe, snoring drifted from Jake's bunk already. Another light flickered across the room, and I rose onto one elbow. The sofa had converted into a full bed. Isaac sat reading

Surfer magazine with a flashlight. I sighed and lay down, then realized that Nick was standing at the foot of our bunk in his boxers, digging in his suitcase.

I seized the opportunity. "Dude, what do you know about my dad?"

A smirk curved Nick's lips. "He didn't make it, jockstrap. Neither will you."

"Shut up, *Black & Dekker*."

Nick grabbed the bars at the end of the bunk and climbed up. The bed shook while Nick got settled. Then he whispered, "Nighty-night, *snitch*."

I reached up and slapped the side of Nick's mattress, glaring at the bars above. What had happened between Nick and me and Kip, Sammy, Jeb, and Paco . . . it hadn't been my fault. We were just dumb kids. We'd made our own gang, called our "bad" selves the *Seis Puños*, thought we could do whatever we wanted.

Besides, the vandalism had been Nick's idea.

I pulled the covers up to my ear, brainstorming ways of getting Nick to talk.

The next morning, by the time I came sniffing, little remained of Lena's breakfast feast. Jensina was the only one at the table. Strands of her tousled black hair were mixed in on the red side: Tinkerbell after the bomb went off.

Acoustic guitar music drifted from the living room where Gabe sat playing and singing. The dude was good.

Kerri, Jake, and one of Gabe's sisters were singing along. Jake looked neat and tidy, as usual, in black jeans, a striped business shirt, and a brown bowtie. What a nut.

Isabel was nowhere to be seen. Beth was doing sit-ups, sneakers tucked under the back of the center couch, her arms, legs, and face coated in a glossy sheen of sweat. Her baby blue T-shirt read "Pretty Tough."

True that.

"Tee goloden?" Lena asked me, pulling my gaze away from Beth. She stood in front of me, her eyes wide and blue, her face pudgy and beaming.

Goloden meant something about food. I nodded and sat at the table with Jensina. Lena set a plate of tortilla thin pancakes and a bowl of steaming mush in front of me.

"Kasha," she said, pointing to the cereal. Then she pointed to the array of fillings on the table. "Choose to fill blini."

The fruit, jelly, butter, potatoes, sour cream, and leftover items from dinner, all spread out before me, gave me plenty of options. I studied Jensina, who was still eating. She'd filled her tortilla thin pancake and rolled it like a burrito. I scanned the table for peanut butter but didn't see any. So I reached for the jelly.

"Aren't they yummy?" Arianna plopped down beside me—blocking my view of Beth—and pointed at my burrito. "They're called blini. Think I could make them if I used thinner pancake batter?"

I shrugged, my mouth full of blini and jelly. They could really use peanut butter. Arianna had brought a gust of that herbal tea smell along with her. She was wearing a long, ruffly brown skirt with beige lace peeking out the bottom. All she needed was a parasol, and we could put her in a time machine and send her back to the Gold Rush.

Arianna snatched a cucumber slice off a plate and popped

it into her mouth, chewing with her lips pursed like she was thinking. I'm pretty sure she was, but who knew about what.

Isaac fell into a chair across from me. His eyes were half closed, and pillow creases streaked across his cheek. "What's to eat?"

I explained the blini then lowered my voice. "The kasha tastes like paste."

Arianna continued to plague me, droning on about a TV show she and Mr. S had watched that discussed the political situation in Russia. She said I needed to understand current events to be a servant here.

I licked jelly off my fingers and scooted to the side so I could see Beth, counting her sit-ups as she went. I didn't know when she'd started, but she'd been at sixty-three before Arianna had blocked my view.

Mr. S clapped his hands. "We're going to start in about five minutes, so finish up what you're doing." He glanced at the table where I was sitting. "'I feel like this is a dream—and I apologize for how I dressed some of you.'"

Isaac chuckled. "Good one, Mr. S. Who said that?"

"Ray Romano. Now, to those of you who are still wearing what they slept in, please get dressed. Five minutes."

Great. I could see I was going to have to get sneaky if I ever wanted a turn at the shower. I jogged into the boys' room, threw on some clean clothes, my Lakers cap, deodorant, and sprayed myself with a cloud of cologne. It reminded me of what Sherry had said every morning of our six-day relationship.

"Spencer, cologne is not a shower."

Yeah, well, sue me.

I fell into the wing chair in the corner just as Mr. S opened in prayer. When he finished, he gave Tatyana the floor.

"Welcome to Leega Missionerov," she said. "In case you have not learned, that is Russian for *Mission League*. I am happy you have come to help in our service path."

Tatyana gestured out the sliding glass doors. "This apartment is central in city on Arbat ulitsa. Also, museum of famous Russian poet, Alexander Pushkin, Red Square, and Spaso House, home to US Ambassador, are not far.

"It is only few blocks to Smolenskaya Metro Station. Remember that name. *Smolenskaya*. You will be taking metro wherever you go. I have metro card and city map for everyone. If *politsia* is stopping you, they are wanting to see passport and visa. Have them with you always. I am sure no one is wanting to spend the night in custody. Mr. Stopplecamp tells me you have buddies. Use them. You are not wanting to be lost in Moscow."

I located Gabe across the room. He was sitting on the couch beside Isabel. Hmm. How long had they known each other, anyway?

"Shops are nearby to buy snacks. City water might be making you sick, so I am recommending you purchase bottle water. My mother will cook your meals here. Do not be spending all your money first week. Prices of souvenirs on Arbat ulitsa—very expensive. End of summer I will be taking you shopping for bargains.

"Also, pickpockets work the metro and target naïve foreign tourists. They will target you. They carry satchels to hold wallets they take, and they'll try to get close or bump you on metro and take wallets. Boys, maybe you will want to keep your wallet and passport in front pocket and keep your hand over it, because pickpockets take from front pockets too!"

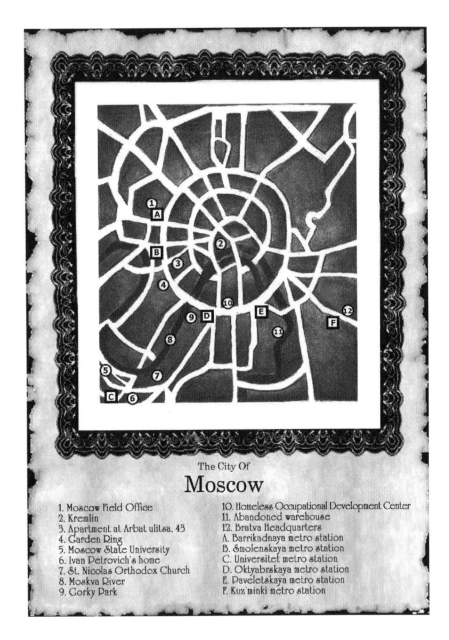

The City Of

Moscow

1. Moscow Field Office
2. Kremlin
3. Apartment at Arbat ulitsa, 43
4. Garden Ring
5. Moscow State University
6. Ivan Petrovich's home
7. St. Nicolas Orthodox Church
8. Moskva River
9. Gorky Park
10. Homeless Occupational Development Center
11. Abandoned warehouse
12. Bratva Headquarters
A. Barrikadnaya metro station
B. Smolenskaya metro station
C. Universitet metro station
D. Oktyabrskaya metro station
E. Paveletskaya metro station
F. Kuz'minki metro station

Dude, if anyone tried to mug me, they'd wish they hadn't.

"Do not reveal to anyone you are agents-in-training. Please say only that you are Americans students helping homeless. Also, it is not likely, but may be necessary to use . . . how do you say, passcode? The code identifies League members to each other in emergency situation.

"If someone is approaching you, claiming to be agent, he should be giving you code up front. That is protocol. If he is not, you can offer code to him. If he is not responding correctly, you have no reason to comply with his demands. Mr. Stopplecamp, you will assist me to demonstrating passcode?"

Mr. S joined Tatyana in the center of the room. "Miss? I have instructions for you to follow me to meet up with your group."

"Ah, yes. Can you tell me: Do you like red?" she asked.

"There's power in the blood," he answered.

Tatyana panned her gaze over each of us, eyebrows raised. "You see? By this, I am knowing he is agent. Is everyone understanding? One person asks, 'Do you like red?' and it is to be answered, 'There is power in the blood.' No right answer, no agent, da?"

Though I couldn't imagine why anyone shady would try and mess with a bunch of churchers, I liked this idea of this secret code. Very Jason Bourne.

Tatyana paced across the room. "After lunch we will take metro to Moscow Field Office for tour. This is special privilege, so please be respectful of agents who are working. Maybe you will see your friend Ryan Matheson there, but you must never approach agents outside League facility, unless they are speaking first. They may be undercover. This applies to Ryan, myself, my father, Prière, and any other agents you are meeting here."

Great. Prière was here? I hoped he didn't have any cryptic dreams involving me and the Russian Mafia.

"Tomorrow we will go to Homeless and Occupational Development Center or HODC," Tatyana said. "There is much work needed. I am thankful you are here and hoping to accomplish much this summer. Now I will show you local area, and we will meet back here for lunch."

Mr. S held up a hand. "I'd like to remind you about my daughters, Mary and Martha. They'll keep busy this summer with Kerri and some local missionaries, but they'll live here and eat here. Try to remember their ears. They already know more than they should about the League. I don't want to burden them further. Thanks." He clapped his hands once. "Okay, time to get going. Everyone get your stuff, and let's go."

I found my shoes at the bottom of the pile in the boys' room. "Hey, Gabe. You ever use a secret code before?"

"Only in district training events." Gabe was crouched over his suitcase, digging for something. "Every two years there's a competition in LA for the Agent Development Program. You can enter areas you're training in. If you start taking LCT, you can compete next spring."

Sweet.

"But Beth is the district LCT champ," Gabe said, "so you probably don't stand a chance."

"*District champ?*" My eyes widened.

"Yeah. Last year she took first out of two hundred. Girls

don't compete separately from boys like they do for sports in school, so they have to be tough to place—"

"She won against guys?" That explained her brutal nature.

"Women face the same odds as guys in the field, so training is no different." He stood. "Beat you to the street."

"Not a chance."

Outside on Arbat Street, Tatyana led us past dozens of souvenir kiosks, restaurants, and boutiques. I couldn't believe there was so much American stuff here. A McDonalds, a Cinnabon, a Hard Rock Café, and of course the Starbucks, where we stopped so the group could get a caffeine fix.

I didn't drink coffee, but I bought a couple muffins and inhaled them while everyone was waiting for their drinks. The girls disappeared into some clothing store, so Gabe and I explored a supermarket and bought a bunch of Russian candy, each buying something different to try as many as possible.

When we returned from seeing the neighborhood, Lena had lunch waiting. Isabel was already sitting with Nick at the counter, so I fell into a seat at one of the tables between Gabe and Arianna and filled my plate. Lena was a great cook. Too good. If I was going to stay in shape for basketball, I'd have to find a way to work out. I shoved a forkful of potatoes into my mouth, wondering if Beth would punch me if I tried to join her for sit-ups in the morning.

The room fell suddenly quiet. People casually raised their thumbs one at a time and glanced around at each other, smiling and snickering. I swallowed and looked from one eager face to the next. What was the joke?

"Spencer!" voices rang out all at once amid snickering.

I jerked my gaze around the table. "What?"

"You pray," Isaac said, fork in one fist, spoon in the other.

Heat flashed over me. *Pray?*

Gabe nudged my arm. "Last thumbs up prays for the meal."

"Go ahead," Arianna said.

"No." There was no way. I hadn't prayed out loud since third grade.

"You *have* to," Arianna whispered.

Isaac, who was sitting at the end of my table, raised an eyebrow at Arianna. "No one *has* to."

"Just do it, Garmond," Nick said with a look on his face I wanted to wipe off.

All eyes focused on me. The food didn't smell so good anymore. Forget this. I pushed my chair back and stood to leave.

Isaac hopped up with me. "Dude, I got this. Sit."

I wanted to leave, but what was I going to do? Go sit in the boys' room and sulk? I was stuck here with these people all summer. I may as well deal. I fell back to my seat and looked at my hands in my lap. My face burned.

Isaac said a quick prayer, and everyone dug in. It was quiet except for the sounds of silverware clinking against ceramic.

Then Isaac said, "Hmm . . . Need a joke to break the ice here . . . Wouldn't want you guys to think I was a *borscht.*"

Thankfully, everybody laughed.

Still, it took a lot of effort for me to pick up my fork again. *Thumbs, Spencer. Duh!* I shoveled potatoes into my mouth, keeping my head and eyes down. When I finally did glance up, I locked eyes with Nick, who smirked and whispered something to Isabel. She giggled.

Great.

REPORT NUMBER: 14

REPORT TITLE: I Steal a Piece of Paper . . . Big Deal
SUBMITTED BY: Agent-in-Training Spencer Garmond
LOCATION: Outside, Arbat ulitsa, Moscow, Russia
DATE AND TIME: Friday, June 6, 12:10 p.m.

THE MOSCOW FIELD OFFICE OPERATED out of an ordinary grey office building a few blocks from Barrikadnaya Metro Station. No sign indicated that the place was a Mission League facility. Inside the small foyer, a guard chatted briefly with Tatyana before letting us pass.

Tatyana turned her back to the elevator and faced our group. "It is blessing to have elevator. But it is small and old and we must be gentle with it. We will split into three groups. Fifth floor."

I found myself in the second elevator group, crowded into the small space with Gabe, Arianna, Isabel, and Nick. The doors closed, and the elevator jerked and crawled upward.

Nick cleared his throat. "You think God makes mistakes, Isabel?"

"No."

Nick's gaze flashed to mine. "Then Prière must be off his rocker, don't you think?"

Man! Why couldn't Nick just let it go, already?

Isabel cocked her head to the side. "He is little strange but—"

"He's only human, right?" Nick asked.

"What's your point, Nick?" Arianna asked. She stood in the middle of the elevator with Gabe and me on one side and Isabel and Nick on the other.

"My point, Mission-Ari, is your boyfriend doesn't belong. Prière screwed up big time on this one."

"Arianna is not my girlfriend." I just felt that needed to be said aloud.

"Prière didn't screw up!" Arianna yelled with more volume that seemed possible for her little mouth, especially in such a small space. "He is a servant of the Lord."

Nick's gaze flashed across the elevator to mine. "You see it too, don't you, jockstrap? You know you don't fit in here."

The word *jockstrap* changed everything. I squeezed my hands into fists. "I'm more than happy to go round two with you, *Black & Dekker*, but not here."

He blew a quick breath out his nose, like a bull getting ready to charge. "Is that a fact?"

"Yeah, it's a fact."

"Es-pensor and Neek," Isabel said, "be nice."

I wanted to obey her, I really did. So I tried to sound mature instead. "Why do you care, Muren? Is this about Cornerstone? Dude, let it go. We were twelve." Not that I didn't feel bad about how it all went down, but seriously. Enough already.

"It's more than Cornerstone," Nick said. "People are paying for you to be here, and you don't want to be. You're wasting everyone's time and money getting trained, and I know you'll quit the first chance you get."

"*Neek*," Isabel sang.

But he'd nailed me on that one. That *had* been my original plan. But that was before I'd found out about my parents. "I don't quit," I said. And that was true when I really wanted something. I only quit when I didn't give a rip.

Nick cracked his neck. "Garmond's dad quit, Isabel. And you know what they say, like father like son, right?"

"You don't know what you're talking about," I said. My dad hadn't quit. He'd turned traitor. Which was worse.

"Besides, it's not a good idea to have atheist agents in the Mission League," Nick said. "Bad for the image, you know."

I glared at Nick. "I'm not an atheist."

"You don't *pray*. Sounds like an atheist to me."

The elevator opened and Nick strode out. I stayed put, shooting Nick down with imaginary *PoP* ray guns and watching his body explode.

"Ignore him," Gabe said.

Before I could inform Gabe that I could handle Nick Muren, Isabel stepped in front of me. Surprised at her nearness, I jerked back against the wall.

"Es-pensor, look at me." Isabel put a hand up on my shoulder, immobilizing me. Except for my hands, which wouldn't stop trembling. I finally had the goddess right here, alone, touching me. Why couldn't I speak?

I swallowed and looked down into her eyes—eyes that I

swear could see me for the loser I really was. The intensity made me want to look away. But I couldn't. I stared so hard into those endless orbs that my eyes began to water.

"God don't make mistakes. He knows you and the story of your life. He has a plan for you. You belong here, *entiendes?*"

I nodded with the realization that, whether I agreed or not, I had no control over my actions. I would have agreed to anything she said.

"Bueno." She wrapped her arms around my waist in a soft, warm hug. The top of her head rested against the middle of my chest. Her hair smelled like a flower garden. All was right in the world.

Sadly, she let go all too soon. She blessed me with one last glowing smile and left the elevator. I remained frozen in place, woozy from the effect the goddess had inflicted upon me.

Gabe stood holding the door open, staring after Isabel with his mouth gaping like a surprised emoticon. The elevator buzzed in protest, banging against Gabe's back every few seconds.

I finally stepped out of the elevator, where Arianna was waiting, arms crossed, a satisfied smirk on her face. What had her so smug?

Gabe let the door close. "I've never heard her talk that way to anyone."

Arianna leaned closer to us and whispered. "One of her spiritual gifts is encouragement."

Isabel now stood between Beth and Jensina, arms linked as if all three might break out into a chorus line dance step. I removed my Lakers cap and ran my hand through my hair. Maybe there was something to spiritual gifts after all. That had been beyond encouraging.

I glanced around. We were standing in a white reception area. White tile floor, white walls, but the waiting chairs, end tables, and receptionist's desk were aluminum. The only color came from the magazines piled on the end tables beside the chairs, the receptionist's red blouse, and our clothing.

Ivan stood in front of a door beside the receptionist's desk with Nick at his elbow. Did Nick really know something about my dad, or was he just messing with me? We looked at Russian magazines until the elevator slid open, and the third group arrived.

Mr. S walked over to Ivan. "Listen up. We're ready to go. Please give Ivan your undivided attention."

Ivan spread his arms as if lecturing. "Maskovskoye Regional'noye Atdeleniye, or Moscow Field Office, has nineteen departments serving city and surrounding areas, including Placement, Defensive Apologetics, Offensive Apologetics, Pastoral, New Cults, Community Helps, and Intelligence.

"An agent in New Cults Department, like your friend Ryan Matheson, he started in entry level Research and Monitoring. Next level is Field Intelligence Junior Operative, then Senior Operative, and so on and forth. Junior and senior agents are to go on undercover assignments."

Ivan swiped a card through some kind of reader on the wall, and the door buzzed open. He led us down a narrow, white hallway, keeping to one side so employees could pass. Long halogen bulbs glared from the ceiling. People bustled past, carrying files, reading documents, and talking on cell phones. I expected to find Russians working at this office, but there were all kinds of nationalities—male and female—of all ages.

Ivan stopped at a door labeled "Placement Department," swiped his ID card again, and showed us around a grid of cubicles where more people were working. Nothing special. Nothing that looked very James Bond. No Moneypenny. No Q.

Ivan led us to another department. I stayed to the back, keeping my distance from Nick. A disparaging commentary ran through my mind, distracting me from Ivan's explanation of the Counseling Department.

Why *was* I here? Maybe I *was* wasting League money. I was no atheist, though. God was up there. He just didn't give a rip about me, and the feeling was mutual. What was the point of following a God like that?

Ivan Petrovich stopped outside the Administrative Department. "This is my office. We oversee all League activity in Moscow. We are to be keeping track of every agent's location and mission. I am holding weekly meetings with department heads to be checking on agent and departmental progress."

Ivan showed us around his office before taking us back into the hall. It was weird to think that Grandpa Earl had once done this same job in Los Angeles. Had his office looked like Ivan's? Had Grandpa sat at a spacious desk surrounded by shelves of books stretching to the ceiling and black file cabinets five drawers tall? Did he have three phones on his desk?

I dragged my feet and yawned as Ivan moved down the hall. Isabel's musical giggle floated down to me at the end of the line. I spotted her brown curls bouncing through the crowd. She clenched the back of Gabe's shirt, trying to keep up as he dashed to the front of the line. I dug my fingernails into my palm.

Pain made a nice distraction.

Ivan stopped in front of another closed door. This one had

a narrow, rectangular window down one side. "It is great blessing to have here a full intercession department. Please take look inside, but try not to disturb."

When my turn came, I quickly surveyed the room through the window on the door. It looked like any school classroom back home. Four men and two women were kneeling at individual altars. Two more men lay prostrate on the floor, nowhere near each other. Beside each intercessor, a woman sat at a small desk with a computer. Three were tying, one looked asleep, another seemed to be praying along with her intercessor, and the last was chewing on her fingernail, staring down at her shoes.

"It's amazing," Beth said when she peeked inside. "This is the first intercession department I've seen. What you think, Nick?"

Nick blew a bubble with bright blue gum and popped it with a smack. He tugged Beth's ponytail and flashed a grin.

She whacked his hand away. "You're the only one of us going for intercessor. You could at least pretend to be interested."

I looked at Nick. Did he think *he* was a good investment of League training dollars? Because if I didn't belong in the Mission League, neither did Nick.

Isabel peered through the window. "Is that Prière?"

"Where?" Arianna pushed back through the crowd to have another look.

"Da," Ivan said. "We are always providing station for visiting intercessors. He prays for you."

Everyone looked again—including me. Sure enough. Prière was lying face down on the floor in the middle of the room.

Bizarre.

"Each intercessor has a praying station and a, how you say, transcriber?" Ivan said. "The transcriber is to record the message, vision, dream, or prophecy the intercessor communicates. That data, called a communiqué, is later being transcribed into reports and sent out over all world."

I inched closer to Ivan, drawn in by two words he had used. "Intercessors get visions and dreams?"

Nick burst into a cackling laugh. "How do you think God talks to them, Garmond? On a cell phone?"

"Nick, come on over here and keep me company," Mr. S said.

I waved to Nick as he walked past.

He coughed into his fist, masking his comment. "Moron."

Before I got a chance to retaliate, Ivan answered my question. "Our intercessors are praying for facility here and city of Moscow, but often they receive word for other agents or locations. Frequently names of people in danger. Their transcriber files a communiqué report, then intercession team prays for individual and agents who are associated with case. Intercession communiqués are updated to League server hourly, giving agents access to most current data."

"How do you decide which transcriber works with which Intercessor?" Jake asked.

I spaced out as Ivan answered Jake's question and leaned against the wall, dazed. If what Ivan said was true, Prière must have had some sort of vision of me and Nick put a report into the system. Whoa.

Again the thought struck me: Could *my* visions and dreams be like the ones Prière had?

Huh-uh. No way.

Ivan moved a little farther down the hall. "Our computer room houses servers for Moscow data. The network is under surveillance from recent security leaks." He swiped his card and held open the door. "So you cannot enter, but you may look."

I snapped out of my daze at the word *computer*. I slipped to the front and peeked inside. "What kind of leaks?"

"Unauthorized access from inside facility. Our biggest challenge with confidential data is making it accessible to authorized users and restricting access to everyone else. Our intelligence computers are having no external drives, so it is impossible to download information directly from computer except from room here. Few days ago, unauthorized download attempt failed, and we increased security."

Questions clouded my mind. Who would want to steal information from here? Christian traitors like the kind Grandma had once investigated? Did this office have an Internal Profiling Department too? Before I could think of which question to ask next, Ivan closed the door and continued the tour.

He led us to the New Cults Department: a gymnasium-sized room filled with low cubicles. A six-foot plasma screen shrouded the center back wall, flashing criminal dossiers. Below the screen a huge, waist-high table was covered with papers and photos. Four men stood around it discussing the contents and shifting them.

We followed Ivan through the maze of cubicles. "New Cults is one of most dangerous fields. Agents conduct surveillance and go undercover to study suspicious organizations and individuals. Cults are very persuasive. Department here seeks to discover their appeal and how to break recruitment processes.

"We encounter some wretched people in cults, so our saying is, 'They are not enemy, they are prize.' Our first goal is always to be winning souls to Christ. Many people think they will find love and acceptance in cults. Sadly, there is only control, conforming, and obedience to sin. I tell you this to stress that the Mission League is not fun and games. Agents are risking their lives daily."

"Do you ever lose any?" Jake asked.

"Agents quit sometimes. Many retire. Some never retire until God takes them home."

Jake tugged at his bowtie with his finger, as if it were too tight. "No, you said that many agents risk their lives. Do any ever . . . lose their lives . . . at work?"

"Da," Ivan said, his wrinkles shifting into a frown. "On occasion in this hostile environment we have lost field agents."

An awkward silence filled the air.

"Hey, guys!" Ryan Matheson, Jensina's old friend, appeared behind the group. He tapped knuckles with some of the guys and hugged the girls until he saw Ivan Petrovich. "Sorry, sir."

"Not at all, Agent Matheson. Greet your friends and show them your station. I must speak with Agent Lindley. We will return in a moment." Ivan and Jake walked toward the big table.

"Where's Jake going?" I asked Gabe.

Gabe shrugged.

Jensina linked her arm into Ryan's. The height difference was like a little girl and her daddy. "Let's see your desk."

Ryan led us to a tiny cubicle sandwiched in the middle of the room. Inside was a cluttered desk with a computer, printer, and a chair. "This is me."

Isaac surveyed the space and nodded. "So this is where the magic happens."

"Oh, yeah," Ryan said. "You know me, saving the world and all."

Isaac elbowed me. "See, Spencer? Didn't I promise we'd see some cubicles?"

I gaped at the twenty-five-inch flat screen monitor on Ryan's desk. "Sweet monitor!"

Ryan's brown eyes flashed to mine. He was maybe an inch and a half taller than me and twice as muscular. "You like computers?"

Not as much as I liked basketball. "Yeah."

"Check this out." Ryan sat at the computer and typed in several passwords. "My department has access to the international server. So I can get information on cult activity around the world. Take Big Robbie's, for ex—"

"The family restaurant?" Gabe asked.

"Yeah. Don't eat there." Ryan typed fast. "They suck in their employees with a scheme that promises they can invest a small percentage of their income and become part-owners in the company. As time goes on, more is required. Members eventually move into apartments owned by the corporation and stop associating with anyone else—family, friends, you name it."

Ryan wheeled his chair to the side so we could see his monitor. "The Moscow office doesn't cover Big Robbie's, of course, but I thought it'd be a neat case to show you since it's going on in America. With this system, I research my assignments and cross-reference them against what's already out there. Try it." Ryan stood and offered his seat to me.

I leapt into the chair to explore the system.

"What kind of assignments you get?" Isaac asked.

"I'm new in junior ops, so I do mostly research. I run my findings over to my boss at the big table where they put it all together. After a while you know what to look for." He paused and grinned wide. "I just got my first outside assignment, though, so I'm real excited."

I already knew. I'd nosed around Ryan's computer desktop, opened his assignment folder, and found a dossier for an Anastasia Vseveloda.

I stared at her picture, unable to breathe. It was the blonde. I could almost smell the fried sausages from my dream. I spotted a printer in the corner of the cubicle and hit print. I wanted a copy of this.

Beth folded her arms. "So what are you going to do? Stake out?"

Ryan chuckled. "Not exactly. My partner, Lev, and I are working together. I've made contact with someone and have to keep an eye on her. Lev monitors everything when I go in. I get to wear a wire."

Isaac crouched beside me. "Cute wahine. Looks like tough work. 'Anastasia Vez-vel-o-dah. Goes by: Anya. Nationality: Ukranian. Processed at Field Homeless Shelter—'"

"Hey! You guys can't see that. Okay, man, enough computer time." Ryan grabbed the back of my shirt and lifted me out of the chair. "You're gonna get me busted! Everybody out." Ryan closed his system and strode out of the cubicle. The group followed single file.

Nick's voice boomed on the other side of the cubicle wall. "Told you Garmond was trouble. You can't trust that kid, Ryan."

"Shut up, Nick," Beth said.

I hung back so I'd be the last to leave. As I went by the printer, I snatched the dossier page I'd printed out, folded it up, and shoved it into my pocket. I had to know who this Anya was. Why I'd been dreaming about her. My heart pounded as I joined the group around the big table where Ivan was describing all the criminals as they appeared on the big screen. He had returned, but Jake was still gone.

" . . . some of the most notorious cult leaders worldwide. Shoko Miake offers peace to followers through meditation, but really she calls on demons. Ekevu Girma recruits through wild parties that are ending by taking oath to Rifaa, an animistic god. Diane Bay MacCormack's groups partake in New Age practices. Pratima Dharmesh leads feminist cult in India that exalts women as gods. That is only a few.

"Many cult leaders are also operating successful, fraudulent businesses to fund their cult organizations. They will try anything to pull people away from God. There are no major leaders in Moscow that we are aware of, but there is plenty activity to keep us busy."

Next, Ivan led us to the Community Helps Department, where Tatyana was waiting.

"I hope you are having informative tour," she said. "I work at this office when I am not at HODC."

Like the other departments, cubicles filled the large room. Instead of the big table from the New Cults Department, Community Helps had a large meeting table in the back. A gigantic map of Moscow and the surrounding areas covered the back wall.

"There are many branches in this department. I work in Homeless Branch. HODC is my first solo project. Homeless tend to gather in tourist areas, metro stations, and parks." She pointed at some of those areas on the Moscow map. "It is huge blessing to have found building near Gorky Park for HODC. Having been open six months, we already are running out of space. We are planning second facility in another part of city to open next year.

"Please keep your League status secret at the HODC as well. Only one employee is agent—my secretary, Marina. All others are hired or volunteers, many right from training program. They receive good job experience there. Tomorrow morning you will see facility, and in afternoon, I will meet with each of you. I will consider requests when assigning job schedules."

"I hope you enjoyed tour," Ivan said. "Does anyone have question as we head out?"

Isaac leaned over and whispered to me. "Yeah, I've got a few questions. Why does the word *two* have a "w" in it but the word *one* doesn't? Why don't hamburgers have any *ham* in them? And if oranges were blue, would they still be called oranges?"

I chuckled. I could get used to Isaac's humor.

"What's the biggest problem you face in Moscow?" Gabe asked.

"That is depending on department." Ivan led us back down the long white hallway. "Homelessness and unemployment are huge problems. The Mafia is also problem, especially with homeless youth."

"Does the Mafia exist all over Russia or only in Moscow?" Gabe asked.

"All over, but mostly in cities."

When we got back to the reception area, there sat Jake,

slouched in a chair. He hopped up, bounced over to Ivan, and shook his hand. "Thanks again for the opportunity, Mr. Petrovich. I'm really excited about this."

"You will learn much, I am sure."

"I only wish I knew which path to take after graduation," Jake said.

"You are working with Mr. Stopplecamp and Prière on that?" Ivan asked.

"Yeah." Jake shook his head. "It's hard to know, though."

"Have patience, God will direct you."

How exactly could Mr. S and Prière help Jake choose a path? Did Prière take Jake into the intercession room? Did Jake sit and wait for Prière to get word from God?

It all seemed a little ridiculous. If I hadn't been haunted by my own bizarro dreams, and if I hadn't had the printout of the mysterious Anya in my pocket, I'd have laughed it off altogether.

I had my thumbs up when I sat down to dinner at the apartment, but this time Kerri prayed. Mr. S kept us busy all evening talking about the Field Office and the neighborhood and the people. I didn't get a chance to look at the dossier. I took it into the bathroom with me before bed that night, but my Cyrillic was too poor to read it. What had I been thinking? If only I could paste it into Google Translate.

Instead, I stuffed it in my suitcase and lay awake in bed, aware of its presence beneath me.

It had been a busy day: prayer disaster, Nick's elevator

attack, Isabel's encouraging hug, the tour, and a stolen dossier. A guilty pressure lingered in my chest. It was only a piece of paper, for crying out loud. I wasn't going to put it on the Internet or anything. I just had to know who this Anya chick was. I mean, she'd been haunting my dreams for years. Still, I doubted Ryan would be thrilled if he knew I'd printed it out.

Seriously, what was I doing here with these people? I stared into the darkness around me and replayed Isabel's words in my head.

God knew I'd be a Christian someday?

Now that I was far away from Isabel's intoxicating presence, I wasn't buying it. I mean, why would I ever sign on to be one of these churchers? I'd always done fine on my own.

But what if my dreams were some kind of message from God? And if they were, what was I supposed to do about it? The vision of Nick punching me on the basketball court had come true. Did that mean I'd meet the blond woman, Anya, here in Moscow?

The idea both terrified and thrilled me.

REPORT NUMBER: 15

REPORT TITLE: I Finally Manage To Read the Dossier
SUBMITTED BY: Agent-in-Training Spencer Garmond
LOCATION: Oktyabrskaya Metro Station, Moscow, Russia
DATE AND TIME: Saturday, June 7, 8:58 a.m.

I UNCAPPED MY PEN AND circled Oktyabrskaya Station on my metro map as the exit to take for the HODC. Tatyana led us all outside the station and down the street. Music chimed in the distance, and the smell of popcorn wafted on the warm breeze. I glimpsed a field of green grass between buildings. A huge Ferris wheel edged the skyline.

"Is there a carnival or something going on?" I asked.

Tatyana nodded. "Da. Always there is something in Gorky Park."

We approached a single story brick building. A sign out front read, "Welcome to the Homeless and Occupational Development Center" in tiny English under big Cyrillic lettering. A scruffy crowd clustered around the entrance. I wrinkled my nose at the rank body odor.

"Tatyana, ya apazdal!" *I'm late!* A panicked woman passed her baby to Tatyana and jogged back toward the metro station.

Tatyana shifted the baby onto her hip and stepped to the door, jiggling her keys into the lock. She glanced around at the grubby crowd. "I am sure you are all hungry." She pushed the door open and stepped inside. "Oksana? Where could everyone be?"

"*Mira!*" Isabel pointed to a note taped to the back of the front door.

Tatyana read the letter, and her expression sagged. "All three of them?" She plopped into a chair in the front office. The baby started crying.

I backed away from the snotty, drooling baby. I didn't want to get sick while I was over here. Kip had told me horror stories of what happened to Americans in foreign hospitals.

"What's wrong?" Isaac asked.

"My girls found jobs. I am happy for them, but I wish they give more notice. The next shift is not arriving until ten." She looked at our group. "Who loves babies?"

"Me," said the girls and Gabe, who flashed me an innocent smile.

"Isabel, take baby Zina." Tatyana handed the bundle off and turned to a list on the wall. "Five more children will be arriving any minute. Who can make coffee?"

Isaac raised his hand. "I can make it, drink it, and take pictures of it."

I sensed I should volunteer too, but for what? The others seemed to have everything under control.

"This way." Tatyana led us through a cafeteria with eight

long tables, two across and four deep. The homeless lined up along a counter that peeked into a large industrial kitchen. We Americans followed Tatyana inside.

"Coffee is here." She opened a steel cupboard. "The rest of you greet people and ask them to sit. Offer fruit and juice, anything you find. I will be back. Girls, this way to nursery."

Gabe forged a pout. "Aww."

"That's reverse sexism," I said. "You should get to play Mr. Mom if you want to."

Isaac pried the lid off the can of coffee. "Don't get me wrong, Gabe is pretty good with the kiddies, but I think his real plan was to spend some extra time with a pair of pretty brown eyes, am I right, Stopplecamp?"

Gabe's cheeks flushed. "You got coffee filters for that?"

I leaned against the cool metal counter and laughed out loud—couldn't help it. So Gabe liked Isabel too. Well, may the best man win.

Sadly, I knew that wasn't going to be me.

An old man wandered into the kitchen. He wore a dirty army-green parka with greyish fur around the hood—much too heavy for summer. His face looked tired and content at the same time. He opened the cupboard beside the coffee, pulled out filters, and offered them to Isaac. His hands smudged the crisp white paper.

Isaac accepted the filters. "Spasiba." *Thank you.*

The old guy shuffled toward me. The hems of his dirty jeans had frayed into tangles that dragged behind his tattered sneakers. "Menya zovoot Viktor." *My name is Viktor.*

That's fabulous, buddy. I forced a grin.

"Menya zovoot Isaac." Isaac's back was turned as he made the coffee. He must have assumed Viktor was talking to him instead of me.

Viktor glanced around the kitchen. "Amerikantsy?"

"Da." Isaac poured coffee into the filter, then poured water into the machine.

Viktor locked eyes with me and gestured to Isaac and Gabe. "Your friends?" he asked in English.

"Sure are," Isaac said, mistaking the question for himself again.

I didn't answer.

Viktor took two wobbly steps forward and put his hand on my shoulder.

A warm tingling cascaded through my body. No, not again. I went rigid, suddenly afraid I was about to see a vision.

None came.

"Remember to lift each other in prayer," Viktor said to me. "Prayer is vital to be in the center of God's will."

"Good advice." Isaac poured a cup of coffee and offered it to Viktor.

Viktor patted my shoulder then accepted the cup. The tingling stopped, and I shivered. My gaze darted around the kitchen. Everyone was busy searching for food. No one seemed to have noticed my strange interaction with Viktor.

Isaac set a tray with bread and cheese on the counter, and the homeless started filling their plates. Gabe added a bowl of fruit. I watched, feeling awkward about not knowing what to do and stupid when someone jumped in and did something obvious. Like Gabe putting fruit in a bowl. Why hadn't I thought of that?

Tatyana returned and helped herself to a cup of coffee. "I am glad you are talking with people. That is part of working kitchen."

Next Tatyana led us to the nursery. The regular volunteers had arrived, so the girls joined us for a full tour. The building consisted of a front office, job-training area, shelter with sixty beds, small sanctuary, donations room, kitchen, cafeteria, laundry room, medical center, and nursery.

"Many are thinking homeless people are all alcoholics or beggars," Tatyana said. "Politsia treat them like criminal because many homeless have no identity documents. Without passport in Russia, you are invisible. Runaways come to Moscow and live at railway stations and street markets. Many have homes but prefer street-life to being abused or neglected by their families. My brother Pasha made many friends here. I am sure he will introduce some."

Tatyana ended the tour back at the front desk just as two teen boys ran out of the kitchen with their arms full of bottled water, apples, and oranges. They looked like thieves.

Now this I could help with. I ran to the door to block their escape.

Tatyana froze. "Pasha! Sch'to tee delaesh'?" *What are you doing?*

A tall, skeletal boy grinned. "Neechevo." *Nothing.*

"Tebe nel'zya brat' etu peeshoo," Tatyana said. *You cannot take this food.*

Pasha glanced at the Americans and shrugged. "It is for some homeless, Tatyana."

I relaxed and stepped aside. Clearly, this was Tatyana's brother.

Tatyana didn't relax, though. "You are taking it to your friends, and they are trouble."

Pasha's friend mumbled something in Russian and bolted out the door.

Pasha started to follow, but Tatyana jumped at him and slapped at the food in his hands. Water and fruit crashed to the floor. Pasha grabbed what water he could and raced after the other boy, laughing. Tatyana screamed in frustration.

I stayed out of it.

Tatyana turned back to the group, red-faced. "Izveeneete." *I'm sorry.*

"Ees not your fault," Isabel said.

Tatyana cleared her throat. "My brother does not always take the HODC seriously. Some of his friends are bad crowd."

I helped Isaac, Gabe, and Isabel pick up the remaining bottles of water. Beth, Jensina, and Tatyana took the fruit to the kitchen to see what could be salvaged.

When the girls returned, Tatyana was in a better mood. She smiled, and her voice perked up. "Time for lunch! We go back to apartment for eating."

The metro ride seemed shorter on the way back. By the time we arrived at the apartment, Lena had lunch waiting. Halfway through the meal, Tatyana announced the start of her evaluations. I helped myself to seconds.

Tatyana peered at the clipboard in her hands. "I will be questioning oldest to youngest. Isaac, whenever you are ready."

"I was born ready." Isaac jumped up and dumped his plate into the sink.

Someone knocked on the door to the apartment, and Ryan entered. Jensina squealed and drummed her palm on the empty chair beside her. Ryan joined Jensina, and the other girls crowded around. I studied the agent with a mixture of envy and awe.

"What are your plans for today?" Jensina asked.

"Yeah, you off or something?" I asked. Ryan's snug long sleeve T-shirt left little room for wires. If he was here, who was watching Anya?

Ryan's brows sank. "I'm on lunch."

"Spies can break for lunch?" I dropped my plate in the sink and turned to lean against the counter. "You must have been in the neighborhood, huh? So where's your partner? Lev, wasn't it?"

"You ask a lot of questions, kid. What I do is none of your business."

"I'm not a kid."

Jensina glared at me and pulled Ryan toward the balcony. "Come see the view, Ryan."

"You done eating, Spencer?" Gabe asked me.

I nodded, and we retreated into the boys' room. Nick was asleep on his bunk. I collapsed onto mine.

"So." Gabe sat on his bed, eyebrows raised. "You have that printout?"

My arm hair stood on end. I hadn't realized anyone had seen me. I put a finger to my lips and pointed the other hand up to where Nick slept. I stood. "I'm thirsty. You want to run get something before it's our turn?"

"Okay."

I retrieved the paper from my suitcase and ran into the hallway and down a flight of stairs. I sat on the top step of the third floor landing.

Gabe settled beside me. "I can't believe you printed that."

"It's just a piece of paper."

Gabe snorted. "That's not what my dad would say."

"I had to," I mumbled, frustrated that I couldn't read it and even more frustrated that I couldn't defend myself, because I wasn't about to tell Gabe about my dreams. I spotted an address—Gasheka ulitsa, #7—at the bottom of the page. I'd look for it on my city map. But I couldn't read anything else. "Can you tell what it says?"

ASSIGNMENT DOSSIER

RESTRICTED ACCESS

NATIONALITY:	UKRANIAN
SEX:	FEMALE
HAIR:	BLONDE
HEIGHT:	5' 4"

PROCESSED AT: FIELD HOMELESS SHELTER, KIEV

DETAILS: TURNED UP ON DOOR OF FHS, KIEV ON 5/10 AT 0942 HOURS. VICTIM HAD BEEN BADLY BEATEN AND WAS HALF STARVED. SHE HAD NO MEMORY OF WHAT HAPPENED. FAMILY IN UKRAINE CHECK OUT. NAME FLAGGED IN SYSTEM- 18 COMMUNIQUÉS TRANSFERRED TO MOSCOW FOR SURVEILANCE

FUGITIVE STATUS: NONE (UNDER INVESTIGATION: NEW CULTS DIVISION, MOSCOW CASE # 763489-03)

CRIMINAL ACTIVITY:

SUSPECTED: CULT INVOLVEMENT MAFIA CONNECTIONS

ARRESTS: NONE

BACKGROUND: RAISED IN RIVNE, UKRAINE REST UNKNOWN

NAME: VSEVELODA, ANASTASIA
GOES BY: ANYA
NICKNAME: UNKNOWN
ALIAS: UNKNOWN

LAST KNOWN ADDRESS:
PARENTS IN UKRAINE
11, SOBORNA STREET,
33000, RIVNE, UKRAINE
PHONE: 380 362 22 10 56

CURRENT ADDRESS:
GASHEKA ULITSA, #7
MOSCOW, RUSSIA
PHONE: 95 832 5206

INTERCESSOR COMMUNIQUÉS:
RISK LEVEL: HIGH
8 DANGER
6 PROTECTION
4 SUSPICION
18 TOTAL COMMUNIQUÉS

E - - - MOSCOW FIELD OFFICE - - - MOSCOW FIELD OFFICE - - - MOSCOW FIELD OFFICE - - - MOSCOW FIELD OFFICE - - - MOS

"I think so." Gabe removed his glasses and spoke in fragments as he translated. "'Came to League hospital, Kiev . . . abused and starving . . . moved to Moscow safe house . . . name flagged . . . eighteen intercessor communiqués?' Whoa. That sounds like a lot. So they transferred this woman to Moscow to get her on her feet. Ryan is supposed to keep her safe."

"Which gives him a reason to watch her." I pointed to a bolded section. "What's it say here?"

"'Assignment: Escort target to and from job training. Gain trust and gather intelligence. Get as close as possible without arousing suspicion.'"

What did *that* mean? The woman I'd been dreaming about for years was right here! "Think she's getting job training at the HODC?"

"I don't know." Gabe put his glasses back on. "Ryan undercover, though? That's pretty wild."

From Gabe's tone, I gathered I wasn't the only one who thought Ryan was a tool. I gazed at the young woman's picture. What did she know worth protecting? What would happen to her if Ryan failed? And what did any of it have to do with me?

• • •

Lena had started dinner by the time my turn came to meet with Tatyana. I sat across from Tatyana on one of the awkward sofas and gave her a bored stare.

"Spencer, how are you liking your first assignment?"

I shrugged, not wanting anyone to know I was having a decent time. So far. "Do I get a real assignment or something?"

"Da. But not what you are hoping for, I think. Only older students receive intercessor assigned missions. I have copy of your gifts assessment test. You like computers?"

"Yeah."

"I have ordered new computers for HODC. Could you connect them?"

I perked up. "Sure—da." I kept forgetting to use the little Russian I knew.

She scribbled on her notepad, scanned the paperwork again, and tucked a strand of brown hair behind her ear. "I wonder, would you like to talk with homeless at HODC, get to know them and their stories?"

I adjusted my Lakers cap, not liking the sound of that. "I'm not so good with people."

"Puhcheemoo?" *Why?* Her amber eyes peered into mine.

I looked away and scratched the back of my neck. "Don't know."

"Have you ever tried?"

"Guess not."

"Well, you must try."

I sighed. "Whatever."

"What else do you enjoy? Hobbies, music?"

I imagined myself playing a guitar surrounded by the girls. *Yeah, right.* "I play basketball."

"Ah." She wrote something down. "I am planning open house event for last week you are here. Perhaps you could organize games? A tournament, perhaps?"

"Sure." A thought came to me. "But you don't have a gym. Where would we play?"

She made another note. "There is court in back of HODC."

Excellent. I smiled inside, excited at the idea of playing ball. I'd worried that missing summer league and conditioning would hurt my game. But this could be a way to keep fresh.

REPORT NUMBER: 16

REPORT TITLE: We Meet Some Homeless Thugs
SUBMITTED BY: Agent-in-Training Spencer Garmond
LOCATION: St. Nicolas Orthodox Church, Moscow, Russia
DATE AND TIME: Sunday, June 8, 9:30 a.m.

SUNDAY MORNING THE THIRTEEN OF US dressed for a Russian Orthodox mass. Mr. S went on and on about how different the service would be and how we were supposed to pay attention so we could talk about it later. Kerri made the girls wear skirts and gave them flowery headscarves, "To be respectful of their customs," she'd said.

We rode the metro to an old-fashioned Orthodox church in South Moscow. It was plain compared to some of the cathedrals I'd seen in the city. A single cupola topped with an emerald green onion dome that stretched into the grey sky.

We met Tatyana, Ivan, Lena, and their son—Pasha, whom I remembered from the drama with him and Tatyana at the

HODC—on the street in front of the church. I guessed Pasha's mom made him come to church too.

Inside, the first thing I noticed was the chanting music coming from a choir of dudes in robes standing in a gold choir box. There was a lot of gold paint in this place. The sanctuary was like stepping into a medieval painting. Shards of colored glass formed jagged images of Jesus on the dozen Gothic windows bordering the sanctuary. A collage of saints stared down from the vaulted ceiling.

Any bit of wall was covered with a framed painting of some saint or Jesus or Mary. There were all kinds of glass cases on stands with pictures of saints inside. Old ladies walked around, kissing the glass. Weird. But all these medieval faces staring at me kind of gave me the creeps.

Also weird: no seats. People just milled around, crossing themselves over and over. The sanctuary was filled with people, the women wearing scarves on their heads. Even little girls wore them, so I guessed Kerri wanted our girls to fit in.

Gabe bought a candle and stood for so long staring at a stained glass image of Jesus on the cross that when I spotted a bench on the back wall, I ditched him and made for it, but Mr. S grabbed my arm and shook his head. Oh kay. Guess I'll stand.

The service started with some guy sing-talking in a monotone voice. Someone else replied in sing-talk. The congregation stood in place and watched, crossing themselves, some bowing, some holding lit candles with little paper drip catchers. The locals parroted back lines in some of the songs. A dude dressed like a king came out waving a fancy gold cross around. Some other guy waved some incense.

"The ritual feels so powerful," Gabe whispered to me, his

eyes moist behind the lenses. "Maybe since it's so different from what I normally do."

It was different, I had to give him that.

They offered Communion, which Mr. S said we could do if we wanted. I passed this time. I mean, everyone going up there and drinking out of the same holy grail. Eww.

The service went on for-ev-er, and everyone but me seemed into it.

Afterwards, Ivan invited us Americans to his apartment for lunch.

"Pasha," Lena said, "why you don't show students around before dinner? Take to see Moscow University."

Pasha shrugged as if there were nothing better to do. "Who wants come?"

Gabe raised his hand, so I did too, relieved that Nick didn't. There were four: Gabe, Isabel—*sweet!*—Arianna, and me. The rest of the group went with Ivan.

Pasha led us back to the metro. We rode for a few stops. I examined Isabel's map with her. We seemed to be heading *away* from the university.

When Pasha led us off the train and out of the station, Gabe seemed to read my mind. "Isn't Moscow University the other way?"

"Where exactly are we headed?" Arianna asked.

"University boring," Pasha said. "I take you to see-sight Moscow and meet real Russians. This, missionaries love to see."

Gabe shot me an uneasy glance, but I wasn't concerned by Pasha's change of plans. I had no desire to see any college campus that wasn't an NCA A school. So whatever Pasha wanted to show us had to be more interesting. It was so hot out that I unbuttoned my dress shirt since I was wearing a white T-shirt underneath. I made a mental note to wear only one layer from now on.

Pasha led us down several back streets and into a dirty industrial area. There were piles of wood, empty crates, and trash everywhere. We crossed a narrow street, and the Moskva River came into view a few blocks away. The overwhelming stench of trash, oil, and urine made me gag. I pulled my T-shirt over my nose to mask the smell.

"We should come down here and do some clean-up." Arianna lifted the hem of her blue and pink floral skirt as she stepped over a puddle of oil. "Maybe see if the city would bring in a few Port-a-Pottys."

Isabel walked alongside Arianna, hand clamped over her nose and mouth, fingers and thumb straight to accommodate her claw-like fake fingernails. Gabe stuck by me, out of his comfort zone, perhaps.

Pasha turned a corner and stopped in an alley with warehouses on either side. Both were covered in some serious graffiti. I don't tag—anymore—but the Seis Puños did our fair share of public art back in middle school.

I admired the scrubs, stickers, and pieces that covered the buildings we passed. Cyrillic letters looked sweet in 3D. One piece had bubble lettering stretched jagged and narrow in red, burgundy, brown, and orange blends like the flames of a bonfire. Cartoon people were crowded around the blaze, warming their hands. I wondered what the Cyrillic lettering said.

Before I got a chance to ask, Pasha said, "Come and see!" He darted through a battered door. Gabe and Arianna followed him inside.

Isabel started after them, but I grabbed her arm. "Let me go first."

I pulled open the door and it creaked. Inside, the warehouse was vast and filled with rows of shelves, overflowing with boxes, most of which had been ripped open. Slices of sunlight stabbed through cracks of broken windows, illuminating trillions of dust motes in the air. I blinked, adjusting my eyes to the darkness, trying to get a sense for movement, where any enemies might be. Pasha stood with Gabe and Arianna in an open space, a few yards ahead.

"Bueno?" Isabel set her hand at the small of my back and peeked around me.

"I think so." I put my arm around her and stepped all the way inside, letting the door close behind me.

The air smelled like the high school locker rooms in downtown LA, damp with a century of mildew and body odor. Urine smelled stronger inside than out by the river. I tucked my nose back into my shirt. It hadn't been much of a shield so far, but it was better than nothing.

Scraps of clothing, wadded newspaper, and cardboard created nest-like beds along the walls. Did people sleep here? Live here? I turned away to shake off a wave of nausea, conflicted by thoughts of a few kids I knew back home that claimed to live on the streets. Did they really? Did they live like this?

"What is this place?" Arianna asked.

"I show you," Pasha said, then shouted, "Bratva!" His voice echoed softly against the high ceiling.

A voice floated from above. "Sch'to tee delaesh'?" *What are you doing?*

A husky blond, who looked at least twenty, climbed down

from a shelf like some kind of monkey. He wore grubby clothes and gripped a cigarette between his lips. He reached the flood and walked past me toward the circle of nests and jumped up on a collection of crates that looked like a throne. I took note of the size of his biceps and pulled Isabel closer.

Pasha extended his arms and turned in a circle. "Giving Amerikantsy a tour!"

The boy laughed, then called out to us. "Privyet, Amerikantsy!" He hollered up to the roof. "Bratva! Come meet Amerikantsy Pasha brought!"

Boys appeared from around corners, out of broken windows, and behind doors, like something from *West Side Story*. They circled around, closing in on where we stood. They wore ragged, dirty clothes with dirty faces to match. A tingle shot up my spine. This looked like it could get bad. Fast.

I turned back to the entrance, but three guys were standing in the doorway.

Arianna sucked in a short breath. "Homeless teenagers."

Gabe spun in a slow circle, as if trying to make sure he could see everyone.

"Que pasa?" Isabel clutched my waist, infusing me with enough superhero strength to save the world.

A short boy swaggered out into the circle of nests, a lit cigarette dangling from his mouth. He had black hair and a white scar on his jaw, like he'd been cut by some Russian version of C-Rok. "Hello, *Amerikanskiye* girls!"

The homeless boys cheered. Somebody wolf-whistled.

The short boy removed the cigarette from his mouth and offered it to Isabel. "Seegaretta?"

"Nyet." She wrinkled her nose. "I don't like."

The crowd erupted in boos, hisses, and awws. I pulled

Isabel behind me and moved us to the outer wall where no one could come up behind us.

The short boy sulked away, over-exaggerating his defeat as if he'd been shot in the heart. His friends laughed, and my tension eased.

"Where you find the Amerikantsy?" the husky blond dude standing on the crate throne asked Pasha.

Pasha lit a cigarette and took a long drag. "Rahdeetyelee." *My parents.*

"Missionery!" the short boy said.

Pasha gestured toward the husky blond on the crates and expelled a cloud of smoke with his next words. "Vlad is leader."

"Leader of what?" Gabe asked.

Pasha drew his hand across the crowd. "Our family."

Isabel raised her eyebrows. "*Su familia?*" Apparently the girl didn't speak English when she was scared, which was fine by me. I'd listen to her in any language.

I surveyed the motley crowd. Did Pasha hang with these people on purpose? He had a pretty great family. Granted, I'd known them for only two days, but Tatyana was nice, Ivan directed the field office, and Lena cooked like someone from *Iron Chef.* Granted, people were always telling me how lucky I was to live with Grandma. So there you go.

Vlad sat down on his throne. "We care for each other how no one care for us."

Dude. Even a homeless, Russian gangster could speak English?

"People care about you," Arianna said. "In fact, we'd like to—"

"No one!" Vlad shouted. "Our country, politsia, our parents—no one care for us. So we care for each other."

"Da!" a stocky boy said.

"Jesus cares for you," Arianna said.

I snorted. That wouldn't go over well with this crowd.

It didn't. The homeless boys burst into laughter. Some jeered at Arianna, one knelt before her and prayed, sarcasm thick on his foreign words.

Three boys sitting on a low shelf sang, "Da, Eesoos lyubit menya!" *Yes, Jesus loves me!*

"Well, He *does*." Arianna bit her lip and studied a pleat in her hippie skirt.

Gabe took a turn playing Christian counselor. "Yeah, but, Pasha's family loves him. I'd bet they'll help the rest of you too."

Pasha's thin lips twisted into a scowl. "You know nothing of my family, missionary. My parents put on show for you, bribe for me to come so you see our *happy* family." Pasha spat on the floor. "It is lies. They not tell you they put me out of house. That I live with Bratva on streets." Pasha dropped his cigarette and crushed it with his heel.

"I don't like it here, guys," Arianna said. "Let's go."

She walked toward me and Isabel, but a homeless guy darted in front of her and cut off her path. She shrieked.

Isabel slid closer to me and gripped my arm with both hands. A few of her dagger fingernails stabbed my side. I put my arms around her so she knew I would keep her safe, but I couldn't very well let anything happen to Arianna either.

I walked deeper into the warehouse, pulling Isabel with me. I walked past Arianna's admirer, and once we had passed him, I grabbed the back of Arianna's shirt and pulled her back.

"We can't stay here," Arianna whispered.

Gabe closed his eyes and moved his lips in silent prayer.

Guess that left me to be the man. "We'll be fine," I told the girls. I looked to Pasha. "Hey, man, the girls are scared here. And we haven't had lunch. How about you take us to your parents' place now."

Gabe opened his eyes and whispered. "Good idea, Spencer. Even if they lead us to a restaurant or a café, then we can find the metro."

"That's what I was thinking," I said, making sure to claim my brilliance within earshot of Isabel.

"The missionaries are hungry," Pasha said to Vlad.

Vlad whistled twice, and the gang scattered, Pasha with them, leaving the four of us alone with Vlad.

He motioned for everyone to sit. Isabel claimed the only other crate. Gabe sat on a cardboard box that caved several inches under his weight. Arianna put a handkerchief down before sitting on a tire. Her flower print skirt covered the tire like a tablecloth. I crouched onto a piece of cardboard, sitting on my haunches so I could be ready for action if need be. Besides, there was no way I was touching the floor Pasha so easily spat on.

Something rustled in the dark. Isabel shrieked. Arianna gathered her skirt and lifted her feet. Thankfully, the sound was human. The short, dark-haired smoker had returned, arms heaped with junk food packages that he dropped on the floor in front of Vlad.

Vlad rose from his crate and crouched to survey the plunder. He nodded at the little dude and yelled up to the rafters. "Yuri is first today!" He tore into a bag of cookies and returned to his throne. He pointed at the food pile. "Eat."

Alrighty then. I reached for a bag of crackers. I ripped them open and ate one. The saltiness about killed me, but I forced a smile and held up my bag in a toast to Vlad's provision. "Yummy."

Vlad looked pleased. See? I had this multi-cultural relations thing down pat. It was all about sucking up to the big guy so he wouldn't kill us. I wondered how long we'd have to play polite before they'd let us go.

Another homeless guy appeared and added an armful of loot to the stash.

"This building stores things no one wants," Vlad said, like a king sharing about his kingdom. "It is our home."

Pasha returned with an armload of bottled water and tossed one to Vlad.

Vlad gestured to Pasha. "Pasha our best supplier of water. Very hard to get water."

"Did you steal that from the HODC?" Arianna asked.

Pig Latin wasn't my greatest strength, but I mumbled, "*Ut-shay up-ay, anna-ariay.*"

She didn't seem to hear me. "Tatyana would give it to you, you know? That's the whole point of what she's trying to do. Help homeless get back on their feet. Unless you just want to mock her sacrifice and—"

I threw my bag of crackers at Arianna.

She yelped and glared at me.

"Shut. Up." I said this slowly, so the nitwit could understand. Thankfully, the Russians weren't listening to her.

The stocky dude returned and added more food to the growing pile. Yuri offered him his lit cigarette. The boy took it and sat beside Arianna on the tire. The look on her face was priceless. I could've tried to help her, but it was fun to see her squirm. If the guy tried anything, I'd step in. For now . . . she'd live.

Two more boys appeared and set foot in the collection.

"How goes life in States?" Vlad asked.

"Good," Gabe said.

"Bueno," Isabel said.

Arianna's face had paled, and she glared at her seatmate's cigarette. Leave it to her to pick a fight with an international gangster over the ills of smoking.

Yuri walked over to me and peered down. "You *bagaht?*"

I shook my head, clueless what *bagaht* meant.

Yuri moved on, stopping at Gabe's collapsing box. "You?"

"No," Gabe said. "I'm not rich."

Yuri squatted beside Gabe and nudged his loafer. "Fancy shoes."

I had to agree. Gabe never wore sneakers, but why loafers?

"How many *mashiny* you have?" the dude asked Gabe.

"Cars? I don't have one. No license yet." Gabe grinned, his braces flashing in a shard of sunlight. "My parents have dva." *Two.*

A chorus of mumbling revealed this to be a bad thing.

Yuri pointed at Isabel and continued his survey. "You— how many car?"

Isabel squeaked and held up three perfectly manicured fingernails, complete with a fake diamond on each. Nice.

"Bagahta!" the Russians screamed.

Yuri loomed over Arianna's crate. "You?"

Arianna folded her arms. "I don't have to submit to your interrogation."

Her seatmate mumbled as he stretched the hem of her hippie skirt out like an opening fan. Arianna snatched it back and tucked it under her legs.

"Bagahta!" the Russians chanted.

"How about you?" Yuri came back to me. "How many car?"

"*Odin*," I said, thrilled to be able to answer in Russian.

"One only?"

I nodded. "My *babooshka's*."

Yuri squinted one eye skeptically. "You father?"

I shrugged one shoulder. "He probably has a car. I've never met him."

"Bagaht!" Yuri sang, and his friends snickered.

The stocky boy pointed at Isabel. "You. How many, what you call, *tooflee*?"

"Shoes? That I brought to Moscow?" She wrinkled her nose. "*Nueve*—I mean, dévyat?" *Nine.*

My jaw dropped. The girl had lugged nine pairs of shoes to Moscow?

The Russians muttered, some shook their heads, some laughed, a few yelled *bagahta* again. The cloud of smoke around us was thick now, and I smelled some weed in the mix too. I scanned the room and counted at least six glowing butts but couldn't tell who was holding what.

The familiar smell of marijuana clawed at my gut. Like I said, I didn't do drugs. Anymore. And I continued to remind myself of that fact as I fought off the craving.

But still . . . Basketball season was a long ways off. One puff would be long gone by then. And just thinking about the look these churchers would give me if I asked for a drag made the whole thing *really* tempting. Really. I chuckled just thinking about it. But I was a good boy. I promise.

"What do you do at America?" Yuri asked Isabel.

She pursed her lips. "Go to school, work at Mami's salon, sing—"

"Salon? What mean salon?" the stocky boy asked.

The short boy pointed at Isabel. "Spoyte nam pyesnyu." *Sing us a song.*

Vlad flashed a lupine grin. "Da, sing!"

"Nyet!" Gabe straightened and tried to stand, but only fell deeper into his box. "She doesn't have to—" He struggled to look at Isabel. "You don't have to."

"No problema, *Gabriel.*"

What? I thought about smoking for thirty seconds and Gabe stole the mantle of Hero?

Isabel closed her eyes, and her voice resonated to the high ceiling. "Amazing grace how sweet the sound that saved a wretch like me. I once was loss, but now am found was blind but now I see."

No one moved or spoke while she sang. I stared, fingering the cross around my neck, transfixed by the sound of her voice.

Vlad stood and applauded.

Just then, another Russian boy raced inside. "Vlad!" he screamed. "Politsia caught Oleg!"

Vlad spat on the floor near the boy's feet. He turned to Isabel. "Sing more."

I looked from Vlad, to the boy, to Pasha, and back to Vlad. "Aren't you going to do something about your boy?"

Vlad glared at me, his eyes flashing. "Oleg stupid. Probably caught on purpose to eat better than us tonight." Vlad laughed, and his gang joined in.

Gabe pushed out of his box and stood. "We should go."

Vlad sprang up and tilted his head from side to side, cracking his neck in the process. Although Gabe stood a good six inches shorter, he puffed out his chest. I had to admire his guts, but he was obviously clueless what he was getting his loafer-wearing self in to. We were on Vlad's turf. It was his rules. And challenging him was not something we were going to do.

"Vlad," I said, "thanks for the food. Do you mind if we leave? We have some people waiting for us."

Vlad looked at me, then to Isabel, Arianna, and finally Gabe. He smiled, inclined his head. "Pasha, take Amerikantsy back."

"*Okay*. We go." Pasha crumpled his cracker bag and tossed it on the floor. He strolled toward the door and flung it open. We scrambled after him. Gabe first, then Arianna, Isabel, and me.

"Thanks for the food," Gabe said without looking back.

I gave Vlad a quick nod. Our eyes met—

I swayed on my feet, engulfed in vertigo. A familiar warmth seized my body.

Vlad pins my arms behind my back under blinding lights.

A second later, it was gone. My eyes regained focus, and I found myself standing with a hand against a sagging box on a shelf to keep myself from falling over. I inhaled deeply through my nose, again aware of the warehouse's stench. I glanced up. Vlad stood across the room watching me curiously. When I made eye contact again, he grunted and took a long swig from a dark bottle.

I took off.

REPORT NUMBER: 17

REPORT TITLE: Everyone Gets Assignments but Me
SUBMITTED BY: Agent-in-Training Nicolas Muren
LOCATION: Metro Train, Moscow, Russia
DATE AND TIME: Sunday, June 8, 2:26 p.m.

SITTING ON THE METRO, I gazed out the window at the grey blur of the tunnel wall, then refocused on the reflection on the glass. It was like watching a misshapen black and white TV. The train-car was pretty much empty. Arianna sat beside me. Pasha, Gabe, and Isabel sat across the aisle.

No sign of Vlad. I relaxed a bit, faced forward, but still felt edgy. Had Vlad been going to attack me like Nick had that day on the court at school? When?

Was this the kind of thing that happened in the Intercession Department? I brushed the thought off with a shake of the head, but it lingered.

Was God giving me these visions?

"How could you do that?" Gabe suddenly yelled at Pasha. The outburst made me jump and yelp a strange non-word. "Ha-yah-yah!"

Five pairs of eyes fixed on me at once. My heart galloped like a horse inside my chest. I straightened and looked back out the window, wishing I'd gotten a chance at that weed after all. I was wound up tighter than a torn ACL. I mean, sure, the visions were freaking me out, but I had to get a hold of myself.

Gabe got back to his beef with Pasha, his voice still louder than its everyday mumble. "What were you thinking taking us there? We had girls with us, no adults. We didn't know where we were. None of us can speak Russian worth our—"

"Speak for yourself," Arianna said.

Sadly Arianna *could* speak Russian better than any of us. Gabe, Isaac, Jensina—they'd been at it all year. Arianna blew them away.

She reeked at Pig Latin, though.

"How were we supposed to defend ourselves?" Gabe said to Pasha.

"They my droozya!" *Friends.* Pasha's nostrils flared. "You were not in danger by my side."

Arianna stood with her hands on her hips, glaring at Pasha like she might incinerate him with her eyes. "I doubt this is what your mother had in mind when she asked you to show us around. I recall mention of Moscow University?" The train lurched. Arianna stumbled and grabbed a pole to steady herself. Her flowery skirt twisted around her legs like a mermaid's tail. "And where do homeless boys get so many cigarettes?"

"They steal them," I guessed. "But how do you score pot with no money?"

Pasha's gaze flitted over me, as if deciding if and how to answer.

"Marijuana?" Gabe's eyes widened behind his Buddy Holly frames, and for a moment, he looked like a Mr. S Mini Me.

"You see good in them, Pasha?" Isabel touched his arm, moving into encouraging mode, which just about broke my heart. I seriously had thought that she'd done that special, just for me. Turns out it was just a line she used on everyone.

Pasha glowered at her hand. "They need me."

"The HODC could help," Arianna said. "Why don't you enroll them in the program?"

Pasha jerked away from Isabel and lit a stub of a cigarette.

"Is smoking allowed on the metro?" Arianna asked.

"You can probably smoke in a hospital in Russia," I said.

"Well . . . I'm telling your parents," Arianna said, almost whispering.

"Ohhh!" Pasha raised his hands, shaking them. "I so scared."

"No, it's okay," Gabe said, his voice back to its low hum. "There's no harm done." He glanced from face to face. "We're safe now."

"Could you at least not smoke that in here?" Arianna asked. "*Pozhaluista?*"

Pasha reached out and flicked ash onto Arianna's feet. She screamed and shook out her hippie skirt. Gabe and Isabel tried to calm her, but she stomped to the end of the train car and sat down. Pasha laughed and took a long drag on his cigarette.

I had a question of my own. "Why do you think Americans are rich?"

"You are Amerikantsy," Pasha said, as if that explained everything. Then he blew a cloud of smoke in my face, which only made me want a cigarette of my own. But I didn't smoke. Anymore.

"I'm not rich," Isabel insisted.

"You have three car, you are rich," Pasha said. "In Russia, we have only what we need. Some have more, but most do not waste money on *nine* pair shoes."

Dude had a point.

Isabel frowned and batted her eyelashes as if she were thinking *very* hard. "But I brought sandals for summer, sneakers for running, heels for dresses, these are my everyday shoes, but brown doesn't go with everything, so I got black—"

"What I say?" Pasha waved his hand around, and Isabel dodged the lit butt as it swung her way. "For Amerikantsy, it is never enough. You convinced you need more. Tatyana think she is helping people to get them jobs. Then they will want homes. Then they will want stuff to fill homes, then more *shoes*." Pasha flicked ash onto the floor. "Bratva cares not for such things. We care only for each other."

"*Oye!*" Isabel took hold of Pasha's arm and glared like she was his mom or something. "Vlad didn't care about Oleg. Making him steal? That's wrong."

"If not today, Oleg would be caught tomorrow. He is bad thief. That is not Vlad's blame to take. Besides . . ." Pasha leaned toward Isabel. Shadows flickered across his face from a passing train. "I rather steal for those who care for me than obey those who care not. I choose Bratva."

Several stops passed in silence. Isabel leaned against Gabe's side, and he put his arm around her. Nicely done, churcher. I conceded the round, but the game was not over.

Pasha led the group to trade trains once before exiting the metro. "Our country is old and tired," he said as we walked along the sidewalk. "The roads and buildings are weak, the people are poor. But with Bratva, I am happy."

"You don't look happy," Gabe said.

Pasha didn't answer. He led us through the gate of a large apartment complex and up a flight of stairs to the front door of his parents' home.

Lena greeted us, beaming. "How was University?"

"Very . . . educational." Gabe went to Kerri, who stood setting the table, and kissed her cheek. "Hey, Mom."

Pasha disappeared down a hallway. A door slammed.

"Can we help with lunch?" Isabel asked.

"Nyet. Food is ready. Please to sit." Lena ushered us to the table.

After lunch, Lena showed family photo albums to the girls while some of the guys talked in the living room. Pasha had returned for food, and now he stood with me and Gabe out on the tiny balcony surrounded by a miniature flower garden.

Pasha lit another cigarette and took a long drag. "Mother likes flowers." He flicked ash in the center of a white lily. It burned a hole through the petal.

"It takes a lot of love to grow flowers," Gabe said. "I tried once. Everything died. Your mom must have a lot of love to give."

Pasha gave Gabe a bored stare and let his cigarette fall over the railing to the ground below. "Paka." He yanked the sliding glass door open and went inside.

"Yeah, see you!" Gabe looked down at the burned lily. "That went well."

I hid a smile. Gabe tried too hard, but at least he tried.

• • •

Monday morning, I sat across from Gabe at one of the kitchen tables and grabbed a blini from the plate in the center.

A familiar French accent drifted over the conversation. I scanned the apartment and saw Prière sitting in the living room with Isaac. I tapped the table in front of Gabe with my fork. "What's Prière doing here?"

"Assignments. See that red card Prière's holding? Blue cards are for test assignments. They come from my dad. But red cards are intercessor-assigned. Some of us get one from the local field office during summer trips. None for you, though."

I eyed the card in Prière's hand. "What kind of assignments?"

"Only Prière knows—and Isaac, Jake, or whoever else gets one. Not even Dad knows what Prière hands out."

"How does anyone know if they pass or fail?"

Gabe swallowed the rest of his compote and set down the glass. "Prière tells whoever needs to know, and it goes in their file. Plus they have to write a report."

Prière handed the red card to Isaac. Isaac studied it and jerked his gaze toward my table. Our eyes met, and Isaac quickly glanced back at the card.

Oh-kay. Now that was weird.

"What kind of assignments do *you* get?" I asked Gabe.

"I'll probably have to follow someone around, maybe draw a floor plan of the apartment or something. Who knows with my dad." Gabe paused to eat a crumb from his plate. "That was freaky yesterday, with those Bratva guys."

"Yeah." I watched Isaac walk into the guys' room with his red card. Beth, looking cute in baggy cargo pants and a black

T-Shirt that read "Just Walk Away," took Isaac's place beside Prière.

"I was glad Vlad didn't get rough." Gabe was still talking. "It would've been ugly. I stink at LCT."

I peered at Gabe before reaching for the juice. "Not much of a fighter?"

"Don't know. Never been in a real fight. I'm a musician." Gabe wiggled his fingers. "Got to protect my hands."

I smirked. Sure. I looked back to Beth and Prière, but she wasn't looking at me.

"I just don't get mad at people, though. Wouldn't you have to be pretty angry to get into that kind of a fight?"

I scratched my fork around my plate and sighed, thinking about Nick and C-rock. "Yes. Yes you would."

REPORT NUMBER: 18

REPORT TITLE: I Meet a Babushka Who Recycles Soup
SUBMITTED BY: Agent-in-Training Spencer Garmond
LOCATION: Medical Center, H.O.D.C., Moscow, Russia
DATE AND TIME: Thursday, June 12, 10:45 a.m.

TATYANA HANDED OUT ASSIGNMENT SHIFTS for what we'd be doing at the HODC this summer. We all had to work each area at least once. I was scheduled in first aid with Arianna the first week because the computers wouldn't arrive until next week.

That was something to look forward to, at least. I was having Internet withdrawals and looked forward to some one-on-one time with a computer again.

After three days of medical center in the mornings, I knew more about first aid than I ever cared to. The medical center consisted of six U-shaped stations with two beds each. A nurse's desk sat in the center of the room.

		M	T	W	Th	F	S
Week 1	AM-	M	M	M	M	M	M
	PM-	K	K	K	K	K	K
Week 2	AM-	F	F	F	F	F	F
	PM-	D	D	D	D	D	D
Week 3	AM-	M	M	M	M	M	M
	PM-	S	S	S	S	S	S
Week 4	AM-	K	K	K	K	K	K
	PM-	B	B	B	B	B	B
Week 5	AM-	M	M	M	M	M	M
	PM-	V	V	V	V	V	V
Week 6	AM-	N	N	N	N	N	N
	PM-	K	K	K	K	K	K
Week 7	AM-	M	M	M	M	M	M
	PM-	L	L	L	L	L	L
Week 8	AM-	CH	CH	CH	CH	CH	CH
	PM-	P	P	P	P	P	P

Key: B- Building & Maintenance; N- Nursery;
D- Donations; F- Front Desk; S- Shelter; K- Kitchen;
L- Laundry; M- Medical Center; P- Job-training area; CH- Chapel; V-VBS

ASSIGNMENT SHEET: SPENCER GARMOND

Arianna had a knack for healing, and the nurses let us work our own station for minor wounds, which made Arianna the nurse and me her trusty sidekick, a role I served belligerently. In between patients, we stocked cupboards, which really meant I watched Arianna work while she bored me to death with lectures.

"You should really learn Cardiopulmonary Resuscitation." Arianna counted out twenty-five Band-Aids and tucked them into a drawer.

I sat at the nurse's desk and spun the chair in a circle, clunking my foot against the metal desk then spinning back the other way. "Why?"

"To save lives. I got certified when I moved to the States and got a job as a lifeguard at Pilot Point Athletic Center. I also teach kids to swim." Arianna paused to count to twenty-five, put the Band-Aids in the drawer, and moved to the next station. As she passed, her thick beige skirt brushed against my leg, reminding me of the straw skirts Hawaiian hula dancers wore—except Arianna doing a hula dance was a mental image I could have lived a long life without.

She started counting out twenty-five Band-Aids again.

"They're Band-Aids, Arianna, not rations for men on the moon."

"I give God my very best offering in all I do."

More like she couldn't function unless things were done her way.

She busied herself in silence. I felt like I should help but knew she'd only let me hold the box. I'd rather sit and do nothing than follow her around like a puppy. I really wanted to work in the front office. It was a great place to see people move around the center, and Beth was stationed up there. Plus I wanted to see if there was a file on Anya Vseveloda. I hadn't managed to find Gasheka ulitsa on my city map and wasn't sure what to do about the dossier.

Arianna opened a new box of Band-Aids. "Now if you'll pay attention, Spencer, I'll explain how CPR works."

"What say we leave that to the professionals?"

Her nasty glare made me grin. "You never know when you might need to help someone and a professional isn't available."

Time to change the subject. "Your dad's in the Mission League, right?"

"My dad, mom, two uncles and an aunt, both my brothers, and a few cousins—"

"You have brothers?"

"Gideon is in League administration in London, and Brandon's a League teacher in France. I was born there, you know."

Whatever. "It's weird that your whole family was called." I ached to tell someone about my parents, but Kimbal had told me not to. But if I vaguely hinted about things I wanted to know and Arianna explained them, that worked for me.

"The League runs in the family, most the time," Arianna said. "You should know that."

I spun my chair around to face her. "What do you mean?"

She hesitated, her face flushed. "I . . . uh . . . you told me your parents were in, didn't you?"

I shook my head, squinting at Arianna, who was exhibiting symptoms of lying. Again.

"Oh." She grabbed a fistful of Band-Aids and shoved them into a drawer. Uncounted. "Well, I must be thinking of someone else." She snapped her fingers. "Nick said it on the plane."

"Nick, huh?" I folded my arms. There was something very strange about Arianna's behavior, but Nick *had* sort of spilled those beans.

"I think maybe we're all descendants of the Israelites or something." Her eyes glimmered.

I burst into laughter, but it didn't last long. I checked the clock again. Please, God, make the torture stop.

With three minutes left to our shift, a patient arrived with third degree burns. The nurses offered to let us observe through lunch. There was no way in Moscow I was staying a second longer than my shift. Arianna stayed. Of course.

I grabbed my water bottle and headed for the cafeteria alone. I strolled down a hallway with windows that faced the makeshift basketball court Tatyana had told me about. Three guys were playing. Pasha, Yuri, and a guy I didn't recognize.

I bolted out into the muggy heat. "Hey, Pasha. Can I play?"

Pasha ignored me and nailed a shot from the baseline. Yuri grabbed the ball from beneath the net and fired it back.

I darted forward and intercepted the pass. "Pozhaluista?" *Please?*

Pasha arched his eyebrows. "You know how, Amerikantsy?"

Oh, this would be fun. "You wound me, Pasha."

He shrugged one shoulder as if pondering whether or not I was a waste of his time. "Okay. Two against two. Alex, you with Amerikantsy."

Pasha gave me the ball first, apparently thinking I needed the advantage. Silly man. He hung back, waiting to see what I'd do. Wide open at the three-point line, I sank the shot.

Alex burst into laughter and applauded. Pasha gave me an

appraising look. "Okay, Amerikantsy. I see you can play."

Pasha guarded me. Alex, short and slow, was the weakest player of the three, but he could pass well enough. Pasha was tough under the hoop, but my outside shot evened things up. The sun was merciless. After fifteen minutes of hard play, Alex begged Pasha for a break.

I took a quick drink from my water bottle and trailed Pasha back onto the court. He pulled off his shirt and tossed it on the ground. I had about three inches over him, and Pasha had no muscle. Milky skin clung to his ribs—the guy needed to eat more. Much more.

Pasha ran his fingers through his oily hair. "Pashlee." *Let's go.*

I passed the ball to Alex, who dribbled around in a circle and lobbed it back. I drove Pasha backward, used Yuri as a screen, and cleared myself for an easy jump shot. Pasha tripped over Yuri and crashed to the pavement.

I grabbed Pasha's arm. As I pulled him up, I caught sight of a huge tattoo on his right shoulder. "Dude, is that thing real?"

Pasha glanced at his tattoo. "Da."

I studied the design that covered Pasha's upper arm. A round intricate maze with a line leading out the top like a yoyo. A star was in the center. "What's it mean?"

Pasha smiled proudly. "Bratva."

King Vlad on his crate throne. "Did it hurt?"

"Nyet." Pasha's pupils dilated.

Liar, liar pants on fire. I pointed at Yuri. "You got one too, man?"

Yuri lifted his sleeve to reveal a smaller version of the same tattoo.

I turned to Alex, who shook his head.

Pasha laughed. "Alex afraid of needles."

"And dyevooshki." *Girls.* Yuri cackled and punched Alex in the arm.

Alex cried out and swung a fist.

Yuri darted out of the way, grabbed the basketball, and threw it hard at Alex's chest.

"Astanovees'!" *Stop!* Alex rubbed his chest where the ball had hit.

"Enough!" Pasha said. "Pashlee."

Yuri chased the ball down and the game continued.

PASHA AND YURI'S TATTOO

After dinner at the apartment, Gabe and I went into the boys' room. Nick was already asleep on the top bunk. Isaac was out in the apartment with Mr. S. And Jake was in the shower.

"I saw you with Pasha," Gabe said. "You're good."

I sat on my bed. Hello? Did no one go to school games? Of course I was good. Freshmen didn't make varsity unless they were better than good. "Thanks."

"Did you beat him?" Gabe asked.

"Even with a handicap." I explained about Alex. "You know Pasha and Yuri have Bratva tattoos? Real ones."

"I don't believe in getting tattoos," Gabe said.

"Well, the design was awesome." But here was another thing that didn't make sense. Tattoos were expensive, weren't they? Just like pot. How did homeless kids pay for this stuff ? They must be pickpockets. Or maybe they were breaking in to houses and stealing jewelry. Some guys in Pilot Point did that to pay for drugs.

Gabe dumped out his backpack on his bed, and a slip of blue cardstock fluttered to the floor. His eyes went wide. He grabbed the paper, studied it for a full minute, then looked at me. "Test assignment."

I eyed the card. "Anything cool?"

"Nah. In fact—" Gabe dug through the pile on his bed and picked up two more cards. One was red. "I'm supposed to destroy them but haven't gotten around to it." He shuffled though the cards and put a blue one in the front pocket of his backpack. He tossed the other two on my bunk. "You can read those."

I grabbed them. "I thought you're not supposed to tell."

Gabe dropped his backpack on the floor. "You're not, but new recruits help with the team assignments anyway, and the other one will be public, so it doesn't matter."

I examined the blue card first.

TEAM: Alpha
SERVICE: HELPS: COMMUNITY: OCCUPATIONAL
Assist Tatyana Ivanovna with
occupational side of HODC.

Big deal. That was the whole reason we were in Moscow. I grabbed the red card.

PARTNER: Isabel Rodriguez
SERVICE: HELPS: COMMUNITY: FAMILY SERVICES
Work closely with Pastor Yegorov to plan a
special worship service for the end of the summer
using your gifts in music.

Nor did a worship service sound like secret agent stuff. But at least he had the lovely Isabel as his partner. Lucky stiff. "That's it?" I asked. "What about the third one?"

Gabe shook his head. "Can't show you that one."

"Oh, come on!"

"Sorry. I'm excited about the worship service." Gabe grinned, his eyes staring dreamily into nothing. "Working with Isabel is always a blast. She's a soprano, but she sings alto harmony with my melody—it's awesome. Plus it will keep her away from Nick—" Gabe flushed, glanced at the top bunk, and whispered. "Sorry. That was lame."

I shrugged, not caring if Nick heard that someone else thought he was a jerk. "Pretty much everyone benefits from steering clear of Nick."

Gabe's whisper lowered. "I know I'm supposed to love everyone, but there's just something about him. And Isabel, she trusts everyone—*hugs* everyone—which is good and bad, you know? You've seen the slimy way Nick treats her. Yet she's still friends with him."

"Beats me." If I were Isabel, I'd have put Nick in his place long ago. And I'd go out with me.

"She can take care of herself, though. We were LCT partners last year, and she creamed me regularly. Still, I worry about her. I don't trust Nick not to sink to a level lower than scum."

Neither did I. Nick lived at the scum level. I found it interesting, though, to hear Gabe get all riled up about something. I'd never heard him say a bad thing about anyone. But I guess Nick just brought out the worst in everyone.

The bathroom door swung opened, and Jake came out dressed in grey slacks, a white dress shirt, and a red bowtie. He walked over to the shoe pile and dug out a pair of lace-up Oxfords. It was almost bedtime. Where was he going spiffed up at this hour?

"Next!" Gabe grabbed his shower bundle and raced into the bathroom.

Jake jetted out of the apartment, leaving me alone. Gabe's backpack lay in the middle of the floor between the two beds. I casually reached out my foot and pulled it closer. I snaked the third card out from the front pocket and read it.

SOLO
FIELD: PROFILING: WORLD
Track and report all movement and
conversations of Nick Muren.

• • •

The next morning I felt like such a jerk, I made myself eat a bowl of kasha as punishment. I had no business snooping around in Gabe's stuff. I almost wished I'd been caught. Now I had to pretend I didn't notice Gabe making notes in his journal when Nick went to the bathroom.

I considered confessing, but alienating myself against the one person I considered a friend this early in the trip could ruin the whole summer.

In the HODC kitchen with Jensina that afternoon, I met the cook, a crabby stout old woman who went by the title Babushka. *Grandmother.*

Babushka's apprentice, Svetlana, was sixteen. The blond, silken-haired beauty with wide, fearful eyes gave me a panic attack every time we came face to face. Tatyana had prepared us for working with her. Svetlana had come to the center six months ago when her kid, Mishka, had a fever. They'd healed the kid, and Svetlana had enrolled in the program, learned sign language and how to cook.

But she'd suffered greatly in her short life. On top of her traumatic past, Svetlana was deaf. At least I didn't have to stress over talking to her. She was prettier than Isabel and Beth combined. Must have been because she was a blonde.

Having lived so long with Grandma, manual kitchen labor came easy. I cleared tables and washed them down. Then another wave of homeless came through, and I did it again. So much for secret agents. This was so not what I'd signed up for.

I carried a tray of dirty bowls to the kitchen window and set them on the ledge. Then I watched in horror as Babushka emptied each one into the pot of soup Svetlana was stirring.

My stomach jolted. My hand flew to my mouth. I breathed in a long breath through my nose but could smell only bleach on my hand. I raced into the kitchen and grabbed the last bowl before Babushka could add it to the pot. "What are you doing?" I asked.

Babushka snagged the bowl from me. "Putting soup away."

Svetlana looked up from the pot, her eyes wide and sparkling.

I groaned. "You can't put that back in the pot—somebody had it in his mouth. Probably spit it back into the bowl."

"Is no go to waste," she said.

I made my way back out to the tables. So I was weird for being grossed out over recycled soup? I was beginning to see that nothing went to waste in Russia. But if not recycling my soup made me rich, I'd be bagaht any day.

REPORT NUMBER: 19

REPORT TITLE: I Tail My First Suspect
SUBMITTED BY: Agent-in-Training Spencer Garmond
LOCATION: Front Office, H.O.D.C., Moscow, Russia
DATE AND TIME: Monday, June 16, 10:02 a.m.

THE SECOND WEEK AT THE HODC, I started working in the office, which sat between the cafeteria and an open area with desks where people could get job counseling.

Tatyana had purchased three new computers, one for the office, and two for clients to use for preparing résumés. I had already set up both client computers in the counseling area and now sat on the floor in a pile of computer parts, boxes, and Styrofoam packing, working on setting up the one for the office. Marina was already helping a Russian woman at one of the client computers. This was my kind of work.

The front door opened, and a warm breeze flowed into the stuffy room. "Privyet, Tatyana," a familiar male voice said.

Tatyana's voice cracked. "Ryan. Kak dela?" *How are you?*

"I'm good."

I straightened my back to peek over the desk. Oh, yeah, Agent Ryan. Maybe I could ask him a few more questions about—

My gaze landed on the blonde standing beside Ryan, and my pulse quickened. No way, no way, no way! It was Anya. From the dossier. And my dreams.

I stared until I realized I was staring, then I averted my gaze just enough to see out of my peripheral vision.

"This is Anya," Ryan said to Tatyana. "Your dad said the computers would be ready today, and we wanted to get started."

"They're *barely* ready." Tatyana cleared her throat. "You must be excited to find a job, Anya. Have you already registered with us?"

Ryan didn't give Anya a chance to answer. "We registered her last week."

Tatyana's face reddened like it had the day she'd caught Pasha stealing water. She turned to Anya. "What is your full name?"

"Anastasia Vseveloda."

That deep, growling voice from my dreams sucked the breath right out of me.

Tatyana scribbled on a notepad. "Marina is working with someone, but there is free computer I can help you on. I will pull your file."

Ryan draped his muscular arm around Anya's shoulders. "We don't want to be a bother, Tatyana. I know you're busy and everything. So, I'll help her."

Anya gave Ryan a flirtatious smile. "Spasiba."

They moved to the free computer. I watched a moment longer before reaching for the printer cable. I shivered, chilled despite the lack of air conditioning.

Tatyana stomped into the office area and dug in a file cabinet behind me, shuffling papers. I peeked at her and made a mental note of which drawer Anya's file had come out of. I'd wanted to look all morning, but setting up the computers had kept me busy.

Tatyana banged the file cabinet shut, marched back to Ryan and Anya at the computer, and slapped the file on the desk. Ryan gave her a curious glance, but before he could say anything, Tatyana whipped around and stormed back to me. Eyes red, she sank into her chair with her back to computer counseling area.

I swallowed, a bit wary of getting involved in this drama, but, since I was such a nice guy. A nice, curiously nosy guy. "Uh . . . you okay?"

"Da, da." Tatyana peered at me and sniffled. "Ryan and I, we . . . how do you say? *Date* for a few months. I ended this. I am not knowing what is wrong with me."

My eyes darted back and forth between the couple at the computer and Tatyana. I didn't get it. What was the big thrill with Ryan, anyway? I stretched my spine. He wasn't *that* much taller than me, and I still had time to grow. He was pretty muscular, I supposed. Was that what girls liked? I'd have to start lifting.

But Tatyana looked completely devastated, like she'd hoped to marry this nut or something. Would it be so bad for me to tell her what I knew? I plugged the printer cable in. "That Anya chick, she's Ryan's . . . uh . . . assignment."

Tatyana's wide amber eyes studied me. "How you know?"

I winced, not wanting anyone to know about the dossier. "Uh . . ."

Tatyana peeked over her shoulder. "Never mind. It matters not. I am not wanting to date *field agent* any way. They are always on assignment." She looked at me fiercely. "Do not expect to keep girlfriend if you become field agent someday."

I pictured myself speeding around in the black Camero I didn't own, Svetlana in the passenger's seat, admiring my mad driving skills. I chuckled silently. Alas, this was not likely to happen anytime soon.

Tatyana dabbed her eye with her sleeve and sighed. "You know, I want to remind you to organize basketball tournament for HODC."

Right. I dug through the mess, looking for the monitor cable. "Who will I get to play?"

She sniffled and shrugged her shoulders. "Make a flyer, see if teams sign up. It could get neighborhood involved."

Oh-kay. "I guess I could do that. I bet Pasha could put together a good team."

Tatyana's expression hardened. "Be careful, Spencer, playing too close with Pasha. I love my brother, but—" She choked up. Sniffled.

Here we go again. I looked away, leaving Tatyana to pull herself out of this one. I couldn't help it. I liked Pasha and, if I was going to have to do this basketball tournament thing, I wanted him in it. Why was that bad?

"He has not lived at home for months," Tatyana said. "He fights with Father then wants to go with him to field office. It is no making sense. And all Mother wants is for him to eat and sleep at home, but he will not do that, even for her. He is always with friends. Unless you want trouble, you will keep away from them all."

Oh, really? Was that a prediction or a threat? I couldn't tell.

I descended into Oktyabrskaya station on the escalator with the rest of the Americans, heading home for the night. As I stepped onto the platform, a familiar face caught my gaze. I froze and scanned the marble pillars until beautiful, blond Anya came into view. She walked onto the up escalator. Alone.

Without Ryan.

Well, hello there, my lovely. Where are you going this fine evening?

I glanced behind me. The rest of my group had already boarded the train. A wild urge seized me, and I jumped onto the up escalator, keeping my eyes fixed on the platinum head near the top.

"Spencer?" Arianna called. "Where are you going?"

"I'm fine. I'll catch the next train." I ran up the rest of the escalator and jogged to keep up.

Anya exited the metro and darted through the crowd, her head turning back and forth as if she'd lost someone or something. She kept a steady pace but went out of her way to kick over a cup of change sitting beside a homeless man.

Rude much?

The man yelled a complaint, but Anya plowed along like a bulldozer, pushing people out of her way, scanning the crowd. She walked into the alcove of some office building and put a cell phone to her ear. I stopped just before the alcove and took a sip from my water bottle.

"Don't know, I lost him." She spoke in perfect English, tapping her finger on the wall. "Look, I'm trying! Those kids aren't as easy to manipulate as American teens." She rolled her eyes. "Of course I do. I've got him wrapped around my finger." She gestured to the wall. "I will . . . I said I will!" Her voice was so loud people were staring. "Fine!" She lowered the phone and stepped out of the alcove. Her eyes met mine. "What are you looking at?"

I swallowed hard, my mind racing through all I had overheard, yet trying to look like I had overheard nothing. "Uh . . . Anya?"

"Who wants to know?"

"I'm Spencer."

She made a nasty face. "Spencer who?"

"Spencer Garmond. From America." Gee, why didn't I give her my Social Security number and home address while I was at it?

She glanced at my Lakers cap, looked me up and down, and her angst vanished. She pursed her lips together, and her eyebrows furrowed like she'd remembered something. "What do you want, Spencer?"

By now I was thinking this was a bad idea, meddling in Ryan's case, possibly blowing his cover. Still, I had dreamed about this woman. There had to be a reason.

"Well, you . . . uh . . . you looked lost. I thought you might be looking for Ryan."

She narrowed her eyes. "How do you know Ryan?"

Like I said, totally blowing the guy's cover. "Well, I just—I mean, I saw you with him at the HODC." Atta boy, kid! Way to save your neck!

Her expression changed again, this time to the flirtatious one she'd used around Ryan. She sauntered toward me, her gaze boring into mine. "Do you know where I can find him? The field office, maybe? Can you take me there?"

Hold up. Was she supposed to know about the field office? "I can take you to the HODC."

She rolled her eyes. "I know how to get *there*." Her gaze flittered over me again. "Your hair is amazing. I've only seen this color once before. Do you mind?" She reached out, pulled off my cap, and brushed her fingernails through my hair.

I shivered and pulled back. This was nuts. I snatched back my hat and turned to the metro entrance. I'd go to the apartment. Anya could do whatever. I ran my metro pass through the slot and entered. I stepped onto the down escalator and glanced back.

Anya stood behind me as we descended, her shoulders level with my eyes. Oh, great. I glimpsed a tattoo on her left arm poking out from her upturned sleeve.

My heart stopped. *Figs and jam!* The thing was a maze—just like Pasha's tattoo—and was stained onto her arm in red ink.

"Like what you see?" Anya gave me a wicked grin and shifted her weight. The tattoo disappeared under her sleeve. "So, Spencer. Where you from?"

"California." Why was I telling her the truth? Her words from the phone call came back to me: *Those kids aren't as easy to manipulate as American teens.* What kids? And was she manipulating me?

"You a surfer?"

"I play basketball." I stepped off the escalator onto the

train platform. No train.

"Yeah, you don't look like you get much sun. What do you do in California, Spencer?"

"You don't have to come with me. The HODC is the other way." I did *not* want her following me to the apartment. Forget the dream. This creepy lady was freaking me out. Stranger danger in a big way.

She tossed her blond mane over her shoulder. "What brings you to Moscow? Something, I hope?"

"Uh . . . school trip." I peered down the black tunnel. Still no sign of the blasted train. Maybe if I took her to the center, Ryan would be there and I could ditch her. "Uh, I'm going back up. I forgot something."

She followed me onto the up escalator, climbing the steps until she stood on the same one as me. Her arm brushed against mine, her skin unnaturally cold. She smelled like cigarettes. It did *not* make me want one.

"Nice cross." Anya ran her fingers along the chain of my necklace and picked up the cross. I'd forgotten I was wearing the thing. "Are you a Christian, Spencer? You aren't with the Mission League, are you?"

Her eyes drilled into mine. Whoa . . . Something was wrong with them. There was no color—only black. Had they always been that way? I tugged the cross from her fingers and tucked it into my T-shirt, wondering how she knew about the Mission League? Could she be in it?

The code! I needed to ask her what color the blood was. No, that wasn't it. *Mother figs and pus bucket jam!* And why couldn't I stop shaking?

"Anya! Slava Bogu!" *Praise God!*

Ryan stood at the top of the escalator, hands on his hips

like a massive Peter Pan.

My hero. Seriously.

"I looked everywhere for you," he said to Anya. "It's not safe to get separated."

Anya ran up the last three steps and tackled Ryan in a hug like some girlfriend whose guy had been stationed overseas. "I sorry. I turn around and you are gone. I am not knowing where you go when *Spin-seer* find me and bring me to you. He is good boy, yes?"

I stepped off the escalator and gaped at Anya. In a breath she'd ditched her perfect English for a bad Russian accent.

Ryan wrinkled his brows. "Spencer? Oh, right . . . Wait, what?" He faltered, but quickly covered. "Hey, thanks, man. You know, you should get back, don't you think?"

"I really should." I had better things to do than hang with a schizophrenic Barbie doll and a wannabe James Bond. I was so grateful to be free that I ran my pass through the metro slot—*again*—and ran down the escalator.

"*Spin-seer!*" Anya called after me. I turned back, and she blew me a kiss from the top of the escalator. "I am thanking you so very much."

Yeah, whatever, crazy lady.

Mercifully, the train to Smolenskaya Station was there. I crammed in with the rush hour crowd and managed to grab a free spot on a hand pole. My heart still raced.

What a stupid thing to do.

Should I tell anyone what had happened? If so, would I get busted for printing the dossier? Ryan might contact Mr. S or Tatyana to find out why I'd talked to his assignment. But she had a tattoo like Pasha's. That had to be more than a coincidence, right? Ryan was probably all over this already. It *was* his case.

I got off the train and sprinted to the apartment. I took the four flights of stairs two at a time and burst through the door into the center apartment.

Kerri, who stood in the kitchen, squealed, hands clasped at her chest. "Oh, Spencer! Praise the Lord! I've been worried sick! Were you lost?"

I glanced at Gabe, then at Isabel who stood beside him. They stared back, expressions slack. "Yeah, I got lost—wait no. I mean, I missed the train and had to catch the next one."

Kerri pulled me against her chest and squeezed. Awkward. She smelled like garlic and onions. "I'm so thankful you're safe. Please be more careful!"

I squirmed, trying to get away from this pillowy hug. "I will. I promise."

She released me. "We're cooking dinner. Why don't you help Gabe peel potatoes?"

Potatoes? "Where's Lena?" I asked.

Kerri went to a bubbling pot on the stove and stirred it. "Pasha isn't well, and she needed to take care of him tonight."

Pasha unwell? "What's wrong with him?"

"Don't worry about Pasha." Kerri steered me to a table where Gabe was peeling a potato. "Let's get dinner on the table, okay?"

Gabe leaned close. "You all right?"

Nope. I'd followed a crazy woman, possibly blown Ryan's cover and mine, and had run away with more questions than answers. I picked up a raw potato with my thumb and forefinger. "Later."

I shouldn't have been surprised, but *Chef Gabe* peeled potatoes fast, four to my one, and practically cooked the meal himself. I was a victim of Grandma's technology denial and barely knew how to use a microwave. If I found myself home alone, I just ate peanut butter sandwiches or cereal—anything before attempting to cook. It was the one chore Grandma never bothered to teach me.

Dishes, sadly, I could do. After dinner, I stood at the sink scrubbing a pot. Isaac dumped a pile of plates into the soapy water then slapped my chest.

"Hey, don't be careless in the city, man. I don't wanna sound like your mom, but if something happens to you, it's my neck and my career. Rule 18b. Stay with the group, and don't miss any more trains. Capiche?"

"Yeah. Sorry."

Once the dishes were done, I beckoned Gabe out onto the balcony, dying to tell someone what had happened.

"So?" Gabe's curious gaze met mine.

Once the glass door was shut tight, I told him all about Anya.

Gabe looked skeptical. "You're sure it's the same tattoo?"

I leaned on the railing and stuck my sneaker between the black bars. "Ninety-nine point nine, nine, nine . . ."

"Maybe it's a popular one?"

"No way." My shoe got stuck, and I twisted it until it came free. "Pasha said it was Bratva."

"But that means brotherhood. Anya's a girl."

"A scary girl." My gaze settled on a Brittany Holmes billboard down the street, the same picture I'd seen on the drive from the airport—a beautiful girl holding a bloody knife. Man, I needed that poster. I turned Gabe to face the billboard. "Like her. Not the type of girl who needs protecting."

Gabe turned his back to the railing and propped his

elbows on top. "Maybe she acts tough because of those things listed on the dossier, getting beat up and everything. Afraid to get close to people?"

No way did I buy that. "Who was on the phone then? Who does she have *wrapped around her finger*? Ryan?"

"Why would she say that about someone who's protecting her?"

I sighed. "I told you. She doesn't *need* protection. She practically beat people up just walking through the crowd. And why fake a Russian accent with Ryan? She can speak perfect English." I couldn't shake the chills Anya had given me. If I were home, I'd jump online and research the tattoo. "You think I could get out to that Internet Café down the street?"

Gabe shrugged. "I don't see why not."

Oh, yes. I liked this plan. "Let's go there tomorrow."

"You need to tell somebody the whole story. Like Ryan—or Ivan Petrovich. He's Pasha's dad. He should know if Pasha is in trouble with Anya."

Yeah, but I wanted more info before I came clean. "All I know is I've never felt so weird around anyone. It was like someone had blacked out the colored part of her eyes with a Sharpie."

"That's creepy?" Gabe said.

Agreed. "Especially if you're the one she's looking at."

REPORT NUMBER: 20

REPORT TITLE: Anya Asks Pasha about Spencer Garmond
SUBMITTED BY: Agent Ryan Matheson
INTERVIEWEE: Pasha Ivanovich
LOCATION: Abandoned Warehouse, Moscow, Russia
DATE AND TIME: Sunday, July 6, 10:27 a.m.

PASHA ENTERED THE DAMP WAREHOUSE and dropped his backpack on the concrete floor. He unzipped it and dumped the contents, allowing the water bottles to roll in all directions. He grabbed one, twisted off the cap, and drank.

"Privyet, Pasha."

He spat water from his mouth and whipped around. Anya stood in the dark corner. A sliver of light from a high broken window cut across her face. He wiped his mouth with his wrist. "You scared me."

"So sorry." Her voice was soft and feminine today, speaking English.

Pasha never knew who to expect. "What do you want?"

Her eyebrows twitched. "Not a very friendly welcome, after all we've been through."

As friendly as she deserved. Pasha sneered at her. "You do not come here unless you want something. What is it?"

Anya swaggered toward him, her high-heeled boots cracking like gunshots in the vast warehouse. Pasha tensed at each sound, swallowed the fear gripping his heart, and stood tall.

She stopped a meter away. "I want to know about one of the American students."

Aw, nuts. Here we go again. "I do not know them," Pasha said, fidgeting with the hem on his T-shirt.

"Then get to know them."

"If I start hanging around, Tatyana will be suspicious."

"Spencer Garmond. The tall redhead. Wears a Lakers cap. Ask him about the Mission League, if he's related to Freidrich Lange. Find out about his parents."

Spencer? Pasha frowned at the mention of his new friend. Freidrich Lange was one of the League founders. There was a painting of him in Father's office. "Spencer is American missionary—the only one who is treating me normal. What are you wanting with him?"

Anya raised one sculpted eyebrow. "I thought you didn't know the Americans. Now you're saying you know him?"

"We play basketball. He likes my tattoo."

Anya put her hand over her own tattoo. "Don't trust him."

Pasha pitched his water bottle at her feet. "Stop telling me that! Do not trust Father, Mother, Tatyana. Do not trust my friends. Trust you, you say. But you are the only one I am not trusting."

"Pasha, I'm surprised at you. I always follow through on

my word."

"Word? You never say words! Normal people have conversation. You are only ever talking to give me jobs. You use me. You use us all!"

Anya took two steps forward, slid her icy hand around his neck, and grabbed a fistful of hair at the back of his head. "Don't take me for granted, Pasha."

Her voice had changed. It was now deep and raspy, not at all feminine, not at all soft. He broke out in a cold sweat, his legs trembled. She pushed his head to one side, and the force knocked him to the floor. He stayed where he fell, not daring to look at her again, not daring to move.

"I want the rest of the files, Pasha. I want the passwords. I want information about Spencer Garmond. And I want it soon. You will be paid."

Pasha shivered on the cold concrete, alone and helpless. Anya could be anyone when it suited her. He preferred the seductive woman he'd met at Café *Moo Moo* to the monster. He counted to fifty before looking up. When he did look, he saw nothing but an empty warehouse. He breathed a sigh of relief. Maybe there never really had been a seductive woman. Maybe it had all been a part of her magic act.

REPORT NUMBER: 21

REPORT TITLE: I Take a Glitter Bath
SUBMITTED BY: Agent-in-Training Spencer Garmond
LOCATION: H.O.D.C., Moscow, Russia
DATE AND TIME: Monday, July 7, 3:10 p.m.

WHITE PASTE GLUED MY FINGERS TOGETHER. I pulled
them apart with a sticky smack and shook my hand, trying to
free a scrap of paper that was stuck to my pinky. Six kids
huddled around Gabe, watching in awe as he helped a girl add
glitter to her picture. She gazed at him like he was a rock star.
The little boy I worked with gave me a pitiful stare.

I held up my mournful attempt at cutting a cross. "Gabe,
help."

Gabe chuckled and held out his hand. "Give it here."

The little boy beamed and ran around the table to watch
the expert. I went to wash my hands, wondering how I'd last a
whole week on crafts. The kids would likely riot if I didn't

shape up.

I couldn't believe the trip was half over already. I'd made my basketball tournament flyer while working in the front office, and some of the HODC's alumnus had already signed up.

But Vacation Bible school made a nice change in the daily *slave* routine at the HODC. Tatyana had asked me to teach a Bible story. I'd begged out of it, but the only other choice had been crafts. I'd hoped this was the lesser of two horrors.

"Can you get some more glitter?" Gabe asked.

I picked up the glitter dish and walked toward the supplies shelf to refill it. Nick was standing there unloading glue bottles from his arms. He mumbled something I couldn't hear.

"You talking to me?" I asked.

"'I can't cut! I can't glue! I can't pray!'" Nick snorted. "Poor widdul baby."

I sucked in a sharp breath and focused on the task at hand, but as I poured the jug of glitter into my dish, Nick bumped my elbow, and glitter went flying.

"You did that on purpose," I yelled.

"Did what?" Nick looked at my shirt. "Wow, you sparkle."

I dropped the glitter jar and pushed Nick into the shelf. Bottles of paint came down on his head like dominoes.

Gabe slid between me and Nick and steered me out into the hallway. Nick tried to come after me, but Isaac grabbed his arm and held him back.

"This is not happening, people." Isaac dragged Nick out the door and toward the front of the building. He turned back and pointed at me. "Don't go anywhere."

Nick shot me a nasty grin as Isaac hauled him away.

"You okay?" Gabe asked.

"Yeah." I dusted glitter from my shirt.

"You can't fight. You signed the contract. And Dad already let it slide once."

I swore and kicked the wall. Someone yelped. I looked to the classroom door and saw Jensina scurry back inside.

"Nice, Spencer," Gabe said. "Now you're scaring the girls."

I sagged with defeat. "I'm sorry!"

"You've got to control your temper. I know you're trying, but my dad will send you home in a second. He's done it before."

"Great." I brushed more glitter off my shirt. I didn't care anymore. Forget Moscow. If I left tomorrow, I could still get into summer conditioning.

"Help me clean up that mess before Isaac gets back. Maybe he'll have mercy on your for doing something right."

Gabe and I cleaned up the glitter and put the paint back on the shelves just in time for Isaac to return and summon me out into the hall.

Gabe shot me an apologetic frown. "See you."

Isaac took me into the cafeteria and pointed at the closest table. "Sit."

I sat.

Isaac sat across from me. A vein pulsed in his forehead. "The Mission League is a non-violent organization. You know that?"

I shrugged.

"So you go postal, you go home. Comprendo?"

"Yeah." Whatever.

"If I report this, it'll be in your permanent file. That means when you want a job someday, they'll know you're a hothead, and you won't get the job."

"They keep files on us?"

"Big brother's always watching." Isaac leaned onto one elbow. His hair fell across his eyes and he shook it aside. "Luke 6:29. It was on the memorization list."

I looked at the ceiling as I dug a speck of glitter from the corner of my eye. "Uh . . . if someone hits you, hide your face?"

"Close enough."

"I don't get it."

"If Nick hits you, don't hit back. If Nick dumps glitter on your head, *don't do it back.* That's what it means. God doesn't want you to take revenge."

"That's stupid."

"No, newbie. That's Christ-like. Put it like this: If Nick hits you, which is harder—to hit him back or to not hit him back?"

I grinned. "Harder for who? I pack a big punch."

"You're probably a wonderful singer too, but that's not the point."

I huffed a loud sigh. "Fine. Not hitting him is harder, but I've been trying to *not* hit him since middle school."

"Well, don't stop trying now."

I stared at my clenched fists. I hated feeling this way. Trapped. Controlled. I tried to not fight, but Nick wore me down with every nasty glance and comment. It wasn't my fault that the cops had played me. I was just a dumb kid, scared out of my mind. And it wasn't like Nick had gone to jail or anything. I don't know why he still made such a big deal about it. Why wouldn't he let it go, already?

Isaac cleared his throat. "Why don't you take LCT this fall? Pour that energy into something useful."

"Beth's fighting class? I plan to." *If I'm still in this thing.*

"Yes, LCT trains agents to defend themselves. But it also

teaches self-control. That's what you need. Now, clean yourself up and get to VBS. I sent Nick to games for the rest of the day so you can both chill."

"Are you going to report us?"

"Not this time. Consider it your warning. Next time I will, though. Then Mr. S can decide if he wants to send you packing."

I trudged to the bathroom and tried to brush the glitter from my hair. That was the second time someone had told me I lacked self-control. First Arianna, and now Isaac. Clearly they were right—but did I care enough to do anything about it? If I got sent home for fighting, would Grandma still send me to military school?

Probably.

VBS worship kicked off each afternoon in the tiny chapel with music. Gabe played his guitar and Isabel sang, and the kids loved it. Even singing church songs, it was easy to see Gabe and Isabel were made for this stuff—and perfect for each other. I sat sulking in the back by myself, doodling on an offering envelope, while Isabel belted out the chorus of *Our God is Big*. Beth sat with Jensina in the second row.

The door banged open, and Pasha and Yuri scampered in, chattering like squirrels. Pasha jumped the back pew and landed beside me. Yuri followed. They smelled like cigarettes and sweat. Both could use a shower. Or two.

"Hey." Pasha's sweaty hair was matted to his head like black slime.

"Been playing?" I asked.

"Da," Pasha said. "You been in Leega Missionerov long time?"

"Couple months," I said.

"You like kiddy God songs?"

I folded my arms across my chest. "They're all right."

"That girl all right." Yuri gawked at Isabel, Nick-style.

I stiffened.

"Nyet, Svet-lah-nah is most beautiful girl here." Pasha closed his eyes and breathed her name.

Tatyana shot them a warning glare from the front of the room.

Pasha stopped laughing, the sound winding down like a nearly empty balloon. "Spencer, you never met your father, is right? How about your mother?"

I squirmed on the pew. "Uh . . . she's dead."

Pasha's smile faded, his face paler than usual. "Izveenee."

Yeah, I was sorry too. For a while no one spoke. Gabe and Isabel were belting out the final verse of a hymn, the crowd singing along.

"You related to Freidrich Lange, no?" Pasha asked.

I leaned closer, holding my breath to avoid Pasha's body odor. "Who?"

"Uh, creator of Leega Missionerov."

"Am I related?" I looked at my knees and blinked. "I don't know. No. What's with the twenty questions?"

Gabe strummed into a fast song. Isabel spurred the crowd into clapping. Pasha and Yuri sang in loud, tuneless voices, swaying with their arms over each other's shoulders. I fought to keep a straight face.

Tatyana's glares screamed, and she crept over. "Why are

you here?"

Pasha flashed her a toothy grin. "I'm in love with VBS."

"Me also," Yuri said.

She pursed her lips into a thin line. "Be serious or leave."

"This church not so friendly," Yuri said to Pasha.

"You are right." Pasha folded his arms. His tattoo poked out from the bottom of his sleeve, just like Anya's had. They *were* the same.

"*Pasha!*" Tatyana's cheeks turned pink.

Pasha looked at Yuri then back to Tatyana. "We go for one thousand rubles."

She gasped.

My eyebrows shot toward the ceiling. That was like thirty bucks.

Pasha threw his arm back over Yuri's shoulder and sang louder than before.

"I only have four hundred," she said.

"That will do." Pasha held out his hand.

Tatyana's eyes glossed with tears. "Please come home for dinner. I will make borscht."

Pasha pushed his hand against her arm. "You have four hundred or not?"

She pulled the bills out of her back pocket and threw them in his face. "I hope it is not for cigarettes, Pasha Ivanovich!"

Pasha gathered the money off his lap, the pew, and the floor. "Paka, Spencer." He jumped over the back pew and bolted for the entrance with Yuri at his heels. The door banged shut behind them. Tatyana gave me a challenging look before trudging away and slouching in a pew near the wall.

My feelings toward Pasha ran hot and cold. When we were playing ball, Pasha was a lot of fun. But here, now, I felt like *I* needed a shower.

I didn't like the way Pasha bullied Tatyana. Despite being a little weepy, she was a nice girl who worked hard to help people. I also didn't like the way Yuri drooled over Isabel or how Pasha leered at Svetlana. Granted, I'd spent a good deal of time watching Isabel myself, but that was different, wasn't it? Had Isabel seen the same hunger in my eyes that was reflected in Nick's? Man, I hoped not. Because it wasn't cool. I'd try not to stare anymore.

One thing was certain: Tatyana deserved better from her brother.

And what about Pasha's questions? Related to Fred Who? How could Pasha know more about League history than I did?

That evening, I dragged Gabe down to the Internet Café. We went through the pair of glass doors and beheld rows and rows of computers lined up like soldiers. I paid ninety-six rubles for thirty minutes and sat down at an empty station. Thankfully, Russian keyboards had English *and* Cyrillic letters on them. I typed in search options.

"Here." I pointed to a round maze symbol. "Something like this . . . or this." I pointed to another.

There were hundreds of maze tattoos online. I looked for images with a line coming out the top, but when I found the right one, it seemed to belong to dozens of groups all over the world. There was El Camino in Latin America, Dakila in Indonesia, Shizuka in Japan, Rifaa in parts of Africa, and the Free Light Foundation in English speaking countries.

My mind raced. "Ivan mentioned some of these in the New Cults Department."

"Bratva!" Gabe tapped the word on the screen. "Like Pasha said."

My new search for *Bratva Moscow* found a website and I had to copy and paste into Google Translate to understand it, though it didn't do a perfect translation by far. I read aloud from the "About Us—English" page. "'Bratva teaches of the power inside the human soul. People hunger for love and acceptance, searching all their lives in vain. Our country provides no security, nor does religion, employment, or family. Bratva provides it. We are a true family. Bratva can give your life purpose.'"

Gabe scoffed. "Only God can give life purpose."

"Says here that Bratva was founded by Dmitri Berkovich. Their motto is, 'Providing a path to love and acceptance and a journey to true power and purpose.'"

Gabe's eyebrows arched. "Sounds like a cult."

"There's a Bratva chat room!" In less than a minute, I signed up and entered the room. After more copying and pasting into Google Translate, I scanned over meaningless and somewhat confusing translations, until my eyes stopped on the words *field office.*

"Gabe, look." I pointed to the screen, reading between the lines of other ongoing conversations. "See db666 and amarx? They're plotting something."

> db666: When can you do to the field office?
> radd45: anyone try the crown on the New Club?
> amarx: soon
> mikael_54: it well. better to stay away from Nova if

you are underage, try B24 or neolit on kalskaya

alexalex2: mio on zemlyanoy is better db666: How soon?

radd45: alexalex2, whys mio best?

alexalex2: my brothers bartender and gives free drinks

amarx: In negotiations.

radd45: lol

db666: Make happen now.

db666 has left the lounge

Gabe squinted at the screen. "666? Freaky."

I locked eyes with Gabe. "Someone's going to break into the field office."

Gabe looked doubtful. "There are probably hundreds of field offices in Moscow. It doesn't mean it has to do with the Mission League."

"There's an e-mail address. I could write and see if I get a response."

"What good would that do? You don't have e-mail access."

"I could do it from the center."

Gabe's forehead wrinkled. "That's a bad idea."

"Why?"

"'Cause my dad would freak if he found out."

"I can register an e-mail with any search engine. If I never get a chance to check my messages, I won't know if they wrote back or not. No one could track it. No one would know."

Gabe groaned, but I knew I'd won. I registered with a Russian search engine and e-mailed Bratva a touching letter about being in a foreign country and needing love and acceptance. I signed it *Biff*, my alias from Arianna and Isabel, which amused Gabe. I paid for my printouts, and Gabe and I took off.

I studied the research as we walked back to the apartment. I had about twenty pages, most of which covered the history and symbolism of mazes and labyrinths. "I should have tried to find a link between the Free Light Foundation and Bratva. I bet all these groups are connected."

"I've never seen a tattoo like that at school," Gabe said.

"PPCS isn't exactly a tattoo-friendly school. Anya spoke perfect English when she made that phone call. She could be American."

Gabe held the door to the apartment building open. "She could be anything."

REPORT NUMBER: 22

REPORT TITLE: I Blow Agent Matheson's Cover
SUBMITTED BY: Agent-in-Training Spencer Garmond
LOCATION: Cafeteria, H.O.D.C., Moscow, Russia
DATE AND TIME: Wednesday, July 9, 12:11 p.m.

THE NEXT DAY WHEN BABUSHK A served borscht for lunch, *again*, I grilled her to make sure it was fresh before I ate any. Gabe took only fruit and bread, apparently not willing to take the risk. We sat a table in the corner of the cafeteria.

Beth swung one leg over the bench across from me and pushed back against Gabe. "Excuse me. Pardon me. Make room."

Gabe slid down, and Beth settled into his spot, propped her elbow onto the table, and gazed at me. My chest tightened. I watched her without looking directly at her, focusing just past her shoulder as if I didn't care that she was there.

I totally cared.

"Can we talk a sec?" she asked me.

I gave up my tough-guy act and looked her over. She wore a red T-shirt that read, "I'm a One Girl Revolution." Two low pigtails draped lazily over her shoulders, and her emerald eyes searched mine.

My stomach lurched. "What?" I yelled. Smooth, Garmond.

"Easy, Tiger. What's got you all riled up?"

Pretty girl. Too close for comfort. I forced down a spoonful of borscht.

"Isaac told me about your fight with Nick," Beth said. "It's tough. I used to get in fights before—" She stuck out her bottom lip and sighed, puffing her bangs in the air. "It don't help. I know it feels good at the time to defend yourself, but it don't change nothing."

"*You* got in fights?"

Beth's grin lit up her face. "Oh, yeah. Most of which I started."

An image of Beth beating up kids in the park popped into my head. "Why?"

Her expression softened. "Well, according to my *counselor* it was psychological. A low tolerance for frustration. My mom died when I was ten. She'd been sick all my life. Then my dad got remarried, and with a stepmom came two sisters—girly girls. It didn't seem fair, you know? I became a bigger tough-girl than ever. It set me apart, I guess. And fighting was something I could win. Made me feel strong—invincible. Deep, huh? Dr. Joe's pretty smart."

I swallowed, intrigued by how much sense she was making. "How'd she die?"

"Leukemia."

The word hung in the air between us, a bridge connecting

my buried sorrow to Beth's overcome grief. I blinked back to the subject. "So how'd you stop fighting?"

"I didn't for a long time, not 'til I became a Christian."

"*Right.*" I stirred my soup, raising the drawbridge at the word *Christian.* "How'd they suck you in?"

Beth flicked her finger against my forearm. "Not fair, Tiger. No one *sucked* me anywhere. You want to know or not?"

I stared at the forming welt on my forearm and shrugged one shoulder.

"We stopped going to church when Mom died. My brother Tony started up again when some girl invited him, and he got hooked. *Sucked* in." Beth snorted an airy laugh. "Few months later he got in a car accident—not his fault. Someone on a cell phone swerved over the line. He was seventeen. Doctors said he'd die."

Beth snatched the roll from my tray, ripped it in half, and dunked it in my soup. "I hated God. He took my mom and now my brother was dying. I was sick of Him picking on our family. Then Tony's youth group came to the hospital and prayed every day for a week. I thought they were nuts, until Tony made a full recovery. It changed my life. I knew God had answered their prayers. Been in church ever since."

Beth ate the soggy roll in one bite, dimples forming in her cheeks as she chewed. "It's funny how people say they don't believe in God but blame Him when something bad happens. He never gets credit for all the good days, just blamed for the few bad ones. That's how I was."

I leaned forward and stared Beth down. "But God could've saved your mom, kept that car accident from happening. How can you be okay with that?"

"God made the world. He made me." She plucked a

strawberry off my tray. "Look at this thing, Tiger, all these little seeds. It's amazing. I don't have a clue what God's up to. I can't make a strawberry. If God wants my mom in heaven, who am I to say no? He made her. She belongs to Him, not me. Besides, what would I have to say to you if she were alive? Me, raised by my dad and three brothers? I'd be a different person if Mom had lived, playing with dolls and getting manicures. That's how God works. Our pain can help others."

Beth had a real positive way of looking at things, one of those glass half full people, the kind I used to hate. But I didn't hate Beth.

"Putting myself in the other person's shoes helped a lot. I know Nick's always hassling you, but there's a reason, even if it's whacked. I've known him a long time. He's not the Antichrist. If you can figure out his deal, maybe you can understand."

"It's because of something that happened in middle school."

"Nah, I don't buy it. That might have started the problem between you two, but there's got to be something more now."

"How can you be so sure?"

"Don't know. Just am." She popped my strawberry into her mouth, cheeks dimpling again. "Mmm. And you—do you believe in God?"

I twitched.

"I'm not asking if you like Him. Just, do you think He's there?"

I glared at the red liquid in my bowl and shrugged one shoulder. She might be cute, but even cute girls could push their luck.

"I'll take that as a yes. Look, stuff happens, Tiger. Bad

stuff. Now, you're a smart guy, tough, talented. I saw that three pointer you made against Bakersfield during playoffs. All net."

I smiled into my soup. Sucking up to me was a nice tactic.

Beth put her hand on my shoulder and squeezed. "Nothing bad happens that God can't use for good. That's in Romans— part of the Bible. So if you think the bad stuff 's from Him 'cause He's a big jerk who wants to torture you and make you suffer, you're wrong. And you're too sharp to be falling for that lie."

I glanced at Beth. The girl had a way with words. But no one had had to feed me lies—I'd always assumed God was a jerk. Could I have been wrong?

Beth looked at her watch. "Wow, I got to run. Think about the fighting thing. I don't want you kicked out of the League before you even get to try LCT."

"Thanks," was all I could think to say.

"See ya, Tiger." Beth walked around the table and slapped me on the back. I waited until she was out of earshot to gasp for air. She was like no girl I'd ever known, and yet she still had the power to make me stupid.

I suddenly realized Beth hadn't cared that I wasn't *saved*. She clearly wanted me to get with the program, but she hadn't judged me or given me any dire warnings of eternity in hell. No big deal. My call.

Relief flooded me. If Beth was cool with me, maybe some of the others would be too.

• • •

The following Monday, Tatyana called me to the Job Placement office to install a new computer program. I was thankful to escape my first day of nursery duty. As the software was installing, I logged onto my Russian e-mail to check for an answer from Bratva.

Marina approached my desk and laid a file beside the keyboard. "Could you print out the résumé we prepared for this woman?"

I checked the name. Anastasia Vseveloda? My heart stopped then began to race as I met her eyes. Black and creepy sci fi eyes.

"Hello, *Spin-seer*."

"Hey." I printed the résumé, watching her in my peripheral vision.

She was like Dr. Jekyll and Mr. Hyde. Since Anya had used the accent, I expected her to play the victim today. She smelled faintly of cigarettes and donned a glowing smile, her mane of blond curls loose around her face.

Clearly, good looks weren't everything.

"I interview today for job," she said.

I snatched the résumé from the printer tray and handed it to her. She wore a long-sleeved blouse, spoiling any glimpses of her tattoo.

She didn't accept the printout. "Could I get copies, please?"

"Uh, sure." I stepped to the copier. "How many?"

"Ninety-nine will do."

My jaw dropped. Tatyana must have a limit on how many—

"Joking, *Spin-seer*. You so serious."

I stiffened. "Your English sure went downhill fast."

"*Spin-seer*, you my metro hero."

I faked a smile.

Anya pulled a cell phone out of her purse and looked at Marina. "Excuse me, miss? You take picture of us, yes? *Spinseer* my metro hero."

Marina rose and took the camera. "Sure."

Picture? Wasn't Anya supposed to be homeless and jobless? Pretty spendy phone for someone in her shoes—make that three-inch-heeled leather boots. Why was I the only one who saw through Anya's charade? Homeless people didn't wear boots like that, right?

Anya trotted around to the back of the desk and tucked her arm around my waist. I should feel thrilled that a beautiful woman was touching me, but her touch wasn't normal. It made me cold and seemed to suck the breath from my lungs like a high-powered vacuum.

Marina aimed the phone. "Say cheese."

"Cheez!" Anya sang.

The flash went off, blurring my vision for a second. Anya clicked back across the floor to take her camera from Marina. My shirt was damp where her arm had been. I itched like ants were crawling all over me. I sank into my chair, squirming and scratching my arms.

What on earth?

Anya eased into the chair in front of my desk and scooted it close. "I interview today to be photographer." She leaned forward, her elbows on my desk, her chin in her hands.

Maybe she was just insane. I pulled her file out from under her elbow. "The interview is soon, I hope?"

"*Spin-seer*, you believe in God?" Her black eyes probed mine.

"I—what?"

"I see doubt in you eyes."

She was like one of Brittany Holmes' demon hunter minions. Beautiful and creepy. I looked away and shivered. "Marina, did someone fix the air conditioning?" The front office and the medical center were the only places in the building with air, but it had been broken since I'd arrived.

Marina smirked my way, her desk fan blowing her hair around. "What do you think?"

Never mind.

Marina stood and walked toward the hall. "I'll be right back, Spencer."

I trembled and wiped my forehead with my sleeve. I'd never understood the term "cold sweat" until now. How long was Anya going to sit there, anyway? What did she want?

She put her hand over mine and squeezed. "You don't talk much, *Spin-seer*. It's cute."

My hand blazed, and a vision flooded my mind.

Anya giggles and sets my Lakers cap over her blond curls. She grabs my chin and forces me to face her, squeezing my face so hard her thumbnail cuts into my cheek.

I yelped, leaped backwards out of my chair, and rubbed the feel of IcyHot from my hand. I darted forward and snatched her file off my desk. "I have to file this." I wiped my sweaty hand on my jeans and stumbled toward the file cabinet. I watched her from behind it, keeping my distance in case she tried to grab my face.

I flipped through her file again—I'd done so over and over every chance I'd gotten—but there was still nothing of interest in it.

"All set?" a male voice asked.

"I am waiting for copies," Anya said.

I peeked over the top of the file cabinet. Ryan stood beside Anya.

The agent looked surprised to see me. "Oh, hey, Spencer."

I gulped, breathing hard for no reason, feeling somehow violated. I mean, what was happening to me, anyway?

"*Spin-seer*, please. My copies?"

"I can't give you that many copies." Telling Anya no in front of Ryan felt so lame.

Anya giggled. "I need only two."

Of course she did. I yanked the résumé back out her file, slapped it on the glass, and punched the copy button. Why were chicks crazy? Could somebody let me know?

A minute later I handed her the copies.

"Thank you, *Spin-seer*. Ryan, I must use restroom. Please wait?"

Ryan nodded.

Anya gazed at me with probing eyes as she strode around the corner.

Ryan looked around the office. "How's it going?"

"Fine." I rubbed my thumb over the pink spot on my hand. It looked like I'd actually been burned.

"Jensina around?"

"Somewhere." My voice quivered slightly. I caught sight of my tournament flyer on the desk. "Hey, Ryan. Tatyana is having this open house and I'm putting together a basketball tournament. She said you might be able to coach our team?"

Ryan frowned. "You don't want me to play?"

"Well, it's just for kids. On Saturday the nineteenth." I handed him a flyer.

He grabbed it and looked it over. "Oh, right. Well, sure. I

can do that."

"Thanks, man." I took a deep breath and figured the guy could use a free tip. "Hey, can I tell you something else?"

"Shoot."

I moved close and spoke low. "When I saw Anya in the metro station the other day, she was taking to someone on the phone in a perfect American accent."

Ryan's eyebrows sank. "The metro is loud. You probably heard wrong."

I hated being shorter than Ryan. "It was quiet," I said with as much attitude as I could muster. "The train had just left."

Ryan shook his head.

"Also—" I glanced toward the hallway, hoping Anya was still occupied. "I think she knows you're following her."

Ryan went white. He leaned forward. "What did she say to make you—?"

"And she has this tattoo that looks like a maze, and Pasha—"

Ryan grabbed my arm and squeezed. "What did she . . . ?" He released me and stepped back. "You know what? No. You stick to your work here at the center and stay out of my way, you got that?"

"But Pasha has—"

"Ready," Anya sang, slinking up to Ryan and closing her purse.

"Great. Let's go." Ryan pointed at me. "Remember what I said."

"Yeah, you too," I shot back. Big jerk, anyway.

Ryan opened the door for Anya, pierced me with once last I'm-the-king-of-the-world glare, and they left.

I fell into my chair, physically exhausted, like I'd just

finished a basketball game. I stared at my pink, stinging hand and trembled. The similarities to Anya having inflicted the burn on my hand and some of the characters in Brittany Holmes' Light Goddess films was just plain creepy.

Marina returned to her desk. "Strange woman, that one. I found her standing around the corner filing her fingernails. I think she was eavesdropping on your conversation."

I took a deep breath and blew it out in a sigh. If Anya hadn't known that Ryan was following her before, she did now. Nice work, Agent Biff.

REPORT NUMBER: 23

REPORT TITLE: Arianna's Theories on Demons
SUBMITTED BY: Agent-in-Training Spencer Garmond
LOCATION: Nursery, H.O.D.C., Moscow, Russia
DATE AND TIME: Monday, July 14, 11:22 a.m.

I COULDN'T FOCUS THE REST OF THE MORNING. I wanted to tell Gabe about Anya, but I wouldn't see him until lunch. When I finished installing the software, Marina sent me back to the nursery, where I found Arianna stacking diapers on a shelf.

The room had bright zoo animals painted on the wall, kiddy toys everywhere, three cribs, and a row of highchairs. There were four babies today. Three could walk, so maybe they weren't babies anymore, I didn't know.

I fell into a rocking chair and watched them play. This would be my least favorite week of the summer. Not that I had anything against babies, it was just . . . What if I broke one?

They were so little.

I glanced at the burn on my hand. Beth had said nothing bad happened that God couldn't use for good. So what if someone else used that stuff for evil? If I was gifted in discernment like I was supposed to be, I'd know the answer.

But I didn't. I didn't have gifts. Not like Gabe, MissionAri, and Isabel had with music, encouragement, and healing. Why didn't I? Beth had said I was too sharp not to fall for any lies, but if I couldn't even figure out my own gifts, I was an idiot. I rocked faster.

Mishka toddled across the room, carrying a toy truck in his fist. I couldn't believe this two-year-old was Svetlana's kid. He tripped over a stuffed bear and fell on his face. A loud wail burst out of him. How could someone so small be so loud? Arianna scooped him up. After a kiss on the hand and a twirl in a circle, Mishka was back on his feet, cruising the room.

"Healing was one of your spiritual gifts, wasn't it?" I asked. "You're good with patients—babies too."

Arianna beamed, showing off her gums. "It *was* my top score."

I folded my arms and stopped rocking. "Everyone's doing something from that test. Isabel encourages, you heal, Gabe sings. I don't do any of mine."

"Of course you do."

"Not like Gabe. He can do anything."

"He can't do computers."

"Didn't see computers on the spiritual gifts list."

Arianna put her hands on her hips. "First Corinthians 12, Spencer. What good is a body with all legs and no head or arms?"

I grinned, clueless to what she was getting at and figured I may as well be cute about my ignorance. "A daddy long-legs?"

Arianna rolled her eyes and pushed a toy car across the floor to Mishka. "It's not a riddle. God doesn't need you to encourage or heal or sing or play guitar. You said yourself, the rest of us do those. God needs you for something else. Trust Him to guide you, and He'll develop your gifts. Just be patient."

A little girl heaved a naked doll onto my lap and slurred Russian baby talk. I handed the doll back. "Being patient is a waste of time. I want to know if I'm supposed to do something, and I want to know when, how, and why."

The little girl dropped the doll onto Arianna's lap and repeated her incoherent babble. Arianna grabbed a dress off the floor and pulled it over the doll's arms and head. "It's okay if you can't be patient. Know why? Because God loves you and knows you'll figure it out someday. I think God knows boys are a bit slow."

"Excuse me?"

She handed the doll back to the girl, who toddled away. "Just try a little prayer here and there. You'll get the hang of it."

Praying had never helped me before. "If God wants me to do something, why doesn't He just say so?"

"'Blessed are those who believe and have not seen.'"

"That makes no sense. I want to hear, not see. It's easy for you and Gabe and Isabel. But I just don't get all this God talk. Nick was right: I'm a fake."

"Spencer, there's nothing fake about you." Arianna rose and walked to the snack cupboard. "A little reckless and impulsive, maybe. I refer back to boys being a bit slow."

I got up and walked to where she stood pouring tiny

cookies into cardboard cups. I grabbed one and dumped the contents into my mouth.

"These aren't for you." She pushed me away and filled another cup. "You tried to hide that you aren't a Christian, you never pretended to be one. There's a big difference. And yes, reckless describes you perfectly. Fighting with Nick, following a strange woman who's being watched by New Cults. You haven't told Mr. S what you did, and you're still poking around where you shouldn't."

I scowled. "Who told you I followed her?"

"I'm a good spy, like my dad." Arianna loaded the babies into highchairs and fed them cookies. More like a good mom than a good spy.

"Okay, *good spy*, Anya came into the office this morning and took a picture of me. Then I think she eavesdropped on me and Ryan." I explained how Marina had found her in the hallway. "Why would she do that?"

Arianna twisted her lips. "Maybe she needed to freshen up. Girls do it all the time."

"In the hallway?"

Her eyebrows arched. "Why not?"

How could she not see this? "Boys might be slow, Arianna, but girls are weird. I can't believe she'd walk three yards to file her fingernails."

Arianna fed Mishka a cookie. "I just said it was possible."

"Aren't you at all curious about the tattoo?"

"Quite, but that doesn't mean I need to solve the case, Joe Hardy."

"Who?" I pulled the rocking chair closer and sat back down, exhaling a long and hopeless breath. "If I come clean, I might get sent home. I need more proof—maybe get a better look at the tattoos. I could be wrong."

• • •

I brought Gabe up to speed at lunch.

He narrowed his eyes. "Why would she take your picture?"

See? Gabe saw that that was not normal. I winced at the memory of her arm draped around my shoulders. "Weird, huh?"

"Ryan didn't believe you?"

"The guy's a joke. Didn't even listen."

Gabe bit into his roll. "Weren't you scheduled in the nursery today?"

"Yup. Tatyana needed me to install a program."

"Did you get a chance to check your e-mail?"

I shook my head. "I was about to when Anya came in. Then I was too freaked out and couldn't think. I'm not scheduled on front desk until our last week here. But someone's going to try something with the field office server before then. I think it was Anya the first time."

I picked at my roll until I had peeled off the glossy brown top.

Arianna's snicker turned my gaze to the end of the table where she was sitting. "You two are hopeless."

I shot her a dirty look. "You think I should tell Mr. S?"

"Yes, but last week when you first decided to play super sleuth."

Gabe rolled his eyes. "Arianna, my dad would go nuts."

"I rest my case. Spencer needs to involve someone qualified. Keeping the information between you two won't help the Moscow Field Office one bit."

JILL WILLIAMSON

I slapped the table. "I *tried* to tell Ryan today. No one's going to believe me!"

"Try again," Arianna said.

"Not without more proof," I said.

Arianna's eyes flashed. "What proof? You getting beat up, kidnapped, or worse? Spencer, it's not worth your life."

I faked a laugh. "My life?"

"I think you're getting a little carried away, Arianna," Gabe said.

"No, you guys aren't putting the pieces together. Ryan works in New Cults and is assigned to Anya. Therefore, Anya is somehow connected to a cult, right? Many cults call on spirits. These things are real. My dad saw this kind of activity in Africa before I was born. The way Spencer feels around Anya is how Dad felt around the witchdoctor. She could be demon-possessed."

I instantly thought of Brittany Holmes kicking butt in the *Jolt* movies. Demons always had black eyes in the movies. Maybe because they did in real life.

Arianna paused for a breath. "If Anya is possessed or into something evil, Spencer needs to stay away from her. He doesn't know how to protect himself from demons. He doesn't know spiritual warfare. Plus, he isn't saved."

Her comment hit a nerve. "What's that have to do with anything?"

"Plenty," Arianna said. "If you're a believer, God is with you and protects you from demonic possession. But if you get yourself killed now, you don't go to heaven."

And the evangelist had returned. "You're psycho, you know that, right?"

She pressed her lips together and stared at me. "If it

242

makes you feel tall to insult me, go ahead. It doesn't make what I said any less true."

I stared at Arianna, feeling like I was way out of my element. "Yeah, well, how do you know so much, anyway?"

"It's all in the Bible," Arianna said, tapping the black book by her tray.

"I disagree, Arianna." Gabe folded his arms. "The Bible may say that, but you're not God. Ultimately God gets to decide when it comes to eternity."

"I'm trying to *teach* him, Gabriel. If he understands the cost, maybe he'll start making better choices."

Gabe wrinkled his nose like a scolded puppy. "You can't bully him into salvation. It's his choice."

"If Spencer wants to risk an eternity in hell, he's crazier than I thought."

Again I was going to hell. "This is exactly why I didn't want to join you people in the first place. You're just making everything worse." I turned to Gabe. "Is that really possible? What she said about demons?"

Gabe shrugged. "Anything is possible."

I looked at my still-pink hand. "So how would you fight a demon, anyway?"

"*You* wouldn't," Arianna said.

Her tone hit another nerve, and I snapped. "Just forget it, Arianna, okay? Gabe?"

Gabe spoke softly. "I don't know much about demons. Arianna could be right about it. You did have discernment on your spiritual gifts test. That could be why you felt so weird."

Arianna smiled. "See? You're using one of your gifts, after all. Now tell Mr. S."

I balled my fists and looked away. If she wasn't a girl . . .

REPORT NUMBER: 24

REPORT TITLE: I Fess Up and Learn To Write a Report
SUBMITTED BY: Agent-in-Training Spencer Garmond
LOCATION: Arbat Ulitsa, 43, Moscow, Russia
DATE AND TIME: Monday, July 14, 6:20 p.m.

DEMONS. YEAH, RIGHT.

I sulked during dinner, mostly because it was Arianna's birthday, and I was mad at her. Her comments from lunch nagged. I'd never given heaven much thought. I was only fifteen, after all. But it was weird to think I might not go there. I mean, sure, I screwed up sometimes, but I was basically a good person. What were the requirements for heaven, anyway? Were they written somewhere?

When Gabe was in the shower, I leafed through his Bible. I'd conveniently forgotten mine at home. I couldn't make sense of it, though, and I didn't see the word *heaven* once.

I was pretty sure God was up there, though He was doing

nothing to stop the pain in the world. Jesus I wasn't sure about. I mean, why become a human? Especially knowing how nuts we are. I thought God had more sense, you know? But could I believe in God and not Jesus? Did that make me Jewish or something? Why did religion have to be so complicated?

And what about demons? I hadn't seen the word *demon* in Gabe's Bible either. But I might've missed it: The book only had fifteen hundred pages. Not exactly a quick read.

I needed some insight on my dreams and Anya. She'd burned my hand just touching me. And those eyes . . . But the daydream—or vision—of her grabbing my face had yet to take place. Nor had the Vlad vision happened yet. I had no desire to see either person again, but the more Anya popped into my life, the more I had to connect this dot-to-dot. And maybe, just maybe, Mr. S would be a good place to start.

After singing the birthday song and eating the cake Kerri had made for Arianna, I sat with Gabe in the living room, watching some Russian game show. When it ended, Gabe got up. "I'm going to bed. You coming?"

I glanced to where Mr. S was sitting in the corner chair, reading his Bible. I sighed. Time to come clean. "In a minute."

Gabe left, and I walked over to his dad. "Hey, Mr. S? You got a second?" I stole a quick glance at Arianna, who was reading at the kitchen table.

Was that a smirk she just gave me?

Mr. S closed his Bible. "'I must govern the clock, not be governed by it.'"

"*Right.*" I wanted this to be quick and painless. "I was wondering—since the tour of the field office, I mean . . . Um, the people who work in New Cults. Do they ever meet, you know, demons?"

"Demons?" Mr. S's eyes swelled behind the thick lenses, like big, brown meatballs. "Why do you ask?"

I fidgeted with the hem of my T-shirt. "Well, how do you know if you meet one?"

"Do you think you've met one?" Mr. S's forehead wrinkled with concern. "You don't mean Mr. Muren?"

I snorted. Good one, Mr. S. "No, not Nick. Someone else. It's . . . hard to describe."

"Panicked? Cold and trembling? Sweating? Smothered?"

The accuracy of his words brought a chill over my arms. I nodded.

"I've felt that sensation, Spencer. Not many have. I can't say for sure if you were with someone demon-possessed or if an evil spirit was oppressing you. There's no common book of answers when it comes to the spirit world. However, people with the gift of discernment are prone to sense supernatural presences. That's one of your potential gifts, right?"

Supposedly. "Yeah."

Mr. S leaned back in his chair. "When did you have this feeling?"

What was that memory verse? The truth will free you? "When I'm around Anya." My stomach lightened the instant the name left my mouth.

"Do I know this Anya?"

The lead weight in my gut returned. "I . . . uh . . . She's Ryan's assignment."

Mr. S scooted to the end of his seat, his face stern. "How do you know about Ryan's assignment?"

I confessed the whole ordeal—leaving out my dreams and visions—and waited for Mr. S to speak.

"Spencer," he began slowly, "the League trains people

246

vigilantly. There's no reason to think Ryan is not doing a thorough job."

"But—"

He put up his hand. "Your concern for Pasha is understandable, but you—we—have no business meddling in real cases. We're here for training. Let the agents do their jobs."

I wanted to melt into the carpet.

"I'll take this dossier to the field office tomorrow and share your story with Ivan. He deserves to know, for more reasons than one. I hope you're wrong about Pasha."

Great, now I'd snitched on Pasha. "But what about Anya and demons?"

"If this woman is being watched by New Cults, it's possible she's demon-possessed or has participated in demonic activity. Remember how you felt around her. It's a good lesson, but please don't try to rid her of any demons. In fact, stay away from her. If you see her again, leave. Find one of our adults. Go to another part of the building and pray. Recite your memory verses, okay?"

Prayer and Scriptures. A Christian's answer for everything.

"'Wise men don't need advice,' Spencer. 'Fools won't take it.'"

I looked at my shoes. "Yeah, okay."

"And no discussing Ryan's case with the others. Who else knows about it?"

"Gabe and Arianna."

"Fine. I'll talk to them. Now get me this dossier."

I slouched away to my bunk. Gabe eyed me as I walked in. I took the dossier from my suitcase, hesitated, then grabbed the rest of my research too. Maybe it would help. Gabe whispered something to me, but I was already out the door. I shoved the paperwork at Mr. S.

He flipped through the pile, eyes bulging. "You printed all this from Ryan's computer?"

"No." I dug through the papers and pulled out the folded sheet. "This is the dossier. I researched the rest at the Internet Café down the street. I could have done more with better access to a computer, but . . ."

Mr. S pointed at another page. "Is this the tattoo?"

"Yeah. It's a maze in the shape of the international symbol for power. You know, like electricity. Input-output? I think it symbolizes a journey to power or something because Bratva's website mentions that. 'Bratva' is what Pasha's friends call themselves. I'm not sure about the star in the center. Witchcraft, maybe . . . anti-God? Different groups use this symbol all over the world, though. They could be connected."

A hint of a smile flashed on Mr. S's face. "Thanks for giving me all this. It's very . . . thorough. Your consequence is to write a report I can give Ivan. I want it before you leave for the HODC tomorrow morning."

My stomach tightened. Newbies didn't do reports. "I don't know how."

"Gabe can help, since he knew about this."

"Also, Mr. S, I tried to tell Ryan about this today, but he didn't believe me. And after they left I found out that Anya had been eavesdropping on our conversation, so maybe you could warn Ryan that Anya knows he's, you know, spying on her."

Mr. S sighed. "I'll do that. Anything else I need to know?"

I wanted to ask Mr. S about the visions and the burn, but something held me back. "Anya took a picture of me. Why would she do that?"

Mr. S pondered a moment. "It's probably nothing. Put it in your report."

I started toward the bedroom then turned back. Though I hated to do it, I was running out of time. "Uh, Mr. S? You think you can referee my little basketball tournament on Tatyana's open house night?"

Mr. S chuckled. "Do *you* think I can?"

I shrugged. "I didn't know who else to ask."

"I can do it, Spencer. Thanks for asking me."

Doing a report turned out to be a nasty chore. Gabe couldn't believe I had to do one my first year, but he helped with the formatting and wording. I even had to sign an official affidavit swearing that my information was true. It was three in the morning when I finished the beast.

I yawned, my mind racing with thoughts of everything that had happened, everything Mr. S had warned me about, everything that still puzzled me. Mr. S had said, "*Don't take it upon yourself to rid her of any demons.*" What did *that* mean? Did I need to pick up a Brittany Holmes demon hunter utility belt? Arianna would probably know. But she still wasn't talking to me and—since I was unable to stomach another hellfire speech—I preferred it that way.

• • •

SWORN AFFIDAVIT

I do solemnly swear or affirm that the information given by me in these reports is the truth, the whole truth, and nothing but the truth. I understand that making a material false statement under oath is a crime, a misdemeanor of the first degree, and punishable as provided under M.L. 875.790.1. My statement is provided willingly. I am of sound mind and fully cognizant of my actions. No promises or threats have been made to me and no pressure or coercion of any kind has been used against me.

SWORN TO AND SUBSCRIBED BEFORE ME THIS ___15___ DAY OF AUGUST

Patrick Stopplecamp   *Spencer Garmond*

LEAGUE ENFORCEMENT OFFICER   AFFIANT

MY SWORN AFFIDAVIT

When I stepped into the bathroom before breakfast the next morning, Nick slipped in behind me and locked the door.

"What are you doing?" I scowled and held up my hands as a barrier. "Get out of here!"

"Tell me about your friend Pasha." Nick leaned in, perfectly groomed and stinking of expensive cologne. "I know he took you to his warehouse gang or whatever, and I know you guys are pals. I want to know everything, about that Anya chick too."

I crossed my arms. "I'm not supposed to talk about it."

Nick's gaze stabbed into mine. "This supersedes protocol."

Yeah, right. "You're not my group leader, Nick. I don't have to tell you squat." I made to exit, but Nick's hand shot out and grabbed my shoulder. He squeezed into a pressure point, sending a paralyzing jolt of pain through me. I elbowed his stomach. Nick's vise loosened enough for me to wrench free.

Nick backed off, jaw twisted like he was biting back some choice words. "Fine. I'll tell you, but if you tell a soul, I'll tell Gabe that you read his assignment card."

"Oh, real nice." Apparently Nick hadn't been asleep that day.

Nick took a deep breath. "It's my assignment. To follow the kid."

"What kid? Me?"

Nick gripped the porcelain sink, his knuckles turning white. "No. Not you, moron. Who cares about watching you? I'm talking about Pasha. Ivan's kid."

I caught on. The whole red card, blue card thing. "You're assigned to follow Pasha? Why?"

"That's not your business, but I need your help. He's slippery, and I can't manage to find out what he's up to."

My eyes went wide. "Oh-ho-ho! So now you need my help? Now you want me to do you a favor, huh? Should've thought about that before, I guess."

His face hardened. "Whatever. I don't need much from you. I just can't seem to find him."

"Maybe that's because you're a bad agent."

Nick's jaw went slack. He glared at me through the reflection in the mirror. "I could arrange an accident that gets you sent home."

I couldn't help but chuckle. "I'm sure you could, Nick." I mean, seriously. What a wannabe mobster. "What do you want to know? Pasha lives in a warehouse with a bunch of homeless guys. They steal junk food. Oh, and he's got a mean jump shot from the top of the key. Guess you can put that in your report."

"You don't know anything about what Pasha and his gang are doing with the field office?"

The question froze my brain for a moment. "Why would Pasha do anything at the field office? He's not in the League."

"But his dad is, moron. You'll tell me if you find out anything, right?"

"Sure." I would rather eat recycled borscht than do Nick's assignment. "Now get lost." I turned around and cranked on the shower.

"What about Anya?"

I turned back to Nick, and an idea popped into my head. I raised my voice over the sound of rushing water. "First tell me about my dad."

A wide grin spread across Nick's face. "Not a chance."

I spun Nick around and shoved him toward the door. "Then get out."

He turned back. "One clue, Garmond. That's all you get.

Twelve or thirteen years ago, a building in downtown LA exploded. Look it up."

I froze, distracted by this clue. Twelve or thirteen years ago was about the time I came to live with Grandma. "That how my mom died?"

"That's all you get."

"Fine." I ran a hand through my hair, pausing to scratch the back of my neck. "Anya is the Russian woman Ryan is assigned to watch."

Nick propped a hand on the wall. "We all heard that much at the field office. What else?"

"She and Pasha have the same tattoo. I'd show you what it looks like, but I already turned in my report."

Nick's eyes narrowed. "What report?"

"Mr. S made me write one."

Nick's nostrils flared, and he mumbled a nasty curse phrase. "Don't mention this to anyone." He slammed the door on his way out.

Good riddance. I locked the door and leaned on the sink. If Nick thought he could blackmail people into doing his job, his future as a spy looked dim. He knew some stuff about my parents, though, and I was going to figure out what.

The train rattled over the familiar route to the HODC, and I sat with Arianna, for once desperate for her biblical wisdom. Wisdom I lacked. I'd asked her a few questions already, and she'd opened up like the chatterbox she was. Guess she wasn't going to gloat about my confession to Mr. S. Girls: Who could figure them out?

"But why would Mr. S say that?" I asked. "How could someone get a demon out of someone else?" I sounded crazy. The words leaving my mouth were insane.

"Because you risked a lot already. Mr. S probably figures you'll try and save Anya. A hero complex from you wouldn't surprise me."

"Save her from what?" I didn't give a rip about helping Anya with anything.

"Demonic possession."

"Why would I do that?" I paused, thinking over what Arianna had implied. "*Can* someone do that?"

"You can do everything through Him who gives you strength."

More Bible verses. I groaned and looked at the ceiling ads. "Yeah, yeah."

Arianna practically sang, "It can't help you if you don't believe."

"I don't know what that means, *Him who gives you strength.* I tune out whenever you talk church stuff. It makes *that* much sense."

She brought a hand over her mouth. "Of course! All this time I *could have* helped you, but didn't know how. You're a Greek!"

I blinked and sat up straighter. Did she just call me a geek?

She laid her hand on my thigh, which, I had to say, crossed a line. "I learned this in church. First Corinthians 1:23 says, 'We preach Christ crucified: a stumbling block to Jews and foolishness to Gentiles.' Historically speaking, when the Jewish people heard of Jesus, since they knew God and lived under His laws, Jesus was a stumbling block to them. You know, something that tripped them up and altered their way of life but wasn't impossible to consider."

She patted my leg to the rhythm of her speech. "But the Greeks didn't know the God of Abraham. They believed in all kinds of false gods. Zeus and Apollo and such. When they heard people talking about Jesus, it sounded like lunacy to them. That's what you're saying, right? When we talk about Jesus, we sound crazy?"

"I guess." She'd gone all mega-preacher on me again, grabbed my leg, and called me a Greek. And she wondered why I thought she was crazy. Why couldn't she just answer my questions?

The train stopped. I bolted out of there and stepped onto the up escalator.

Someone tugged at the base of my T-shirt. I turned. Arianna stood on the step behind mine. "That's how the people are in Japan, Spencer. You need to understand God from the beginning. Did you know you're a sinner?"

My sigh turned into a yawn. "Japan? Arianna, I'm done with this conversation."

"Oh." She bit her bottom lip. "Okay."

Figs and jam. I'd hurt her feelings again. I was such a jerk. "You can tell me sometime, just not now." I didn't know why I was getting soft all of a sudden.

But her silence brought more guilt as we exited onto the street. She only wanted to help. And I'd brought it up. Maybe she was right. Maybe I was a Greek. An interesting idea, maybe, but I'd really rather research this stuff on my own, without Arianna around to interrupt all the time and give me her take on everything. She wasn't the only one with a brain.

255

I attempted a peace offering. "You were about to tell me how to get a demon out of someone?"

She wouldn't look at me.

Come on, girlie. Give me something I can use. "So, how do you do it?"

A crisp breeze hit, sending her bangs straight in the air like some sort of sideways Mohawk. "God does it. If your faith is strong enough, you cast it out in Jesus' name. My dad's done it more than once."

"What's 'cast'? How do you cast?" I pictured Foggé Grief, Sammy's *PoP* magician, casting an inferno spell. Arianna's dad was Special Forces. Is that what Special Forces Agents did?

"Command it to leave by calling on God's authority over it."

"I command it?"

"Well, not you. A follower of Christ. A true servant. Someone gifted in prayer and in sync with God."

I pretended not to notice her snide tone. "How do you get *in sync with God?*"

"Become a Christian. Then pray and read your Bible."

The idea that Mr. S thought I may try and do this demon thing made me laugh. Did the man know anything about me at all? "You really believe all this stuff, don't you?"

"Of course."

"Why?"

"Because it's true. It's my reason for living. Do you think I'm crazy?"

"Duh."

She punched my arm, though it was pathetic compared to the wallops Beth dished out. She tapped me with another one.

I laughed, feigning fear and pain. "Okay, okay, I get that

you think it's true. Just don't hurt me anymore!"

"I don't *think* it's true, Spencer, I *know* it's true."

I took in a deep breath. I so didn't want to go here. But I couldn't afford to alienate her intelligence. Obnoxious as she could be, I needed to stay on her good side. "And how do you know?"

"I can't prove it to you, Spencer. I have no logical, factual evidence to present. I just know in my heart because of the joy I have. I know because I've seen His miracles. I know there's a better place after this life, and I know I'll be there because I've accepted Christ."

Fine. I'd humor her. The time had come to make peace. I groaned in my head before the words left my mouth. "And how do you do that?"

She smiled, eyes twinkling in the sunlight. "I thought you'd never ask."

REPORT NUMBER: 25

REPORT TITLE: Some Homeless People Scam Us
SUBMITTED BY: Agent-in-Training Spencer Garmond
LOCATION: Cafeteria, H.O.D.C., Moscow, Russia
DATE AND TIME: Tuesday, July 15, 3:32 p.m.

I PLUNGED THE GRIMY RAG into the bucket. My eyes watered from bleach and lack of sleep. I'd tossed and turned last night after dreaming that Mission-Ari had cast a demon out of me. I hoped it was a regular nightmare and not the kind that came true.

"Tables never stay clean, do they?" a raspy male voice said. I looked into the tired and friendly face of Viktor. "Nope. I've cleaned these same tables all summer."

Viktor laughed, a wheezy chuckle. "People keep getting hungry."

"Spencer!" Jensina called from the kitchen.

"Aren't you hot?" I mean, I was melting, yet Viktor still

wore that parka.

He patted my shoulder as he walked by. "Take your troubles to the Lord in prayer. It is unwise to face the enemy alone."

Unwise to face who?

"Spencer!" Jensina yelled. "Come here!"

"Hold on!" I turned back to Viktor, but the old man was shuffling toward the exit. Whatever. I went back to washing the table. It was my last—

"Get in here and help me dry these dishes!"

Oh-kay. That girl could stand to OD on chill pills. I stormed across the cafeteria and entered the kitchen. Svetlana stood at the stove, stirring the pot of soup. I smiled at her and forced my gaze to where Jensina stood at the sink. "What is your problem?" I asked.

She gave me a bored stare. "Can you help me now?"

I pitched my rag into the sink; water splashed up onto Jensina's face.

She squealed. "Spencer!"

Svetlana walked up to me, signing something.

The girl had my full attention. I shook my head. "I don't understand."

Jensina wiped suds off her cheek and flung them at me. "She said you're angry."

I crossed my arms. "What? You know sign language?"

"My little brother is hard-of-hearing," Jensina said. "Signing is really different here, but I've learned some of it hanging out with Svetlana."

Svetlana's hands moved fast and stopped, crossed over her chest.

Jensina giggled and signed back to Svetlana. Then both

girls looked to me. "She said, 'You hair is fire . . . Your heart must not burn. Pray, and God will melt your anger with His love.' Aww." She signed to Svetlana. "That was beautiful."

Svetlana held out a dry towel. I snatched it from her and staggered to Jensina's pile of wet dishes.

Everybody wanted me to pray.

Arianna's get-saved speech played in my head every time I saw her. One Saturday, I tried avoiding her by going to the Arbat McDonald's with Gabe, but she invited herself along. Then she had the gall to try to talk us into going to Café *Moo Moo*. Didn't work. It was free time, and we wanted the familiar greasy, salty goodness of the Golden Arches.

I think Arianna expected me to say the Jesus prayer just because she'd explained it, as if her words were some magic spell. I might not think they were all crazy anymore, but that didn't mean I wanted to sign on for full membership.

"Smells like home." Gabe sat at a table outside and stuck a long French fry in his mouth.

I wasn't hungry—overwhelmed by my list of worries. The creepy feeling Anya gave me, the picture she'd taken, the burn on my hand, the vision of her squeezing my face, the vision of Vlad holding me. Viktor's cryptic statements about the enemy. Nick's taunting about my dad and blackmailing me about Pasha. Svetlana's telling me to pray. The fact that Pasha hadn't come to play ball in days. Gabe spending every second working with Isabel on their assignment, and leaving me with Arianna, who was bent on converting me.

Gabe stopped chewing and stared over my shoulder.

I turned. Nick was sitting at a table with a blonde who wore more skin than clothing.

"Who's that with Nick?" Arianna asked.

"Polina," Gabe said, pulling a notebook out of his backpack. He started to write.

I smiled. Nice work, Agent Bo Sto. "Polina! My new best friend."

Arianna dipped a fry in ketchup. "You know her?"

I seized the opportunity of Gabe's distraction to grab a handful of his fries. Hungry or not, eating provided an excuse not to talk to Arianna. I'd never heard of Polina, but if she kept Nick from harassing me, I loved her.

A young boy with a broken arm approached the table, his eyes all zombie-like. He mumbled something, then reached for the food on Arianna's tray.

"Hungry?" Arianna held out the food she'd bought to take back to Isabel.

The boy snatched the bag and raced off, whistling sharply. People swarmed him from four different directions. Two little girls, a teenage boy, an old woman, and a young woman holding a baby. They huddled in the street around the boy, whose arm was *completely* fine. The old woman took the bag of food and inspected the contents. The children waited until she nodded her approval. Then they devoured Isabel's meal in seconds.

My jaw dropped, and I grinned at Arianna. "They scammed you!"

The old woman bowed to Arianna. "Blaga Slovenia." *God bless you.*

Arianna looked at me, her bottom lip trembling. Tears

261

welled in her eyes. Within seconds they trickled down her cheeks. She buried her head in her arms on the table and sobbed. Should I do something? Say something?

She jumped up suddenly. "Come on." She sniffled and gathered her trash. "We're going back."

Gabe glanced at Nick and wrote something in his notebook. I swiped another one of his fries. Eating one had made me hungry.

"Pay attention, Gabriel Stopplecamp!" Arianna said.

Gabe looked up slowly, his eyes a white blur behind his glasses.

Arianna pointed at the family. "Did you see they sent the boy over, faking a broken arm?"

"I saw," Gabe said.

She clapped her hands. "Now! Move it! This is an emergency! We have to talk to Tatyana."

We? I glanced at Gabe, who shoved his notebook and pen into his backpack. He stood and tossed his pack over one arm. Arianna pulled me to standing and pushed me in the direction of the apartment. I stepped back to the table and shoved one last handful of fries into my mouth. So good.

Back at the apartment, Arianna spilled the whole story to Tatyana. "How can we help them? They need a home and jobs, maybe daycare for the baby so the mother can work. Did you know people do that to get food?"

"You mean scam people?" I said.

Arianna shot a scowl my way. "I mean, so desperate for food they make their children lie."

"It is problem," Tatyana said. "That is why we start HODC, to help."

"How can you be sure you're serving everyone?" Arianna

asked. "Clearly these people have slipped through a crack."

"We cannot help everyone," Tatyana said. "Not everyone is coming to us."

"You're giving up?" Arianna's voice shook. "But those children . . ."

Tatyana frowned. "I am understanding how you feel, but panhandlers, especially children, do well in tourist areas. Why work if they can eat for free?"

Eating sounded so good. I went into the kitchen and opened the fridge. If people wanted free food, the HODC was open. If they didn't, what did I care? I grabbed a banana.

"But where do they live?" Arianna sniffled, and I hoped that she wasn't about to explode into hysterics again.

"Is difficult to say," Tatyana said. "Some share apartments with other families. Some sleep in the park, subway stations, alleys, abandoned buildings . . ."

I pictured the Bratva boys snuggled in their mildewed nests.

Arianna's voice quivered again. "There must be something we can do."

"Give them a flyer or something," I said over a mouthful of banana.

"Great idea," Tatyana said. "We can only help those who are wanting help."

"Why not make them come?" Arianna's eyes grew wild. "The politsia could make people take the program at the HODC if they're caught stealing or panhandling. Once they're there, they'll see how great it is and want to change."

I went to the living room. I sank into the sofa beside Gabe, who was scribbling in his Nick notebook. Isabel and Beth came out of the girls' room and sat at the table beside Mr. S.

"Arianna," Mr. S said, "the fact that your heart breaks for the lost is evidence of great love and mercy. But please understand that God doesn't force people to love Him. Some choose not to. You can share the gospel and love others, but you can't decide for anyone."

"He's wasting his time," I whispered to Gabe. "She'll never grasp *that* concept."

Arianna looked around the room with big puppy-dog eyes. "I guess I see what you're saying. We shouldn't force them to come to the center . . . because God doesn't want us to control others."

"Exactly," Mr. S said.

"But my word for the year is 'service.' How can I serve those people?" Arianna asked.

"'It is a very difficult job, being the servant of two masters.'" Mr. S said. "To truly serve God, you must sacrifice your agenda for His. Love people, give to them, pray for them, but remember, it's God's will be done, not yours."

Tears ran down Arianna's cheeks, and she wiped them away. "Can we pray right now?"

I groaned inside and eyed the door to the boys' room. But Beth and Isabel were here, so leaving now would make me look bad.

"You bet," Mr. S said. "You open, I'll close."

Everyone circled around Arianna, holding hands. I ended up between Gabe and Beth, whose natural grip was a little strong. I gripped back and instantly regretted it when Beth crushed my fingers.

Arianna prayed for the homeless. Gabe prayed for Pasha and his friends. Isaac prayed for the HODC. Isabel prayed for our group to get along. Beth prayed that evil would be far from us. Jensina prayed for Ryan. There was this ominous silence then, and I knew they were waiting to see if I was going to take a turn. No way. So finally, Mr. S closed, praying we would all use discernment to make good choices.

I winced, and not from Beth's iron grip.

REPORT NUMBER: 26

REPORT TITLE: I Discover a Traitor
SUBMITTED BY: Agent-in-Training Spencer Garmond
LOCATION: Backyard Basketball Court, H.O.D.C., Moscow, Russia
DATE AND TIME: Saturday, July 19, 9:12 a.m.

MY BASKETBALL TOURNAMENT DISTR ACTED ME from my long list of burdens. I couldn't wait to play a real game. Gabe and I hauled folding chairs out to the court and placed them along one side.

Four teams had signed up to compete. Isaac, Jake, Nick, Beth, Jensina, and I comprised the American team. Jensina told me Ryan had backed out of being our coach after all my meddling in his case, but she'd convinced him to coach anyway, since it was for a good cause. Whatever.

The second team included people who had gone through the center in some way. People from Tatyana's church made up the third team, and the fourth team, I was glad to see, was

Pasha and his Bratva friends. Maybe Pasha would get his friends involved in the HODC now that they'd been here.

I shook the thought from my mind. I was starting to think like Mission-Ari. At least the open house had brought out a few spectators. All my chairs had bodies in them, and there were more people standing around. Sweet!

With only four teams, it was a pretty short tournament. Our team and Pasha's team crushed our opponents and moved on to play in the final game.

The scrappy play of Pasha's team had me bruised all over, but I fed off the adrenaline and pushed myself harder. The game went back and forth, each team fighting for the lead. Mr. S wasn't a half-bad ref. At halftime, we were behind by five. My team joined Ryan on the metal chairs. I paced and guzzled water.

Nick rubbed his arm and glared across the court at Yuri. "What's that little guy's problem? Spencer should guard him, they both play rough."

"If you'd pass the ball," I said, "he wouldn't be all over you."

"I'd pass the ball if there was someone to pass to," Nick said.

Beth crushed an empty paper cup with one hand and tossed it under her feet. "Tiger's been wide open like six times already."

"Me too," Jensina said, panting. She looked like a tough Anime chick with her hair done in two stubby braids: one black, one red.

Nick smirked at me. "Let me rephrase: I'd pass the ball if I saw anyone *worth* passing to."

I clenched my jaw and stalked a safe distance away from

Nick. He was the one who wasn't worth it.

Ryan clapped his hands in a symbol of motivation. "Beth, go in for Nick."

"Oh, come on!" Nick yelled.

"Let's get the ball to Isaac and Jake down below," Ryan said. "We're taller than they are! Let's use that."

As I took my position on the court, I heard Ryan speak to Nick. "This is a team sport. If you can't play with the team, you can sit on the bench. It's supposed to be fun."

Ryan's words upped my opinion of him. Just a smidge.

I brought the ball down and checked my teammates' locations. Pasha rested on the Bratva bench, and Yuri now guarded me. He stayed back, waiting for me to make a move. I stopped and faked a pass to Jensina. Yuri tried to intercept it, so I pivoted around him and lobbed a shot-like pass to Isaac for an easy layup.

Cheers erupted from the small crowd. I took my defensive position at the other end of the court, accepting high fives from Beth and Isaac.

"Nice pass," Isaac said.

"Nice shot."

The pass to Isaac recharged me. I swiped the ball from Yuri and scored on the fast break. Arianna and Isabel cheered my name. I grinned. Surprisingly, Jensina had a great outside shot, and if the ice fairy could get open—and manage to *catch* the ball—she scored every time. Beth was a powerhouse on rebounds, knocking Vlad and Yuri to the ground with mad elbows. We took the lead and began to pull ahead.

Late in the game, while waiting for the ball to be inbounded, I overheard Gabe and Pasha having a heated discussion on the bench. What was Gabe doing on the Bratva side, anyway?

Rough as they were, Bratva couldn't keep up and lost the game 68–55. After we all shook hands, the girls came out to congratulate us.

Isabel gave me a wide smile. "You were awesome, Espensor! I would hug you, but you're all sweaty."

Beth hugged me despite the sweat. I didn't know if that made me like her more or less.

"Well done, all of you." Arianna swept out onto the court in a red, white, and blue striped skirt and gave out awkward high fives. "Jensina, your aim is really good."

"Thanks." Jensina smiled bigger than I had ever seen.

Tatyana addressed the crowd in Russian, so I didn't catch all of it. Something about thanks for being here, food in the cafeteria, and please go back and tell people about us. Maybe she meant "come back sometime" or "go out and tell people." Hey, I was proud that I caught that much.

Gabe and Pasha were talking under the hoop. I started toward them, but Gabe's words slowed my steps.

"Tatyana's worried. Your parents are worried. They love you."

Pasha folded his arms. "They care only that I follow their rules, always comparing me to Tatyana."

"Tell them how you feel," Gabe said. "Maybe they'll understand how unhappy you are."

"Nyet!" Pasha screamed. "I am done wasting life there. They did not see me before, and now they ask why. They care only how they look to others. I have real family now. Life is better with my brothers."

I walked closer. Gabe was trying to help again, but Pasha didn't want it.

"Sleeping in a warehouse and breaking the law is no life," Gabe said.

"*Perestan'!*" *Stop it!* "You know nothing of Bratva. We have power no one can hurt."

"That isn't true," Gabe said. "You're hurting yourself."

"You are same as them, judging, pretend to know everything. No more!" Pasha jogged away.

Gabe stepped after him but stopped when he saw me. He grimaced. "I tried."

"Let it go," I said.

"I should at least apologize."

"What for? You did all you could."

"No. I want him to know I don't judge him. I'll be right back."

Gabe started away, but I grabbed his arm. "Hold on. We're not supposed to leave without telling someone. Your dad will have a fit."

"You're one to talk. Look, I'll catch him before he gets too far."

Gabe took off after Pasha. I joined him. In the distance ahead, Pasha's legs carried him in marathon strides toward the metro station.

Taking the train without permission was a no-no. Not that I minded. I was just supporting Gabe. We ran onto the waiting train and it started to move. The air conditioning chilled my sweaty skin.

I grabbed a handhold near the door. "I hope he was on this one."

When the train stopped, I poked my head out the doors and scanned the platform without getting off. I shook my head. "Don't see him."

I sat down beside Gabe, and the train pulled away.

"Nice game, huh?" Gabe said.

"Yeah. It felt good to play again." As the train slowed to a stop, I stood and approached the doors. "Paveletskaya Station." I marked Pasha taking the escalator steps two at a time. "Bingo."

We chased Pasha through the city until the smell of oil and urine jogged my memory. "He's heading for the warehouse."

Gabe put out his hand. "Let's slow down a little, then. I don't want any trouble."

This from the guy who just broke his dad's rules.

The sound of voices brought me to a halt. I crouched behind a dumpster that stank of rotten food, and I peeked around it. Pasha greeted some familiar faces and gestured at someone sitting on a wooden crate.

Gabe elbowed me in the ribs and pointed. Pasha moved to the left and the figure on the crate became visible. I froze.

Anya!

I waved a fly away from my ear and strained to understand their conversation, wishing I'd studied Russian harder.

All I could make out was that Anya wanted some kind of code and Pasha would get it from his father.

My heart raced. All this time Pasha had been helping Anya? What a fool I'd been to miss that. The same tattoo, Pasha claiming his parents hated him. But a traitor to his dad? Why?

Anya stood up and Pasha and some Bratva boys crowded around her crate. Pasha pulled a knife from his pocket and pried the lid. He withdrew a carton of cigarettes and ripped it open. He shoved a couple of packs into his pocket and tossed the carton to the guy beside him. He spoke Russian to a chunky dude, who heaved the crate onto his shoulder and carried it into the warehouse.

Anya mentioned the code again. Pasha asked when she was going someplace. And Anya said tonight.

Then Pasha walked into the warehouse and Anya followed. Gabe pulled my sleeve. "Let's get out of here."

"I can't believe it." I put my head into my hands and pulled my hair. Gabe and I sat on the metro, heading back to the apartment. "What's Pasha's problem? Ivan and Lena and Tatyana are nice people. He could have a perfect life, and he gives it up for cigarettes?"

Gabe gazed out the window. "He really believes they don't care."

Moron. *My* dad didn't care. "What are we going to do? I promised your dad I'd stay away from Anya. He's going to flip."

"You didn't follow Anya. I followed Pasha, and Anya was there."

"He's not going to believe me. Grandma never believes me." She'd branded me the trouble-making jock for years.

"My dad will."

I shot Gabe a skeptical look and clenched my fists. Emotions fizzed out of me like steam in Grandma's kettle. Pasha was a traitor, like my dad. "Why do people hurt their family?"

Gabe looked up, his expression blank.

"You're supposed to love your family. Look out for them. Why does God let this stuff happen?"

"God doesn't force people to be nice. I think He hopes we can take the bad things in life and use them to help others."

Help others with bad things? "I don't get it."

Gabe shifted in his seat. "Take Pasha. I feel bad for him because I know he's hurt. I tried to help, but I couldn't. Coming from me it's just another goody-goody Christian trying to boss him, telling him to obey God and his parents. But from you it would be different."

I stared, slack-jawed. "Are you kidding me?" Where was Gabe going with this?

"Your dad left or whatever, which was horrible. I'm just saying—and I could be totally off-base—but what if God wants you to use that experience to help you connect to Pasha in a way I can't."

That was crazy talk. "You think God let my dad betray my mom and leave me without a father or a real family so thirteen years later I could tell some Russian gang kid I know how he feels?"

Gabe smoothed out a wrinkle on his polo shirt. "Maybe. Sort of."

We rode in silence for several stops before Gabe spoke again. "Look, you never said what happened, but God didn't make your dad do what he did. For whatever reason, your dad made that choice. God knows it hurt you, though, and He knows your pain will help you relate to Pasha. Suffering makes us stronger, and pain teaches us, if we let it. So . . . you should be way smarter than me." Gabe stuttered out an awkward laugh.

I took in the words but didn't respond. Beth had said God

works through all things for good. So how could God possibly use Pasha and Anya's little chat? Maybe the good was that Gabe and I could warn the field office. Then what good had come from my dad's betrayal? My mom was dead. Talking to Pasha wouldn't change that. I still had to live with Grandma instead of Kimbal. I stared out the window into the tunnel's blackness, tuning out the voices and the sound of the train, trying to act like the ache in my gut wasn't really there.

"Spencer, you okay?" Arianna asked again.

I nodded, staring into space. I'd been sitting in the chair in the corner of the living room since Gabe and I had returned. Gabe had confessed to his dad, who had immediately called Ivan. Isaac had gotten in my face about running off without telling him, like Isaac was my grandma or something. Then Arianna had wanted to know if I was okay. After that, Nick had asked what Pasha was up to, and now Arianna was back. I didn't want to talk.

"Why is everyone grilling me?" I snapped at Arianna. "Gabe was there too! Ask him!" I hadn't done anything wrong. *I* wasn't the traitor.

I still wore my game clothes, which were stiff with dried sweat. Numbness filled every pore, like I was recovering from a wound I couldn't see or feel. Emotional paralysis, maybe. Breathing took all my strength. Even sleep seemed too difficult. Movement would not come, words would not come. I was empty.

The thing was, Gabe's words from the train made sense. I

blamed God for the bad things in my life. I took great care to avoid getting too close to people so I wouldn't get hurt. But it didn't always work. I couldn't control Pasha or Nick or my dad. And playing video games and goofing off with Kip and Sammy was fun, but it was a way to ignore dealing with my issues. I saw that now.

I hated the idea that God might have a plan He wasn't sharing with me. At the same time, the idea brought a strange comfort. Why worry if God was in control? Maybe I was trying too hard to live. Maybe I should just go with it, checking everything against the handy-dandy Bible, of course, or praying or whatever. Arianna would be thrilled.

A door clicked shut, and silence filled the room. I scanned the apartment and stood. Where had everyone gone? I walked to the kitchen. Muffled voices drifted from the girls' room. I strained to hear but couldn't make anything out. Voices were clearer at the boys' door.

"We lift up . . . shield him . . . ask You for help . . ."

They were praying. I put my hand on the doorknob to go inside when a new voice began.

"Jesus, please help Spencer . . . He doesn't understand . . ."

Gabe's voice. I froze, my stomach churning. The voices rose a little from the girl's door. I whipped around, realization dawning.

No way. They were all praying for me.

Heat rushed over me. The hair on the back of my neck danced. I bolted out the front door, down the stairs, and out into the comfort of the noisy city.

REPORT NUMBER: 27

REPORT TITLE: The Bad Guys Nearly Catch Me
SUBMITTED BY: Agent-in-Training Spencer Garmond
LOCATION: Outside, Arbat Ulitsa, Moscow, Russia
DATE AND TIME: Saturday, July 19, 4:47 p.m.

I WANDERED THE STREET, my blood boiling in my veins.

God, I know I haven't said any prayer that makes me a Christian, so I guess You can't help me. I mean, I'm not perfect like them.

There is no one perfect. Not one.

Tell them that. They seem to think they've got it all figured out. I mean, why make this difficult, God? Why not prove it if You're there?

Blessed are those who believe who have not seen.

"Stupid Bible memory verses," I mumbled aloud.

I hesitated at the entrance to the Internet Café.

I could catch her.

It's not your job.

I went inside and paid for the use of a computer. I sat at an empty station and signed in to my Russian account. The screen blinked: You have one unread message.

My muscles tensed. Here we go.

I don't need prayer. I need them to believe me. I'm right about Anya, and I can prove it.

They won't listen to you. They know you're not a Christian, and they don't want you looking better than them.

That's not true.

Yes, it is. how would it look if a kid solved Ryan's case?

I'm not a kid. I can catch her. I can prove it. Then they'll see I'm not just a moron in sneakers. Then they'll have to admit that God gave me an ability he didn't give them.

They'll think you're crazy.

I'm not crazy!

They think so. That's why they're praying. They probably think a demon possessed you.

"Shut up!" Several heads turned and stared my way. I slouched in my chair and opened the message.

Dear Biff,

Life can be hard and cruel. People who misuse their power over others are the cause. Bratva can teach you to connect with this inner power and master it—for good purposes. We are a family that takes care of each other. We accept you, whether you are homeless, a criminal, handicapped, male, female, or lost for whatever reason. We accept all people. Bratva does not discriminate.

We invite you to a free informational meeting at our headquarters this Saturday at 6:00 p.m. Come hear our offer. If you need a family to love you as you are, we are that family.

You are in our thoughts, Biff.

Sincerely,

Dmitri Berkovich, President

Volgogradskiy prosp., 92

Nice form letter. The name Dmitri Berkovich rang a bell, though I couldn't remember why. If only I still had the research I'd given to Mr. S.

The computer clock read 5:02 p.m. An hour until the Bratva meeting. Coincidence? God telling me to go? I logged onto the chat room, but it was empty. I mapped the location of the meeting and printed it out.

Two metro trains and forty-five minutes later, I exited Kuz'minki Station on the southeast side of Moscow under the alias Foggé Grief. *Biff Gar* didn't sound like a real name, so I borrowed Sammy's *PoP* character.

I made my way along Volgogradskiy prospect and stopped in front of number 92, trying to regain the confidence that had subsided during the lengthy train ride. An impressive stone building loomed over ten stories high. The top tapered into a point, tier upon tier like a square wedding cake. A large staircase marked the entrance.

I checked the address again. No floor or suite number. Strange.

I tucked my cross necklace into my neckline and climbed the stairs. Midway through the revolving door, I caught my unkempt reflection in the glass. I straightened my Lakers cap over my matted hair and smoothed my wrinkled T-shirt and shorts. It would have to do.

Three steps into the lobby I understood the lack of specifics on the address. Bratva seemed to own the whole building. I stopped in the center of a vast lobby and fixed my eyes on the large graphic logo staring down at me from the vaulted ceiling, less detailed, but identical to Pasha's tattoo. Around me, receptionists answered calls and people waited in lines.

Posters of the tattoo logo hung six feet apart around the lobby ceiling. Every fourth one read "Find the power within" in English beneath the labyrinth logo. TV monitors hung between the posters, running footage of testimonies of what Bratva had done in people's lives.

Looked like Bratva consisted of a whole lot more than Vlad's warehouse gang. An eerie indigestion spiked in my gut. What was I doing here?

A young man in a red blazer approached. "Can I help you?"

I fought to keep my voice smooth. "I'm here for the meeting at six."

"Amerikantsy?" I nodded.

"My name is Filipp. The meeting is on the tenth floor. I can take you there."

"Spasiba." *Thanks.*

Filipp led me into a crowded elevator that zipped to the ninth floor in less time than it took to do five at the field office. Bratva must be loaded.

On nine, the doors opened to a party. All but Filipp and I exited onto a dark floor where throngs of people flickered under strobe lights. Two giddy young women stumbled into the elevator. As the doors slid shut, I glimpsed a boy my age in a room across the hall getting an injection in his forearm. I choked on my own breath and clutched the handrail. I was an idiot. I'd be lucky not to be arrested.

One of the women nudged me and spoke in slurred Russian, her eyes bloodshot, her breath DUI-worthy.

I didn't understand her, so I said, "Ya ne ponimayu." I stared at a cotton ball taped below the inside of her elbow and wondered what she was on. Meth, maybe?

When the doors opened on ten, Filipp escorted me past a large ballroom crowded with people, and into to a smaller room. I counted at least thirty people milling around, chatting. The familiar sound of English met my ears in every direction, calming me some. Pastries and pitchers of water filled a table in the corner. My stomach growled, reminding me that I'd skipped lunch, and I headed toward the food.

A round, balding man approached me at the buffet table. "Have you done this before?" His twangy accent was like a cowboy's. "I was in a similar group in Alabama and haven't received connection since I left. I sure need it."

Connection? I tensed at the man's phrasing and grabbed a cream-filled pastry.

"We are to begin," a female voice said through a microphone. A young woman dressed in a red jacket, like Filipp's, stood at the podium at the front of the room.

People scrambled to sit. I took a second pastry and sat in the back row.

"Welcome," the woman said in English. "We are happy you have come. Please forgive my poor English as I speak. It is not mistake you have come here. Please to feel welcome and to find what you are searching for."

I bit into my pastry. What am I looking for? Anya? Demons?

"I am Nadejda. I want to share with you my heart. When I became thirteen, my mother marry horrible man. His fits caused so much pain, and Mother lost job from too many days sick. Not many days later, this man kill my mother and so I run away to live on streets.

"I begged for money and did much drugs and prostitution. I wanted death. My father of birth abandoned me, my mother abandoned me, God abandoned me. Many days went by and a man brought me here, to Bratva. When I made connection with power inside me and unleashed my light, my life had meaning."

I shoved the last half of the pastry into my mouth. What kind of power did people have inside them that unleashed light? It sounded like a crock.

The woman went on. "Maybe you are also lost and hurting. You are not victim. Many religions will teach a God who controls life on this earth. I ask to you, what kind of God hurts? What kind of God is silent?"

Her words had transfixed me. I braced myself for her claim that there was no God. It seemed to be where she was headed, but she didn't go there.

"Bratva can teach ways to personal inner power and strength. I have felt this. Many do not know about this inside power. At Bratva, we care about each other without asking questions of judgement. Come to us.

"Dmitri Berkovich is the founder of Bratva. He will speak in moment. We now will pass out information about Bratva programs of scholarship. Please complete registration so you can start process today. If you allow, Bratva will provide path to inner power and love. Thank you."

Scattered applause broke out. Nadejda nodded in thanks

and walked around to the back of the room, joining two more redcoats at a table.

A bearded redcoat handed me a red folder. The tattoo logo stared up at me, embossed in gold on the glossy surface. The room was silent except for shuffling papers. The girl in front of me scribbled on her registration like she was being timed.

Creepy knots cinched in my gut. This place was Bogus City. What kind of people partied this early? Why were people getting injections? What had the balding dude meant by receiving connection? And what power did these people think they had inside them? A door up front opened, and a huge man dressed like a secret service agent, with black hair, dark eyes, and black suit, bounded toward the podium.

"Good evening. I am Dmitri Berkovich." I shivered at his deep growling voice. His English was much better than Nadejda's. "Welcome to Bratva. We are in the business of helping people. We ask nothing of you but to allow us teach you to use the power you already have, so you can experience life the way we do, with joy and control over your destiny. I will be here to answer any questions you may have. Thank you."

People clapped. Dmitri marched to the table in the back and sat beside Nadejda. I wrinkled my nose. Was I supposed to be impressed with that pathetic speech? The crowd flooded toward the table, so I jumped up too. Since I was in the back, I got there first.

The balding Alabama man bumped into my back as people crowded the table.

"Do you have your registration ready?" Nadejda asked me.

"No. I uh . . . wanted to ask if you know a friend of mine. Her name is Anya. She told me to come by." My voice came out smooth despite the pounding in my chest. Oscar performance, baby.

Until Dmitri's dark eyes probed like x-rays, and my hands trembled. I clenched them into fists as the creepy chills Anya gave me returned, stronger this time. Dark and cold. Sweat prickled my brow, and my breathing quickened. I coughed to hide it and broke eye contact, and the intensity faded some.

Dmitri's voice purred. "A friend of Anya's is dear to me. What is your name?"

"Spen—Grief. Foggé Grief."

"Nice to meet you, Foggé. What brings you to Moscow?"

"T-tourist." *Breathe, dude.*

Dmitri tried to look in my eyes, but I turned to Nadejda. "Do I have to get the tattoo? I've got a thing about needles."

Dmitri's booming laugh vibrated the table. "No, Foggé. That is a mark of appreciation and loyalty. It is a choice. Everything here is *your* choice. The power is within you to decide, however, you may change your mind about needles to receive connection."

I paled.

"Are you joining us today?" Dmitri asked. "I would love to connect with you. Have you seen our ninth floor?"

I accidentally glanced into Dmitri's eyes, and this time I couldn't look away. Something in the man's stare held me immobile. Petrified. Something black and moving.

Dizziness plowed through me like a point guard on his way to the hoop.

"Are you okay?" a woman asked.

I gasped and found myself kneeling on the floor, woozy and nauseated. I blinked my eyes into focus. "What happened?"

Nadejda was crouched beside me. "You fell. Have you

JILL WILLIAMSON

eaten?"

"I don't feel good." I swallowed and tried to stand. "I should go."

Nadejda helped me up. "What about your registration?"

I shook my head and backed away. I wanted to leave. "Some other time."

Dmitri stood, an immense shadow to my left. The man's powerful gaze chased me out the door. In the hall, I forced my legs toward the elevator. Voices raised in the room behind me.

Okay. Please, God. help me get out of here.

Strength wrapped around me like warm-up sweats. I beat the down button several times with the end of my fist.

Come on! Come on!

Eternity seemed to pass before the doors slid open and I fell inside. My reflection in the glossy elevator wall looked worse than before. My shirt clung to my chest. My cheeks were feverish. Thankfully, the elevator went straight to the lobby without stopping. I stared at the doors, willing them to open. When they finally parted, Filipp and a uniformed guard blocked the exit.

Mother pus bucket!

"Excuse me, sir," Filipp said. "I believe you forgot something upstairs. Would you come with us for a moment?"

I forced a calm expression. "I didn't forget anything."

"Are you Mr. Grief?" Filipp asked.

"No."

Filipp glanced at the guard and frowned. "What is your name, sir?"

"Spencer Garmond." I winced as my real name left my mouth, wishing I could catch the words and stuff them back in.

The portly guard stepped forward. "Pokazhite vashi

pashport."

My heart raced. I'd left my passport at the apartment. "Are you politsia?"

"He is security for the building," Filipp said.

"Um, sure, hold on a sec." I walked out of the elevator and fumbled with the folder they'd handed out upstairs, as if my visa was tucked inside. I dropped the folder, flipping the pages onto the floor in as big of a mess as possible. "Whoops! Sorry about that."

"Let me help." Filipp stooped to gather the papers.

The guard crouched beside Filipp. With both men distracted, I pushed Filipp hard into the guard. They lost their balance and fell to the floor.

"Izveenee!" *Sorry!* I called over my shoulder. I sprinted from the building in the direction of the metro without looking back.

I leaped down the escalator steps and squeezed between the closing doors of the train just before it pulled away. My heart rattled around inside me like a pinball. This train would take me all the way to Barrikadnaya Station, but should I get off at the field office or transfer back to the apartment? Either way, I had to get off at Barrikadnaya. The field office could be closed, so it was probably best to return to the apartment.

As the train sped along, I couldn't shake the evil sensation choking my breath. Was this how discernment felt? Smothered, like Mr. S had said? I shoved my hands between my knees and glanced around the train, observing the other passengers. Was I being followed?

Several times now I'd heard the word *connection*. Anya had said it to Pasha, and the balding man and Dmitri had said it to me. Did connection have something to do with drugs?

Was it the name of a drug? Was that how Dmitri had wanted to *connect* with me on the ninth floor? I forced deep calming breaths out my nose. I'd been so stupid to go there.

Barrikadnaya Metro Station overflowed with people. I darted through the crowd like a cricket. But I'd never entered the station from this direction and was totally turned around. I followed the crowd up an escalator and realized too late that I was exiting the station. I'd have to go back down to make my transfer to Smolenskaya.

A woman's voice, angry and familiar, shouted in Russian. I whipped around. Anya stood in the center of a group of four large men at the foot of the escalator below. In my mind I cursed like a trucker, all attempts at cleaning up my mouth lost to fear. Anya's voice grew softer as the escalator carried me higher.

I faced forward just as three men stepped onto the down escalator. My stomach lurched, and I squatted, pretending to tie my shoe. The creepy, evil Anya-Dmitri feeling coursed through my veins. Crouching, I stepped off the escalator. Someone grabbed my arm.

I jumped back into a group of people and tried to pull away.

"Don't be afraid, Spencer. It is only me."

Viktor. I breathed a sigh of relief as the warm, familiar tingle flowed through me at Viktor's touch. "I can't talk now, Viktor. I'm kind of in a hurry."

"Take my hat and coat." The old man pulled a fur hat over my Lakers cap. He shook off his parka and helped me into it. "They are looking for you. Go on foot, and you will be safe. Take Novinsky Boulevard all the way."

My mind blinked a dozen questions at once.

"Don't ask questions. Just go." Viktor pushed me toward the doors.

Fleeing the station, I ran for Novinsky Boulevard. I sprinted, jogged when I got winded, and ran some more when my breath returned. It was only a mile to the apartment, but I couldn't get there fast enough. Viktor's parka stuck to my arms, but it increased my girth, and I welcomed the disguise. It also shrouded me in that same strong, warm feeling.

I stopped at a crosswalk and waited for the signal. Jaywalking, although tempting, was a bad idea. Cars didn't stop for pedestrians in Moscow. Still, I made good time, even with slowing to look over my shoulder every five steps. Ten minutes later, I zipped into the apartment building on Arbat Street and trudged up the stairs.

I hoped that no one had missed me, that I could sneak into the boys' room and climb into bed. I tried the boys' door and found it locked.

I paced back and forth outside the apartment. I had no clue what time it was—dark. I'd been gone for hours. I hadn't bothered to take my key with me when I'd left, either. Defeated, I cranked the knob on the main door. The warmth and smell of something meaty weakened my knees. I stood motionless in the doorway as every face in the apartment stared at me like I was a ghost.

REPORT NUMBER: 28

REPORT TITLE: I Confess My Late-Night Outing
SUBMITTED BY: Agent-in-Training Spencer Garmond
LOCATION: Arbat Ulitsa, 43, Moscow, Russia
DATE AND TIME: Saturday, July 19, 8:42 p.m.

"SPENCER!" KERRI RUSHED TO EMBRACE me. She grabbed my cheeks and looked me up and down. "You're burning up!"

Mr. S stormed over, face as red as if he were the one who'd just run a mile and a half in a parka. "We've been worried sick! It's been nearly four hours!"

Isaac ran across the room, bare feet slapping on the tile. "Didn't we talk about going solo? I need your location at all times!"

"Whose coat and hat?" Gabe asked.

"You look like a bum!" Nick called from a sofa in the living room.

Mr. S yelled, "Everyone, to bed!"

Jensina stood from the sofa, holding a thick book against her chest. "It's not even nine o'clock!"

"You don't have to sleep, just go to your rooms." Mr. S shot death glares around the room like lasers that made the students scatter.

Arianna towed Mary and Martha into the girls' room. I remained in the doorframe, mortified that everyone had witnessed my latest blunder.

Kerri pulled me inside and shut the door. "Did you eat? Are you hungry?"

My emotions caught up with me like a slap to the face. I leaned against the door frame and slid to the floor. I clutched my knees and buried my face into them. I couldn't explain why I felt so vulnerable. Maybe the fact that I was now safe from the evil I'd faced had shattered my tough-guy exterior.

Kerri sat beside me and wedged her arm around my shoulder, pulling me close. Her affection didn't help me fight off my emotions. I held my breath and steeled myself against a total meltdown.

At the sound of metal scraping on tile, I looked up. Mr. S had pulled a chair over from the table. He sat and propped his elbows on his knees. "I'm sorry I yelled. I'm glad you're safe, Spencer. It was a while before anyone realized you were gone, then we split up and looked until I received an urgent call from Ivan.

"Every intercessor at the Moscow Field Office had received your name in the last few hours. And that's a pretty big deal. This hasn't happened since . . . well, never in my experience. So I panicked, and we prayed for the next hour, all of us. We didn't know what else to do."

My body went rigid as everything came back in a rush. "You *prayed? Again?*" My voice shook. "Look, I know I don't belong here, but I'm not crazy, and I don't need everyone praying for me like I'm some kind of helpless freak!"

Mr. S's forehead wrinkled. "Spencer, we only prayed after Ivan's call. I understand how you feel, but under the circumstances, prayer was perfectly justifiable. We were all very worried."

"I'm not talking about then! I'm talking about before— about why I left in the first place. I can't be around a bunch of people who think I'm nuts."

Mr. S shook his head. "Spencer, I—"

"I *heard* them praying!"

"'It is a wise father that knows his own child.' Just a minute, okay?" Mr. S stood, walked to the boys' door, knocked, and went in, leaving me alone with Kerri.

"I'm sorry you're sad," she said. "Did someone say you were crazy?"

"No."

"Then why do you think that's how everyone feels?"

"I heard them praying for me like I'm some kind of idiot loser who isn't as smart as them with all their memory verses and perfection and good grades. Arianna thinks I'm going to hell. And Gabe thinks I'm a player. And Nick has hated me for years."

"Oh, don't worry about him." She squeezed my shoulder." I think maybe there's some confusion in all this. Pat will figure it out. He's good at that."

Prickles stabbed behind my eyes. I'd never known what it was like to have a mom. I was torn between giving her the silent treatment and hugging her and bawling my eyes out.

The boys' door opened, and Mr. S returned to his chair. "A simple misunderstanding, I believe." He gave Kerri an exasperated look. "Apparently, Gabe was worried about you—something he said on the train? He felt guilty about upsetting you and said when you sat quietly for nearly two hours he couldn't take it anymore and just had to pray." Mr. S pursed his lips, suppressing a smile.

Kerri snickered and clamped her hand over her mouth.

I looked from Mr. S to Kerri and back and forth as they giggled at some inside joke. I forced a scowl, but it twitched into a grin. Their laughter was contagious. "This isn't funny!"

Kerri exhaled a musical sigh. "Oh, I'm sorry, Spencer. But you have no idea the things my boy gets into his head sometimes. He's a riot. Once he wanted to join the community choir instead of the school choir. I asked why, and he said that the school choir was already made up of Christians, and he needed to evangelize through music. He loves you, Spencer. He talks about you like you're his brother."

Me? Gabe thought I was a womanizing troll. "Wait, *Gabe* got them all to pray for me because he was worried about me?"

Mr. S nodded.

I relaxed a bit, knowing that Gabe had been the ringleader and not Arianna. "Well, he could've said something."

"He did," Mr. S said. "A few of us tried talking to you, as you may recall, but you didn't want to talk."

Gabe had worried about me, like a brother. Gabe was so good to me though, and I'd already betrayed him once by looking at his confidential assignment. I was sure to ruin it. And I didn't want to hurt people like my dad had, but how could I guarantee I wouldn't? Being a jerk ran in my blood.

Worrying about it only exhausted me further. Maybe Mr. S

would let me go to bed. "I'm guess I'm pretty tired."

Mr. S held up a finger. "I'm afraid you don't get off that easy. First of all, they've doubled security tonight at the field office and changed the passwords. Last I heard, there's been no breech." He adjusted his glasses. "I know how Anya makes you feel, so I wanted to ask—are you all right?"

I took the furry hat off my head and adjusted my Lakers cap. "She doesn't bother me unless she touches me or looks into my eyes. Since she didn't see us watching, it wasn't a problem."

But Dmitri's probing stare did float into my mind's eye, sending a shiver up my spine. I should probably confess that whole episode, get it over with. "I did something stupid tonight."

"Something besides running off?" Mr. S said.

I studied a scratch on the floor. "I went to the Internet Café to check my e-mail. Back when I researched the tattoo, I set up a Russian account and e-mailed Bratva. An answer to my e-mail said there was an open house tonight. I was mad and wanted to prove I wasn't crazy, so . . . I went."

Mr. S's eyes bulged. "You *what?*"

"Where was it, Spencer?" Kerri asked.

"Across the city, southeast of the Kremlin."

Kerri whimpered and put her hand over her heart.

"You thought it would be a good idea to go across a foreign city, alone, to the open house of a cult?" Mr. S stood and paced around his chair. His scalp flushed pink. When I didn't answer, he said, "I'm listening," in a tight voice.

"Bratva has their own building. It's huge. Some guy took me to the tenth floor for the meeting, but we stopped on nine where some kind of party was happening. I think people were doing drugs. *Connection*, I think they call it. It might be meth. Anyway, at the meeting this lady said Bratva would help us connect to our 'inner power.' A lot of what she said sounded good, actually. Too good, I guess. The place weirded me out. Then the founder came in. Dmitri Berkovich."

Kerri gasped.

Mr. S stopped pacing. His nostrils flared, and I hoped he wouldn't explode. "Try 'mobster,' Spencer. Dmitri Berkovich is the head of the Russian mafia. There's no proof, of course, but it's common knowledge he's in charge."

My mouth slowly fell open. "Yeah, he looked like a mobster." I huffed a laugh at my own stupidity. "I told him my friend Anya asked me to come."

Kerri brows wrinkled. "Spencer, you didn't."

"That's when it happened again. When he looked at me, I felt the way I felt with Anya, only worse." I told them about blacking out, escaping from the building, and Viktor's help.

Mr. S cupped a hand over his mouth and massaged it. "And who is Viktor?"

"A homeless guy from the HODC. This is his coat and hat. He said he knew I was being followed. That was weird too, now that I think about it. Though Viktor's always been a bit strange."

"You ran all the way from Barrikadnaya Station?" Kerri asked.

"Well, at least now we know why the entire Moscow Intercession Department received your name." Mr. S continued pacing. "I knew he'd be a handful when I read his file," he mumbled. "Ivan should know you're safe and what happened." He left his circle and reached for the phone.

I scrambled to my feet. "What's in my file?"

Mr. S didn't answer. He was already talking on the phone.

I looked down at Kerri. "What's in my file?"

She shook her head and got to her feet. "Nothing that matters."

"Of course it matters! And what's in my dad's file? My mom's file?"

Tears formed at the corners of her eyes. "Oh, honey. We don't have access to your parents' files."

Of course they didn't. "Well, what kind of stuff is in someone's file?"

"Information. Your background, family history, training successes and failures, assignments, communiqués—that sort of thing."

Isaac's warning popped into my mind. "Like if I got in a fight?"

"Yes. Pat makes those notes and sends in a quarterly report. And Isaac and Jake write group reports that Pat sends in with his. If something happens at the student level, and it's not reported by one of those three people, International isn't informed, and it's not in your file. Unless another agent is watching you." She wiggled her eyebrows as if the very idea were a joke.

But I didn't find it funny. Kimbal had been watching me for years. My report was likely as thick as the Los Angeles phone book. "Is that pretty rare? An agent watching a kid?"

"Anything is possible if International thinks it's important."

I thought of Nick spying on Pasha. "How do they know what's important?"

"International has its own intercession team. God gets word to the right people."

I tried to imagine a room filled with intercessors like the one at the Moscow Field Office, only bigger.

Freaky.

Kerri squeezed my shoulder. "Let me get you some dinner. Are you hungry?"

My eyes got big, and I smiled. "Starving."

When I finally went to bed, the room was dark except for Gabe's book light and the dim glow drifting in the window from the streetlamp. Gabe set down his Bible and apologized profusely for his intense prayer vigil.

"It's okay." I sank onto my thin mattress. "I just misunderstood."

The sharp shadows the book light threw off made Gabe's face ghostly. "Dad said it was a bad idea to do what I did the way I did it. But you got to know I meant well."

It didn't matter anymore. I didn't need to hear it. "I know. I . . . you know . . . thanks."

Gabe smiled in relief. "Anytime, man."

"Hey, Garmond," Nick said from his bunk, "if it makes you feel any better, I didn't pray for you. All that praying put me to sleep. I took a nap."

"You know what, Nick? That does make me feel better." After tonight, Nick's brand of evil just wasn't a big deal.

The black silhouette of Nick's head hung over the edge of the top bunk. "They're not kicking you out?"

"Nope. Sorry to disappoint you. I'm not even going home."

"*Man!*" Nick's silhouette shook then disappeared.

"Where'd you go?" Gabe asked. "Dad freaked out. Then Ivan called, and Dad freaked out more."

I filled him in on the whole night's adventure.

Gabe just stared at me when I finally stopped talking. He looked so strange without his glasses on. "You're fearless."

"Nah. I'm just crazy—reckless, like Arianna said." I chuckled at the irony of my words. Now I was claiming my own craziness. "I guess everyone knows me better than I know myself. And now I have to write another report tomorrow while you all go to Tolstoy's house."

Gabe wrinkled his nose. "That stinks. Tolstoy's house is supposed to be cool."

"Yeah, well, I'll just have to wonder."

"It's weird about Viktor," Isaac said. "One day we're going to find out that he's an angel. That no one has ever heard of some homeless guy named Viktor."

I jerked my gaze across the room to Isaac. I'd thought everyone else was asleep. "What do you mean?"

Isaac sat up. The yellowish light from the window lit the back of his head. "Not everyone's seen that dude. I saw him. You and Arianna saw him. But not Jensina or Beth. Tatyana's never heard of him. The other day he said something to me that he couldn't possibly know about. It's weird. This guy could be playing shortstop for Anaheim." He waited for us to react. "Get it? The Angels?"

"Har har," I said. "But just because some homeless dude is hard to keep track of and says freaky things doesn't mean he's an angel." But I pondered this further. Viktor *did* give me a strange feeling when I was around him. Different from the one Anya and Dmitri gave off, but kind of the same in some ways. If demons existed, then why not angels? "Viktor knew they were following me and—"

He wants me to pray.

A chill ran over me, creating goosebumps on my arms. Viktor saved me tonight.

God saved me.

"When did you meet this Viktor guy?" Gabe asked.

"Will you guys stop talking?" Nick yelled. "I'm trying to sleep."

I reached under my bunk and slid out my suitcase. "Few weeks ago," I whispered to Gabe, digging for my mom's letter.

"Why didn't you tell me?"

"You were there. The first day we went to the HODC."

"Shut. Up!" Nick yelled.

"I don't remember him," Gabe whispered.

"What? You and Isaac were right there the first time I met him. Isaac talked to him."

"Okay, guys." Isaac jerked the window blinds closed. "Lights out."

A tiny click of Gabe's book light, and the room went black. I slogged through the darkness toward the bathroom.

I closed the door before turning on the light, sat on the edge of the tub, and scanned the letter my mom had left me.

Trust God always. He's in control ,and His plans are perfect. Stay close to Him in prayer, for that relationship will be your best protection in any circumstance and your only hope of seeing me again.

I marveled at the confirmation in my hands. My mom had wanted me to pray too.

Maybe I should.

REPORT NUMBER: 29

REPORT TITLE: I Have the Worst Nightmare Yet
SUBMITTED BY: Agent-in-Training Spencer Garmond
LOCATION: Arbat Ulitsa, 43, Moscow, Russia
DATE AND TIME: Saturday, July 20, 8:02 a.m.

SINCE EVERYONE ELSE WAS EATING BREAKFAST, I took my time getting dressed. The tile floor felt cool beneath my feet, but it wouldn't last. Only the mornings were cool now. By day, the summer heat of Moscow would blaze.

Still embarrassed over yesterday's pray-fest, I entered the center apartment and shot straight through the kitchen to my chair in the corner. I plopped down and stared at the TV. A figure grew in the corner of my eye, heading my way. I pretended to be engrossed in the morning news. The form stopped.

Ryan. Hands on hips, ready to fight. I kept my eyes glued to the TV.

"Just so you know, nothing happened last night," Ryan said in a baby-like voice. "There were no break-ins, no attempts to hack into our system."

I dared to look up. "That's good."

Ryan's expression was lethal. "How am I supposed to do my job when you keep blowing my cover?"

I tensed. "I didn't blow anything that—"

"Stay out of my way." Ryan stalked back to sit beside Jensina at one of the kitchen tables.

I sized him up and figured I could take him. That might be delusional, but Ryan was wrong. I hadn't blown his cover. Anya had known what she was doing when she went to that hospital in Kiev. She was playing everyone to get info the Mission League had, and Ryan couldn't see it. If she had tried Pasha's passwords last night, they'd failed. But she'd try again. If anything, I had stalled her. Given Ryan more time.

When Ryan left, I made my way into the kitchen to see if there was any breakfast left. I really wanted a jar of peanut butter. As I scraped the remains of a potato dish onto a clean plate, Isaac's head poked over my shoulder.

"Hey, newbie," Isaac said. "You trying to muck up my perfect record?"

I frowned and licked the serving fork clean.

Isaac squeezed my shoulders. "I'm just saying a dead person looks bad in a team leader's file. Rule 18b, man. Don't die."

"I *didn't*."

Isaac grinned big. "Perfect! Keep it that way, will ya?"

I sat at the counter with my breakfast, and Arianna stopped by to take her turn lecturing me.

"You need to study spiritual warfare before going near a

situation like that. Oh, and it might help if you were an adult. And a believer. I mean, what chance does a fifteen-year-old non-Christian have against a mobster possessed by a demon?"

I ignored her, and she went away mumbling about my stupidity. I devoted the day to my report while everyone toured Leo Tolstoy's house. Because of me, Mr. S had to miss out as well. He and I didn't talk much. It took me close to four hours to get the report right, and I was still working on it when the group returned.

With only two weeks left of the summer, Mr. S spent the rest of the day discussing the trip, the group projects, and the people we'd met so far. Arianna shared her persistent attempts to invite the homeless family from the Arbat McDonald's to the HODC.

My mind wandered in a field of confusion. Clearly Anya was involved with Dmitri at Bratva Headquarters. Dmitri must have sent her to follow me last night on the metro.

If it hadn't have been for Viktor . . .

Had God sent Viktor to help me? Why? Did God know I'd get into trouble? Had He given me the vision of Anya and the vision of Vlad? Were they simply a glimpse of future events, like the time I'd seen Nick punch me on the basketball court, or did they mean something else? Ivan had said that intercessors had visions, like the one Prière must have had about me and Nick getting into trouble on the basketball court.

Was I going to turn out like Prière someday, limping around and stroking my moustache? Prière was a freak. I didn't want to be a freak. I wanted to be normal.

Nice wish, I know.

I heard Mr. S say Svetlana's name. The image of her signing to me in the kitchen flashed in my mind. I was supposed to pray, but I didn't know how.

Uh . . . God? Hello? If you're listening . . . uh . . . help?

I snickered, but before I could try again, Mr. S's voice jolted me from my hopeless attempt at prayer.

"You find Svetlana's situation humorous, Spencer?"

Heat crept into my face as all eyes focused on me. "Uh . . . no." I hadn't heard what they'd said about Svetlana. I forced myself to pay attention.

The more I learned about Svetlana, the more in awe of her I became. She'd lived a harder life than anyone I'd ever known. Her mother, a homeless prostitute, had died on the streets when Svetlana had been nine. Svetlana had lived seven years alone in the city before finding the center. She'd been raped and beaten and—wretched things.

Yet she held no grudge. She proudly shared her past—her *testimony*, Gabe called it. That confused me. Why would she want to talk about something so horrible? Wouldn't she want to forget about it? Move on? Or make those who hurt her pay? And what about Mishka? Would he ever wonder who his father was? Would Svetlana tell him the truth?

I hoped not.

The topic switched to Gabe and Isabel's worship service scheduled for the next evening. Everyone was looking forward to it but me. It was just another opportunity for Gabe and Isabel to shine together. I really liked Gabe, but I could never compete against someone like him. The dude was a saint. He even talked Svetlana into helping with a special song, though I had no clue how a deaf girl would sing.

• • •

From where I sit in my car, I watch Anya enter her apartment. I relax when the door closes, and I switch on the microphone in my ear. By the sound of things, she is putting away her groceries. I catch my reflection in the rearview mirror. I'm—Ryan?

The car door creaks open, and a man with a blond ponytail climbs in with me.

"Privyet, Aleksey," Ryan says.

"Tee goloden?" Are you hungry? Aleksey smiles a huge smile, revealing a large chip in his front tooth.

"Da." I feel Ryan's stomach growl.

"Teremok is around the corner. My treat." Aleksey climbs back out and pokes his head in the open door. "Be careful."

Ryan laughs. "Ne volnooytes'." Don't worry.

Aleksey shuts the door and strides away.

Ryan's stomach growls again. "Bring on the blini, Aleksey!" He watches his partner until he turns the corner, then increases the volume. Muffled sounds, like paper. Anya is still putting away—

Anya screams. Ryan cowers, clutching his ear.

"What you want?" Anya yells in her broken English. "Get out my home!"

Odd that she'd use her fake accent in the comfort of her own home.

A deep male voice laughs. Glass shatters.

Anya screams. "Get out!"

Ryan scrambles out of the car and crosses the street. No sign of Aleksey. "Lord, help me."

I stay with him, trapped inside his head as he runs to the door, clearly not fazed by Anya's use of a fake accent. I mean, wouldn't she only use a fake accent for an audience?

Then it hit me. Ryan still didn't believe that Anya was faking her accent. He was walking into a trap.

Ryan rings the doorbell. Low voices hum through the walls. Footsteps on linoleum. The door opens. Anya's eyes widen.

"Privyet, Anya. Uh . . . can we talk?" Ryan asks.

"Is not good time." Yet Anya opens the door farther, dark eyes sparkling.

Ryan enters, looking everywhere but at Anya, whose poker face is terrible at the moment.

Anya closes the door behind him, still protesting. "Ryan, please."

He walks into the living room.

I float free from Ryan and look down on the room from above. A dark figure steps out from the hall behind Ryan, clutching a ceramic figurine like a baseball bat.

Dmitri!

Ryan is speaking to Anya, oblivious to the looming shadow on the living room wall. I can't hear their voices anymore.

"Behind you!" I scream, but Ryan doesn't respond.

Dmitri breaks the figurine over Ryan's head. Ryan slumps to the floor but stirs, trying to rise. Anya slips into the kitchen and returns holding a syringe.

"Ryan! Get up!" I yell.

Anya plunges the syringe into Ryan's arm. Slowly he stops struggling and drops to the floor again, this time to stay.

Suddenly I'm someplace else, strapped to a chair in a

white room. My body aches and the back of my head stings. Anya paces before me, hands perched on her hips. Her lips move, but no sound comes forth, like someone hit the mute button. I study my tan arms that are bound to the chair with canvas straps.

I'm Ryan again.

Images flash through my mind: Riding in a car—an elevator—being bound to the chair—another syringe—Anya questioning me—being struck with the figurine—darkness—a white room—Anya answering her apartment door—the figurine—the figurine—the figurine—

Someone shook my shoulder. "Spencer, wake up!"

I opened my eyes. Mr. S sat perched on the edge of my bed, eyebrows pinched together. Gabe and Jake stood behind Mr. S, eyes wide and peering over his shoulders. Nick's face hung down from above. Isaac stood at the foot of my bed, shaggy head threaded between the bars. Kerri, Arianna, and one of the twins gazed through the doorway from the center apartment. My heart thudded in my chest. It had been a dream?

"Are you okay?" Mr. S asked. "You were having a nightmare."

I opened my mouth to talk, but it was parched, and I just croaked. Kerri disappeared. Isabel and Beth stepped into her vacancy.

"Why is everyone staring?" I whispered.

"You were screaming like a girl," Nick said.

"To bed, Mary!" Kerri chastised her daughter then brought me a glass of water. I sat up and guzzled it without pausing for breath.

"Okay, everyone to bed." Mr. S looked at me. "You going to

be okay?"

I glanced around the room and whispered. "I dreamed about Ryan."

"Oh?"

"Anya and Dmitri attacked him and took him somewhere. Sometimes I was him, and sometimes I watched. Crazy, huh?"

"'Dreams are today's answers to tomorrow's questions,'" Mr. S said. "Where did this happen?"

"At Anya's apartment at first. She tricked Ryan into going inside, then Dmitri hit him and—" I took a deep breath. "Then they were at some office building. The field office, maybe. Torturing him. And they injected something into his arm."

Mr. S patted my pillow and took the empty glass from my hand. "Go back to sleep."

"Should I tell Ryan?"

"I will," Mr. S said. "Don't worry. We'll get to the bottom of this. Good night."

I lay awake, eyes darting at shadows around the room. One moved, and I sat up in a panic. My hair got caught in the springs from Nick's bed. I winced and yanked it free. The blinds on the open window rustled in the breeze, creating the shadow. I lay back down, my mind racing with images of Ryan in pain.

Was Ryan really in trouble? The dream of Anya at the foreign restaurant hadn't taken place yet, as far as I knew. Could these things have happened long ago? Were they glimpses of the future, maybe, or just my crazy imagination? Terrified, I rubbed sleep from my eyes, desperate to be in my own bed in California.

REPORT NUMBER: 30

REPORT TITLE: Pasha Wants Out
SUBMITTED BY: Agent Ryan Matheson
INTERVIEWEE: Pasha Ivanovich
LOCATION: Chapel, H.O.D.C., Moscow, Russia
DATE AND TIME: Sunday, July 20, 9:55 a.m.

PASHA SAT IN THE BACK CORNER of the sanctuary and watched the people in the front row. The Americans were trying to blend in to the Protestant worship service. Amusing. He allowed himself a hint of a smile, but it didn't last.

He could think only of Yuri.

His friend had come back from Bratva Headquarters late last night, high from connection. And he'd woken Pasha at three in the morning, having some kind of seizure. Pasha hadn't known what to do but call Father. Now Yuri was hooked up to a machine in the hospital, barely alive.

This was Anya's fault.

He watched the pretty American girls. Even the annoying

one wasn't so bad. Calling them ugly on the metro had felt good at the time, but it had ruined his chances with any of them. No matter. Svetlana was still his favorite. She looked like Anya, only nice.

Anya! Thinking about her made his skin crawl. She'd used him again and again, yet he kept helping her. What power did she hold over him? He'd never be her boyfriend—he'd realized that a long time ago. He saw how she worked on the new recruits. He brought poor, lost souls to her, and she played with them, promising a warped and dangerous power and a future together that didn't exist. They were toys to her. Wind them up, point them in the right direction, and they would come back to be wound up again. The energy she gave them never lasted long, even with Bratva connection. They always needed another charge.

But Yuri had taken too much.

Spencer was sitting, slouched down in a pew three rows away from the rest of the Americans, looking alone and out of place.

Just how Pasha felt.

Pasha could not let Anya destroy his American friend the way she had destroyed Yuri. He hated how she ruined everything. Sure, Pasha had had many problems with his family before Anya had come along, but he'd have gone back and made peace by now if she hadn't convinced him otherwise. He desperately wanted to go home, but everything was out of control. He'd burned bridges. Besides, the gang he'd helped create would never let him leave. Neither would Anya. He shuddered to think what she'd do if he tried to leave Bratva.

He would end up like Yuri. But it would be no accident. And if by some chance he did manage to escape, what of the power? Could he survive without connection? It preyed on his mind, a hopeless addiction.

There must be a way.

The music ended, and the prayers began. Pasha stared at his parents. Would they pray for him today? Light a candle in his name? The ache in his chest proved how much he missed them. Father had been right all along, of course. How could Pasha go back now that Father had been proved right?

Svetlana opened her Bible and turned the pages, her golden hair spilled forward like a veil obscuring her face. He'd wasted this summer.

Pasha studied one of the stain glass windows above. Jesus hung on a cross, His loved ones mourning at His feet, a crown of thorns on His head. God was the enemy in Anya's world, and Pasha had allowed himself to drift away. Did God understand this? Would God still offer help if Pasha wanted his life back?

He wanted to sit in that pew with his family.

Eesoos, I want to go back. I'm sorry. Set me free. Send a sign. Please, help.

REPORT NUMBER: 31

REPORT TITLE: I Make Peace with Pasha
SUBMITTED BY: Agent-in-Training Spencer Garmond
LOCATION: Arbat Ulitsa, 43, Moscow, Russia
DATE AND TIME: Sunday, July 20, 12:42 p.m.

EVERYONE SEEMED EXTRA QUIET around me the next morning. Apparently, I'd screamed and yelled in my sleep for five minutes before Gabe had gone and awakened his dad. Talk about embarrassing. But the dream had felt so real. I sat by myself at church and fingered the back of my head every so often for a lump, but I found nothing, of course.

That evening, I dressed quickly for the Gabe and Isabel worship service. I settled into my corner chair and watched TV, waiting for everyone else. Mary stared at me from the kitchen and giggled when I made eye contact.

I pretended not to notice.

Tatyana and Ivan arrived, and together our group filed out

the door, with me at the back of the line. Mr. S pulled me aside before I could leave. He sent the others ahead with Tatyana and Kerri, then closed the door, leaving me alone with him and Ivan, the three of us standing awkwardly in the kitchen. I had a bad feeling I was about to be sent home for meddling in Ryan's case.

Mr. S gestured to the nearest dining table, and I sat. "Spencer, Agent Ryan Matheson is missing. The field office lost contact with him last night."

Tingling peppered my body. No way.

"Normally," Ivan said, "we would not be concerned overly until more time is passing, but Ryan was on stakeout with his partner. When Mr. Stopplecamp told me your dream, I recognized link at once. Have you meet Ryan's partner, Aleksey Andreich?"

"No."

"Could you describe him based only on your dream?" Ivan asked.

"Real skinny and tall. Long blond hair in a ponytail. Chipped front tooth."

Ivan pursed his lips and nodded at Mr. S, who leaned forward and placed a recording device in the center of the table.

"Please tell us your dream in detail, Spencer," Ivan said. Both men stared at me intently. "Leave nothing out."

By the time Mr. S and I got to the HODC chapel, the service had begun. The tiny sanctuary was packed. I stood in the back doorway reluctant to enter at all. As usual, the Americans had claimed the front row. Svetlana was there too. Gabe stood center stage, playing guitar like a rock star. Isabel sang along as backup. Both looked blissfully happy. I slid into the back pew, feeling like I'd just jumped in with C-Rock and the King Coats gang.

Ryan was missing, and I'd seen it. I felt like I should do something more, but what? I tried not to think about it, to focus on the music. But even after the whole summer, I still didn't fit in with these churchers. But that wasn't a surprise. What surprised me was this: Why did I care?

Isabel's eyes were closed, one hand stretched above her head as if reaching for something. Gabe's eyes were also closed, but that didn't hinder his guitar playing. The song was slow—God was supposedly here, in everyone's midst. I wanted to believe it was real, that God was here, but I didn't feel anything.

If God had gifted me with prophecy, I was supposed to use it to help people, right? So telling the dream to Ivan had been good. Why, then, did I feel so lousy? Gabe had said I should talk to Pasha, that I could relate to him because of my past, but none of my dreams or visions had involved Pasha. Had they?

I didn't know how to use this dream stuff for God.

Gabe picked up the tempo, and people jumped to their feet, bouncing and lifting their hands in the air. It used to make me laugh. Now I felt like I was missing out. Voices burst together in song. Without mine.

The loneliness practically suffocated me.

The song finally ended, and Gabe called Jensina, Arianna, and Svetlana onstage to sing a song that Svetlana had written. The deaf girl stood beside Gabe, signing the words as he sang.

Tears streamed down her face, yet she smiled as she mouthed the words. A fury melted through me from anger buried deep inside that had resurfaced first at Kimbal's confession about my dad, then with Pasha's betrayal, but why now?

Because horrible men had hurt Svetlana. Pasha had hurt Tatyana, Lena, Ivan, and the field office. My dad had hurt my mother and me.

"Your heart must not burn," Svetlana had signed to me that day in the kitchen. *"Pray, and God will melt your anger with his love."*

I closed my eyes. I felt like I had when Nick had hit me on the basketball court, but this was a different kind of attack. It came from all sides. I wanted to fight back and beat it away, but I didn't know how.

My stomach churned.

How could Svetlana, a deaf girl, homeless and hungry, a victim of rape who'd kept her baby—how could she be happy? I didn't get it. Somehow she loved God despite what had been done to her. She was beautiful, and I was ugly. Not physically, maybe, although I never did care for my neon hair and freckles. But I was ugly in my heart with my negativity, anger, jealousy, hate. I could go on and on, but it was too depressing.

God? are You listening? I'm sorry I'm so mad, but I don't get why I have these dreams. I don't want them. Give me a different gift—something easy—something I can deal with. I hate not understanding. Why can't You just show me?

I have shown you.

I opened my eyes.

True. I'd seen things others hadn't. God *had* showed me, given me these dreams, these . . . prophecies. Was God sending me after Ryan? I'd been warned to stay out of it, and I was sick of getting into trouble, but if God wanted me to go, I didn't really have a choice, did I? Maybe He wanted me to show these churchers what I could really do. Then they'd have to accept me as I was.

•   •   •

The next day, I stood at the windows overlooking the back of the HODC. Pasha was out there alone, shooting hoops. I watched, haunted by Gabe's words from the subway and Svetlana's testimony. I was ticked at Pasha for betraying his father, but who was I to hold a grudge? I was no better. Hating my dad, hating Nick, being jealous of Gabe, liking all the girls because they were pretty without thinking about them as friends.

I forced myself out to the court. "Hey, Pasha."

Pasha whipped around. Deep circles under his eyes led me to believe he hadn't slept in days—or maybe he'd just missed his *connection.*

Pasha held out the ball. "Want to play?"

"Nyet." I folded my arms and leaned against the pole holding up the hoop. "See Anya lately?"

Pasha stopped dribbling and looked at me, eyes fearful. "How you know Anya?"

"We've . . . met."

Pasha tucked the ball under his arm and walked toward me. "She ask questions about you."

My breath caught. "What'd you tell her?"

"That we play ball. You come from California. You in Leega Missionerov four months. You asked of my tattoo. You went at Bratva warehouse and Father's field office. I am not

313

knowing your parents' names or if you are being relative of Freidrich Lange."

I gaped at Pasha. He'd asked all those weird questions for Anya!

Pasha shot a lay-up. The ball slid through the hoop, and he caught it. "She does not like you. Puhcheemoo?" *Why?*

I shook my head and blinked, reminding myself that my goal in talking to Pasha was to make peace not war. He sure wasn't making it easy. "I don't know."

"You trust her?" Pasha shot another lay-up but missed.

I rebounded the ball and held it under my arm. "Are you kidding? She's a fake and a liar. Plus she uses people. Pasha, why do *you* trust her?"

He shrugged and said in a small voice, "She is Bratva. We take care of each other."

Wow. "She sure picks some strange ways to take care of you: putting you in danger, getting you to betray your family and the field office and"—I looked away—"me."

That seemed to startle him. "How you know about the field office?"

"It doesn't matter. Bratva isn't what you think. They don't care about you. They want to control you. I met some of them, and they aren't normal." I bounce-passed the ball to Pasha. "What's on the ninth floor?"

Pasha's eyes flickered to mine. "She took you there?"

"No, but I saw it, just for a second."

Pasha actually looked relieved.

"Is that were you get the *power within?*" I asked.

"Da," Pasha said, his tone wistful. "Once you connect to the power and invite it inside, you have total control. It is amazing and frightening all at once."

"Sounds pretty risky." Not that I hadn't done some pretty risky things in my life.

"There is no risk . . . at first."

"What happens?"

Pasha's eyes flicked to the street as if he thought someone might overhear. "Only Bratva can know. Is for your own protection."

On a hunch, I seized Pasha's arm and twisted it over. His forearm was rosy purple with track marks. *Mother pus bucket . . .* How had I not seen this before? Because I'd been too obsessed with the tattoo. "Do they force people to do this?" I asked, releasing Pasha.

He rubbed his arm. "Sometimes. Most want it, though."

"Dmitri had wanted to connect with me," I said, mostly to myself, shivering at the realization that they would have forced it on me.

Pasha traced the black line on the ball with his finger. "You met Dmitri?"

Seriously? Did Pasha actually look jealous? "He's no one I'd want in *my* family."

"You have big family?"

"Just my grandma. My mom is dead and my dad . . . He left."

Pasha furrowed his brow. "Zachyem?"

"I don't know. It's not the same, but please don't hurt your family by leaving. They're nice people."

Pasha pitched the basketball hard across the court, and it rolled all the way to the building. "You do not know them!"

"Nyet, but at least tell them how you feel before you give up on them forever. Give them a chance to make it right."

Pasha pointed at his chest. "I am only one of my family not

chosen for Leega Missionerov. Still they force me to work with them. No one asks if I want to help Tatyana. They tell me."

"So tell *them*."

Pasha looked up to the sky and shook his head. "Father never listens."

"Then talk to your mom or Tatyana."

Pasha slouched and blew out a heavy breath. "Is too late. I done many horrible things."

"It doesn't matter. They'll forgive you. I know they will. That's what Christians do. But Anya and Dmitri . . . they're bad news. They'd let you rot in jail to save their own skins."

"She *is* controlling. And violent."

"She's up to something bad with Dmitri. Do you know what they're trying to do?"

"I no think they are working for same goals. Dmitri is promoting Bratva here in Moscow. Is growing army of loyal followers. But Anya, she come from the States. She want information on the Leega Missionerov. Anything. Name of agents, procedures, passwords . . . That is why she pretending to be homeless. Leega gave her apartment and access to young, naïve agent."

Ryan. And now the guy might be dead.

"She promised me job with Dmitri if I did well. I wanted to make Father angry, so I broke in at his precious office and planted her computer chip. It no work, though, and she is angry to me ever since. I thought she care for me. I thought she was to be my . . . But I am fool."

"Where did you meet her?" I asked.

Pasha's cheeks flushed with a reminiscent smile. "Café *Moo Moo*."

I froze, suddenly connecting the red and white décor of the

restaurant in my dream to the Russian café. Pasha had been the one Anya had spoken to in my dream. It *had* been a prophecy. So Anya and Dmitri had probably kidnapped Ryan too, just like I'd seen.

Pasha went on. "She was beautiful and mysterious. She show me how bad my family treat me and joined me with Bratva. Then she gave jobs. I went along. I know she used me. I was perfect, how you say, mole? Inside man? She gave me tattoo. She likes marking people."

"*Marking* people?"

"Is hobby to her. I want to go home, but do not want to face Father. I do not like being wrong."

I could totally relate. "Yeah, me neither."

"How are you wrong?"

I chuckled at his loaded question. Where to start? "Mostly I was wrong about the whole God thing, and I don't really want to deal with that." Though I'd have to soon. I folded my arms again. "What are you going to do?"

Pasha looked different. Content. "Start with Tatyana. I treated her bad. I want my life back, and she is first step. I am glad you spoke to me. You are my sign."

I scoffed. "A sign of what?"

"I prayed God would send sign to show me what to do, and here you come. But I fear Anya and Bratva will not let me go."

"The program at the HODC is good. Try to get your Bratva friends over there, away from Anya and off the streets. At least they could come for meals and wouldn't have to steal." I couldn't believe I had just said that. I sounded like a missionary. Like Gabe.

Pasha ran to where the ball had rolled by the building. He turned, jogging backward. "Maybe I will."

I just stood there, dumbfounded. Gabe had been right about Pasha listening to me. And there had been more to Pasha's story than him being simply a traitor. He hadn't been malicious about the things he'd done. He'd been hurt and weak, where Anya had been strong. He'd been used. That didn't make it right, but—I couldn't help but wonder—had something similar happened with my dad?

And what was I going to do to help Ryan before he ended up like my mom?

REPORT NUMBER: 32

REPORT TITLE: I Break the Rules . . . Again
SUBMITTED BY: Agent-in-Training Spencer Garmond
LOCATION: Outside, Arbat Ulitsa, Moscow, Russia
DATE AND TIME: Tuesday, July 22, 7:20 p.m.

I SWALLOWED A LUMP OF ice cream while I waited for Gabe to finish paying. "Don't you eat anything but chocolate?"

Gabe grinned and shoved a paper bag under his arm. "Not if I can help it."

I followed Gabe out of the store, sucking the bottom of my ice cream bar. It had started dripping the moment I'd opened it. I clumsily dodged pedestrians, paying more attention to my snack than where I walked. As we passed the Internet Café, a sudden thought came to me.

I stopped in front of the door. "Gabe. Something Pasha said has been bugging me. He said Anya likes to mark people. She did his tattoo."

Gabe made a face. "You told me. It's disgusting."

"Remember when we saw those people talking about the field office in that chat room? One was db666 and the other was *amarx*. Do you think amarx could be Anya—Anya who likes to put *marks* on people?"

Gabe stuck out his bottom lip and shrugged. "Could be."

I snapped my fingers. "The other one has to be Dmitri Berkovich. It makes perfect sense. Anya wants to break into the League server so Dmitri can get information on agents." Though something about that felt backward. "I have to check this out."

"Spencer, you'd better leave it be. I saw grey stubble on my dad's head the other day, and I didn't do anything to put it there. If you keep pushing, he may have a heart attack. You did awesome talking to Pasha. Can't you be satisfied with that?"

"I'm just going to look." But the expression on Gabe's face told me that now was not the time. I'd have to do this later, when Gabe wasn't around. We walked on without going in.

My chance came Friday afternoon. Tatyana called me from the laundry room to watch the front desk while she ran errands with Marina. I logged onto Bratva's website and into the chat room.

The odds were slim that Anya would be on. She wasn't. I pasted the text from the past few days into Google Translate and found one conversation from 2:14 a.m. this morning.

amarx has entered the lounge:
amarx: you are there, v?
vlad14: yes
amarx: well?
vlad14: not seen him all the week. think him trying to get

out. Take oleg and alex and trying to take more

amarx: he can't

vlad14: what I should do?

amarx: nothing , I must worry over bigger things. i'm out of time.

vlad14: how you will get passwords?

amarx: i have reliable and handsome methods. meet on 11 at 10:45 tonight. I need you to guard.

She had Ryan! She would force him to give up the passwords. The pieces had come together. If Vlad14 was the same Vlad who led Pasha's Bratva friends, he and Anya must have been talking about how Pasha wanted out and had taken Oleg and Alex to the HODC for meals. Anya wasn't giving up.

Neither would I. God had put this challenge before me so I could show these churchers what I was capable of.

I would *not* fail.

I printed two copies of the chat and shoved one in my back pocket. Then I searched the HODC until I found Mr. S working on a computer in a back office.

"Mr. S! It's happening tonight!" I told him everything and gave him the chat. "You've got to tell the Field Office to expect a break-in. And once they catch Anya, they can make her tell where she's keeping Ryan. Plus they might be going after Pasha too."

"Spencer, calm down. I'm going to call Ivan right away, but why are you still poking around in this? I asked you to keep out of it."

"Because I couldn't stop thinking about it, and I thought that amarx had to be Anya."

Mr. S took a deep breath. "I appreciate your honesty this

time, Spencer. But you need to let the grownups take it from here. Is that clear?"

"But I can help! I'm the only one who knows what I saw in my dream. Let me come with."

"Absolutely not."

I opened my mouth to argue but stopped myself. Did I really think I could convince this man to let me help? I hadn't exactly proved myself to him this summer. "Fine." I walked out of the office.

"Spencer?" Mr. S called.

"I have to get back to the front desk," I said.

I dragged my way back to the front office. I couldn't believe Mr. S wasn't going to let me help. I mean, I had dreamed about all of this. I had also dreamed some meetings with Anya and Vlad and me that hadn't happened yet.

What did *that* mean?

I should at least call Pasha. That wasn't breaking any rules. Tatyana had mentioned that Pasha had come home yesterday. I grabbed the phone to warn Pasha then hung up when I realized I didn't know the phone number. Where would Tatyana keep her home number written down?

Beth strutted into the office with a file tucked under her arm. "Hey, Tiger. Can I get some copies?"

I minimized the chat window on the computer screen. "Help yourself."

Beth looked at me like I had two heads. "I can't work this thing. Me and technology . . . not so good."

I joined her at the copier. She smelled nice, like vanilla. "How many do you need?"

"Five."

I punched the buttons, and the old copier started clanging

and beeping. The first copy spit out. Beth stood whacking one forearm against the other, again and again. I could hear the smack of bones hitting under flesh.

Yowzers. "Why do you do that?"

Beth looked at me, then down at her arms. "Sorry. I do it so much I forget. It's body conditioning. Since I can't train this summer, I'm keeping myself in shape however I can."

"I get why you do all the sit-ups and pushups. But why hit yourself?"

"It toughens my skin and the tissue underneath so it doesn't hurt when I hit or get hit. Basically, I'm turning my skin into armor, like leather."

"Can I do it?"

Beth twisted her lips to one side. "I'd wait 'til we get back and Boss Schwarz can show you how. You could hurt yourself otherwise."

"*Isaac* is the LCT guy?"

"Isaac's dad is the advanced LCT instructor. Everyone calls him Boss Schwarz. You be sure and take the advanced class with me when you sign up, not the easy class Gabe takes. That boy's a wimp."

"Ouch."

"Hey, I speak the truth. He can play a guitar like nobody's business, but I can kick his behind into next week."

No doubt about it. And Gabe would likely agree. I pondered this as the last copy spit out. A thought came to me. Beth was practically Tatyana's assistant; maybe she'd know the number. "Do you have Tatyana's home number? I want to call Pasha."

"Yeah." Beth scribbled the number on a scrap of paper and handed it over.

955-07-55? "Uh . . . could you dial it? I don't know how to use these phones."

Beth rolled her eyes and dialed. "I thought *I* was the techno moron here." She handed me the receiver.

"Thanks." I put the phone to my ear. It was already ringing.

"Thank *you*." Beth whacked the copies on the top of my head and plodded out of the office.

Man, I liked her scary ways.

The phone rang three times before Pasha answered. I explained what I'd seen in the chat room, how Anya had captured Ryan. I tapped my foot through a long pause, waiting for his reply.

"Why you are looking at Bratva chat room?" Pasha asked.

"Long story. Was it Anya and Vlad? Were they talking about you? Are they going to try something tonight, or am I wrong?"

Pasha sighed heavily. "You are not wrong. She is dangerous. Vlad is not knowing what he is doing. I must be stopping him."

"I'm coming with you." I hated to go behind Mr. S's back. Again. But I'd seen the future. I was involved in this thing somehow. And maybe it was the only way to prove to everyone that God could use some *jockstrap* like me.

"I will be outside apartment at 10:15. Dasvidanya." "Bye." I hung up and sighed. I was *out* of my mind.

• • •

It was the longest day of my life as I sat in the apartment and waited for ten o'clock, especially with the nagging in the back of my mind to stop this ridiculous plan. Had I learned nothing? Proving to everyone that God had chosen me for this special task wouldn't keep Mr. S—or Grandma—from killing me.

I certainly didn't *want* to go after Anya. But that didn't matter. I'd seen myself with her and Vlad in the future—I was the one who'd seen the locations in my mind. So there was no way out. It had to be me. I was the chosen one. I'd seen enough time-travel movies to know that much. So I was going through with it, even if it meant getting sent home or kicked out.

I hoped they all felt bad when I was gone. I hoped they realized how their long lists of rules alienated regular guys like me.

Dinner came and went. Everyone gathered to pray for Ryan, as they had been doing every night since his disappearance, although I was the only student who knew why. I turned down going to a movie with Gabe, Isabel, and Jensina and watched TV in the living room, waiting.

Arianna sat beside me, her long red skirt billowing over my knees. "Have you thought any more on our discussion?"

What was she talking about? She never stopped talking. "Which one?"

Her gaze darted to mine, tentative and guilty. "Jesus dying for your sins."

Why couldn't the girl leave me alone? I had too much going on at the moment without Arianna dragging up all this emotional, repeat-after-me, saved business. "Can't you just drop it?"

"But Spencer, it's your life."

I slapped my knees. "Exactly! You finally get it! *My* life, not yours. Weren't you listening to Mr. S when he said you can't force those homeless people to go to the center?"

Her eyebrows sank. "I listened."

"It's the same with me, Arianna. You can't make me your clone. The more you try to, the more I want to push you off that balcony. Just be my friend. If you can't do that without nagging me every second, I don't want to be yours."

I stomped off to the boys' room and tried to take a nap. Stupid, annoying girl. Drove me nuts. Drove everyone nuts. She was probably crying too. All girls ever did was giggle or cry. Well, I didn't have it in me to be Mr. Nice Guy tonight.

I couldn't sleep, though. I was worried I'd oversleep and miss my time to go. So I did push-ups and sit-ups for the next half-hour. After that, I ran up and down the four flights of stairs until my legs threatened to fall off. Then I showered and put on jeans and a black hooded sweatshirt—the darkest clothes I had.

By the time ten o'clock rolled around, Gabe had returned from the movie, which was unfortunate. I didn't want him in on this plan. It was a stupid plan that would probably get me in all kinds of trouble. Gabe didn't need that.

But how could I get away without being seen?

I finally came up with a plan. I pulled my Lakers cap on and stepped into my sneakers. "I'm going to run get some junk food. Want anything?"

Gabe closed his Bible and jumped off his bed. "I'll come with."

Gah! Total backfire. "Nah, it's okay. I'll be quick." I opened the door.

"Where you going, newbie?" Isaac's sharp voice punctured my plans like a pin in a balloon. He was standing in the doorway to the center apartment.

"Candy run," I said.

Isaac shook his head. "Not by yourself, you're not."

Gabe stuffed his feet into his loafers. "I said I'd go."

"Fine. Let's go." But I bit the inside of my cheek. This was not going to work. Guilt nagged at the back of my mind as I traipsed downstairs with Gabe at my heels.

We stepped outside into the cool night air. Someone whistled. Pasha motioned to me from a boxy blue Russian car with rust on the fender.

Gabe squinted behind his glasses. "Is that Pasha?"

I took a deep breath and explained the situation.

"Are you crazy?" The look Gabe gave me was the same one his dad gave me the night I'd gone to Bratva, pink face and everything. "You forget about Dmitri already? No. There's no way!"

"I have to do this."

"Why?" Gabe stared up at me.

I scratched the back of my neck. I hadn't told Gabe about my visions. Revealing all that now could be a great way to kill the friendship. I wanted to wait until I was a hero before confessing my secrets—in case that backfired too.

"I can't explain it right now. I just have to."

Gabe shook his head. "Not good enough. Tell my dad and let the professionals handle it. They have security at the field office, you know. Good security."

"Then we'll tell security our theory when we get there."

"Tell my dad now!"

The door to the apartment building swung open, and Jake cruised out, again dressed for some fancy shindig. He gave me and Gabe a quick smile and bounced toward the metro station.

"See? Jake goes places by himself."

"He's a junior, and you're—"

"Spencer!" Pasha called from the car.

"Just a sec!" I held up my hand to Pasha and turned back to Gabe. "I can't let Pasha go alone. He just patched things up with his family. Besides, it's all a hunch. I don't want to send a bunch of field agents after nothing."

Only that was a lie. Tonight *was* the night to live through these visions. There would be no turning back. I hoped my pupils hadn't dilated. If they had, Gabe wasn't paying attention.

"If I'm not back in two hours, tell your dad," I said.

Gabe scowled and folded his arms. "One hour."

"It'll take us a half an hour to get there."

Gabe hesitated and checked his watch. "Hour and a half. Quarter 'til twelve, final offer."

"Fine. We'll probably get there, and everything will be normal. Remember what you said. Sometimes bad things have to happen for good things to happen." Like me breaking the rules to save Ryan and prove I wasn't a nutcracker.

Gabe's jaw dropped. "That's *not* what I said or what I meant." I turned away, but Gabe grabbed my arm and whispered, "I don't trust Pasha."

"I do. He wants out, which is why Anya's using Vlad. You're the one who said I should talk to Pasha. You were right. Now we've got to talk to Vlad."

"Dad will send you home."

"We're all going home in a week."

"They'll kick you out."

That gave me pause, but I'd been over this already in my mind. "I have to do this."

"You *are* crazy." Gabe folded his arms. "Before you go, tell me the passcode."

"What code?"

"In case you get in trouble. What is it?"

For Pete's sake. I'd forgotten that stupid passcode two seconds after Tatyana had said it. "Something about blood?"

"Do you like red?" Gabe said in a flat voice. "The countersign is: there's power in the blood."

"Got it." I left Gabe standing on the sidewalk, looking ten years older with his head in his hands, praying aloud.

I ignored my own screaming conscience and climbed inside Pasha's vehicle.

REPORT NUMBER: 33

REPORT TITLE: Pasha and I Sneak into Bratva Headquarters
SUBMITTED BY: Agent-in-Training Spencer Garmond
LOCATION: Car Headed North on Arbat Ulitsa
DATE AND TIME: Friday, July 25, 10:17 p.m.

I WATCHED THE APARTMENT'S BALCONY SHRINK away
over my shoulder. "Whose car is this?"

"Mother's." Pasha veered to the right of the Kremlin, away
from the field office.

My pulse quickened. "Where are we going?"

"Bratva Headquarters," Pasha said, as if it were obvious.

"What!" I had no desire to go back into the dragon's lair. "I
thought Anya and Vlad were breaking into the field office then
making Ryan give them the passcodes?" The field office, where
the good guys would be close at hand to make a multitude of
arrests.

Pasha stopped at a traffic light and shook his head. "*Hack* into field office *server*. She can get files without going there. Is much safer that way. Bratva Headquarters has great computers. Is only taking the passwords, and she can download or upload anything."

That made too much sense to argue with.

The light turned, and Pasha hit the gas. "Still want come with me?"

"Yeah." I did. But while rescue was a good plan in theory, my boiling stomach made me want to run back to the apartment and confess everything to Mr. S.

I reminded myself that I'd been given these visions. With great power comes great responsibility, and all that.

Pasha parked a block away from Bratva Headquarters and led me down a dark alley, approaching the building from the rear. "This way is no cameras."

See? It was all about looking on the bright side of things. No cameras. Bonus.

Pasha jogged toward a small window that rested at ground level. He yanked a pair of gloves from his back pocket and pulled them on. Kneeling, he felt around the window in the dark. He removed a small piece of cardboard, and the window swung open.

"Bratva never sleeps. There are many people here, especially on ninth floor. We will sneak in and use service elevator at back of building." Pasha swung the window to its widest point and smiled. "After you."

I gazed at the dark hole in the wall, wishing I were back in the apartment laughing with Gabe. All I had to do was find Anya, then the visions I'd had of her grabbing my face, of Vlad holding me, and Ryan in the little room would happen in real life. After that, I'd be free.

"This place gives me the creeps." Gabe was right. This was a *very* bad idea.

"Vse harasho." *All is well.* Pasha turned to grab the window with his other hand. "I know this place well. Go on."

I got down on my stomach and backed feet-first into the opening until my foot located something firm. I shimmied the rest of my body through the window into darkness and wrinkled my nose at the faint smell of urine and ammonia. I was standing on a toilet inside a bathroom stall. I climbed down and waited for Pasha.

When Pasha was inside, he led me out into a hallway. My eyes adjusted to the dark, but I could see only shadows. I stayed close to Pasha, following the sound of his sneakers on tile. Excitement and dread filled every pore. Mr. S would freak—that was certain—quote a bunch of dead guys, and hopefully not have a heart attack. Light outlined a bank of elevators ahead. Pasha put a hand out to stop me.

"What?" I whispered.

"Anya will be on floor eleven. Only—there are cameras on upper floors, in stairwells, and in elevators. Probably no one is watching, but they will see tapes tomorrow. We must disguise." Pasha pulled a black ski mask out of his back pocket and put it on.

Whoa. "Where'd you get *that*?"

"Came in useful for Anya jobs. Here." He pulled my Lakers cap low, drew the hood of my sweatshirt over the cap, and cinched the ties. I felt like an Eskimo. "Keep head down."

Adrenaline threatened to immobilize me. We were walking into a bad situation. I'd seen it. Vlad would grab me, and Anya would squeeze my face. Why go into it willingly? I'd ignored God for years—why start listening now? And if God wanted me here so badly, why like this? Why force me to break the rules and get caught? Did God have some twisted sense of humor?

I frowned as a new possibility crossed my mind. What if God had meant for me to stay away and the visions had been warnings of what might happen if I didn't?

Mother pus bucket! Why had I considered that option only now? This prophecy thing needed a users' manual.

Pasha paused and peeked around a corner.

I danced around on my toes like I had to use the restroom, cursing my idiocy. If only I'd told Mr. S about my visions, he would've set me straight. Now, even if I did manage to save Ryan's hide, I'd still be busted. "What's the plan?"

"Get upstairs without being seen. Pashlee." *Let's go.*

I kept my head down and followed Pasha's sneakers to the elevator.

Pasha hit the button, then turned and pulled my sweatshirt sleeves over my hands.

"Fingerprints," he whispered. "Touch nothing. Walk backwards into elevator. Camera is in back corner. I forget what side. Keep head down."

I mirrored Pasha and turned around. I tried to swallow, but my mouth was dry. I wiggled my tongue, trying to make enough spit to soothe my parched throat.

Ding!

I practically jumped out of my skin. The elevator doors whooshed open, and I backed inside. The doors closed, and Pasha hit the button for eleven with his thumb. I went rigid and stopped breathing, aware only that the camera was watching. My heartbeat pounded in my head, which now sweated under the layers of disguise. Finally, the elevators opened to the eleventh floor.

Pasha grabbed my sleeve and led me through the darkness. We followed a twisting hallway a little ways before Pasha ducked into an alcove and removed his mask. He glanced around the corner. "She will be in computer room at end of the hall, where you see light. What we planning to do?"

"It was your idea to warn Vlad!" I peered at the dark door outlined in glowing light. What *could* we do? It had seemed like a great idea to come when I thought we were going to the field office.

Gabe! Nausea flooded me at the realization that help wasn't coming. If I didn't return in time, Gabe would send Mr. S to the field office, not Bratva Headquarters.

I cursed myself silly inside my head. "Should we make sure they're in there?"

"Anya is there." Pasha flexed his jaw. "Are you good fighter? We could try taking her down. With two of us maybe we could, but if Vlad is there, it will be impossible to explain anything. He will help Anya first, ask questions later."

"Are you nuts?" I had no desire to fight Anya or Vlad. "What else you got?"

"I could say I saw their chat and want to help, but you must wait here."

I shook my head. "No way." I needed to be in there for the visions to come true.

"We fight or lie or leave."

Those options stank. "What about the truth? Tell her we've come to stop her?"

Pasha wrinkled his nose. "We could try, but it cannot work so good."

"Do you think Dmitri's in there?"

"Nyet. Anya is working on stuff he knows nothing about. Is only her and Vlad and the Amerikanskiy agent. Does not he work in Special Forces?"

My eyes narrowed. "He works in New Cults. What do you know about Special Forces?"

"Cults often crossover to Special Forces. If we find him, he could be helping us."

"Maybe." I recalled the trouble I'd already caused for Ryan and his first big case. I wanted to ask Pasha more about Special Forces, but this was not the time. I scratched my throat where the ties of my hood were chafing. "Do you have a cell phone? Can you call your dad?"

"There is phone in office down hallway." Pasha winced and glanced down the hall the way we'd come. "I would have to go downstairs to open front doors. You should be coming with me."

I shook my head. "If she leaves, someone needs to follow her."

Pasha licked his lips thoughtfully and finally agreed. He pulled the mask back over his face. "I will make call and come right back." Pasha crouched low and crept back the way we'd come.

I waited in the alcove, bouncing and fidgeting like a boxer about to enter the ring. No doubt Pasha would be in trouble when his dad got the call. I blamed myself. It was bad timing and bad interpretation of my visions.

I stilled and checked my watch. An hour had passed since I'd left the apartment. Gabe wouldn't nark for another half hour. Only I wasn't at the field office, so unless Pasha's call got through, no one would know where I was. Super.

Pasha had been gone only a couple of minutes, but I was

anxious for him to return and overwhelmed with an ache in my gut. A shadow flickered on the wall. The floor creaked. I turned to see if Pasha had been successful, but someone grabbed me. One strong hand pushed my face against scratchy wallpaper and another pinned my right arm behind my back.

"Stoy!" *Don't move!* A male voice commanded. "Tee k'to?" *Who are you?*

My captor forced my arm further up my back until I cried out.

"Dveegaisya!" *Move!* The guy released my head, grabbed my other arm, and pushed me in the direction of the computer room. I squirmed, but my captor's grip tightened.

I didn't want to go into the room with the light. Not yet. Not without Pasha. I put a foot against the doorframe to brace myself, but my captor turned and dragged me through. The brightness blinded me.

"K'to eto?" *Who is that?* Anya's raspy voice scraped over the pounding in my head.

I kept my gaze down, blinking wildly to adjust my eyes to the light. Heels clicked toward me. My eyes regained focus as white leather boots with silver spiked heels appeared on the beige tile in front of my feet. She carried a chill with her, and I shivered.

Anya yanked the cap off my head, pulling out some of my hair with it, and choking me with the drawstring of my hood. I met her eyes, dark and black, and offered a weak grin.

"Spencer Garmond." A pensive smirk crossed her face. "This *is* a surprise. I wondered when we would meet again. Didn't expect it to be so soon."

I didn't miss her phrasing. She'd said *when* we would meet again, not *if*. "I . . . you can't . . ." I shook, cold and trembling. I broke eye contact, but the trembling continued. It felt like my heart was stopping and starting again, beating wildly, irregularly, like a generator running out of gas.

I needed to calm down. Help was coming.

Anya giggled and set my Lakers cap on her own head, her blond curls coming out from under it. She grabbed my chin and forced me to face her, squeezing my face so hard her thumbnail cut into my cheek.

Just like I'd seen in my vision.

"Look at me."

I kept my eyes down, gritting my teeth against the stinging pain and burning cold.

"Look at me!"

I glanced up into dark moving eyes.

"Do I make you nervous?" The voice wasn't hers. It was deep, unnatural.

I squeezed my eyes tight and shook my head. I distracted myself from fear by overanalyzing the situation. I mean, it was a relief the vision had finally happened. Vlad must be holding me. That only left the image of Ryan in a small room, and I'd be all caught up on the vision front.

Sweat trickled down my temple to the tip of my chin. I squeezed every muscle to fight the trembling, but it overpowered my will. Thankfully, Anya released me and sauntered away. I opened my eyes, instantly warmed. The room was the size of the Internet Café. Six rows of desks, five computers per row.

Anya slid onto a chair at the end of the first row and clicked the mouse. When she next spoke, her voice sounded normal. "You came here once, Spencer, but to come again . . . You're not a smart boy. But it's going to make me look very good to my boss. So, thank you."

Two positives I clung to: First, I hadn't had any premonitions involving Dmitri. Hopefully that meant I wouldn't see him. Second, Pasha would be here any minute and help me.

I turned my head. Vlad was holding my arms. Excellent. "Hey, Vlad. How's the warehouse?"

Vlad glared at me and tightened his grip.

"Can he let go of me?"

"I don't think so, darling. But please, tell me why you've come. I'm intrigued."

"To stop you from hacking into the field office."

She cackled like a Disney villain. "How cute! And what are your plans, now that you're here?"

When I didn't answer, she picked up a phone and dialed. "Dmitri. Privyet . . . Oh, I'm fine. Listen. I could use your help down here." She twirled her finger in her hair. "I know. I'm sorry. It'll only take a minute. Could you bring a jolt?" She winked at me. "Thanks a million." She hung up and smiled. "Dmitri is coming. Won't it be nice to finally get us all together?"

"Can't do anything without your boss?"

Anya's expression froze. "I work for no man. Dmitri is a bead on a very intricate necklace. One city in a world waiting for a leader to unite it. You cannot hope to understand what we're trying to accomplish. But you will, in time, be educated. I've asked Dmitri to bring you a little gift, though. Something special."

I didn't want Dmitri's *gift*. I wanted Pasha to burst in with the cavalry. Vlad's grip had slacked. I scanned the office, planning my escape. A door, slightly ajar, stood to my left. The lights were off inside. There was no way to know where it led, but it had a deadbolt. They might just lock me inside. Was that better than where I was now? A multi-plug power strip stuck out from under the desk holding Anya's computer. If I could switch it off . . .

"Sch'to zdes' praees-hodeet?" *What's going on here?* Dmitri's voice was a Klingon growl. Vlad shifted. Dmitri stood in the doorway, holding a small, silver suitcase.

Figs and jam on a stick. So much for not seeing Dmitri. I needed to get out of here and fast. I wrenched away with all my might and swung Vlad into Dmitri in the process. I flew to the desk, unplugged the power strip from the wall, and, just to be safe, yanked out each of the plugs attached to it, along with the modem cable.

"No!" Anya slapped at me from the other side of the desk.

Vlad scrambled forward. His fingertips grabbed at my hood, but I lunged out of reach, sprinting to the door with the deadbolt. I pulled a trashcan over behind me but tripped on an extension cord. I crashed onto the floor a foot away from the room.

Vlad grabbed my hood and pulled me up. I kicked and whacked him with the power strip, but he was too strong. The clicking of Anya's steps and her coldness neared. Vlad hoisted me to standing, and Anya bashed me across the face.

The force rattled my jaw and seared my cheek.

"That was very naughty." Anya yanked the power strip away from me. "It's no use, though, darling. It will only take a moment to reboot. If you wanted to go in the conference room, you only had to ask. Dmitri will bring in your *gift* momentarily." She clicked back to her desk. "Put him in with Ryan."

Vlad pushed me through the door, and the deadbolt clicked. Darkness. At least I was away from Anya and Dmitri, if only for a moment. I slid my fingertips along the wall until I found a light switch. I flipped it up, and halogen bulbs flickered on with a low buzz.

My eyes darted around. I stood in the small white room from my dream. A long oval table surrounded by chairs took up most the space. A man with short brown hair sat with his back to me in a chair at the end of the table, facing another door, which was locked, no doubt.

"Ryan?" I inched forward. "That you?"

REPORT NUMBER: 34

REPORT TITLE: I Jump Off a Building
SUBMITTED BY: Agent-in-Training Spencer Garmond
LOCATION: Bratva Headquarters, Moscow, Russia
DATE AND TIME: Friday, July 25, 11:40 p.m.

STILL TREMBLING, I HELD MY BREATH and made my way toward the chair. Sure enough, Ryan sat slumped over in the seat, head lolling forward, arms and legs secured with strips of cloth. Unconscious? Dead? What would Arianna do?

Check his pulse.

I reached over and put two fingers to Ryan's wrist. Warm. That was good, right? But I couldn't feel anything like a pulse. Frustrated, I pulled away.

"Hey." I nudged him. "Ryan!"

Nothing.

Now I wished I'd paid attention to Arianna's CPR lecture. I took a deep breath and was about to freak, when I saw Ryan's chest moving. If he was breathing, he had a pulse, right?

Relieved, I stepped toward the other door and tried it. Bathroom. Blast. How was I going to get out of here? Where was Pasha? I went back to Ryan. The top of an ink pen stuck out of his shirt pocket. Spy tools! I pulled it out and clicked it. A slender knife jutted out of the tip. I jumped. I'd been expecting a flashlight, but this was even better.

I cut at Ryan's bindings with the pen knife, willing my fingers to stop shaking long enough to do the job. There wasn't much time. Dmitri would soon bring me his *gift*.

I accidentally twisted the shaft of the pen, and a light shot out the top.

Sweet. Ryan's pen gadget was cooler than Kimbal's, unless Kimbal hadn't shown me the knife on purpose. I shook the thought away and kept cutting.

When Ryan was free, I leaned against his torso and hoisted him over one shoulder.

"Aargh!" My knees buckled under his weight, and we crashed to the floor. "What are you, made of stone?"

I twisted out from under the limp body and rolled Ryan onto his back. I slid my hand into Ryan's front jeans pocket—awkward, I know—and removed an allergy pill and a squashed stick of gum.

Excellent.

In Ryan's other pocket I found a ruble coin, the night vision contact lenses, and the paperclip. I pocketed the paper clip and allergy pill and examined the ruble. Would it work like the penny? I set it on my finger and pressed my thumbnail into the number one. Nothing. I flipped it and tried each eagle's head. Then I tried the center tail feather.

Click.

"Ha!" I pulled out the tiny listening device. I crawled to the wall and stuck the suction cup to the white paint. I uncoiled the wire and placed the sticky foam into my ear. I heard nothing. Maybe it was broken. Then I heard a phone ring.

"Da?" Anya spoke so fast in Russian that I couldn't understand. I did catch the names Pasha and Dmitri.

The phone clattered against its base and she said, "Pashlee." *Let's go.* Her boots clacked across the floor, and Vlad's softer, sneaker-steps followed.

What if they were going after Pasha?

I pulled the device off the wall and crammed it into my pocket along with everything but the gum. If Pasha had failed to reach anyone on the phone, help wasn't coming, and I'd have to get out on my own. I dragged Ryan halfway toward the door that led back to the computer room and slowly opened the chewing-gum-that-was-really-C4. My hands were shaking.

What if it didn't work? What if it exploded too soon? What if Dmitri was still in there, waiting with his gift?

I crouched in front of the door, mashed the C4 inside the foil wrapper and shoved it in the crack by the doorknob.

I scampered back to Ryan and covered my ears. The cheek Anya had cut was warm against my palm. I counted to ten. Eleven. Twelve. It wasn't working. Thirteen. Fourteen.

KABLAM!

I cowered, covering my head with my elbows. I peeked through a smoky haze and saw the door swinging free on its hinges. Scattered drywall littered the charcoal carpet like chalk. Whoa.

I ran back, reached under Ryan's arms, and linked my fingers across his chest. I pulled him to sitting then dragged him into the computer room. It was empty. They'd likely gone after Pasha. I wasn't sure if Anya had gotten the info she was after or not, so I used the pen knife to slice all the mouse and keyboard cords. That ought to keep her from hacking into anything.

I dragged Ryan into the dark hallway a yard at a time. We wouldn't get far at this rate. Raised voices gurgled in the distance—Anya and Dmitri, by the sound of things. I peeked around a corner but couldn't make out anything in the dark. A tiny red light glowed from the ceiling.

I'd forgotten about the cameras. Judging from the amount of dough Bratva seemed to have, I bet they worked just fine in the dark.

I leaned against the wall to adjust my grip on Ryan. I squinted and could barely make out the dark shape rotating above. I needed to find a place without cameras.

The bathrooms.

Voices drew close. The camera landed on my corner again. As soon as it started away I followed, a pace out of its view, until I stood directly under it. I searched the hall, and my gaze fell on the white shape of a stick girl. A girls' bathroom. It would have to do.

When the camera pointed away again, I jogged backward as fast as possible, hauling Ryan with me. Thankfully, the door opened easily as I backed against it. Inside, an exit sign beamed overhead, casting pale red light over the sinks and stalls.

I dropped Ryan and pulled the pen light out of my pocket. I twisted it on, held it between my teeth, and fiddled with the contact lenses for what seemed like an eternity until I had both in my eyes. A glowing green bank of stalls illuminated to my left, one larger than the others. I shoved the pen back into my pocket and dragged Ryan into a stall. I propped him between the toilet and the wall and locked the stall and climbed onto the toilet.

"Smells better than the warehouse," I said to Ryan before climbing out.

The contacts were stiff and dry in my eyes. I blinked twice as often as usual. I opened the bathroom door a crack and watched the camera turn. It looked much different now, in green. My leg wiggled—I was anxious to run. At the right moment, I bolted out the door and down the hall. I took two left turns before an exit sign loomed ahead. I sprinted toward it, hands ready to push against the handlebar.

I hit the door like a bird on a windshield. I bounced off and fell onto my rear, wrists stinging.

A static giggle pierced the silence. I scanned the deserted halls, looking for the source.

"Poor Spencer. A mouse in a cage. Shall I offer you some cheese?"

Anya's voice was broadcasting over an intercom. I looked up. Circular speakers dotted the ceiling every three yards or so.

Anya said something in Russian that I couldn't understand. I whipped around, looking for who she might be talking to. Vlad? Dmitri?

"I've locked down the eleventh floor," Anya said. "We've captured your dear friend Pasha, so help is not coming. There is no way out."

I backed into the corner near the exit door. The hall stretched out on either side, but Anya was watching. Where could I go?

A glowing green form appeared at the end of the hall to

my left, and the beam of a flashlight blinded me. The neon shadow jogged my way. The hair jumped on my arms. I scrambled to my feet and sprinted to the right. I slammed into the wall at the end of the hall just as a shot cracked into the surface six inches from my right shoulder.

A dart stuck out of the plaster. I glanced over my shoulder. Vlad's fluorescent form stood halfway down the hall, flashlight rolling at his feet, gun in hand. I took off, safe for a moment, but Vlad would turn the corner any second and shoot again.

Anya's cackle droned overhead. I tried to blot it out and think.

Where could I go? She was everywhere. I whipped through a random door and closed it softly behind me. I stood in a copy machine room. The growing sound of doors opening and closing in the hall sent me scampering toward a door in the back.

Anya's muffled voice carried from outside. "Spencer," she sang. "Come out from hiding. No more games."

I wrenched the door open and went inside an office. Everything was outlined in electric green. Three big desks, several file cabinets, dozens of monitors, circuit boards, external drives, and cables had been stacked in every free space. Moonlight flooded in from a window. I bolted toward it and peered outside.

The moonlight made it hard to see with the contacts. I was in one of the upper tiers of the building. Outside the window, a ledge about two yards wide stretched out at floor-level. Black bars fenced the bottom half of the window, probably to prevent people from climbing outside and falling off the building. I reached up to pull down the window but couldn't quite grab it.

A light turned on in the previous room, spilling a glowing

beam through the crack of the open door. I squinted and pulled the pen knife from my pocket. I scampered under a desk and crouched on my toes, one hand pressed into the stiff carpet to keep my balance, the other clutching my weapon.

Vlad's deep voice broke the silence. "Vse harasho, missionery." *All is well, missionary.*

I watched the carpet in front of the desk, squinting as Vlad's flashlight beam swept the floor. Then his ratty sneakers appeared in front of the desk. As his knees started to bend, I slid back, keeping low, and ducked under the second desk. When Vlad's feet appeared in front of the next desk, I slid under the third. When Vlad's feet appeared again, I pressed past the file cabinet edging the desk, flattening my back against the wall, still squatting. I held my breath and tensed, ready to jump out at Vlad if I had to.

The sound of the door opening brought a hint of joy to my heart, yet I dared not move. It could be a trick. Vlad could be bluffing, waiting for me to reveal myself. Forever passed before I decided it was safe to move. But just as I willed my knees to push me up, the door opened and slammed shut.

I froze. Had Vlad been waiting, or did he just return?

Anya's voice came over the intercom out in the hall, speaking Russian. I couldn't understand a word but figured she had to be yelling at Vlad. I rose, my thighs burning from having crouched for so long. I peeked over the top of the file cabinet. The room was empty.

I dragged a chair back to the window, climbed up, and pulled the window down. Cool night air enveloped me as I leaned my torso outside. There was another ledge on the tenth floor, but I'd have to drop to it. After that, there were no more ledges. It was straight down to the sidewalk below. This was crazy. Falling would mean death, no question, but if I didn't try, that might happen anyway.

I pulled myself back inside. I'd never bothered to learn the phone number to the apartment, so even if I found a phone, I couldn't use it. Did Russia have 911? If I survived tonight and didn't get kicked out of the Mission League, my first priority for my next foreign country would be learning to use local phones.

Worry for Pasha clouded my mind. What would they do to him? I weighed the options but decided going for help was more constructive than trying to rescue Ryan and Pasha myself. I had to get out of the building.

I turned on the chair and scanned the piles of computer equipment. Anya was still barking orders though the hall speakers. I jumped down and looped a coiled orange extension cord over one arm, hoping to use it as a rope that would keep me from falling to a messy death.

I climbed back onto the chair and took a deep breath. I placed one sneaker on the corner of the window ledge and swung my other leg up through the window. Not an easy task with my height and lack of flexibility. I might be an athlete, but I was no acrobat.

I also wasn't about to dive head-first out the eleventh floor window.

After much struggling, I managed to get both legs out. I teetered on my stomach on the windowsill. I gripped the top of the sill and dropped back onto the ledge.

My heart thundered in my chest. I had to all but pry my own fingers off the windowsill. When I finally let go, I pushed the window up as far as I could. It still gaped a few inches. Hopefully Vlad wouldn't notice. Pretty easy so far, right?

Dropping down a whole level would be trickier, but to get to the elevators, I had to get to the tenth floor.

It had been eight years since Cub Scouts, but I managed to tie a nice square knot with the extension cord around one of the black bars that caged the window. I tied three extra square knots on top of the first, just in case. Then I threaded the other end of the cord through all my belt loops and tied four knots in the front to hold it.

I sat and scooted to the edge until my legs dangled over. I wiped my hands on my jeans three times, but there was no drying the sweat. I suddenly realized the cord was longer than I needed. I should redo the knot. I should also take out the contacts. I shook both thoughts away with a long exhale, then turned onto my stomach, legs hanging into space. I gripped the cord as tightly as I could, one hand on top of the other. I'd just lower myself down to the tenth floor ledge. Nice and easy.

Second thoughts assailed my mind. The cord might not hold my weight. The bar might break free. I tugged at the cord to test its strength, eyes focused intently on the knot at the bars. It was holding. It should work.

Okay, God. on the count of three. I jump. You make sure I don't die. Got it? One . . .

My breath started to come fast and short.

Two . . .

Vlad's face appeared at the window. I met his eyes and pushed back.

I fell fast and hard, gripping for the cord, but it wasn't in my hands anymore. My feet smacked against the tenth floor ledge sooner than expected, and I stumbled back. My heels dipped over the ledge. For three long seconds, I circled my arms to keep from going over.

Gravity won. I fell.

I screamed until the cord jerked taut. Fabric ripped. My belt loops! The cord, now free from my jeans, burned as it slid up my torso, pushing my T-shirt out of its way. My body slammed into the crusty stucco wall.

I tried to move fast, knowing Vlad could be untying the window knot right now, but my vision blurred, and my head spun.

I grappled for the knots at my chest, my body twirling from one side until it hit the wall then back to the other. My fingers trembled as I reached up the cord.

A steady bass beat pulsed from the ninth floor. Blinding lights flashed through nearby windows as I twirled on the cord. *Don't look down.*

Stupid me, I looked anyway, and my remaining courage fell out the bottom of my shoes. I was dangling off the front of the building! No more ledges below me. I started to hyperventilate.

Beneath my sneakers, three vehicles sat parked in front of the building like glowing green toys. People down there were staring up at me, waving their hands and yelling, but I heard nothing other than my own throbbing heart. I twisted and turned trying to make out who it was. A shaggy-headed guy in shorts looked a lot like Isaac. The thought puzzled and distracted me from my fear—until I remembered Vlad above me.

I gripped the cord and pulled myself up, one hand over the other like climbing the ropes in gym class, only that fat hairy rope was easier to grip than this thin plastic or rubber or whatever it was. With every pull, my hands slipped some. My palms seared and my forearms burned, but I ignored the pain.

Pain meant I was still alive.

Soon, my eyes peeked over the ledge where the cord—and the cluster of wires inside it—was shredding against the sharp edge of the tenth floor tier. That visual sparked me into action. I climbed faster, arm over arm, until my knees swung onto the scratchy surface.

I crawled to the wall and collapsed. My body shook so much that I couldn't untie the cord from my waist. I took long deep breaths to block out the horror of hanging off the building, the shredded cord, Vlad and his gun.

I rolled onto my back, and the bass beat from the party floor thumped against me. My heartbeat slowed to match its tempo. My body calmed. I thought about removing the contacts but didn't have the energy at the moment. Besides, I'd likely enter a dark office room or something and need to put them back in.

When I finally managed to untie the cord, I stood and tried the closest window. It wouldn't budge. I took slow steps to the next window. Nothing. I inched around the ledge, stepping over bird poop and checking windows until I found an open one on the backside of the building. I grabbed the top of the sill, pulled it down, and stepped up onto the black bars. I dove inside, head first, my body twisting as my hands held on.

My head hit the inside of the window, and my right forearm scraped against something sharp. I hit the floor hard.

I lay flat on my back on a concrete floor inside some kind of cage. Aluminum chain-link fence rose to the ceiling on all sides. Garments hung on bars that stretched across the enclosure. Some kind of clothing warehouse?

I crawled a few paces, then stood and slogged to the fence. I followed it until I came to the wall then followed it back the other way to the door. Through the aluminum chain links, the elevator gleamed, taunting me from across the room. I twisted the latch on the door, and it swung open.

I stepped through just as the elevator dinged.

"There you are, Spencer," Anya said over the speakers.

I froze and shifted my eyes to a camera overhead.

"How clever you are to get out of my cage, but then, you poor dear, you walked right into another."

Her laughter mocked my struggle. I fumed.

Vlad exited the elevator and glanced around. Anya yelled in Russian, and Vlad's gaze fixed on me. Since the chain-link door locked from the inside. I darted back in and pulled the door shut. I twisted the lock and ducked behind a row of shirts.

"Ahtkroy!" *Open up!* The aluminum door rattled.

I peeked between the shirts. Vlad's fingers poked in and out of the links around the lock, but a metal plate guarded it. He ran around the perimeter of the cage until he and I were face to face.

"We don't want to hurt you, Spencer," Anya said in a sweet voice.

"Sure, you don't," I yelled at the camera. "Vlad's gun is just for fun, right?"

"I can't hear you, dear, and you look pretty silly from my view, mouth moving all angry with no sound coming out. Remember, this wasn't my idea. You came to me. But now that I have you, I intend to keep you. You are too valuable a prize to let go."

"I'm not a prize!" I screamed whether Anya heard me or not.

Anya spoke three words I didn't understand. I snapped to my senses, having forgotten about Vlad with all of Anya's talking. I turned just as a sharp pain pricked my chest.

I looked down at a glowing dart sticking out of the basketball logo on my sweatshirt. I gulped and looked back to Vlad, who blew across the end of his gun and grinned.

I staggered a few steps, lightheaded. My left side went numb, and I fell to my knees. I pulled the dart out and studied the needle that had delivered the poison. Should I swallow the allergy pill? It would make me puke, right? But the poison was in my veins, not my stomach.

My eyes crossed slightly. Was I going to die?

Arianna's warnings filled my head. Would I go to heaven or hell?

Please don't let me die. I need more time to understand.

The sound of Anya screaming in Russian wiped across my mind, but when I tried to cover my ears, my hands didn't obey. I stared at them dangling at my sides. Why wouldn't they move? I sat back on my heels. I couldn't understand a word of Anya's ranting except:

"Pashlee, pashlee!" *Let's go, let's go!*

I blinked once and slumped to the floor.

REPORT NUMBER: 35

REPORT TITLE: I Get Interrogated
SUBMITTED BY: Agent-in-Training Spencer Garmond
LOCATION: Bratva Headquarters, Moscow, Russia
DATE AND TIME: Saturday, July 26, 1:40 a.m.

I WOKE TO THE CLANGING OF THE CAGE DOOR.

"Hello?" a man's voice called.

My head jerked up. Everything glowed. My eyes stung, begging to close again. The contacts. Someone had turned on the lights. I rolled to my side and managed to remove one contact, but the other wouldn't budge. I shut that eye and gazed at the dart in my hand. I was alive, but the banging rattled my aching head.

"Hey, kid! Over here."

With one eye open, I glanced across the cage.

A dark-skinned man stood outside the door. East Indian, maybe? He was dressed in the same tan military-like uniform that Kimbal and Mr. S had worn during my recruitment. This one had a matching helmet.

"Spencer Garmond?" The man's voice boomed with authority.

"Yeah?"

"Special Forces. Open up."

Was this a trick? I blinked my eyes rapidly, trying to get the other contact out. No luck. It hurt to think. "Uh . . ." I paused, feeling stupid. "Do you . . . like . . . uh, red?"

"There's power in the blood."

Nice. I rolled onto my stomach and tried to stand. My legs were numb, but they obeyed. I stumbled to the door and flipped the lock, still squeezing one eye shut. The door swung open to the Indian man.

He reached out and grabbed my necklace, examining the cross. He turned and yelled over his shoulder. "Found Garmond!"

"Wheels found Garmond," a muted voice repeated somewhere else.

Oh-kay. That was weird. I stepped out of the cage and followed "Wheels" to the elevator, where four more men in uniform were milling around. Although the uniforms were identical, each face was different. Two with Russian coloring, an Asian guy, and the last one . . . Arab, maybe? Instead of names on their uniforms, they had nicknames. Punch, Bullet, Spinner, Ash. There was no sign of Anya, Vlad, Dmitri, or Pasha. Wheels led me into the elevator with the other men and reached for the first floor button.

"Wait!" I grabbed Wheel's wrist. "Ryan's upstairs. He's a field agent."

"Where is he, kid?"

"In the ladies' room on the eleventh floor."

"What? Better show us." Wheels hit the button for eleven, and the elevator sailed up a floor.

It took ten minutes for me to find the bathroom in the winding hallways, but I managed to remove the other night vision contact, so at least I wasn't squinting anymore. I climbed on the toilet in the neighboring stall and peeked over.

"He's still here!" I hoisted myself over the stall and jumped down. My knees buckled on landing, and I crumpled to the floor. I sat stunned for a moment, still feeling the effects of Vlad's dart. I unlocked the stall door and crawled out.

Wheels rushed inside. A moment later he poked his head out the stall. "Spinner, Matheson needs a medic. Ash, take the kid."

The two men jumped to their tasks. Ash, the Arab man, grabbed me by the elbow and pulled me down the hall. I gritted my teeth. My body ached all over.

"Where's Pasha?" I asked.

"That's classified." Ash had no hint of any accent but American.

"Classified? We came here together. Is he okay?"

Ash shook his head. "Sorry, kid. That's how it goes."

I jerked my arm free. "Don't call me *kid*."

Ash looked me up and down and said nothing.

Outside, the three vehicles I'd seen from the roof sat at the curb. Two black sedans and a van. A massive Russian man in the same tan uniform stood on the sidewalk, radio in hand. He must have been seven feet tall. Ash marched toward him, and the man glared down. The name on his shirt read Goliath. Perfect.

Ash stopped before him. "Captain, this is Spencer

Garmond. Agent Matheson's inside."

"Right. Put the kid in with Schwarz."

I perked up. "Isaac Schwarz?"

No one answered. Ash dragged me away from Goliath, who remained in position like a statue. As we approached the second car, the back door opened, and Isaac jumped out.

Without a word, Isaac steered me inside the car then slid in beside me. Ash got into the passenger's seat. Another man, who was already in the driver's seat, started the vehicle and drove away.

"Where's Mr. S?" I asked.

"He's dealing with something," Isaac said. "I'm on dawn patrol. You cool?"

I nodded and leaned my sore cheek against the cool window, observing the Moscow city lights as we drove. Again we were not traveling where I'd expected. "Are they taking me to the airport—sending me home?"

"They wanna question you at the FO." Isaac nodded toward the men in the front seat. "We'll talk there."

An icy pang engulfed me. Did they think I was working with Anya?

The rattling of the car engine grew to overwhelming on the silent drive.

We pulled up at the field office—which, I finally realized, was what FO stood for. Ash escorted me and Isaac to the fifth floor and led us to a section of the facility that Ivan hadn't included on the tour. Ash swept an ID card at a door that read "S.I.D. Scene Investigation Department" in tiny English letters under large Cyrillic ones.

Jake met us at the door, lips puckered and speechless. "What are you doing here?" he asked.

357

"Just out for a midnight stroll," Isaac said.

Ash and Isaac handed me off to Jake and sat down in a waiting area. Jake led me into a tiny white room.

"Why are *you* here?" I asked.

"I'm an intern. Two day shifts and three night shifts a week."

A woman entered and coached Jake along. He carefully combed me over, taking hairs and fibers, and swabbing my wounds. He placed the dart and the contact lenses—which I'd been clutching in my fist—into separate plastic bags.

"What is all this, Spencer? I've never heard of an agent-in-training doing something like this." Jake opened a cupboard and tossed me a blue hospital gown. "Put it on. Your clothes are evidence now. Ha ha."

The woman turned around while I changed. Jake continued to snicker as he folded my clothes into another plastic bag. He raised an eyebrow at each new gadget he found in the pocket of my jeans.

Jake held up the pill. "Are your allergies acting up?"

"No, and . . . don't take that pill, okay?"

"Why? What is—"

A doctor came in. He inspected the cut and swelling on my cheek, the cord burns on my hands and waist, the scrape on my arm, and the place on my chest where the dart had hit.

In the end, I was given a tan Special Forces T-shirt and cargo pants to put on. They let me keep my own socks, shoes, and underwear. Anya had stolen my Lakers hat, the evil thief.

Jake took me back out to Ash, who led me and Isaac through the New Cults Department, past the cubicles, to a dark hallway—another place I hadn't seen on the tour. Dozens of tiny rooms sprouted off the hall. We passed one that Pasha was sitting in. I was both relieved and petrified to see him here. At least he was okay.

I followed Ash into one of the rooms. It was not much bigger than a walk-in closet. A tiny table sat in the center. I trembled, this time from fear alone. Ash stopped inside the door and motioned for me to sit. Isaac pulled out a chair and sat beside me on the same side of the table. I was glad he was here even though he looked more nervous than I felt.

A large, black window covered half the wall facing us. Butterflies had a war in my stomach. A window like that was so some suit could watch while detectives played good cop bad cop on me. While they tricked me into betraying my friends. I took a deep breath. Been there, done that.

A dull ache rattled inside, reminding me that I should be sleeping. I glanced at my watch. It was three-fifteen in the morning.

Seventeen more minutes crept by before the door opened. Goliath entered, and Ash left. I slid down in my chair. Why'd it have to be this guy?

Goliath sat across from me and Isaac and opened a file. "Agent Schwarz, when did you lose your target?"

Isaac blew out a short breath. "He went outside with Gabe Stopplecamp at twenty-two hundred hours. I followed but hung back when I saw them talking outside the entrance to our apartment. When Gabe opened the door, I ran upstairs so they wouldn't spot me. I came into the boys' room ten minutes later to check. No sign. But someone was in the bathroom, so I thought it might be Garmond. Before I could check again, Gabe confessed to Mr. S, and I knew Garmond had given me the slip."

I squinted at Isaac. *I* was his target?

Goliath made a note. Then he looked at me. "Agent Garmond, you forget you're in a foreign country?"

"N-no no." The words popped out like a glitching MP3.

The captain's voice squashed mine. "Even in your own country, trespassing and breaking and entering are crimes, aren't they?"

"Yeah." I peeked at Isaac, betrayal seeping in.

"They're crimes here too, Agent Garmond. You have your passport on you?"

I grimaced. "No."

"Breaking and entering, trespassing on private property, no passport." Goliath sighed like a disappointed father. "We confiscated surveillance footage of you and Pasha Ivanovich in a building owned by Dmitri Berkovich. Why were you there?"

My throat burned. I met Goliath's stubborn gaze and swallowed. I'd only been trying to do what God wanted. Rage swelled inside, transforming fear to defiance. "We didn't do anything wrong!"

Isaac jumped.

Goliath raised one bushy eyebrow and opened his file. He ran a finger down the paper, exaggerating the length of the list. "Breaking and entering, trespassing, no passport . . ."

I bolted to my feet. "I *had* to!"

Goliath glared back. "Sit down, Agent Garmond." His words were bullets pelting into my chest, knocking the wind and confidence out of me. Someone squeezed my arm. I turned to see Isaac pulling me down toward my chair.

I gulped and sat. "I didn't want to go to Bratva Headquarters. I thought we were coming here. Pasha wanted to warn Vlad not to get involved with Anya, and I wanted to keep her from stealing information from the League server."

"And you felt this was your responsibility?" Goliath asked. I didn't answer.

"Why didn't you report your theory?"

"Because I didn't know it was true. I printed the conversation, though." I felt for the wad of paper in my pants pocket and groaned. "It was in my jeans pocket, the printout of the chat room conversation. Jake took my clothes."

"What chat room?"

"Bratva."

Goliath scribbled something down. "Tell me about this chat room."

I explained how I'd come to find the chat room and how I'd realized who *amarx* was. "I also thought Dmitri was db666, but now I'm not sure. Anya is involved in something bigger than Bratva or the Mafia, and she's using them all to help her. Dmitri works for her, I think. She used Pasha to break into this place."

Goliath picked his teeth with his tongue. "What happened tonight?"

I told the whole story. "Anya tricked Ryan. She'd been faking the homeless thing all along, but he didn't believe it. I tried to warn him, but . . ." I shrugged. "When Pasha stopped helping her, she and Dmitri kidnapped Ryan to get the passwords. Hey, is Ryan okay?"

"Was the room you found him in the same room from your dream?"

I nodded. Goliath made a note on his paper. If these guys already knew everything, why ask questions?

"Agent Matheson will be fine," Goliath said, and I relaxed. "We received a call from Mr. Stopplecamp at twenty-two forty-five concerning your intended trip to the field office. We searched the area and found nothing, so we ran a scan on your necklace and picked up the signal at Bratva Headquarters. We got there just in time to see your little roof stunt. Pretty gutsy."

I fingered the cross around my neck, and my face flushed. "My necklace?"

Goliath gestured to the chain. "Standard issue."

Grandma had given me a gadget?

Goliath went on. "Dmitri Berkovich was found unconscious in the lobby. We caught an unidentified male in the service elevator with Pasha Ivanovich and a tranquilizer gun. I'll assume he's Vlad. They are all in custody and will be questioned.

"We found the remains of a computer, the hard drive removed, and no sign of Anastasia Vseveloda. The Moscow Field Office server showed an unauthorized download of 43 percent. That's devastating. Thankfully, that percentage excluded files which would have compromised field agents around the world. Hopefully, your pulling the plug knocked down the 43 percent further. We can only pray at this point."

Goliath slapped his file closed. "We have agents trained to go into situations like this, Garmond. As you saw tonight. If you had come straight to us with your theory, we may have been able to prevent the whole thing."

I clenched my fists: 43 percent was a lot of information.

Goliath's stern expression sobered. "What you observed and researched this summer was a help to this office. I want you to know that. We were not aware of Pasha's connection to Ms. Vseveloda or the tattoo connection to the Bratva organization until Agent Stopplecamp gave us your research. After looking into it, we began to monitor the group's activities."

"Ryan said he already knew about the tattoo."

"He knew she *had* a tattoo but never looked into its significance. You have good instincts, Agent Garmond, and some impressive gifts, but you lack the wisdom or training to use them. Without wisdom and training, actions can be destructive even when you have the best intentions. Learn to follow protocol and you could be a great field agent someday. You've got the guts for it."

Goliath stood and slapped me on the back on his way out. It was meant to be endearing by the smirk on his face, but the wind rushed out of me. I wondered if he was any relation to Beth.

In the car on the way back to the apartment, Isaac finally broke his silence. "Dude, what were you thinking chasing people all over Moscow? The Mafia? Jumping off buildings? I almost wet my pants when I saw you up there. You nearly ate it."

"Oh, yeah? Why am I your target?"

Isaac looked out the window and heaved a sigh. "Because following you around, making sure you're safe, it's my red card assignment."

I frowned. "Why? Nick said no one cares about watching a kid."

Isaac shrugged. "When you grow up and get your own international spy organization, you can run things however you want."

Kimbal *had* said there would be plenty of people to keep an eye on me in Moscow. "Did they know I was going to get in trouble?"

"Told you. Big brother knows all."

"So, did you fail?"

Isaac grinned and leaned his head back on the seat. "Rule 18b, baby. You're alive—no thanks to me—but that's something."

I cracked a reluctant smile. It was a big something.

When we entered the apartment, Mr. S was waiting at a kitchen table, his face creased with fatigue. Isaac went to bed, and Mr. S pointed to the seat across from him.

Oh, boy. I had another urge to defend myself in spite of the facts. As if making a closing statement of some kind could help my case.

I burst into argument. "Mr. S, you don't understand. All summer I had these visions. I figured God wanted me to do them since they proved I'd be there. When I saw what they were planning, I had to warn Pasha. I couldn't—"

"Spencer." Mr. S's voice was a whisper. "I'm glad you're safe."

I hung my head, cowering like a bad puppy. I'd rather he yell and scream.

"I had hoped you'd learned something from your first visit to Bratva Headquarters."

I looked up. "I didn't know we were going there, I swear. I never would've gone if I knew that."

"No need to swear." Mr. S cracked a weak smile. "Your place in the League at this point is to learn and observe. God didn't give you prophecy and discernment to embrace danger but to warn you of it."

"How was I supposed to know that?"

"Well, if you'd have talked to me about this, I could have helped you. Plus . . . and I don't want you to take this the wrong way, but you're not a typical recruit. Most kids in this program have a relationship with God already. It's like you're using your gifts without a license. And spiritual gifts don't tend to work right without God's guidance. He has a plan for you, and when it's time, you'll only be useful if you're obedient to what He teaches you along the way."

I slouched back in the chair. "But Gabe said God can turn bad things into good. Doesn't that mean this too?"

"Of course. Good did come from this, but the opportunity for greater good was missed because of foolishness. An actor once said, 'You always pass failure on the way to success.' If you continue making rash choices and ignoring the lessons, you choose not to grow. Understand?"

"I guess." I examined the cord burns on my hands. "So you don't think God wanted me to go tonight?"

"I think He wanted you to take what He'd given you and bring it to your team so we could work together to figure this thing out."

"Tell you my visions, you mean?"

Mr. S exhaled a long breath. "I only know about one nightmare, Spencer."

Right. "The day I met Vlad in the warehouse, he looked at me, and I saw a glimpse of what happened tonight. Then that day Anya took my picture, I saw another one. The same thing happened before Nick punched me in gym class when we got suspended. And I've been dreaming about Anya for years. Just her and Pasha at a restaurant, over and over, only I didn't know it was Pasha until last Sunday."

Mr. S leaned back in his chair and rubbed his chin. "Why

didn't you tell me?"

I picked a piece of dead skin off my palm. "I didn't want it to be real. But when Ivan said intercessors had visions, well, the more I thought about it, I figured God gave them to me. And I can't go against God, right?"

Mr. S took off his glasses and rubbed his eyes. "First of all, for intercessors, every glimpse or dream is reported and prayed over for accuracy. It's not that we don't trust an intercessor's instincts—protocol is for their safety and the organization's— but prayer is the only way to know God's will. Yes, He may give you glimpses or dreams, but without prayer, you decide how to interpret God's message. It becomes your will, not His.

"Secondly, any intercessor will tell you that prophecies are confusing. An intercessor submits his report, then communicates with the necessary agents for interpretation and to determine course of action. That holds the intercessor accountable and keeps everyone safe. Had you disappeared tonight and Pasha not called in, without that necklace, no one could have found you."

"But I had to go because I saw I was already there."

Mr. S nodded. "I understand where you're coming from, but tell me, how might things have ended differently had you come to me with all the facts?"

"Uh . . . Anya might be in custody right now, and all the data would be safe in the server." My face burned. I couldn't believe what a mess I'd made of things. "I really blew it, huh?"

"It's not just you. Many agents break protocol. Ivan did by telling Pasha, a non-agent even if he's his son, the confidential details about his job and allowing him access to the field office."

Mr. S stood and pushed in his chair. "I want a full report on this, just like the last two reports. Plus I want amendments to your other reports detailing anything you left out, especially glimpses and dreams." He shook his head at me. "Frankly, Spencer, if we weren't leaving next Friday anyway, I'd send you home. When school starts, you're on probation. That means: You mess up, you're out. So, don't mess up. You'll start the year at negative fifty points. You'll have to work hard to get out of that hole."

Mr. S came around the table and squeezed my shoulder. "I believe you have a future in this organization, Spencer, I really do. Remember, 'A smart man makes a mistake, learns from it, and never makes that mistake again. But a wise man finds a smart man and learns from him how to avoid the mistake altogether.' Next time, come to me first, okay?"

I blew out a long breath. "You got it."

REPORT NUMBER: 36

REPORT TITLE: I Write the Longest Report of My Life
SUBMITTED BY: Agent-in-Training Spencer Garmond
LOCATION: Arbat Ulitsa, 43, Moscow, Russia
DATE AND TIME: Saturday, July 26, 11:52 a.m.

I SLEPT THROUGH THE TEAM'S morning trip to the Pushkin Museum and woke in time for lunch. I was going to leave Moscow having missed every single one of the tourist sites. There was so much I hadn't had a chance to ask Mr. S last night. I'd deserved the lecture, though, and I didn't feel justified bringing the subject up again.

I was still working on my reports when the group returned.

Arianna scurried toward me, staring at my cheek where Anya had dug her fingernail. "Are you okay?"

"It's just a scrape." I flushed as my classmates crowded around.

"What happen?" Isabel asked.

Arianna disappeared and returned holding a bottle of alcohol, which she dabbed onto some gauze and pressed against my cheek.

The cold liquid seared into my wound and stung. I growled and batted her hand away. "I'm fine!"

The concern on her face deepened. She set the bottle and gauze on the table and took my hand in hers. She examined the cord-burns on my palms. "*Spencer!*"

Beth's eyes swelled. "Nice battle scars!"

Kerri cleared her throat, and everyone but Arianna dispersed.

"Kerri, Spencer needs to get a check-up."

"He's had one, dear," Kerri said.

Arianna grabbed her alcohol and stomped away. Was she mad because I'd yelled at her last night, because I'd snuck out, or both? I felt like a museum exhibit with everyone staring in meditative silence. Nick was an exception, of course.

"You really blew it this time, Garmond," Nick said. "Guess you won't be back next year, huh?"

I brushed it off, but Nick's taunt nagged. On the train to Gorky Park that evening, I wondered if I really *was* too much trouble to be in the Mission League. One more mistake, and I was out. What kind of mistake? I should be relieved to be on the way out, but the thought of no Mission League vexed me. Was that for my mom's sake or something else?

We went to the paddleboats at Gorky Park. It was a nice day, and there were lots of birds singing. Once Gabe and I were paddling our boat across the pond, I finally got a chance to talk to him alone. "Are you ignoring me too?"

Gabe's somber gaze was fixed on the water. "That was a

lousy thing to do, to make me choose between you and my dad."

My gut wrenched and I pedaled harder. "I know."

"Ever since you joined, Dad was worried you'd influence me. He was right. I compromised my standards to cover for you."

Ouch. "I'm sorry. You were right about me. I'm a jerk. You want to hit me? Push me into the lake? I deserve it."

"No." Gabe shot me a disgusted glare. "I forgive you. Just . . . don't do it again."

The setting sun came out from behind a cloud, instantly warming my face. "Can you really get kicked out of the Mission League?"

"I've never heard of that happening," Gabe said "People quit, and people get sent home, but they always come back in the fall."

"Nick said they'd kick me out for sure."

Gabe tipped his head back and laughed. "Oh, yeah, like he can talk! Nick snuck out last night too."

My eyebrows shot up. "What?"

"Yeah, with *Polina*. Except no one noticed. Dad got a phone call around midnight. I overheard him telling Mom. Nick went to a nightclub, and someone stole his wallet and passport. Dad had to go rescue him. They spent the morning at the consulate trying to get him a new passport. Dad may be stuck here with him until it's sorted out."

My mouth hung open. I scanned the boats for the one Nick and Jake were riding in. Nick was laughing as if nothing in his life was totally messed up. He'd always been good at faking.

"So don't let him bug you," Gabe said. "He's busted. Think

I should put it in my Nick report?"

A chill crept up my arms. "What?"

Gabe raised his eyebrows and pedaled so hard we turned in a circle. "I know you know."

"How?"

He stopped pedaling. "You put the blue card back in the wrong pocket."

"How come you never said anything?" I couldn't believe Gabe hadn't gotten mad or treated me differently when all this time he knew I'd snooped in his stuff.

Gabe shrugged and peddled again. "It was only a test assignment. And I should've destroyed the card."

I stared at my friend, awed that he was so forgiving. "You sure you don't want to hit me? I promise I won't hit back."

Gabe gazed out over the lake again. "You don't get it, do you? You want me to punish you? It's not going to happen. I forgave you. It's over."

At that moment, Arianna and Isabel's boat rear-ended ours, jerking us forward. We peddled like Lance Armstrong, trying to come around and catch up to the girls.

"Don't tell anyone about Nick," Gabe said. "I shouldn't have said anything. That was gossip. His dad's my pastor, you know."

I didn't bother to hide my grin. Maybe Nick and Arianna were right. I'd never have Gabe's mercy or nobility. The guy was in a class above me. "Don't worry. I talk to, and about, Nick as little as possible. Did your dad get any sleep last night?"

"Not much. First he was on the phone looking for you, then he went out to get Nick. He left Isaac in charge in case a call came while he was out. I didn't hear Isaac leave, but Dad yelled at Nick for a while before Nick went to bed. That's all I remember. When did you get back?"

"A little past four. Isaac came for me. Your dad was waiting when we got back."

"It must have been a surprise to see Isaac."

"You have no idea." I told Gabe about Isaac's assignment.

"Weird." Gabe paddled the boat furiously in the direction of Arianna and Isabel. "Isaac wouldn't tell you why he'd been told to watch you?"

"Said he didn't know."

We rammed the side of the girls' boat. Isabel screamed and splashed us. Once we were out of earshot again Gabe said, "Sorry I didn't wait to tell Dad. I broke after twenty minutes."

I blew out a long breath. "Good thing you did. We never went to the field office."

"Where'd you go?"

"Bratva Headquarters."

Gabe stopped pedaling. The boat drifted aimlessly as I recapped the events of the previous night. I shuddered when I came to the part about dangling off the building.

"You are insane. So that's what happened to your hands?"

I looked at my cord-burned palms. "I was so lucky."

Gabe huffed. "It wasn't luck. It was God."

My jaw flexed. "God isn't with me, remember? I'm not *saved*."

"Whatever. He created you. He's with you even if you're not with Him. He can help you if He wants to."

"Not according to Arianna."

"Forget Arianna. Call it prayer coverage. Dad and Mom prayed last night. I prayed. Arianna and Isabel prayed. And don't freak out—it just means we like you, okay? Ivan called and said the intercessors had received your *and* Pasha's names. After all that, if you still don't believe God answers prayer, I don't know what to tell you. Maybe God was helping Ryan, and you just got lucky."

I chuckled. I did believe . . . a little. How could I not? Intercessors calling my name twice in the same summer before I almost died wasn't something to scoff at. Prayer was weird. It was better than weird, but I wasn't sure what to do with any of that yet.

Tuesday afternoon, as I showed Tatyana how to run a virus check on the computer, Marina bustled in.

"Tatyana, I need you in the nursery right away. Natasha is here."

Tatyana's expression fell. She rose to follow Marina down the hall. "I will be right back."

I took over the mouse and opened my Facebook page. But before I could do anything, the instant message window popped up and chimed.

Ash Blonde: Guess you got out of your little sanctuary, then?

The profile picture was of a blond woman tossing her hair so that her face didn't show. The computer chimed again.

Ash Blonde: I can see you. I knew you'd come on Facebook the minute she left. You're so predictable.

My stomach knotted. I looked around the office. There was only a chubby man in the computer center. I scanned the ceiling for video cameras but didn't see any. Wait. This monitor had a built-in webcam. I ripped off a sticky note and taped it over the little circle.

Ash Blonde: Such a clever boy. Well done!
Spencer Garmond: Leave me alone.
Ash Blonde: But you're so much fun! I was hoping you'd chase me again.
Spencer Garmond: It's over. You didn't get what you wanted.
Ash Blonde: I got exactly what I wanted, plus a bonus. You.

What did she mean by that? This woman was insane.

Spencer Garmond: You didn't get me.
Ash Blonde: I suppose you're right. I *found* you, though. That's what's important. Look under your keyboard. I left you a gift.

I held my breath and lifted the keyboard. A glossy business card with a phone number. American. Area code 310? That was West LA.

Ash Blonde: The number can't be traced or anything, so it won't do your friends at the field office any good. You've helped them enough. Ruined my Moscow contacts.
Spencer Garmond: Thanks for the compliment.
Ash Blonde: I don't like to fail, Spencer.
Spencer Garmond: Then you should join the winning side.
Ash Blonde: Oh, did you become a believer then?

Was she implying that she was on a side that opposed God?

Ash Blonde: Your silence gives me hope. I'd like to talk sometime without you running away. That's rude. Didn't your Grandma Lorraine teach you any manners?

Who was Grandma Lorraine? What was she talking about?

Ash Blonde: Save that card until you're ready to chat.
Spencer Garmond: Why would I ever *chat* with you?
Ash Blonde: I thought you knew! See, you and I will work together someday. I know who you really are and who you're supposed to become. Believe me, you're better off on our side.

Again she'd managed to completely fluster me. What did that mean?

Spencer Garmond: I don't think so.

Ash Blonde: We'll see. She's coming back. Better close your Facebook. I'll see you around, *Jonas*.

I grabbed the business card and shoved it in my pocket just as Tatyana fell into her chair. Something thick felt lodged in my throat. Anya knew my real name. How?

"Parents can be crazy," Tatyana said on a sigh. "Natasha had a fit because she thinks no other children like her Nikki. She wants us to make sure Nikki has friends."

"Tatyana."

She looked at me. "Da?"

"Can you call Mr. S for me? It's really important."

Her eyebrows sank. "You are okay?"

"Yeah, I'm great." Only, Kimbal had kept me safe from something for thirteen years, and it looked like I'd pretty much blew my own cover in one summer. Anya knowing my real name was probably bad. If I told Mr. S, would he tell Kimbal? Would they make me and Grandma move? Make us get new fake names?

I didn't want to move. I didn't want a new name or new friends. PPCS wasn't so bad. Anymore. I already had a place on the varsity team.

But I also wanted to do the right thing . . . for a change.

Tatyana handed me the phone, I stared at the receiver. I wasn't going after Anya. In a few days I'd go back to California, and everything would be fine. I paused for a moment, carefully choosing the words that would determine my future.

"Hello?" Ms. S' voice came through the phone. "Hello?"

"Mr. S? Anya just IMed me on Facebook."

"Are you okay?" Mr. S's voice sounded concerned. "What did she want?"

"I'm fine." I took a deep breath. "She said I failed to stop her. Told me I ruined all her contacts at the field office. Asked me if I was going to come after her again. Told me she wanted to talk still."

"And what did you say?"

"I told her to leave me alone."

"That's it?"

"Pretty much." Not exactly a lie, right?

Mr. S sighed. "All right. Thanks for letting me know. I'll need your Facebook username and password to print your chat history to put on file. You can change it after."

"I'm not in trouble?"

"Should you be?"

I opened my mouth to speak, but I didn't know what to say.

"We'll talk more tonight," Mr. S said.

The *talk* consisted of Mr. S warning me to be careful for the next few days, meaning I was practically under house arrest until we left Moscow. I could leave only with Mr. S or Ivan's supervision. I'd given over my Facebook information, so they'd all know about the Jonas thing soon enough. I'd even given him Anya's business card. After I'd scanned it and emailed myself a copy. For my report.

Secretly, I was relieved to stay inside. At this point, I'd rather hide than worry about some mobster trying to grab me every time I left the building.

That night, as I tossed and turned in my bunk, I pondered Anya's visit. So much of what she'd said puzzled me. Who was I—who was *Jonas*—supposed to become? Was Grandma Alice's real name *Lorraine*?

Had I been wrong to give Mr. S my login information? I hoped not.

• • •

Two days before we were scheduled to go home, Tatyana and Marina threw a goodbye party for us Americans in the front office of the HODC. Babushka cooked a feast, and I stuffed my face. I was on my third helping of pelimini when Tatyana pulled me aside.

"I am grateful for our new computers. If something goes wrong, I will have to e-mail you. I will not know what to do." She smiled, tears welling. "I am wanting to thank you for Pasha. He said you spoke to him, and now he is living at our house. I cannot tell you what it means to have him home. He was so stubborn, and I had given up hope. Thank you for what you did."

I shrugged. "I didn't do anything."

Regardless, she grabbed me in a suffocating hug. "Ryan is thanking you also, though he is too shy to do so himself. He is healthy and resting, and I'm going to be taking him some of Mother's borscht for dinner along with a movie."

"Oh? You thinking of giving an agent another shot?"

She pushed my arm. "Spencer, you are teasing me."

I chuckled. "Hey, have you seen Viktor around? I want to return his coat and hat." I'd brought the filthy items along in a plastic sack.

She shook her head. "I can't find any record of a Viktor meeting your description. Maybe he goes by different name?"

"But he knows you."

"That's what Isaac says too, but I am not knowing him."

A surge of frustration swept through me. But if Isaac was right about Viktor being an angel, he probably didn't need a coat. "Can I leave his stuff with you then? If he doesn't come back, maybe someone else could use it?"

"That would be fine."

Beth grabbed my arm and dragged me away. Her T-shirt read *Self-Saving Princess*. "Isaac mentioned your stunt off the top of that building. He knows I eat that stuff up."

I glanced at my shoes then up at Beth. "It *was* pretty stupid."

"Wish I could've seen it. It sounded awesome! You have to tell me everything later" Beth punched my arm. "Not that I condone breaking protocol. What you did was just dumb. Awesome, but dumb. A smart agent never acts alone." She grabbed my hands. "Rope burns?"

I glanced into Beth's eyes—wide, green, and framed in dark lashes. "Extension cord."

She released a wistful sigh. "Sweet. Remember. Advanced class. This fall. You'll pick it up in no time."

Oh, I so wish I could. My next words were painful. "Uh . . . I kind of blew it. Lost fifty points. I need at least a hundred for LCT, right?"

Beth gritted her teeth and poked me in the chest. "*That's* why you don't break protocol, Tiger." Her eyes lit up with a scheme. "*I* could train you, if you want. So you don't get behind."

"Really?" One-on-one time with Beth? I tried not to look too eager.

"Sure. They have an open floor time at C Camp. We'll work out a schedule when school starts, okay?" She slapped my shoulder.

"Yeah, that'd be great." I looked over as Arianna appeared at my side. Ug. She *would* show up now. Couldn't she see that Beth and I were having a moment? At least a conversation that hinted at a future moment.

I willed Arianna to go away.

It didn't work.

"Can I speak with you?" Arianna pursed her lips and glanced at Beth, as if Beth should take a hint a get lost.

"We'll talk later," Beth said. "I want that story."

No, Beth! Stay, please. I'll tell you the story now. Or you can share more about LCT.

Yet Beth darted away. Tragic, that.

I watched her go, then reluctantly turned my gaze to Arianna.

She took a deep breath. "Well, here we are."

I'm sorry. She sent Beth away for this? I shoved my thumbs into my pockets and raised my eyebrows, waiting.

"Right. Well, I'm apologizing," she said in a near whisper. "You were right. I'm sorry for nagging you about your faith. I'll stop, okay? I think God wants me to serve you by being your friend."

I was taken aback by her honesty. "Thanks."

She bit her bottom lip and looked at me timidly. "Really?"

"Yeah. It's fine."

"Thanks, Spencer!" She threw her arms around my waist and squeezed.

I froze, hands out to the side like some kind of scarecrow. I hoped she'd let go soon. People were beginning to stare, and I didn't want anyone jumping to conclusions.

Especially Beth.

The next two days in Moscow were spent sightseeing and shopping. I finally got to see some touristy things in Moscow. Mr. S stayed glued to me like glitter on a VBS cross, though.

Lena took requests for food, and I savored every last home-cooked Russian meal. The nights were free, but I spent most of my time watching TV. When I packed up my stuff, I found the pile of Grandma's afghans and gave them Pasha, who promised to take them to the kids at the warehouse.

The night before we left, the group sat in the living room, discussing the summer and the changes we'd seen. Arianna was ecstatic that the homeless family from the Arbat McDonald's had enrolled at the center. Svetlana had found a paying job as a cook and was saving for an apartment. I didn't contribute to the discussion. I still had a lot of processing to do.

Mr. S cleared his throat. "There is one last item to discuss before we close the chapter on Moscow. 'Discretion is the perfection of reason, and a guide to us in all the duties of life.' This organization—"

"Sir Walter Scott!" Jake yelled, pointing at Mr. S.

Mr. S smiled and inclined his head to Jake. "Correct."

Jake pumped his fist in the air. "I should get some points for that."

"You may have twenty," Mr. S said. "Now, as I was saying, this organization depends on discretion. When you talk about this trip, it's important to leave out of your stories our visit to the Moscow Field Office and what you saw there. Also, anything dealing with Ryan's case, Anya, Pasha, and Spencer's involvement in the whole thing is off limits. That's a classified case you all became privy to. It's important to keep the information confidential. Spencer, are we clear on this?"

My cheeks flushed. "Crystal."

• • •

Friday morning I filed out to the row of black sedans and loaded my bags. Ivan had pulled some strings, and Nick was able to leave with us. I was thankful, for Mr. S's sake.

I took in the city one last time as we drove to the airport. At five in the morning it was deserted, quiet, and dark, except for the Kremlin and a couple of churches, which were lit up beautifully. I looked out the car window, feeling like a different person was leaving than the one who'd come eight weeks ago.

Maybe I was becoming Jonas after all.

At the airport, I said goodbye to Ivan, Lena, Tatyana, and Pasha. Pasha promised to Facebook me. Kerri helped me fill out my declaration forms, then I watched Gabe and Isabel share an ice cream. I was surprised they weren't holding hands yet. But maybe Gabe thought that was crossing a line.

Seventeen-plus hours later, I gazed out the airplane window at the sprawling city of Los Angeles below. The traffic resembled scurrying ants, busy and obedient. Was Anya down there in West LA? What was she doing? And why did she care about me?

Still, for the first time in years, I was excited for school. Excited to train for LCT with Beth, excited to tell Kimbal about using Ryan's field ops kit, excited to get a nice, peaceful, non-Arianna-lectured look at a Bible. I wanted to understand the God stuff better so I'd be prepared in case another vision came. Whatever was in my future, I wanted to be ready for it.

THE END

Spencer will return in *Chokepoint*

Cast of Characters

ALPHA GROUP:
Spencer Garmond, a six-foot-three freshman; red-haired, varsity basketball player; grandson to Alice; sarcastic, quick-tempered, and not interested in God.
Gabriel "Gabe" Stopplecamp, sophomore; black curly hair; glasses and braces; son of Mr. S and Kerri; honest, good-hearted; musician.
Jensina Han, junior; adopted Asian girl with half scarlet and half black hair; loves to read; straight-A student; seeking the Administration path.
Isaac Schwarz, senior; blond, tan; home-schooled; surfer; leader of Alpha group; plans to attend Mount Olive Special Forces Training Camp in the fall.

DIAKONOS GROUP:
Arianna Sloan, freshman; small, twiggy missionary kid; lived in France, England, and Japan before moving to the States; loves languages and medicine.
Isabel Rodriguez, sophomore; petite; Cuban native with curly brown hair; speaks fluent Spanish and English; loves to sing and work in her mami's beauty salon.
Nick Muren, sophomore; dark-haired, wealthy, arrogant pretty boy; father is a pastor at a mega church; dislikes Spencer; enjoys acting, partying, and chasing girls.
Beth Watkins, junior; brown-haired; tough girl; former district champion in League Combat Training; plans to attend Mount Olive Special Forces Training Camp after graduation.
Jake Lindley, junior; bowtie-wearing, straight-A student with cornrows; leader of Diakonos group; loves academics and debate; seeking the Public Corruption post.

ADULT AGENTS:

Prière, mid-fifties; tall and thin with black hair; wears suits; native of France; never married, former field agent; now serves as a Level One intercessor.

Dave Kimbal, early forties; tall, pale, and muscular with red hair and freckles; never married; field agent assigned to protect his nephew, Spencer Garmond. His cover is a school resource officer.

Patrick "Mr. S" Stopplecamp, late forties; out of shape, pink-faced; bald; tiny double chin; thick glasses; serves as a Level One teaching agent in Pilot Point, California.

Jeannette "Kerri" Stopplecamp, mid-forties; short, round, with black curly hair and glasses; wife of Patrick; mother of sixteen-year-old Gabe and twelve-year-old identical twins Mary and Martha; serves as a teaching agent with her husband.

Ivan Petrovich, late fifties; grey-haired Russian; serves as the Administrative Director of the Moscow Field Office, husband of Lena, father of Tatyana and Pasha.

Tatyana Ivanovna, early twenties; slim, brown-haired good-hearted Russian; daughter of Ivan; serves as an agent in the Moscow Community Helps Department; current project is the Homeless and Occupational Development Center outside Gorky Park.

Ryan Matheson, early twenties; tall, muscular, brown-haired cocky American; serves as a field agent in the Moscow New Cults Department; current assignment is to watch and protect Anya Vseveloda.

RUSSIANS:

Pasha Ivanovich, sixteen-year-old runaway; skinny and pale with black hair and a big nose; son of Ivan; enamored by the beautiful and mysterious Anya Vseveloda.

Anastasia "Anya" Vseveloda, late twenties; confident, beautiful, and mysterious blonde; Anya is being watched by the Moscow New Cults Department.

AMERICANS:

Grandma Alice Garmond, mid-sixties; petite with spiky, short, white hair; dresses in bright, gaudy colors; grandmother to Spencer; former Los Angeles Field Office Internal Profiler.

Glossary of Russian Terms

Americans—Amerikantsy
Are you hungry?—Tee golodna? (f.), Tee goloden? (m.)
aunt—tyotya
bye (see you later)—paka
car—machina (s.), mashiny (pl.)
cigarettes—seegaretta
Don't move!—Stoy!
Don't worry—Ne volnooytes'.
friends—droogee (s.), droozya (pl.)
fruit juice—compote
gang—bratva
girls—dyevooshki
goodbye—dasvidanya
grandmother—babushka
hi—privyet
homeless and occupational Development Center (HODC)—Tsentr pomoshchi bezdomnym i bezrabotnym (TPBB)
how are you?—Kak dela?
How was your flight?—Kak bil polet?
I am late—Ya apazdal
I don't understand—Ya ne ponimayu
I'm sorry—Izveenee
All is well/It's ok—Vse harasho
Jesus—Eesoos
let's go—Pashlee.
Mission league—Leega Missionerov
missionaries—missionery
Moscow Field Office—Maskovskoye Regional'noye Atdeleniye
Move!—Dveegaisya!

My name is . . .—Menya zovoot . . .

my parents—rawdeetyelee

nine—dévyat

no—nyet

nothing—neechevo

one—odin

open up!—Ahtkroy!

pancake—blini

meat filled dumplings—pelmini

piano—peeanino

please—pozhaluista

police—politsia

praise God!—Slava Bogu!

rich—bagaht (m.), bagahta (f.)

shoes—tooflee

Sing us a song—Spoyte nam pyesnyu.

stop—astanovees'

street—ulitsa

thank you—spasiba

three—tri

two—dva

Welcome to Moscow—Dabro pazhalovat' v Maskvoo

What are you doing?—Sch'to tee delaesh'?

What's going on here?—Sch'to zdes' praees-hodeet?

Who are you?—Tee k'to?

Who is that?—K'to eto?

why—zachyem

yes—da

Yes, Jesus loves me—Da, Eesoos lyubit menya

You cannot take this food—Tebe nel'zya brat' etu peeshoo

You guessed it—Atgadala

You're beautiful—Tee krasivaya

Author's Note

The Bible says in 1 Corinthians 12 that spiritual gifts are given by the Holy Spirit for the common good. God determines what gifts He will give each of us so the body of Christ will be built up (Ephesians 4:11–12).

In the Mission League series, Spencer's abilities are exaggerated in order to entertain and to make readers think about what it means to follow God. His prophetic gift was inspired by Joseph from the Book of Genesis. I believe that God bestows all types of gifts as He sees fit, and it's my prayer that you won't compare your own gifts with others or seek gifts that you haven't been given.

I encourage you to study what the Bible has to say about spiritual gifts. It may also be eye-opening to take a spiritual gifts survey. Talk to your parents, pastor, or youth pastor if you have questions. Here are some verses to help you study what the Bible has to say about spiritual gifts:

- Romans 12:6–8
- Ephesians 4:7–13
- 1 Corinthians 12
- 1 Peter 4:10–11

If you want to hear more from God, I encourage you to read your Bible daily. God has much to say to each of us through his Word. Many people don't read the Bible very often. But it is the best means we have of hearing God's voice. I pray that each of you will seek out a personal friendship with God. He will change your life for the better.

God bless!
Jill

Acknowledgements

Since this was the very first book I wrote, and since I've rewritten it many times over the years, it's impossible for me to recall everyone who helped me with this story. But I'll try.

Thanks to my husband, Brad, and my kids, Luke and Kaitlyn, for your patience, love, and support. I couldn't write without you three.

Thanks to Pastor Joe Torosian for reading my first chapters, encouraging me to stick with it, and coming with me to my first writing conference. You are the master.

Thanks to Rebecca LuElla Miller for doing an early edit on this manuscript. You taught me so much!

Thanks to the members of my old critique group. You know who you are! And to Chris Kolmorgen, John Otte, Rachel and Holly Bentz, and Leighton Hajicek for reading the rewrite. Thanks to Kirk DouPonce for another amazing book cover, to Jeremy Gwinn for being an awesome cover model, to Levi Mansuetti for starring in my book trailer, to Kareen Mansuetti for scouting locations, to Jon Maiocco for his musical genius, and to Daniel, Wyatt, Sam, Emily, Heather, and Janelle for being extras. Thanks to Nichole for her amazing map of Moscow and to Keighley Kendig for her fabulous character sketches.

Special thanks to Rick Barry, Kendra LaLonde, and Mindy Chumbley for all your last-minute help.

And a big thanks to Jeff Gerke for publishing this book and to Amanda Luedeke for your constant encouragement. I appreciate you both.

Jill Williamson is a chocolate loving, daydreaming, creator of kingdoms. Growing up in Alaska led to a love of books, and in 2010 her first novel, *By Darkness Hid*, won a Christy Award. Jill writes fantasy and science fiction for teens and adults. She loves working with writers and blogs about writing at www.GoTeenWriters.com.

Jill is a Whovian, a Photoshop addict, and a recovering fashion design assistant. She now lives in the Pacific Northwest with her husband and two children Jill's full list of books can be found on her website, where adventure comes to life.

To be notified of new releases, subscribe to Jill's Sanctum ezine on her website and get a free short story.

Look for Jill online at:

www.JillWilliamson.com

www.facebook.com/jwilliamsonwrites

Readers of Jill Facebook Group: http://bit.ly/1RAwWuK

www.twitter.com/JillWilliamson

www.instagram.com/jill_williamson_author

www.pinterest.com/jillmwilliamson

Come hang out with us!

GO TEEN WRITERS

honesty, encouragement,
and community for writers

www.GoTeenWriters.com
And join the community of writers on Facebook:
http://www.facebook.com/groups/goteenwriters

ONE CHOICE COULD DESTROY THEM ALL

THE SAFE LANDS
CAPTIVES
JILL WILLIAMSON

A young man must find
a cure for a deadly disease
by befriending a beautiful
woman who is his enemy.

Printed in Great Britain
by Amazon

33920401R00228